HEART SET ON YOU

A small-town friends to lovers romance novel

LILY MILLER

Heart Set on You is the third novel in the steamy and addictive Bennett Family series!

He's a Hollywood heartthrob - sexy, talented and a *total* player (I've read the tabloids). And me? I'm a small-town girl who knows better than to fall for America's hottest bachelor.

That is, until an unforgettable chance encounter in the rain makes me re-think everything I thought I knew about Miles Bennett. Maybe he's worth the risk after all.

It turns out there's a lot more to Miles than the gossip rags let on. Yes, he's drop dead gorgeous, but he's also funny, sweet and thoughtful. And the really crazy part? He could have any A-list actress, but he wants me.

But despite a picture-perfect, whirlwind romance, the truth is our lives are still a world apart. His skyrocketing career means his home is in L.A. while my responsibility to my family is calling me back to the farm where I grew up.

Am I destined to lose the only man I've ever really wanted? I soon realize that taking a chance on love is the easy part. Holding on to it is a whole lot harder…

A small town, friends-to-lovers, full length romance featuring a swoon-worthy Hollywood heartthrob, a country girl with a past and a happily-ever-after.

Heart Set on You

Cover design/Illustrations: Jayde Ubels

Editing: Carolyn De Melo

Publicity: LitUncorked, Katie and Brey PA

For Carolyn
whose friendship and patience I could never repay.
I'll give it my best shot regardless.
I seriously love you.

Chapter One

Miles

I have a bit of a reputation, and honestly, I've probably earned it. According to the tabloids, I'm a Hollywood playboy. Life of the party, up for anything, a different girl every week. Some of that is true. I'll try anything once – even when I shouldn't. As for the girls, well, I don't kiss and tell. But believe it or not, there's more to me than you read in the headlines.

Take right now, for example. I am currently in my trailer, the one with my name on the door: Miles Bennett. I sit with my eyes closed listening intently as Kate, the makeup artist who has been assigned to me while I'm shooting in Vancouver, powders my nose and tells me incredibly detailed stories of her 7-year-old son, Casey. Casey just happens to be the greatest second grader to ever walk the planet. Or so I'm told.

My eyes open as the makeup brush softly dusts down my neck. I watch Kate beam with pride as she tells me Casey is competing in a swim tournament this weekend. His backstroke is killer – as is his competitive streak, which he inherited from his dad. As far as I can tell, it's the one and only good trait from her ex-husband's shit DNA donation. The guy sounds like a real dick-bag. I know this because I'm a good listener.

"All done. Damn, I'm good," Kate says, throwing the brush into her kit and then sliding the cape from my neck. I stand and she straightens the collar of my shirt and hands me my navy-blue suit jacket to match the dress pants I'm wearing. She smiles my way. "Knock 'em dead, Miles."

"That's the plan. Thanks, Kate. Give Casey a fist bump for me and tell him to break a leg," I say, shooting a smile right back at her. I like her. Not in *that* kind of way – I *am* capable of interacting with an attractive woman in a purely platonic way. Kate's just nice to talk to. Thankfully. It helps, seeing as we'll be spending a lot of long days together over the next two months while I shoot this film. She's also born and raised here in Vancouver, which makes her my go-to personal Google for the best restaurants and hotspots to visit.

"Not so fast," Tori from hair says, eyeing me in the mirror. She points to my chair with a look that says, *I'm not done with you.* I lower myself back into the chair and she smoothes her fingers through the ends of my light brown locks with a styling gel, then sprays an obscene amount of hairspray over my head. "*Now* you're ready."

"Thanks, Tori. I may need a lung transplant in the near future." I mock cough and then check myself out in the mirror. *Yup, I look good.*

Seconds later I'm called to set. My current project is an action-comedy movie directed by Josh Lucas. I see him now, standing just off-set going over the script with my co-star Violet Michelson. Violet's eyes appraise me as I approach them and she flashes me a smile that is equal parts confident and naughty. The look in her eyes seems to say that she'd like to see what's under the suit. I nod coolly, knowing I need to keep this professional. I've never been one to dip my pen in the company ink and I don't plan on breaking that rule now.

"M.B." Josh addresses me by my nickname, clapping my shoulder. "Perfect. You're ready. I was just telling Violet I've made a slight change to the script." He hands me the sides script and fills me in. Violet leans into me, listening intently. She is arguably the most famous actress in America right now, having starred in some of the biggest movies of the past couple of years. A household name with over 12 million social media followers, Violet is supermodel gorgeous and unlike your boy, absolutely loves mixing business with pleasure. That's hardly uncommon in this industry. But these days Violet is dating Emilio Ricci, the biggest name in race car driving. The tabloids love the two of them, it's hard to find a magazine that doesn't have their faces plastered on the cover.

After going over the script changes, Violet and I take our positions on set. My PA, Georgia, who has been my personal assistant for years, hands me my water bottle and after a good, long drink, I hand it back to her and take a deep breath in. The rush of adrenaline I've come to fiend for rushes through my veins. I feel alive. I get ready to do what I do best.

I open my eyes to see Violet staring my way, a slow smile on her face. There's no doubt she's stunning, with eyes the color of caramels, long blonde hair and creamy pale skin. *Nope. Not happening, Violet. Nice fucking try.*

I relax my shoulders, get into position and wait for my cue.

"Quiet, please," the 1st AD shouts from behind a monitor. The 2nd AD steps in front of the camera and calls the scene and take number. With a whack of the clapper board, the 1st AD calls action and it's showtime.

It's no hardship working with Violet, and our scenes are going smoothly. She's playing nice, toning down the sassy, sultry edge she accosted me with earlier. I feel good. I'm on my game. Josh seems to agree, which obviously makes me happy. The man is a genius, a legend in Hollywood, and there's no way I'm going to let down the one director I've been dying to work with.

A few takes later, we wrap for lunch. Georgia is waiting for me on the edge of set to escort me to my trailer. I barely get out a "hello" before she's telling me my return call time after lunch and making sure everything on my preference sheet is just right. Georgia is mid-sentence when I feel a tap on my shoulder. I stop and turn.

Violet.

"Violet, hi. Everything okay?" I ask her. My eyes shift to her mouth, to her tongue that wets the corner of her lips. *Fuck.*

"We were magic together today, Miles," she practically purrs, with a look in her eyes that clearly says she wants to bang me until next Tuesday.

"It couldn't have gone smoother," I tell her with a smile, then realize quickly that may have not been the best choice of words. I don't want to give her the wrong impression. Having Violet Michelson in my bed would feel like sipping my favorite tumbler of whiskey: smooth and sexy. But I don't do other men's women. A media scandal is low on my list of shit I need right now. This guy is going to be on his best behavior for the next two months. Scout's honor.

I know for certain Violet *did* get the wrong impression when she leans in close to me, her breath dancing across my neck, and whispers in my ear, "Can I join you for lunch?"

I take a step back, running my hand through my hair. *Tori from hair is going to be pissed.* "Sorry, Violet. Sounds lovely, but I have a call I need to make. It may take some time." I try to keep it light, knowing we will be working together for the next couple of months and I need to walk a fine line here. But getting involved with Violet is a mistake I won't make. No way, no how. First of all, sleeping with your co-star is never, I repeat *never*, a good idea. Second, getting involved with her male co-stars is sort of Violet's M.O. There was Hugh Dempsey from the pilot movie, Blake Dalton from the casino film. Oh, and the bodyguard when she was on set in Hawaii. I'm sure there are others I'm missing. It's a long list, and I really don't need my name added to it. Third, she's fucking taken. And finally, even if she wasn't seeing Emilio, I'm just not that into her. I mean, the girl is gorgeous, but I've been with women like Violet. Hell, I've dated plenty of models and actresses, all stunning and sexy as hell. Some of them I truly cared about, others bored me to tears – I could definitely stand a lot fewer selfies and TikTok videos. But even when I was into it, it was never enough to make me want more. Something was always missing. Those relationships were fun for a while, but in the end they lacked depth and excitement.

Nope, not a fucking chance, Violet, I say silently.

I notice Georgia watching us. Her eyes are wide, like she can't believe what she's seeing. She looks like she's waiting for someone to hand her a bucket of popcorn.

"Maybe another time then," Violet says, looking completely unaffected by my rejection. She turns, giving me a perfect view of her round ass floating from side-to-side as she saunters away.

Georgia tries and fails to reign in a smirk when I turn my gaze to her. She motions to the exit, falling in line with me as we walk towards my trailer. "As I was saying, Miles. Be ready in 60. I'll be at your door to escort you back to set. I'll knock. We'll walk. I'll also need you to sign-"

Georgia is still talking, but I'm no longer paying any attention to what she's saying. My attention is completely captivated by the woman standing to my right. She's with Josh, the two of them chatting as I openly stare at her. I can't help it.

Who is she?

My eyes take her in. She's small, just barely over five feet. Her hair is the darkest shade of brown, almost black, falling to her shoulders in lush, loose waves. Her skin is a warm olive, her cheekbones high and angled, her full lips a soft shade of pink. She's wearing a simple black dress that ends at her knees, a fitted leather jacket and a pair of white high-top Converse on her feet. It's casual and understated. *I like it.*

But it's not what she's wearing that has me enthralled, it's the way her soulful, big eyes lock on mine when she glances up from the iPad she's juggling in her hand. She's looking at me the same way I'm looking at her.

Fascinated. Interested.

I'm definitely intrigued.

Suddenly, it's a silent game of who will break eye contact first. I raise my brow a fraction and smile. Her lips part, curving up in a shy grin, the briefest hesitation and an emotion I can't quite pinpoint dancing across her face.

Surprise. Curiosity. Or is it attraction?

Seconds later, Josh says something to her, and she breaks the spell, shifting her gaze from me back to my director. Just like that, the moment is lost. I shake my head, returning to reality as I continue through the doors,

Georgia still at my side, and walk the two steps up to my trailer. After promising her I'll be ready for the 1 p.m. call-back, I shut the door, flop onto the couch and close my eyes, replaying every second of what just happened in my mind.

What the hell *was* that? In my line of work, I'm around beautiful women all the time. But after just one look at this girl I have tingles covering my skin and my chest feels all fluttery.

I decide it must just be a case of the first-day-on-set jitters. I dig out my cell phone to distract myself and see I have a message from my agent, one from my publicist and one from my brother Liam. Swiping the screen to life, I scroll to check the last one.

> Liam: Good luck today, movie star.
> Remember to keep your hands to yourself.
> See you next week.

I laugh to myself. Smartass. But man, I'm excited to see my oldest brother Liam and his fiancée Ellie when they come here for a visit. My other brother Parker, who's two years older than me, and his wife Olivia will be coming as well. I can't wait to see them all.

In the meantime, though, I have lines to run and a turkey clubhouse to eat. And a text to send.

> Miles: Hey Jackass, you must have me
> mixed up with someone else. This movie
> star is, wait for it, a gentleman.

My brother texts back almost immediately.

> Liam: I just spit out my drink. I've heard you
> called a lot of things but a gentleman? I
> doubt that word has ever been used in the
> same sentence as your name before.

Miles: They are practically synonymous.

Liam: On what planet?

Miles: Mine. The one you get to live on
with me.

Liam: A gentleman with an ego the size of a
large state.

Miles: You love me. Admit it. Can't wait to
see you guys.

Tossing my phone on the couch beside me, I smile. Liam is living proof that people really can change. My no-strings-attached older brother, former purveyor of one-night stands, is now engaged to be married and expecting his first child. He's hopelessly in love, his balls firmly held in his fiancée's hands, and he wouldn't have it any other way. No one saw that coming. But I guess that's how life goes… always full of surprises.

Chapter Two

Rylee

I've never been that girl who throws herself at a man.

I don't bat my eyelashes, or wear outfits so tiny I risk being arrested for indecent exposure or slip men my phone number. That's just not me. Not going to happen.

I think that's in part because of the way I was raised. I grew up in a small town outside of Nashville and I was always taught to respect myself, to treat others the way I would want to be treated, to honor my family. These life lessons extended to my romantic life too. Don't chase after a man, my gran always told me. If he's not interested enough to pursue you, he isn't worth having.

Words to live by. Until today, that is.

I'm tempted to ignore them entirely now that I've been in the same room as Miles Bennett. *Forgive me, Gran.*

Miles Bennet. The man so many women fantasize about late at night. The man whose face graces the cover of almost every magazine on grocery store shelves. The man who has every woman in the city drooling since his plane touched down at the Vancouver International Airport four days ago.

Miles is the definition of a sex symbol, with those piercing hazel eyes that draw you in and own you the minute his gaze lands on you. I try to shake the memory of that moment between us from my head. I'm here to *work*, not to be swept up in ridiculous fantasies.

Returning to set, I adjust my walkie talkie headset and stand amongst the camera crew in video village. I'm never too far away from Josh Lucas, the film's director. I take my job as his PA very seriously, as I do most things in my life. I've always worked hard, and I've never been afraid to get my hands dirty. Growing up in the country definitely helps with that.

I stand off to the side and can't resist sneaking a peek as Miles and Violet film, drinking him in. One of Hollywood's leading men and *People* magazine's "Sexiest Man Alive" winner, not once but twice. Gossip rags don't do him justice. He's tall with broad shoulders and thick brown hair. His skin is tan, his lips look soft and pillowy – perfectly kissable, with a smile that gives me goosebumps. This man would look good in anything, but right now Miles happens to be in a suit. *Ho-ly!*

"How is he real?" Abby gushes from beside me, tapping her chin with a blue fingernail, gazing at Miles. She's fixated, clearly loving every bit of him. Any woman in the world with a pulse, I'm sure, does. "He's even better looking in real life."

"I have no idea. I'll bet he gives grown women heart attacks every time he leaves the house," I whisper back. "One look at him and they're goners."

"He must have groupies knocking down his door at all

hours of the day, hordes of them wearing nothing but trench coats," Abby says, absentmindedly twirling a few loose strands of her bright pink hair.

"Don't forget the supermodels," I remind her. "And the actresses. I wouldn't leave out JLo. I've heard it's a very long list." We've all read the articles – there have been plenty of them over the last few years. Miles is photographed with a different woman on his arm practically every week.

"I can't promise you I won't assault him with my tongue if he comes within arms-reach of me," Abby says, her eyes narrowing in Miles' direction.

"Gross," I say, wrinkling my nose in mock disgust. "But I wouldn't blame you if you did."

Abby opens her mouth to say something else then stops, apologetically raising one finger in my direction as she listens to someone through the earpiece of her headset. Shooting me a look that says *duty calls*, she briskly walks away.

Although we only met a few weeks ago, I really like Abby and the friendship we've struck up. We clicked right from the start, probably because we have a lot in common. We both relocated to Los Angeles from small towns, and both work as PAs in the movie industry. While working in Vancouver, we are staying in the same downtown hotel and plan to make the most of whatever down time we manage to get. We'll be taking in the incredible Vancouver scenery, eating the most mouth-watering sushi and spending our nights in one of our hotel rooms bingeing *YOU*. That's another thing we have in common: An unhealthy obsession with Penn Badgley. *I know we're not the only ones.*

It feels like I won the jackpot meeting Abby. Days on set can be very long and nights can feel pretty lonely when you have no one to keep you company. FaceTiming my grandparents, my nieces and nephew or my best friend Meg helps to pass the time, but nothing beats having a friend to meet for coffee or drool over the talent with.

Even though I've repeatedly checked in with catering, ran over the preference sheets too many times to count and confirmed with our transpo drivers on times and location, I still can't relax. If it's not one thing, it's another. It's just the nature of the job.

I have to stick around set to make sure Mr. Lucas has everything he needs for tomorrow, so I take the opportunity to watch the last minutes of filming. Miles' and Violet's characters are in the kitchen, sitting at the dining table. They're arguing over another man, Miles appearing effortless in the role. In between takes, Violet looks at her sexy-as-sin co-star like she wishes he was laid out on the dining table in front of her, naked on a platter.

Abby's eyes find mine through the lenses of her thick-rimmed glasses from where she's standing a few feet away. It's hard to miss Abby. Today she's wearing an oversized band T-shirt, lavender pants and a pair of cherry-red Doc Martens. Combined with her rose-hued hair and the multiple earrings looped through her ears, she's a buffet of bright colors and accessories. She shoots me an *are-you-seeing-this* look and I raise my eyebrows back at her and nod.

An AD announces 15 minutes until we wrap for the day, so Abby and I both switch off our tablets and she heads over to where I'm standing.

"From the looks of it, our leading lady has her sights set on our leading man," Abby says as we watch the last scene of the day.

I roll my eyes. "She couldn't be more obvious if she tried."

Abby nods. "Yup. She's as obvious as Kylie Jenner's nose job."

"Is she not with that super-hot Formula 1 guy? Emilio something?"

"Last time I checked," Abby shrugs.

"I think she may have forgotten about him."

"Yeah, the eye-banging is getting out of control. I'm surprised she's not already on her knees unzipping his jeans."

"You just couldn't resist, could you?" I grin, elbowing her gently in her side.

"Nope," Abby laughs. "But with anyone other than you, I will deny it until my last breath."

She turns to face me as the producer announces we're done for the day. "At last. So, dinner at that ramen place we both wanted to try after work?"

"Great idea."

I'm exhausted and hungry, and right now noodles sound like the cure for everything. But first I need to talk to Josh and regroup for tomorrow. I knock on the open door of his trailer and Josh waves me in, his eyes on the stack of papers in front of him. His trailer is well laid out, with a workspace, a small conference table, and multiple monitors.

"Have a seat," he directs, so I take the chair opposite him. "Excellent work today, Rylee."

"Thank you, Mr. Lucas," I say nervously, uncomfortable with the praise. I've never been great at accepting compliments. Anything resembling a spotlight makes me squeamish, I much prefer to blend into a crowd.

"Rylee, we've been over this. Call me Josh, please," he says, looking up at me for the first time since I entered his office. I meet his eyes and smile.

"I'm sorry. It's a habit. Will do."

Josh hands me the shooting schedule for tomorrow, quickly going over locations and times.

"Got it," I assure him, tucking the paperwork neatly into my bag. "And is there anything else I can do for you today?"

"I'm fine," he says, with a quick shake of his head. "I'll need you here for seven tomorrow. It's going to be a long one. Enjoy your night."

I stand from my chair and turn back towards the door, ready to go. Then I freeze. I hadn't heard him come in, but suddenly here he is, standing in the doorway right in front of me, one hip leaning against the frame. *Miles Bennett.*

Even in my surprised haze, I register that he is the most beautiful man I've ever seen. His hazel eyes are filled with mischief as he tips his head in a silent hello. The corners of his mouth tilt up in a sexy, confident smile. My pulse speeds and heat barrels up my spine, my body reacting to him on impact.

This isn't the first time today those eyes have been on me. I know it's nothing, he's just being polite, but I can't ignore the look he gives me. It feels dangerous, intimate. My heart hammers in my chest and I can't help picturing his body close to mine, his lips marking a path from my collarbone down to my stomach and then farther. I'm sure every woman on this set feels it when he looks in their direction. He probably makes it a habit to flash that perfected Hollywood smile wherever he goes, so it's silly to think it's any different when it's aimed at me. I swallow the giddy feeling in my chest, pushing aside the images in my head.

Miles steps aside just enough for me to squeeze my body past his. He smells so good. My body shivers in response but I keep my gaze forward, not daring to make eye contact, not wanting him to see how he's affecting me.

I meet Abby outside and tell her I want to walk the 10 blocks to the restaurant instead of calling an Uber. It's late spring, the air is cool and for some reason I feel hotter than a house on fire.

Chapter Three

Miles

If I thought she was breathtaking yester-day, she's somehow even more stunning today. Fitted jeans hug her slim legs and the plain white T she's wearing looks anything but plain on her. She's wearing her white Converse again and her thick dark hair is ironed straight past her shoulders, accentuating her eyes. They appear hazel, almost golden, sparkling and bright. In just jeans and a T-shirt, she somehow manages to be the most captivating woman I've ever laid eyes on.

I need to know her name.

But it will have to wait. Josh has noticed me and is currently beckoning me to him with a raise of his brow. *When the director calls… yada yada.*

I possess patience in spades. I can wait to find out who she is. I know what I want, and I'll take my time working for it.

My morning is spent shooting a bedroom scene, followed by a brief meeting with my publicist Matthew, who has met me on set to go over Vancouver media. The local outlets are hungry for anything they can get on Violet and me. There are photos. The two of us were spotted leaving The Ivy after a working lunch with Josh not long ago, and then again slipping into a town car after drinks at The Roosevelt last month. There were three other cast members with us, but the press conveniently opted to keep them out of the shot. They want something they can put their spin on, the first photo, the next new Hollywood romance. "Viles," I've been told, is our couple name. *Fuck my life very much.*

"Stay away from her, Miles. I mean it. You're on top right now. You're George Clooney level right now, but you fuck up, and they'll turn you into Charlie Sheen."

"Jesus, Matt. Do you have that little faith in me?" My publicist side-eyes me without answering my question.

"Fuck you, Matthew. I know how to keep my dick in my pants."

"Good. Then prove it. Oh, and before I forget, Wednesday is the children's hospital visit. You should be there a couple of hours then straight to set. There will be cameras, so wear something nice."

"Do I usually look like a vagrant?"

"I'm just busting your balls," he smirks. "Just don't forget what I said. Be a good boy." He lets those be his parting words, leaving me to think.

Is this really what people think of me? Even my own publicist? I love women as much as the next guy. Okay, maybe more. Sure, I've had my fair share of one-night stands, I've slept around a bit. But I *am* capable of a real relationship. I'm not afraid of commitment. I see how my two older brothers have found lasting love, and that's definitely something I want. Matt can kick rocks. I know how to behave myself.

When I want to.

I shouldn't have left my trailer. I definitely shouldn't have gone looking for her, checking my teeth and hair in the mirror like some dumb teenager. But I couldn't help myself. Apparently I have zero restraint when it comes to this girl. The pretty PA.

I didn't expect to spot her so quickly, standing on the steps of Violet's trailer. I swallow hard, taking in her dark golden skin glowing in the sunlight. My fingers itch to touch her, to trail down her slender arms from the edge of her short-sleeve T to the dip of her wrist.

And therein lies the problem. I *want* her. A woman I've barely met. A woman I know absolutely nothing about. Hell, I don't even know her name. But for some reason, I want her. I know it's crazy, but I can't seem to make it stop.

I watch her for a second as she listens to Violet go on and on about some minor annoyance. The pretty PA's fingers type furiously over the screen of her iPad. She smiles weakly while Violet doles out a hefty amount of bitch at her. She seems to be holding her own, but even so, I find myself at the bottom of the steps before I know it, standing beside this girl whose name I need to know, her gaze turning to meet mine. There's a quick hitch in her breath when she registers that it's me. I make a mental note of it.

This close to her I can see the true color of her eyes. I was wrong. They aren't hazel, they're green. So green they look like emeralds. There's the faintest sprinkling of freckles over her nose. It's been a long while since I've seen freckles, most women in Hollywood pay makeup artists to cover them up. God, she is gorgeous. The attraction I feel towards her is so strong it physically hurts.

She holds my gaze for a few seconds before turning

back to face my co-star, who isn't done with her yet. Violet may not be done with this, but I certainly am.

"Your 14 PAs aren't enough, Violet? You need the assistance of Josh's too?" I say with a cheeky smile, resting my hand on the railing just behind the pretty PA's back. I have to restrain myself from tracing my fingers down her delicate spine.

"Seems like it," Violet huffs. "Nobody here is capable of making a decent cup of coffee or getting my lunch order right. So Josh sent me this one."

She nods her head in the girl's direction.

This one. I've heard that Violet can be difficult, but I'm starting to see that *difficult* doesn't begin to cover it. I watch the PA do everything in her power to keep calm. She doesn't have to say anything, the cold look in her eyes is enough. While Violet works on mastering the art of resting bitch face, the PA manages to keep her cool. It doesn't matter. I still feel the need to do something.

"I tell ya what. You tell me what you want for lunch and I'll happily fetch it for you," I say to Violet, who smiles like a petulant child who's just been rewarded for bad behavior.

The pretty PA seems unsure what to do, her eyes swinging from me back to Violet. She looks panicked, off-balance. "It's fine, Mr. Bennett. I can handle this." Her voice is pretty and soft; it sounds like a song. *A song? Did I really just think that? Where did my balls disappear to?*

"There's no doubt you can, but I'm headed that way anyways," I say with a shrug. I don't normally lie, but I feel it's fair in this case. "So, what will it be, Violet? What would you like for lunch?"

"Thank you, Miles. A turkey-and-cheese croissant with tomatoes. Mustard, no mayo. A Diet Coke would be nice too. I'll wait for you inside," she says. Gesturing over her shoulder to her trailer, she adds, "There's plenty of room for you to eat with me."

That won't be happening, but I'll break that news to her when I return with her order.

I sneak another look at the woman who I'd rather be picking up lunch for – scratch that, I'd rather we were heading out for lunch together – and see that she's clearly uncomfortable. This is her job. Kind of. And I'm sure the thought of the lead actor on set running an errand for the lead actress is not sitting well with her. She catches me looking at her and pulls her device into her chest, unknowingly obstructing my view of her smooth, tan cleavage. *Jesus, Miles. Eyes up. Don't be a perv.*

"Mr. Bennett. It's really fine. Honestly, I don't mind at all. Y'all need a break. I'm happy to help." *Y'all.* Why does that sound so hot? Does she know how hot that sounds?

"That'll be all, thank you," Violet interrupts us, waving her hand in the air like a flapping fish, signalling the PA to skedaddle. I watch her stiffen, unsure how to handle this shit situation.

Lowering my voice, I try to reassure her. "Please, I've got this." A silent understanding passes between us and she smiles a shy smile and accepts.

This should be my cue to go. I need to fetch my co-star her lunch, after all. But I can't get my feet to move. The pretty PA solves that problem when she says, "I'd better be going," and turns to leave. In her eyes is a mix of appreciation and uncertainty.

"Wait," I say with zero chill, because apparently that goes out the window when I'm in this woman's company. "One question."

Turning to face me, her emerald irises make my skin pebble.

"Will you at least tell me your name?"

I watch her clutch her iPad to her chest a little closer, but she straightens her back and looks me in the eye.

"Rylee," she says a little nervously. "Rylee Brookes." I can't help the sudden grin that takes over my face. Her name suits her. It's so… her. Pretty, different. And suddenly Rylee Brookes is my new favorite name.

"Rylee Brookes. It's good to meet you. I'm Miles."

"I know," she says. Rylee takes a few steps backwards, smiles, then turns to walk away.

Even the slam of Violet's trailer door doesn't knock the huge grin from my face.

Chapter Four

Rylee

Toeing off my sneakers, I hop onto the queen size bed at the hotel, focusing on the two people on my little phone screen – the two people on this earth who love me the most. My grandparents. We have our routine. At night, we FaceTime, and in the morning, I email them to say I love you and to remind them to take their medications. On weekends, we chat on the phone, catching up on the week. It's not perfect, but it's the best I can do living 2,500 miles away from home and from my family.

It's not enough to say that I'm close to my gran and gramps. It's so much more than that. After all, they practically raised me.

My mother was a Sunday school teacher and my father worked in construction. They were high school sweethearts, and the love between them never seemed to fade. They held hands wherever they went, and most days ended with them watching the sunset from the porch swing, my dad's arm wound tightly around my mom's waist. There was always a bouquet of flowers on the kitchen table, my dad bringing home a fresh bunch as soon as the last ones had wilted.

My childhood was beautiful. We drank sweet tea on our porch, listened to Dolly and Kenny while we made pecan pies and green bean casseroles, and we never missed a Sunday sermon. It sounds idyllic because it was. Until everything changed.

This June will mark 11 years since I saw them last, since my two brothers and I moved in with my mom's parents.

I had just turned 13 the week before and my two brothers and I were at our grandparents' farm. We were spending the night, our parents attending a party at a friend's house. I had been sound asleep for a few hours when the knock on the door came. The voices were loud enough to wake me – especially my Gran's cries, which I could hear echoing off the walls. When I stumbled out of the bedroom with sleep still in my eyes, I saw a police officer standing in the doorway. My Gran was hunched, folded over her knees with her face in her hands, my Gramps' sturdy arms wrapped tightly around her. I didn't know then what had happened or why they were talking in hushed tones. I only knew that something was wrong.

There was never a question about who we would live with from that day forward. The farm became our new home, our grandparents became our legal guardians. Looking back, I wouldn't wish that first year on my worst enemy, but in time we made it through to the other side.

In the years since, many memories of the time before the accident have faded, others lost forever. But some remain imprinted so clearly in my mind that they feel like yesterday. I'll never forget how Mama looked when she worked in her garden. Wearing her favorite faded yellow sundress and a wide-brimmed hat to protect her fair skin from the sun, her feet bare, toes dusty. Or when Daddy came home from work in the evenings, going straight to the kitchen, pressing a kiss to the top of her head. If I close my eyes, I can still taste the Herbes de Provence, her secret ingredient in her chicken pot pies.

Now, sitting in a Vancouver hotel, that heart-shattering day that changed my world forever feels like a lifetime ago.

I giggle as Gran fills me in on the latest gossip from back home. Deer Lake may have a population of 7,300, but it is home to more than its share of small-town drama.

"You wouldn't *believe* the way Linda Baker treated my friend Marcy when she went to the Sunny Side Up for lunch last week," she tells me, dishing on the owner of Deer Lake's busiest diner. She sighs. "Bless her heart. But Linda wouldn't know southern hospitality if it fell out of the sky, landed on her face and started to wiggle."

"Never a dull moment," I laugh. "I miss you guys. So much."

"Rylee." She looks at me with her you-better-quit-that face. "Don't you be worrying about us."

"I never said I was," I say, knowing that Gran can see right through me. Sometimes she knows me better than I know myself.

"You think I can't tell when my only grand-baby girl is worrying? What's the worst that could happen here? We're just fine."

"If you ever need me, I can always leave here early," I insist. I'm supposed to be in Vancouver for 8 more weeks, until the film is scheduled to wrap, but I find myself worrying about them a little more every day. "Anyone could do my job here-"

"Rylee-Jay." Gramps stops me. "Don't you sell yourself

short. You would be absolutely irreplaceable and I'm not just saying that because I've loved you all your life."

I fight the urge to get all weepy. He's definitely biased, but it still feels good to have someone believe in me.

Gran chimes in, always wanting to have the last word. She leans in closer, her neatly coiffed gray hair filling the screen. "We have lived our life, now it's your turn. We will not be the reason you don't live out your dreams. This world needs you."

My Gran was the one who told me to leave Deer Lake. She took my hand in hers, her grip strong and her voice full of love, and said I needed to find my place in the world. It's what my parents would have wanted and there was no way she was going to hold me back. That was four years ago.

My best friend Meg had moved to Los Angeles to be closer to her dad shortly after we graduated high school. Her parents had divorced when we were kids and her dad moved to West Hollywood for a job in the film industry. As soon as Meg arrived, he put her up in a two-bedroom condo, all expenses paid, while she was going to film school. She had been begging me to come live with her and after that talk with Gran the time finally felt right. I left for the west coast, moved in with Meg and started film school a month later. It wasn't something I ever saw myself doing, but I needed a change, and it sounded interesting at the time.

"I know," I say quietly, shifting my gaze to the window of my hotel room. The sky is dark, the streetlights flickering through the sheer curtain. I drop my head, feeling the familiar push-and-pull on my heart at the thought of my grandparents needing me and me not being there. It's a guilt that has panged in my chest every day since I left

Deer Lake and seems to only grow stronger the older they get.

"You know that I worry about you two," I tell her. "I just hate that you are at the farm all by yourselves."

"We aren't alone, sweetheart. We have Cole and Cara."

"But they don't live with you. What if something happens and you need me and I'm so far away?"

My oldest brother Cole lives three miles from my grandparents with his wife Cara and their three small children. They'd gotten married straight out of high school, Cole taking a job at the largest automotive garage in town. Five years later, he's still there except now he owns it. The day I left Deer Lake, the responsibility of taking care of our grandparents fell straight onto Cole and Cara's shoulders. I'm grateful they took that on, but I know they could use a break. They have three little kids and a business to run, and our grandparents need more help than they used to. My other brother Walker feels the same way I do, and wishes he was around more to help. He calls whenever he can, but that isn't often seeing as he's in the military and living overseas.

I can't ignore the fact that my grandparents are getting older. At 76, they are starting to slow down, and my gran is becoming more forgetful. I've noticed it in our conversations, and my sister-in-law has filled me in on a few incidents as well. Cole won't dare tell me because he's afraid I'd jump on the first flight home. And he's right.

I've already decided that this will be my last film. I have to listen to my heart. I need to go home and take care of the people who took care of me when I needed them most.

"You have nothing to worry about. So shush, sweetheart, and tell us more about that hunk of a man you're working with."

"I'm not working with him, Gran. He's the star. I'm just the one running around set like one of those chickens in your yard."

At the mention of Miles, my mind drifts immediately to our run-in today. There's no doubt he is the sexiest man I have ever seen, with those long, dark lashes and chiseled features. He looks like every one of my fantasies come true – he even *smells* delicious. That's not what stood out the most though. It was the way he looked at me, like he wanted to know me. *Me.* Like somehow, he cared about the no-name PA who was getting an earful from his co-star. Violet Michelson can be a lot to handle, but there's no denying that she is drop-dead gorgeous and totally glamorous – in other words, she's everything I am not.

"With a face like yours, you should be the one starring opposite him if that director you work for had half a brain," my gramps says, interrupting my thought spiral.

"Thanks, Gramps," I say with a smile. "You're sweet, but there's one big problem with that idea."

"What's that, sweetheart?"

"I don't know how to act," I tell him, and they both laugh. They're the cutest.

A few minutes later, I yawn, nestling my head into the pillow. My gran notices and tells me to get my beauty sleep, so I look my best for "that handsome movie star" tomorrow. I shake my head at them. They never let up on me finding my soulmate and giving them great grand-babies. But a man like Miles Bennett falling for a small-town, country girl like me? *Bless their hearts,* as Gran would say.

After saying our goodbyes, I change into my pajamas, wash my face and snuggle into bed. Then I close my eyes and replay my run-in with Miles. Over and over again.

It had all been a lot. Miles' charm. Being that close to

him. The rush of desire I felt was so strong, it took hold of my chest and made it hard for me to breathe. There's a reason why it's *his* face that pops up when you Google "America's hottest man." He is heart-stoppingly, breathtakingly handsome.

Or maybe it's just been a while. It's been two long years since any man has kissed me, touched me. Not since Eric, a guy I met in film school. We dated for two years and not even he had ever made me feel this way.

I set my alarm for tomorrow morning, rest my cell phone on the nightstand beside me and turn off the lamp. I push any thoughts of Miles Bennett and my non-existent sex life out of my mind and try to get some sleep.

The next morning, I am sitting in the craft services tent, jamming a raspberry scone into my mouth and scrolling through my Instagram feed. I like a photo that Cara has posted of my nieces and nephew around the fire in my gran's backyard. They're roasting marshmallows, my youngest niece perched on Gran's knee. As always, my heart does a free fall in my chest at the thought of missing these moments with them. I keep scrolling to a photo of Meg with a margarita glass covering the bottom half of her face, the caption reading *Fiesta, siesta, margarita. Repeat.* She's in between jobs so she hopped a plane to Cabo with her boyfriend. Tapping the comment button, I type, *What I wouldn't do to be sipping a marg beside you.*

Meg and I have always been close. I don't remember a day as long as I've known her that we weren't. When we met, she was the funny, loud, popular girl who lived four houses down from me. I was the quieter one who stayed happily in her shadow. Meg knew how to play the piano, do front and back walkovers and always loved hanging with the boys. She was also in my class every year from grade three right through to our high school graduation.

Over the years, we'd done just about everything together: gone to Nashville on weekends to watch the latest bands, poured our hearts out to each other about crazy ex-boyfriends and been there for each other when times were tough. And they have been, like when my parents died and I cried in her arms every day for weeks. Now, we're both 24, still each other's best friends and the ones we always turn to when life gets tough.

"You missed a good night," Abby says, flopping down in the chair beside me. It's 7:15 in the morning and filming has been delayed due to an urgent last-minute meeting between Josh and the production company. "I hope that FaceTime call with your grandparents was worth it. You missed out on a game of Would You Rather? with a bunch of the crew. The cute blonde key grip guy likes threesomes and leather, by the way."

I raise my eyebrows at her. "Sounds wonderful," I say, tucking my phone into my pocket.

I pick up my coffee with two hands and am taking a sip when Abby and I both turn to see Miles walking into the tent with his PA. They're in the middle of a conversation, neither of them looking up as they head straight for the breakfast buffet, picking up plates and filling them. He's wearing a pair of black joggers with a gray hoodie, his hair and makeup already done. His PA leans into his shoulder. I watch them, because it's impossible not to. I swear half the room is staring. His head bends toward her, his laugh floats through the room and I know in this moment – a big aha! moment – that I can't let what happened yesterday happen again. Talking to him, being that close to him, is a very bad idea. I wince when I think of that glimmer of hope I felt when it seemed like he had noticed me. Just the idea that Miles Bennett would be interested in me is ridiculous. He's a born charmer and I can see now that I'm no different than every other girl who's felt that spark of hope when he's looked her way.

Now I'm sitting in a tent, probably with raspberry preserve on my face, pathetically watching the way his arms flex when he pours coffee from the carafe into his Styrofoam cup. The move of his muscular thighs as he reaches for a napkin. I inwardly cringe at myself for ogling the talent, but I'm positive I'm not the only one. Every woman here is following his every move. If Miles notices, you can't tell.

His gaze sweeps over the room, eventually landing on me. He pauses, then smiles. It's a different smile than the one he'd given me on set the first time or the one when he saved me from Violet. This smile feels deliberate. Genuine. Despite my best intentions, something flickers in my chest.

Abby looks from Miles to me, her eyes wider than the highway, kicking my ankle under the table with her boot. I nudge her very gently to stop her from making a scene. Thankfully, she can take a hint.

He walks in my direction and even if I couldn't see it, I can *feel* his eyes move to my mouth, my jaw, my shoulder, and finally back up to meet my stare. I can feel it like a feather, softly brushing over my skin. I hold my breath, and the room goes silent. And then it's over, as suddenly as it started, our connection interrupted by a crew member who approaches Miles with a question. They chat for a few seconds, giving me an opportunity to get a closer look. I look at Miles' hand, the one holding his coffee cup. His fingers are long and tan, his nails perfectly groomed.

Abby's voice cuts through my train of thought. "What the hell was *that*?" she demands. "What is going on between the two of you?"

"I have no idea what you're talking about."

I force myself to tear my eyes away from Miles. I have to before I am consumed by him.

"I've got to go," I tell Abby, crumpling up my napkin, pushing it onto my plate.

"But I haven't finished telling you the rest of the story," she protests. "You would never believe-"

"Oh, I think I can imagine," I say. But just because I *can* imagine whatever outrageous gossip she's about to spill, it doesn't mean that I want to.

Abby licks the icing from her cinnamon roll from her index finger. "It's okay. I'll fill you in at lunch."

"Thank goodness. I'm not sure I could survive not hearing the rest," I tease, pushing back my chair. She gently grabs my arm as I stand.

"And we are also circling back to whatever it is that is happening between you and Miles Bennett."

I stand, my knees wobbly. I take my plate and coffee cup from the table and grab my clipboard of sides that I need to go over. I slip through the tables full of crew and assistants, past the craft services bar, and out the door.

Chapter Five

Miles

I didn't see her leave, but by the time I'd dealt with the crew guy's questions, she was gone. I didn't see her again for the rest of the day.

I can't seem to shake her from my mind. When I met with Josh about a script change this morning, I found myself scanning the room, searching for her. At lunch, I was distracted by the craziest shit, like wondering if she had brought her own lunch, or was she eating in the craft services tent? Or maybe she ran out and picked up take-out. Did she prefer Thai, or maybe tacos? Is she a vegetarian? And when I filmed the big kissing scene today with Violet, it was Rylee's lips I wished were kissing me back.

What the hell is happening to me?

I've had my fair share of women. When I first started getting noticed in Hollywood, I couldn't get enough. I got used to women falling at my feet, and I slept with many of them. For a time, I lost myself in it all, hooking up with girls who only cared that my name was Miles Bennett. I had a different model or actress by my side every month, but that shit gets old, fast. I know it had disappointed my parents – especially my father, who has always been a family man, madly in love with my mother. I grew up in a home where family, morals and values are much more important than wealth and privilege. I've always looked up to my parents, and it felt shitty knowing I had let them down. They've been nothing but supportive of me, encouraging me to follow my dream of becoming an actor rather than join the family business. And I felt like shit knowing that I had let them down.

My dad owns the Seaside Hotel chain. High-end, luxurious boutique hotels across eastern New York. Parker is the C.O.O and my sister Jules runs the marketing side of things. My other brother, Liam, is a lawyer, but he works with Dad pretty regularly, reviewing contracts and evaluating potential business deals. I think I knew working in the family business was not in the cards early on and I'm grateful that my father never pushed it.

Acting had become my passion in high school. When I landed my first major role, Dad was the one who talked through it with me, making sure the deal was in my favor. When the series released a year later, both my parents were there to make sure fame didn't go to my head. My dad taught me to stay focused, to keep my eye on the prize and not be distracted by the shiny things that could quickly derail my career. I didn't always follow his advice, sometimes losing myself to Hollywood and all of its temptations. But I was young and successful, and settling down was the furthest thing from my mind. I just wasn't ready. In the past few years though, the hookups and one-night stands have gotten old. At 25, I've had my fun and now the novelty of a different woman in my bed every week has lost its appeal.

When the time is right, I'd love to bring *the one* home to

my family. Someone who wants me for me and not my bank account or my fame. Someone who values family as much as I do.

More and more, I find myself wondering what it would be like to have someone to call mine. Someone to come home to after a long day on set. A girlfriend in the seat beside mine at family dinners.

Settling into the back of the town car I often use to travel to and from set, I dial my dad's number. I wait for him to pick up as the car pulls out into downtown Vancouver traffic. The time difference and my hectic schedule have made it more complicated to get in touch with my family who live in Reed Point, a few hours outside of New York. The car heads north towards the Lion's Gate Bridge and my rental home 20 minutes outside of the city. When he picks up, I feel the tension in my shoulders after a long day ease. My dad has always been able to center me.

"Miles, how are you, son?"

"I'm good, Dad. On my way home. How are you and Mom?"

"Everything's fine here. Your mom misses you. You know how she gets when her kids are gone for too long," he says. I've gotten used to being away from home more than I'm there, but I know it always takes its toll on my mom. "She's been busy with Ellie, getting everything ready for the baby. It helps that she has something to focus on."

"You better be careful," I tell him. "She's going to spoil that kid rotten."

"It's true," he chuckles. I imagine him in his leather chair in the family room watching a baseball game on TV. "The baby is all she ever talks about. It's beautiful. I still have a hard time believing your brother is going to be a dad. How's filming going? Everything running smoothly?"

"So far, so good. Josh is a machine. You'd appreciate the way he does business. I'm hoping to introduce you."

"I'd like that. We'll find a time to come out and see you," he says. "Any plans tonight?"

"Not tonight. Just a workout, then I need to get organized for next week. Josh has a few of us visiting the children's hospital here. I had Georgia clean out most of the Vancouver Canucks merch to bring along with me."

"Good work, son. I'm proud of you. That's what it's all about."

He's right. Seeing the kids' faces light up for a few minutes was always worth the heartache these visits brought. It always puts things into perspective.

"I'm home now, Dad. I'll let you go. I'll call you this weekend. Say hi to Mom."

"I will. I love you, Miles."

"I love you too."

The sun is setting when the car stops in front of the large house on the ocean. My home away from home. Come to think of it, I'm not sure where home is anymore. I haven't spent more than three weeks in Reed Point with my parents and siblings in the past six years. I own homes in Los Angeles and London, but I never seem to live in either of them for more than a few days at a time.

I walk the stone pathway to the front doors. The house is quiet and dark, but it won't stay that way for long. My brothers and their significant others are arriving on Tuesday from Reed Point, staying with me here in my rental.

I strip off my clothes, changing into an old T and gym shorts, and hit the downstairs gym. I do reps followed by a gruelling run on the treadmill and by the end of it my shirt is soaked, my chest heaving. Thirty minutes later, I'm sitting on the balcony attached to the master suite, taking a sip from my whiskey. I tilt my head to the jet-black night and the stars I always miss when I've spent too much time under the smog-filled skies of LA.

I find myself wondering what the pretty PA is doing tonight. Having a drink at a bar? In bed reading a good book? Her faint accent is still crisp in my mind. The way she says "y'all." It's such a fucking turn-on.

Tomorrow I plan on bringing my A-game.

Chapter Six

Rylee

The rain Vancouver is known for is coming down sideways. I'm juggling a coffee in a to-go cup in one hand and an armful of shopping bags in the other, the plastic digging into my skin as I exit Choices Market. It was dry when I left the hotel and I'm not prepared for the downpour, wearing jeans and a T-shirt. It's Saturday afternoon and I have the day off. Abby wanted me to go for lunch, but I have too many errands to run to get ready for the week ahead.

I also needed this day off to reset, to put distance between me and the man I've found myself way too caught up in. I can't seem to erase Miles from my mind. I keep seeing his big hazel eyes, feeling the heat of his stare. I tossed and turned all night trying to make sense of it all. How can he be into a girl like me? A girl he doesn't even know. I tell myself I must be reading this all wrong. It must be my imagination. But I know what I feel every time our eyes meet. There's something there. It feels real.

Standing under the awning, I mentally prepare myself

to make the dash in the rain to my hotel, which is located 10 or 12 blocks from here. I could have called an Uber, but I need to watch my spending. When I return home to Deer Lake, I want to contribute to my grandparents' expenses, and who knows how long it will take me to find a good job that will pay me anywhere close to what I'm making in the film industry.

I release a heavy breath, dashing out from under the awning and into the pelting rain. I'm instantly soaked, my cotton T-shirt sticking to my skin, a shiver rolling over me. I make it roughly one block when a car speeding down the street plows through a puddle, splashing water up one side of me. *Dammit.* This is not how I saw my day going.

Hiking the bags higher up my arm, I keep going.

I'm startled when a voice shouts my name from somewhere in traffic. I turn to face the road, where a large, black SUV has pulled over to the side. The window is down and when my eyes focus through the rain, I see him in the driver's seat. *Miles.*

"What are you doing here?"

He doesn't answer me, instead shifting his car into park on the busy street, getting out and quickly rounding the front of it.

"Hand me your bags," he says, arms outstretched. "I've got these. Hop into the car. I'll take you wherever you need to go."

My first instinct is to hold on tightly to the armful of bags attached to my body. So, that's what I do. "I'm fine. My hotel is only a few minutes from here. Thank you anyways. I'll see you Monday."

"Rylee." He sighs, taking a step closer. "Please. Let me help you. It's just a ride. It's no big deal. "

"That's really sweet of you, but it's not necessary. A little rain has never killed anybody."

He doesn't take his eyes off me. He steps closer. My skin heats and my heart jumps, a nervous little leap.

"I insist," he says, reaching for the bags. "Besides… you'll hurt my feelings if you don't hop in with me. I'll assume you don't trust my driving and I'm sure you've heard how actors can be. Our egos bruise easily. Come on. Get in. You're soaked."

His point is adorable. I can tell I'm not going to win this argument and in the meantime we're both standing here getting even more drenched. I reluctantly loosen my grip on the shopping bags. He raises his eyebrows and smiles a sexy smile, gently taking them from me. With his free hand, he opens the passenger door, guiding me in. He's determined. I'll give him that.

Once he's loaded my bags into the trunk, he slides into the driver's seat, looking casual and cool despite the downpour. I try to stop myself from openly staring in appreciation at him. His profile shows his chiseled jaw, long dark eyelashes and full lips. I wonder what they would feel like on mine, then quickly shake the thought from my head. Two more seconds of this and I would qualify as a fatal attraction stalker. I realize quickly that being in this small space with him is going to be tricky. My heart is pounding. I'm nervous he'll notice how turned on I am.

"Hey," he says, glancing over at me. "So, where to?"

"The Executive," I reply. "I'm sorry. I'm sure you have better things to do today than drive me to my hotel." I place my coffee into one of the cup holders, wrapping my arms around my chest in an attempt to warm up. My skin pebbles, and I'm not sure if it's due to the wet clothes or the close proximity to Miles. Probably both.

Miles looks at me and smiles. I must look like a Golden Retriever after a swim through a mud puddle, but it doesn't seem to faze him. He's looking at me like there's no other place he'd rather be. I, on the other hand, am mortified.

"Here, put this on. You look cold." Miles removes the ballcap he's wearing, pulls his sweatshirt over his head, hands it to me, then puts his hat back on. He's wearing a short-sleeve gray T-shirt that looks one size too small for him. Not that I'm complaining. It shows off his athletic build, his defined pecs. It takes every ounce of willpower not to stare.

"I'm fine, honestly. You don't need to do that."

"Rylee, you're shivering. Put it on. Here, let me warm up your seat." Miles reaches towards the dash, tapping my seat warmer button while I throw the hoodie he gave me over my damp T-shirt. His scent lingers, making it hard to think straight. *How does he smell this good?*

He finally pulls into traffic, thankfully moving his eyes off of me and onto the road. I'm not sure what to say or where to look, so I stare at the shops and apartment buildings lining the streets. Silence fills the space between us. It seems like every resident of Vancouver is on Georgia Street this morning. A traffic jam of BMWs, Audis and Priuses crawl along at a snail's pace. My entire body feels hyper-aware of the small space we're sharing, of how close he is to me. I'm not sure I can do five more minutes of this.

Fortunately, we reach my hotel before I spontaneously combust right there in the passenger seat. Miles pulls his car up to the front entrance and kills the engine.

"I've got it from here. Thank you again," I say, unbuckling my seat belt, desperately needing some space to calm my racing pulse.

"I'm happy I could help," he says, then reaches towards me, tucking a loose strand of my hair behind my ear. His head tilts to one side at a 45-degree angle, and his lips tip up in the sexiest smile. I feel a flutter in my chest, but the moment is over as soon as it began, leaving a zip of electricity in its wake.

"Let me get your bags." He moves from the car, meeting me at the trunk, and begins to unload my shopping. For a second I almost forget that this is the man so many women obsess over. It feels like we are just two regular people, out running errands on a Saturday morning. Then I look over at him and remember there is nothing normal about this situation. I begin to remove his sweatshirt when he stops me, looking me dead in the eye with a smoldering gaze. He probably doesn't have a clue what that look is doing to me. Resting hot-as-hell face is his usual state. He moves a little closer to me and with every inch, my heart thuds a little harder in my chest. "Keep it, Rylee. It looks good on you. I like you in it."

I am knocked off balance, my emotions all over the place. I tell my silly little heart to calm down. Miles Bennett can have anyone he wants and Rylee Brookes from Deer Lake, Tennessee is nowhere near his league. I'm not even in his galaxy.

"I'll carry these to your room," he says, already moving towards the front doors of the hotel. I open my mouth to protest when he turns his head around to face me and adds firmly, "Don't bother trying to argue." Then he smiles a red carpet-worthy smile that lights up his entire face and it feels like I'm living a scene from one of my favorite rom-com movies.

I shake my head at him. "You are relentless." Then I follow him inside, trying my best to play it cool. I take a second to shamelessly stare at him. He's wearing a baseball hat to hide his face, the snug T-shirt that's just fitted enough to hint at the muscular, toned chest underneath it. A pair of faded jeans and leather sneakers complete his sexier-than-any-man-should-be-allowed-to-look look.

That's enough, Rylee, I tell myself. I need to do my job on Monday morning, and that does not include swooning over this incredibly attractive man.

When we reach the door to my room, I fumble in my purse for my key card. Miles is standing behind me, just inches away. So close that I can smell the cologne on his skin. It takes me an extra minute to find the damn key in my bag thanks to my brain being fried by his scent.

"Can I help you?"

"I'm good, but thanks. You've already helped enough. I've got it." I finally find the key and open the door to my room. Miles heads straight for the dresser, dropping my bags on top.

"This is nice," he says, looking around, first at my view of the city then to the queen size bed, reminding me I am all alone in a bedroom with Miles Bennett. Something about that realization makes me conjure up all sorts of racy fantasies. I allow myself to indulge in them for just a moment before coming to my senses and putting an end to it.

I watch his gaze stop on the bureau. "Is this yours?"

"It is. The camera was my mother's. She took it with her everywhere she went. I guess I'm sort of following in her footsteps." Photography is a hobby that I took to not long after I lost her. I thought if I took pictures with her camera, I would feel closer to her. I think it's helped.

He picks up the Canon, taking a closer look. "What do you take photos of?"

The room suddenly felt too small. Miles looks so handsome standing there, wanting to know more about something that interests me. I'm not sure why he cares, but it feels like he actually does. I swallow hard, trying not to get caught up in it all. Trying not to lose my cool.

"Anything really. Landscapes, architecture, portraits. I

find inspiration in the simplest things. You'd think I'd run out of things to capture but it never seems to happen."

"I'd love to see some of your work one day," he says.

His genuine interest leaves me flustered. Why in the world would he ever want to look at my photography? I'm not sure how to answer him, so instead I stand there like a dummy, my clothes soaked through and my hair still dripping, mascara probably smeared under my eyes. I fiddle with a necklace I'm wearing, suddenly incapable of speech. I'm sure I'm making a *really* great impression on him.

He must notice the silence that's fallen over the room, because he sets down the camera and turns to face me. "Are you hungry?" he asks.

"A little," I answer without thinking. Then it dawns on me. *Wait. Why is he asking me if I'm hungry?*

"How about sushi? There's a great place not far from here with small rooms that offer privacy," he stumbles. "From fans and the paparazzi, I mean, not…" He lets the sentence trail away, suddenly flustered. It's the first time I've seen a crack in his calm, cool demeanor. It's cute, and it makes me cringe a little less about my own nervous fumbling.

"Are you asking me to go with you?" I say, feeling a bit bolder now.

"I'm asking you on a date," he says flirtatiously, once again all charm. "What do you think? Game?"

I've never felt anything like this before. There's a flicker in my chest, a warm, tingly sensation covering my skin. I try to shake it off. Clearly, going on a date with a man like Miles would be a mistake – one I know better than to make. For him, dating a girl like me would be a fun distraction. For me? Falling for Miles Bennett would shatter me into pieces.

I open my mouth, resolved to give him the safe answer,

the one I know that I should. But when he absentmindedly runs his hand through his hair, I lose my resolve.

"Okay, game."

Before I have a chance to change my mind, I grab some dry clothes from the closet and quickly slip into the bathroom to change. I pull my still-wet hair into a bun at the nape of my neck, apply a fresh coat of lip gloss and then return to the room, where Miles is waiting for me.

With a fluttery feeling in my chest that I can feel right down to my toes, I walk out of my hotel room for a lunch date with Miles Bennett.

***

I'm sitting in a little room across from Miles in a tucked away Japanese restaurant. We're hidden from other diners behind walled panels, sitting on top of floral-printed pillows on wooden benches. With his baseball cap pulled low, I doubt either the hostess or our server has a clue who just walked into their restaurant, and the other diners didn't seem to notice Miles as we slipped by.

"Is it always this easy for you to be out in public?" For some reason I thought Miles would be mobbed every time he stepped foot out of his house.

"A hat and sunglasses usually do the trick," he says looking at me over his menu. I thought being alone with Miles would make me feel awkward. Instead, it's comfortable and easy. "Unless the media has been tipped off, I can usually blend into a crowd."

"It's not what I would have expected. I just assumed you wouldn't be able to leave your house without being mobbed everywhere you went."

"It seems that way when you see photos of celebrities in magazines or on TV entertainment shows but typically an agent has tipped off the photographers for publicity. I guess it's the name of the game in show business."

Miles flips his hat so it's backwards on his head and my pulse races. I had no idea a backwards hat could spark a physical response in me, but apparently it's my thing.

Luckily our server arrives at our table to take our orders, so I have something other than Miles to concentrate on. When it's my turn, I can feel Miles looking at me. The waitress takes my order, collects the menu and leaves. When I turn my attention to Miles, he's grinning.

"What?" I blurt, suddenly self-conscious. "Do I have a bug in my hair? Food in my teeth?"

"No, not at all," he laughs. "The opposite, actually." He pauses, clearing his throat, looking down at the table then back up at me. "You're beautiful, Rylee."

You're beautiful, Rylee.

He can't really mean that. I need to remind myself not to fall for his charm. He's used to gorgeous blondes with size zero bodies, perfect boobs and oversized, injected lips. This man is just the world's biggest flirt and I happen to be in his vicinity. I shift my gaze away from him and remind myself that a man like Miles will always end up with a girl like Violet. That's who he really wants. But just the thought of Miles Bennett and Violet Michelson together gets me annoyed. I try to shrug it off.

I know I should thank him for the compliment, that would be the polite thing to do, but I can't quite get the words out.

"You're making me blush, Miles," I say honestly. "I'm not great at accepting compliments."

He's smiling when I look up and it's thrilling. I take in his rich, deep eyes, and how they seem to be laser focused on me. I feel a flutter in my stomach.

"I'm sorry if I made you uncomfortable. I assumed you'd be used to hearing that a lot."

I'm not sure how to answer him and thankfully I don't have to. The waitress appears at our table with green tea and a bowl of edamame, causing the tension in the tiny tatami room to ease. Over tea, we slip into an easy conversation, Miles telling me about his two brothers and sister, about his childhood in Reed Point. I share my own stories of small-town living, of my grandparents' farm. He seems fascinated.

"Goats and chickens. A few cows and horses," I answer when he asks the kind of animals we had on the property growing up.

His eyes are as wide as vinyl records. "You are kidding me."

I laugh. "I swear on my life," I say, crossing my heart with my fingers.

"You don't look like you grew up on a farm. I never would have guessed."

I cock my head to the side. "And what is that supposed to mean?" I ask him. "Please tell me you're not picturing pigtails, Daisy Dukes and cowboy boots?" My voice is laced in sarcasm.

He begins to laugh, shaking his head, "That's not how I meant it."

I look back at him with an *oh really* expression and he laughs again. It makes me feel happy. I want to hear his laugh on repeat.

Our conversation is so natural, so easy, but as we chat about our families a small part of me waits for Miles to ask about my parents. It's not something I talk about with anyone. After all this time it's still so difficult for me to revisit, so I don't. Ever. But the question never comes, and I'm thankful for it.

Our waitress stops by our table with our food, setting down small plates of rolls, tempura and sashimi. We rip open the paper chopstick packages, diving into our meals.

"Do you miss it?" Miles asks, after a mouthful of a sushi roll.

"The farm?" I ask, and he nods. "I do. It's peaceful being so far away from a big city. The fields, the stars at night. There's a small lake not too far from my house that is perfect for swimming. My brothers built a rope swing one summer and the three of us would take turns cannon-balling into the water, over and over and over. I'd go there to read. I'd bring my camera and take photos of the field flowers or the red squirrels – but they were usually too quick to let me get a good photo. My gran would always get mad at me for staying out there too long. She'd send my brothers to come and get me and they would be so irri-tated about it."

"I feel their pain. My sister Jules is the rebel of our family, believe it or not, and my brothers and I were always having to cover for her. She was always getting into trouble. She felt like a full-time job sometimes."

I laugh. "I am team Jules on this one. I know first-hand what it's like to have a couple of older brothers who constantly interfere in your life. It drove me crazy. Everyone in school knew I was Cole and Walker's younger sister because they made sure of it. I hated it and wished they would mind their business."

"They were just doing what any good brothers would do. I bet I would like them." He leans back in his seat, taking a sip of his green tea. "Are they both back home in Tennessee?"

"Cole is. He's the oldest. He lives not far from my grandparents with his wife and three kids. Walker lives overseas." I tell him about Cole and Cara, and about

Walker, who is a Marine Corps infantry unit leader. Walker is the serious, always-in-control brother who craves structure and an itinerary and all of his ducks in a row. I tell Miles how I look nothing like either of my brothers, who both have lighter hair and tower over me. He tells me his brother Liam, who is a lawyer, reminds him of Walker. Both serious, over-achieving and brooding. He says his brother Parker, the oldest of his siblings, followed in their father's footsteps, working in the family hotel empire with his sister Jules.

Everything he tells me feels so personal, like he's letting me in on little secrets that the tabloids, the media and entertainment reporters don't know. I have to pinch myself to make sure that this is really happening. How is this my life? I'm sitting across from a Hollywood heart-throb, in a Vancouver sushi restaurant, listening to the intimate details of his life. It all seems too impossible to believe.

Using my chopsticks, I take the last bite of my salmon nigiri. "That was really good sushi."

"Vancouver gets it right when it comes to sushi," he says, stacking his chopsticks across his empty plate. "I'm glad you liked it."

"I should really get back. Thank you, Miles," I smile at him, a little sad that our lunch date is coming to an end, that whatever just happened between Miles and I is over. Then he surprises me.

"I want to see you again. Can I have your number?" he asks.

What did he just say? I would have to be a sucker for punishment to spend any more time with a man so utterly out of my league.

"You will see me... on Monday, at work," I tell him.

"I want to see you outside of work. Just the two of us.

We could have dinner. Or if you prefer, we could grab coffees and walk the seawall."

Looking across the table at Miles, I'm really wishing I was the kind of girl who was okay with a one-night stand because let's face it, that's what this would be. But that's never been me. I need commitment, but even that isn't something I'm looking for right now.

I watch him tip back his glass of water, his Adam's apple bobbing as he swallows. Any other girl on the planet would probably jump at the chance to go out with Miles Bennett. But I know better than to believe he really means what he's saying. I'm just not sure how to say no.

"You're persistent," I say, stalling.

"I know what I want," he says, his hazel eyes narrowing in on mine. It sounds flirty. I wish I didn't like it so much. He also sounds completely genuine. "Rylee, I want to get to know you. From the minute I laid eyes on you, I haven't been able to stop thinking about you."

He thinks about me?

My heart leaps. He hasn't even touched me, and I find myself practically drowning in lust. I tell myself it's only because I haven't been with anyone since Eric. That has to be it. Two years is a long time to go without the touch of another person. I try to convince myself that it's the only reason I have this strange, fluttery feeling in my stomach.

"Why don't I give you my number and we'll take it from there? I can't make any promises." I say, hoping he'll go with that. My voice sounds hesitant and a little shaky and I'm mad at myself as soon as I hear the words leave my mouth. Giving him my number is a horrible idea, but I've said it and there's no turning back.

"I'll take it," he says, reaching for his phone, unlocking it and handing it over to me. I reluctantly type my number into his contacts and hand his phone back. His fingers brush mine as he takes it, and a blanket of goosebumps rush across my skin in response. I'm not sure whether I'm more nervous or turned on.

"We should get going," I manage to say, needing to put distance between us. His charm is too much, his good looks are more than I can take.

"We should," he says. "But I don't want to."

What am I supposed to say to that? I sit frozen in place. I need to get up and go, but if I'm honest with myself, I don't want to. I want to stay here with Miles and his crooked smile, those hazel eyes that have me on edge. Caution signs are flashing in my mind. *Go, Rylee. You need to go back to your hotel room. He's an actor. He probably says lines like this every single day, to just about every girl he meets.*

Digging into his pocket, Miles pulls out his wallet and pays the bill. Thankfully, my body finally regains the ability to move, and I turn and slide off of the bench. He stands before I do, flipping his ballcap around, pulling it down low on his head. He offers me his hand. Without thinking, I take it, his palm warm and large against mine.

We head towards the exit and only when we step out onto the sidewalk do I realize I'm still holding his hand. I release it quickly and he chuckles.

The rain has finally let up, and I look up, squinting against the sun peeking out from beneath the clouds. Did I really just have lunch with Miles Bennett? Did that really happen?

Chapter Seven

Miles

Fuck me, I can't get enough of this girl. I'm following her back up to her hotel room like a lost puppy. She told me she was fine and didn't need me to walk her to her room, but any extra time I can get with her I'm going to take.

There's just something I find so compelling about this woman. I want to figure it out. I want to figure *her* out.

My hand rests on her lower back when we enter the elevator. I lean against the wall, watching her press the button to her floor. The door closes shut and we're alone in the tiny box. Turning to face me, she dips her chin, hiding a shy smile. It's ridiculously adorable, and vulnerable too. I feel my insides melt a little. I like it. I like her.

There are a lot of things I like about Rylee, but right near the top of the list is the fact that she really couldn't care less that I am Miles Bennett. A lot of women would be hiking up their skirts and begging me to bang them – literally, it's happened before. But Rylee is down-to-earth, she doesn't seem to want a thing from me. She didn't even seem to want to join me for lunch. It's refreshing. I like that I can just be Miles when I'm around her, and not the guy that everyone wants me to be.

It makes me want to get to know her. I need to figure out how to get her to open up and talk to me.

The elevator doors open, and I lower my ballcap on reflex, following her down the hall. When she reaches her room, she hesitates for a second before opening the door.

She turns to face me, and I have to fight the urge to kiss her. I want to feel her lips against mine. There's something about this girl that has me tied up in knots. Maybe it's the effortless way she always looks sexy or the look in her eyes when she catches me staring at her. Rylee genuinely has no idea how gorgeous she is. I already know I'll be thinking about her later tonight in the shower, with my dick in my hands.

"I had a great time with you today," I tell her. I decide to leave out the part about how much real estate she's been taking up in my brain lately or how happy I am to finally have gotten a chance to be alone with her. "Is it weird that I'm sort of grateful for the rain today?"

She blushes – like *actually* blushes. Her cheeks turn the softest shade of pink and it lights me up inside knowing that I did that to her. It makes me wonder what else I could do to her. What color would her cheeks be after sex? What would she look like underneath me, with her dark hair fanned out over my pillow, her lips swollen from my mouth on hers?

Fuck. With images like that in my brain, how the hell am I supposed to focus? My dick is at half-mast just imagining the things I want to do to her.

"I had a good time too. Thank you for lunch, and for saving me from the rain, Miles," she says, her faint drawl a little more prominent. I try my hardest to hide my grin, but it's impossible. That faint southern twang is so fucking hot.

I don't want this day to end, but I know it has to. I want her to invite me in, but I know she won't. I'm also aware that it probably wouldn't be a good idea to be alone with her in a hotel room right now. I've been fighting a hard-on all afternoon just listening to her talk.

So, I lean in and kiss her cheek. When I pull back, her eyes open slowly, her lips are parted. Her tongue traces her bottom lip. Her green eyes linger on my face for a little longer than normal. Fuck, I want to kiss her mouth. I want to run my fingers over her jaw, down her neck to her chest. I want to do a lot of things I know I shouldn't do. The anticipation is *killing* me. But a wariness flashes through her deep green eyes. I can see she's scared, I'm just not sure why.

I lean in closer to her, my lips millimeters from her ear, and whisper, "I want to kiss you." Her chest rises. Her breath hitches. "But I promised myself I'd be good."

I watch her skin flush again. I'm hard as a fucking stone now.

"I…" Her voice is quiet. She glances away for a moment, then back at me. "I really need to go. Thank you again." Her hand pushes the door to her room a little further open, but she pauses before closing the door. An expression of uncertainty flashes across her face.

"Goodbye, Miles."

I wink. "Goodbye, Rylee."

Later that night I'm lying in bed, thinking about Rylee. It's only been six hours and I already miss her. I miss her smile and the way her eyes sparkle when I say something that makes her nervous. I know without a doubt I want to see her again.

I ran 10 miles after I dropped her off, then lifted weights for half an hour in the home gym at my rental, needing to work off some pent-up sexual frustration. When that didn't work, I took a cold shower and jerked myself, shooting all over the white-and-gray marble tile. After I cleaned up, I got into bed and picked up my phone, sending Rylee a text. *Zero restraint.*

> Miles: I had a great time with you today. Is it too soon to ask when I can see you again?

I wait for her reply, tapping my phone against my chin. I wonder if she's been thinking about me too. I hope so, but maybe that's wishful thinking on my part. I sneak glances at the screen every so often, willing those bouncing bubbles to appear. Finally, after what seems like forever, she's typing.

> Rylee: Thank you for lunch. I had fun. You weren't what I expected.

> Miles: A conceited actor with a superiority complex?

> Rylee: I wasn't going to say that.

> Miles: It's okay. I've been around my fair share.

> Rylee: I've seen enough of it too working on sets.

> Miles: I'm not like that, Rylee. I hope I've never given you that impression.

Rylee: You've never. Every person on set
seems to agree you're one of the nice guys.

Miles: Then go out with me. I'm free
tomorrow. Can I take you for dinner?

My grip on my phone is turning my knuckles white as I wait for her to respond. My heart beats a little faster in my chest. It feels like I'm coming unglued. How is she doing this to me already? I'm staring at my fucking phone praying for her answer to be yes. Her response appears.

Rylee: Can I ask you a question?

Her reply is unexpected. She has me curious.

Miles: Anything. Of course.

Rylee: Why me?

I hesitate for a second, wondering how much I want to tell her. How honest I want to be with her. The truth is always the best policy, my mother taught me. She always tells us to say what we feel. So, that's what I do.

Miles: You're beautiful. And I can't get you
out of my head. I want to get to know you.

Rylee: My life isn't that exciting. I would
hate to disappoint.

Miles: So is that a yes to dinner tomorrow?

Honestly, I don't remember the last time a girl told me no.

The perks – or drawbacks, depending on how you look at it – of being famous. No one says no to me, ever. But I can already sense that Rylee may be the exception to that rule. It makes me nervous as hell, but it's also refreshing and exciting.

Miles: Nothing fancy. Just dinner. Don't overthink it. Say yes.

The three dots bounce around on my screen, then they're gone. I anxiously wait, wondering if I'll need a plan B to get this girl to go out with me. My phone lights up with a text a second later.

Rylee: Yes :)

Thank fuck. I blow out a breath.

Miles: I'll pick you up at 7. I'm looking forward to it. Night, Rylee.

Rylee: I am too. Night, Miles.

Dropping my phone to the bed, I'm grinning like an idiot. Like I won some sort of prize. I wore her down. I'm going to dinner with her tomorrow and that's fucking exciting.

I reach for my phone, typing a message to my assistant Georgia, asking her to have flowers sent to Rylee. I wish I could do it myself but using my name and my credit card is a risk I can't really take. If the delivery leaked to the press, I'm pretty sure Rylee would be scared off and there's no way I'm taking that chance.

Georgia responds with a thumbs up emoji. Then she sends a second text with a cheeky message. *Don't think I'm sending this girl flowers for you without knowing who she is. I'll be expecting details tomorrow.*

I laugh to myself, setting my phone on the nightstand. Seven o'clock tomorrow can't come quick enough.

My date with Rylee has been all I've been able to think about. I'm sitting in the backseat of a town car on my way to her hotel, consumed by thoughts of this girl.

She's waiting outside when the car approaches. I do a double take. She's wearing a fitted black dress that ends at her knees. The straps are narrow, highlighting her shoulders and collarbones. Her legs are perfectly tanned. The sight of her makes my mouth water. I suddenly realize this is the first time I'm seeing the shape of her body. A rush of adrenaline courses my veins. She's incredible in every way.

When the driver parks in front of The Executive, I can't wait to get to her. The car has barely come to a stop when I open the door and step out.

"Hi." I lean in and kiss her cheek, leaving my lips on her skin for a few seconds too long.

"Hey," she says, sounding a little breathless. "Thank you for picking me up."

"Of course, and you look amazing."

Her gaze shifts to the ground for a second and I let my eyes move over her. She's clearly uncomfortable when I compliment her. She meets my eyes, a shy smile on her face. "Thank you. You look very handsome."

"Here, let me get the door for you."

When we're both in the car, I am all too aware of her proximity to me. We're sitting so close her knee brushes against mine and even that little bit of contact is enough to set me on fire. It's quiet in the car, but not uncomfortable. I fight the urge to touch her, to take hold of her hand. I want her comfortable and at ease with me. I want to make a good impression but the scent of her perfume filling the back of the car isn't helping. The desire to get my hands on her intensifies, but for now, I settle for sneaking peeks at her when I can.

The drive takes minutes, and soon I'm holding her hand, walking her into the restaurant.

"Good evening, Mr. Bennett," the hostess greets us, then escorts us to our table. The restaurant is dark and moody, with suede upholstery and soft jazz music spilling out through the speakers. Candles flicker around the room, white linen tablecloths and crystal water glasses fill the space. We are led to the table at the back, which I asked Georgia to reserve for us.

"It's so pretty here," Rylee says as she takes a seat. Her dark hair is tucked behind her ears and it's the first time I notice her earrings. She has two small hoops in each ear. They suit her.

Our waitress glances at me, then not-so-subtly takes a second look. She welcomes us to Cardero's and it's obvious she recognizes me. She seems nervous, her voice taking on a higher pitch.

"It's our first time here," I say, looking her straight in the eyes. She tells us about the menu, but I don't really hear any of it. I'm too busy looking at Rylee and the way her skin glows in the candlelight. How her long, slender fingers play with the ends of her hair as she listens to our waitress. I notice the dip of her cleavage and the slender column of her neck. I would give anything to run my tongue down it. *Snap out of it, Miles.*

I order a bottle of wine, and our waitress leaves to grab it. Rylee fusses with her silverware then picks up her napkin.

"Thank you for the flowers," she says, placing the white linen napkin across her lap.

"I wondered if you got them."

"They're beautiful. I love them, but I'm worried you didn't leave any for anyone else in the city."

I laugh because I may have gone a little overboard. "I told them I wanted all of their roses. Was it too much?"

"My hotel room smells like a garden. It's nice." She smiles and her eyes sparkle behind the flicker of the candle between us.

Just then our waitress interrupts us with our bottle of wine. After pouring us each a glass, she tells us about tonight's features, disappearing again once we've ordered.

"You're not wearing your baseball hat," Rylee says, picking up her water glass. "Aren't you worried about people noticing you?"

"Not really," I reply, grinning. "No one on my team tipped off the paps, so the coast is clear. Besides, the driver will pick us up right in front of the door. I think it'll be okay."

We made it easily into the restaurant, but I am aware of the other diners in the restaurant glancing over at us. I've grown use to the attention over the years, but I'm sure it's all kinds of wild for Rylee. Having strangers stare at you is something that takes years to get used to. I pick up my glass and clink it against hers. Rylee licks her bottom lip before taking a sip of the rich, dark red, and my eyes follow the motion. I'm dying to taste the Merlot on her lips. But of course, I don't. I behave like a gentleman. I am, however, curious about something.

"Can I ask you a question?" I lean in closer to her across the table, my elbows resting on the surface.

"Okay."

"How are you feeling about being here? I sensed you weren't sure about coming to dinner with me."

She considers the question for a second before answering. "Are you worried I'm going to suddenly freak out and bolt for the door?"

I laugh. "The thought has crossed my mind."

She smiles. "I promise I won't. But I *am* nervous. Okay, terrified might be a better word."

I love that she's forthright about it. She doesn't make me guess at how she's feeling and seeing as I've never been one to play games or read minds, it turns me on.

"Why is that?" I ask.

"I'm not really sure. Maybe because I can't remember the last time I went on a date, or maybe because you and I have very different lives. Also, it feels a little shocking to be sitting here with you. You make me… nervous," she admits.

"We're going to take things slow," I reassure her. "There's so much I want to know about you. And maybe we'll find we're not as different as you think."

Rylee meets my eyes and nods. It's sexy and so is her response when she says, "Maybe so."

Our appetizers arrive moments later. I ordered the tomato and bocconcini and Rylee ordered a garden salad. I pick up my fork and take a bite.

"How was your day?" she asks.

I pause mid-bite. I don't remember the last time anyone has asked me that, with the exception of my mom. People are usually more interested in my schedule, or my lines, or what party I'll be attending. Or what I can do for them.

"It was good," I tell her. "I slept in later than I have in weeks. Went for a run. Memorized lines and did a quick radio interview for a news station in Australia. And that's about it."

"Not too bad," she says, spearing a cherry tomato in her salad with her fork. "I slept in too. It was nice."

"And what else?"

I pop a bite of tomato and cheese into my mouth while she answers. "I went for a walk with Abby, got my nails done and called my grandparents."

This is the second time she's talked about them, and it makes me wonder if her parents are in her life. Something tells me she doesn't want to talk about it, so I leave it, wanting to enjoy this time together with her.

"How are they doing?"

Over wine and appetizers, Rylee tells me all about them. How they raised her and her two brothers from the time she was a teenager. She says that her grandmother knows every last bit of gossip coming out of Deer Lake and that the two of them have been happily married for 50 years. She tries her best to visit them on holidays and long weekends, she says, and I can tell from her voice that she's very close to them.

We continue to talk about our families, our jobs, our likes and dislikes. I tell her about Parker getting married to his high school sweetheart after eight years apart. She tells me how much she loves the outdoors and about her passion for photography. The mood is flirty and fun, and I already find myself wishing this night would never end.

Our waiter sets our meals on the table in front of us. My veal piccata looks cooked to perfection and Rylee's chicken looks good too. I spread my napkin across my lap and take my first bite.

"How is it?" she asks. "Mine is incredible."

"Mine too. Here, you need to taste this." I stab the veal with my fork and run it through the lemon and caper sauce, and without thinking twice, I reach over the table with my fork and offer it to her. Her eyes widen for a brief second, then she leans in and takes my fork in her mouth. Her lips run the length of it and my dick stirs in my pants.

The *mmm* sound she makes next is enough to give me an erection the size of the Empire State Building.

Rylee swallows the tender meat then sips her wine. "So good," she says. "How did you know to come here?"

"Kate from makeup was raving about it. Josh had told me about it too. He comes here whenever he's in Vancouver," I say, cutting into my veal. "I think they have his picture somewhere on the wall."

"I'm sure they'll also want yours up there after tonight."

After dinner, Rylee and I ordered dessert, deciding to share the lemon cake and the tiramisu. As we sink our forks into the desserts and make small talk, the restaurant around us seems to have faded away. It feels like it's just the two of us, like this is where we are meant to be.

"Tell me what you're thinking." My fork hovers over the plate when I ask her.

She tilts her head to the side as she's carefully choosing the right words. "I'm thinking I hope you don't take the last bite," she says with a grin. "I'm also thinking that I'm happy I said yes to tonight. It's nice being here with you."

"Really?" A smile spreads across my face. I want her to say more. I want to know every single thing that's crossing her mind.

I swirl the red around in my glass, hoping she'll expand.

"Really," she says. "I wouldn't bother telling you something that wasn't true."

Fuck. Why does everything this girl says turn me on? My skin is crackling with lust. I am so fucking attracted to her. "I like that about you. I hope you will always tell me what's on your mind."

"My gran tells me my ability to open myself up to people is both a blessing and a curse."

I can't help but smile. "I'd go with the former. Not many people can be that honest. You seem to wear your heart on your sleeve and it's sexy."

"That's a nice thing to say," she says shyly. "Now, it's your turn to divulge something."

"Okay," I say, my eyes focused on her green irises capturing her attention. "I know I said we could take it slow, but I don't really want to."

I swallow, hoping I haven't made her uncomfortable. "I mean, I can and I will take things slow, but it doesn't mean I want to. There's something about you that makes me light-headed. I like talking to you. You're down-to-earth and funny. And I think you're the most beautiful girl I've ever seen. I mean it, Rylee. I wouldn't bother telling you something that wasn't true," I say, using the same words she just spoke to me.

She smiles and shakes her head slightly. "You're just not used to girls like me who live regular lives. I'm sure I'm interesting now, but that will fade."

"I don't think it will."

She just stares at me, her eyes a little hopeful but mostly cautious. I love it when her eyes are on mine, even if they're not looking at me with absolute certainty. I'm not sure how I can convince her that she means something to me.

"I appreciate your optimism."

I take a breath. "Does that mean you'll go out with me again?"

"Don't push your luck," she says with a devastatingly beautiful smile, before taking the last bite of the cake and licking her fork clean. *Lucky fork.*

"I'll wear you down," I tease and I don't think the innuendo is lost on either one of us. I watch her cheeks flush pink.

Tonight has felt good. Being with her is fun, easy and a total turn-on. She's beautiful and captivating and that combo is enough to keep any man interested, wanting to know more. And I do. I want to know everything there is to know about Rylee Brookes. I want more time with her, more dates. I want to know what makes her tick.

Eventually plates are cleared, and the date is over way too soon. I pay the bill and our driver takes us back to her hotel. I walk her to her room to say goodnight, not expecting anything more than that. My God, I would love a hell of a lot more, but I can be patient.

She opens her door, leaning against the doorway to stop it from closing.

"I should go to bed. We both have an early call time tomorrow morning," she says, fiddling with her key card in her hand. "Thank you for tonight, Miles. I had a really good time."

I try to think of something, anything to say, of some way to extend the night, but I come up blank. Between the smell of her perfume in the air and the overwhelming desire to touch her, I can barely think straight. So I settle for, "I had a great time with you too."

She's looking up at me with her beautiful face and big, green eyes and she still hasn't moved from her position against the door. I realize now how close I am to her. I can't take it one second longer. There seems to be an electrical current running between the two of us, an undeniable attraction. Without thinking, I lift her face with my finger under her chin so that her eyes find mine. Her gaze hazy like my mind feels, swimming in lust. I want to cover her lips with mine but instead I leaning forward, dusting my mouth over the edge of her jaw. Then softly kiss her right below, on her neck. Soft, lazy kisses while my fingers find the back of her neck. She tilts her neck to the side just slightly, granting me access, giving me permission to keep doing what I'm doing. She whimpers as my fingertips find the groove at the back of her neck. The sound drives me crazy.

"You should stop touching me like that," she murmurs as I run my fingers down the back of her neck. Her gaze roams over me, and the longing in her eyes is definitely not just my imagination. We are both drowning in lust.

I want more of whatever this feeling is.

"Is that what you really want? For me to stop doing this?" I say in a low voice, continuing to trace my finger in the opposite direction, back up her neck and towards her ear.

"I-" her voice trails off as my mouth kisses the long, slender column of her neck then traces over the edge of her ear.

She grips my hips with her hands while I back her into her room. The door falls closed, and I turn her and press her back against it. Even in my blissed-out state, I know I don't want an audience for this goodnight kiss.

"I've wanted to touch you since the moment I saw you. You have no idea what you do to me." My lips are so close to her ear, my breath against the flesh of her ear lobe. "Tell me you wanted this too."

"Miles. I-" Her head tips back against the door and her breath catches. I watch her eyes close shut as my mouth sucks on the soft skin just behind her ear. I'm taking my time, kissing her neck slowly and carefully until I make it to her mouth, where I'm aching to be. She shivers.

Arousal takes hold of me, making me want more. I need her mouth. I need to taste her. I want my hands all over her body. I moan under my breath, needing to touch her more.

"Ryls, you're killing me. I want to kiss you. So if-"

"Do it," she says, smiling at the nickname that slipped from my mouth without thinking. "Please, Miles. I want you to." The rasp in her voice makes her plea sound illicit. She used my name when she asked for it. It's erotic. I'm fucking aroused like she's seducing me with her mouth, with her words.

I don't bother to hide my grin when I cup her face with both hands, lean in and brush my lips against hers. Her lips are soft and feel so fucking perfect against mine, a rush of electricity courses through me. I feel my heart beat faster in my chest when her lips part and I take it as an invitation to push my tongue into her mouth. I moan into the kiss and her hands tighten around my waist. Everything about this kiss is perfect and different than any other kiss I've ever experienced.

We're both dazed and breathing heavy. Her fingers roaming up to my arms, gripping my biceps, our tongues tangled together. When I pull back to look at her, her eyes are still closed, her lips parted like she's wanting more. The kiss ended too soon and all I can think about is getting my mouth back on hers.

"I'm losing my mind," I breathe. "I can't stop thinking of you."

"You think about me?" she asks, her eyes open wide now, her expression in disbelief.

"I do. A lot," I admit, which is an understatement. If I had a dollar for every time Rylee has crossed my mind, I'd have enough money to purchase a small island.

I can't stop thinking about taking things even further, being inside her, but that will have to wait. I promised her we'd take things slow and I want to honor that. Kissing her up against this door will have to be enough, and it is.

"If I stay, I won't be able to stop at just kissing you. I better go."

"I think that's a good idea." She whispers the words, her hands letting go of the grip she has on me as she opens the door to her hotel room. "I'll see you tomorrow, Miles. Thank you again for a nice night."

"See you tomorrow. Night, Rylee," I say, before kissing her. Her chest heaves as I pull my lips from hers. She smiles, seeming to have enjoyed the kiss as much as I did. I walk past her, down the hall to the elevator, my whole body covered in goosebumps.

No one has ever left me feeling like this.

No one has ever even been memorable. Until Rylee.

I couldn't forget her even if I tried.

I send her a text, so she knows how much that kiss meant to me.

Miles: Kissing you is better than anything.

Chapter Eight

Rylee

I shouldn't have let him kiss me. I should have said no. In my head, I knew I should stop it. But I couldn't. In that moment the only thing I could think about was the pleasure that took hold of me. On a scale of 1 to 10, that kiss was a 20.

Apparently I can't resist him. Miles is all I want. I've never been kissed like that, with such passion and intensity. I could kiss him forever. Even now, just thinking about it, it's enough to take my breath away. I try to shake off the memory of last night but can't. I'm not sure that I'll ever be able to forget how that kiss felt. My skin heats up remembering the way his tongue found mine when he deepened the kiss. The way my knees felt weak and my back arched into his touch.

Everything about letting go and giving in to Miles was wrong. Nothing good can come from it. But despite knowing that taking things further with him would be a terrible mistake, every part of my body, every single nerve ending, is begging for more. I wish I didn't want him, but I do.

I tried to steer clear of Miles on set today, finding some reason to be wherever he wasn't. If he was in hair and makeup, I was in craft services. If I knew he was filming, I made sure to be sending emails for Josh in his trailer. My attention span was dismal, but somehow I managed to do my job. I felt off all day, unsure of how to act around him, how to be with him in front of everyone at work. Avoiding him was easier.

That was today. But it may not be possible to avoid Miles tonight. It's Jared Kennedy's birthday and we're gathering at a little Italian restaurant to celebrate. Jared is an actor in the movie we're shooting, playing opposite Miles and Violet as "the other man." I wasn't planning on coming, but it became clear that any answer other than yes was not going to cut it with Abby. I finally said I'd go with her under the agreement I would be home and in bed by 11 p.m.

The restaurant is cozy, tucked into the Yaletown district of downtown Vancouver. The walls are brick, painted royal blue, with gold sconces and black shaded chandeliers hanging from the ceiling. We are in a private room with its own white marble bar, brown leather barstools and a bunch of leather booth seats around the edges of the room. Smaller marble high top tables are scattered through the center of the space.

Abby and I are sitting at one end of the bar chatting. We're sipping the restaurant's signature cocktail that tastes like Meyer lemons and sugar.

"I'm so glad you came tonight," Abby says, clinking her glass against mine. I'm tempted to down the sugary drink in one gulp to calm my nerves. My eyes nervously dart around the private room, waiting for Miles to show up. The thought of seeing him for the first time since our date, since that kiss… it might just be the end of me.

"I'm not sure there was any other option. You did threaten to 'end me' if I stayed home," I tell her, popping exaggerated air quotations around the phrase to remind her of her exact wording. Abby's a sweetheart, but apparently she's not above resorting to threats of violence to get her way.

"Well, it got you here, and that's what matters," she says with a sly smile.

Miles texted me after work, offering to give me a lift to the restaurant. I declined. It all felt like too much, showing up to an industry party with him at my side. I didn't want to deal with the stares or the questions. It was just easier if I arrived with Abby.

I knew Miles was coming, but I still feel unprepared when he walks into the room.

He's wearing a tailored navy suit and white dress shirt open at the collar. His hair is perfectly styled, and he has a five o'clock shadow – definitely my weakness. My eyes can't get enough of him, of his strong jaw and gorgeous, tanned skin.

It takes about 10 seconds for his mischievous eyes to find mine and as soon as they do, he flashes me a smile. He's looking at me like we have a secret, which we most definitely do. I smile back. His eyes gleam, lingering on me for a moment, and somehow it feels like he's touching me from across the room. My heart drops to the floor as his eyes shamelessly trail over my body. The thought of actually being with Miles is crazy, but try telling that to my ridiculous heart. This is all so easy for him. His heart is certainly not on the line like mine is. This would be fun for him. For me, it can only end in misery. I have to be careful.

Our moment is lost when the birthday boy clasps Miles

on the shoulder and brings him in for a hug. Jared takes him by the arm and ushers him across the room.

Despite what happened between the two of us last night, I'm keeping my distance. He called me this morning, but I didn't have the courage to answer. Then I avoided him all day on set. Looking at Miles across the room, at his easy smile and the way his fingers hold his rocks glass, I'm not sure if I have the strength to steer clear of him.

We are on opposite sides of the bar, but I can still feel him looking at me, sneaking glances that are setting my skin on fire. When I look in his direction, I catch him staring at me, mid-conversation. He smiles and I smile back, then quickly turn my attention back to Abby.

Needing a minute to collect myself, I excuse myself and go to the restroom. It's located just outside the private room and I'm thankful for that. The space was beginning to feel like it was closing in on me. Locking myself in a stall, I take a few deep breaths to calm my racing pulse, then stand in front of the mirror, washing my hands in cold water. I open the door and take a step into the hallway, where I'm immediately stopped by a warm hand on my wrist. I turn around. *Miles.*

"I'm sorry you weren't the first person I said hello to," he says, rubbing his thumb softly over the inside of my wrist, piercing me with his hazel eyes.

"You don't need to apologize for that. I saw Jared greet you. You didn't stand a chance."

Miles laughs. "I'm glad you're here. I was hoping you'd come."

I look over his shoulder to make sure we're alone. He lets go of the grip he has on my wrist and I miss his touch immediately. "To be honest, I wasn't going to, but Abby talked me into it."

"I hope I'm not the reason you didn't want to come."

"You... I just didn't want things to be awkward between us. I didn't think I could pretend in front of everyone we work with like I didn't just have the most incredible night with you."

I watch his shoulders relax. He lets out a breath. His eyes focus on mine and he grins."Incredible?"

A smile takes over my face.

"You said incredible. I heard it with my own two ears," he teases. " And for the record, I'm not asking you to pretend. I feel the same way. Last night was the best date I've ever been on and I can't wait to do it again."

I'm not sure what to make of this, but his words make me happy. The restaurant and everyone in it seem to go dark. Then his fingers find mine and he holds them there for a second. "Miles, I'm not ready for people to know that we're... about whatever this is. I'm sorry if that hurts your feelings, that's not my intention. I just feel a little over-whelmed."

He sighs. "I understand. That's fine with me, but so we are clear, if it were up to me, the whole world would know that I'm seeing you."

I feel my face heat, and I know that I'm blushing. "We should get back to the party before someone sees us whis-pering in the hallway."

Miles doesn't argue. He's a few steps behind me when we return to the private room. I take my seat next to Abby at the bar, feeling buzzed though I've barely touched my drink. I love how assertive Miles is, how he's not afraid to tell me how he's feeling. His confidence is sexy as hell.

A little while later, Violet arrives with red lips I could never pull off, her eyebrows perfectly plucked and her hair pulled back dramatically in a tight ponytail. She struts into the restaurant like she has all the time in the world despite the fact that she is almost two hours late. I watch her make her entrance in a little black dress, with a heavy emphasis on the "little." She looks flawless with her perfect smile and supermodel body. The only thing she doesn't have going for her is a personality to match. I've never met anyone more intolerable. I deserve an Academy Award for masking the sheer disdain I feel for this woman on a daily basis.

Her eyes dart over to Miles at the bar and I bite my bottom lip, watching her find what she wants. Like a heat-seeking missile, she goes in for the kill. Her gaze is penetrating and full of desire.

I feel sick at the way she's looking at him. I want to tell her to stay away from him, to remind her that she has a boyfriend in Europe. But Miles isn't mine and I have no right to dictate who he talks to, or who he flirts with. So I look away and try to ignore the pang of jealousy. I hate that Violet has the ability to make me feel jealous.

"We should go sit with them over there," Abby says, gesturing to two guys sitting in a booth across the room. "Remember the cute blond crew guy I was telling you about, the one who likes threesomes? That's him. He's hilarious. Come on."

I could use the distraction, so I follow her, and we slip into the booth with them. My back is to Miles, saving me from the torture of watching him with Violet.

I introduce myself to Craig and Steven, who I've seen around set but haven't had the chance to meet. They're nice, easy to talk to, and soon we are deep into a debate about useless skills each of us possess. Abby is emerging as the clear winner as she describes her ability to chug anything cold and never get brain freeze when Miles appears at our table. He asks if he can join us and I notice everyone sit up a little straighter, like Prince Harry has just arrived. He sits opposite me and it takes everything in me not to openly gawk at the man. He's so beautiful it hurts.

He introduces himself to the table, and I laugh when Abby plays dumb at his introduction. "Oh, I'm sorry. I thought you work here," she says. Everyone, including Miles, laughs at her joke.

"Well, I do know how to make a mean gin martini. Maybe I'll apply for a job if my other one doesn't pan out."

"Damn," Abby laughs. "Miles Bennett has jokes."

I take another sip of my drink through a smirk. If Abby only knew. The man has a hell of a lot more than a sense of humor. A wave of guilt passes over me thinking about the secret I'm keeping. I can only imagine the look on Abby's face if she found out I've been seeing Miles Bennett. But I'm not ready to talk about it so I push away the thought as a waitress brings over a tray of tiny appetizers. We all take one.

"This is incredible," I say, after swallowing a bite of the tuna poke stack.

Miles stares at me, his gaze focused on my lips. His eyes have darkened, the look in them making my heart pound. I shift in my seat, nervous that Abby or one of the guys might notice the way he's looking at me. Needing something to do, I pick up my drink and take a sip.

I'm setting the glass back on the table when Violet approaches.

"Room for one more?" she asks, sitting down beside Miles, forcing him to scoot over. Craig and Steven's eyes just about pop out their heads, not that Violet notices. She hasn't acknowledged anyone else at the table besides her co-star. Miles makes a point of introducing her, and I take notice of the fact that he remembers everyone's names.

"Oh, I didn't expect to see either of you here," she

says, briefly letting her attention fall to me and Abby. She's looking at us like we're peasants. I straighten my spine, refusing to allow her to ruin my night.

"Jared was kind enough to invite most of the crew. He really is a great guy," I say, hoping she gets the hint that you can be mega-star famous *and* still be kind to the people around you. I doubt it will actually sink in, but a girl can try.

"Is it cool in here or is just me?" Abby says, wrapping her arms around her middle, rubbing her arms. I bite back a laugh, pretty sure she's referring to Violet's chilly personality. "I should have brought a sweater," Abby continues, "but I couldn't find one in my rush to get here."

"I'm sure you could find what you're looking for at Target," Violet snips. "I've heard girls like you love it there." My hand flies to Abby's knee, squeezing it before she has a chance to jump across the table and throttle her. She takes the hint, blowing out a breath and sitting back in her chair.

"So, where are you from, Miles? L.A.?" Steven asks, attempting to move the conversation along. I'm starting to wish I stayed home with a face mask and a chilled glass of wine. It seems much more enjoyable than sitting here suffering through Violet's childish behaviour.

"No, actually I'm from a small town three hours outside of New York. Reed Point. I moved to L.A. when my acting career took off."

"And that it did. I'm a big fan. I've seen all of your movies. I have to tell you I was jazzed to hear you were the lead on this project. I'm really excited to work with you."

"Thanks, man. It's not a career I ever saw coming, but I love it," Miles answers before asking if he can get anyone a drink from the bar. It's rare for the star of a movie to hang out with the crew, let alone serve them drinks. But

Miles isn't like other celebrities I've met. For instance, I happen to know he doesn't have one item on his preference sheet on set, which is a testament to the type of man he is. Someone raised him right.

"If you're going anyways, I would love a glass of water," I say, and he nods.

"A dirty martini would be amazing," Violet adds, as she scoots out of the booth to let him pass. I expect her to follow him, but she doesn't seem to be going anywhere. She sits back down, lucky for us.

"Consider it done." Miles winks, disappearing to the bar to get our drinks, leaving us alone with Violet for a minute. Abby and I glance at each other, exchanging mental eye rolls. Neither of us can think of a thing to say to her.

Miles returns a few minutes later, handing me my drink and then Violet hers before taking a seat at the end of the booth opposite me.

"Thank you," I say, a hitch in my voice. I wonder if it will ever feel normal to be around Miles. The physical attraction I feel for him is undeniable. It feels like it radiates off of me, totally obvious to the rest of the room. I'm hoping I'm doing a decent job of hiding the way I feel about him, but acting differently than how I feel has never been my thing. And it's not just his looks that draw me in, but the fact that he is so real.

"So, Violet, where are you from?" Abby asks, and I'm impressed by her attempt to engage the actress.

Violet seems bored. Bored with the company, the music, the drinks. Or maybe she's just irritated that she has to share Miles with the rest of the table. She answers Abby's question with zero enthusiasm.

"I'm from California. I grew up in Orange County, but

I wanted to leave since I was little. My dream was always to move to Hollywood and become an actress."

"You accomplished that. Your parents must be proud," Abby says, trying her best to make conversation.

"I guess they are. My father is a surgeon, and my mother owns a woman's clothing store. They're both very busy. You know how it is?"

Abby smiles wanly. As for me, apparently I do not exist. Violet hasn't looked in my direction once since she's sat down. I have no idea what I've done to make her to treat me this way. I probably shouldn't care, but I do.

"It sounds like we grew up very differently," Abby replies. "I'm from the south. A small-town girl. Rylee too."

"Well, that explains things."

What is that supposed to mean? I can't hold my tongue. "I had the privilege of living most of my life in a small town," I say, adding as sweetly as I can muster, "As did Dolly Parton, Brad Pitt and Meryl Streep. You've heard of them, I guess?"

Miles smirks and Abby shoves her thigh against mine under the table.

Violet must notice Miles looking at me because her eyes narrow in on him. Her hand glides over his bicep as she leans into his neck just a little too close. She starts to giggle at everything he says like it's the funniest thing she's ever heard. Every time her hand travels a little further up his arm, I cringe.

I don't know what bothers me more: watching her put her hands all over him or the fact that he's doing nothing to stop it. It hurts that Miles would allow her to flirt with him right in front of my face. She looks across the table at me, her expression making it clear that she's got him right where she wants him. I'm beginning to hate her with a passion.

Standing up, I say to no one in particular at the table, "Can you excuse me?"

A girl can only take so much. I walk away, not able to stand two more seconds of this. The idea of Miles and Violet together is enough to make me vomit. I know I'm behaving like a jealous girlfriend, but I don't care. I feel like an idiot for even thinking there was something between Miles and me. How stupid am I? I don't dare look behind me as I head straight for the door, my heart racing, tears threatening to fall.

I push my way through the crowd of people, reaching the door and exiting onto the darkened street. I round the corner and pull my phone from my clutch, needing to call an Uber.

"Rylee, wait."

Miles' hand reaches for me, wrapping around my wrist, and it causes the same reaction as it does any time he touches me. That spark. It's a thrill. It's electric.

"What are you doing?" I ask, narrowing my eyes at him.

"Looking for you. You just got up and left. You didn't say goodbye."

"You were busy. I'm surprised you even noticed." I hate myself for the clipped tone in my voice. This is not me. I don't speak to people this way. Jesus, what is wrong with me?

"Noticed? I always notice you. Haven't you figured that out by now?"

I'm not sure what to think. How does he expect me to believe him when he's famous for not only his acting but for his social life too? Let's face it, he has a different girl on his arm every week. I remind myself I was happy before I kissed Miles Bennett and I will be happy without him, but he needs to know how I feel. "Miles, what happened yesterday can't happen again. It was a mistake."

"Come here," he says, taking my hand, pulling me into a darkened corner, away from people loitering in the street. "Is this about Violet? Because she doesn't mean a thing to me. I swear."

"Look, I'm sorry. I didn't mean to give you the wrong impression."

"And maybe I didn't give you the right one. I want to get to know you better. I'm not interested in anyone else, least of all Violet. Everything I said to you last night and tonight? I meant it," he says, taking two steps closer to me. My pulse speeds and my cheeks burn, and I can feel the flush spread down to my chest. Instead of backing up, I stay where I am. His body is so close to mine, my chest is almost touching his. The look in his eyes makes me want to dig my fingers into his hair and kiss him, but I don't. I'm still hurt.

His eyes flash. "I'm asking you to get to know me. That's it. We can take things slow. I'm not going to push you, but you're going to have to trust me. Can you do that?" His voice is low, but there's an intensity in it. It's only Miles and I, standing here in the dark, and that thought alone is sending shivers over my skin. My legs are shaking, and I've forgotten every reason I stormed out of the restaurant. All I care about right now is what Miles would taste like if he kissed me.

His hands come up to my jaw, taking my face into his hands. "Can you trust me, Rylee? I promise I won't hurt you." I know what I *should* do, but there's no part of me that wants to move. Maybe I did overreact. Miles is a nice guy, maybe he didn't want to embarrass Violet in front of everyone at the table. He seems genuine. I shut my eyes, regretting that I let Violet get the best of me. I want to trust Miles but even more than that, I want him to kiss me.

I might get my wish. He looks like he wants to push me up against the wall and tear off my clothes. And I want him to. I want him to do so much more than that. I couldn't care less who might walk by.

My legs continue to tremble. "You're blushing," he says, brushing a thumb over my cheek. *Oh my God, how is this man real?* Five minutes with him in the dark and I'm spinning out of control.

"Say yes, Rylee." His voice is barely above a whisper, it's hypnotic. I suck in a breath. I feel as though I'm submerged in water, deep in an ocean. The way he's looking at me right now makes it hard to breathe.

I'm in a daze, drunk on Miles, the scent of his after-shave doing crazy things to my libido. I whisper, "I want to say yes, but-"

"No buts," he counters, his hands moving slowly from my jaw to the sensitive area behind my ears. "Give this a chance."

I really do want to say yes. I want him to kiss me. His lips are so close to mine, but he holds back. He just watches me with a smoldering, alpha-male look. His eyes are focused on my lips and he's waiting for me to answer. He won't give me what I so desperately want until I tell him what he wants to hear.

"Stop looking at me like that," I say, unable to think with his eyes locked on me this way.

"I can't. I'm so fucking attracted to you. Please don't make me beg."

"I must be crazy," I say, my breath catching as he looks at me, my whole body now nearly trembling.

"Only crazy not to give this thing between us a shot. Say it. I want to hear it, Rylee. Tell me we're going to get to know each other and see where this can go," he whispers, and his gaze intensifies. His fingers hold me tighter, excitement shivers over my skin.

My heart is pounding. A slow smile widens across his face. There's no way I can answer him with anything but a yes. So I say it, giving in to him, to the idea of seeing where we could go. It feels absolutely terrifying.

"Yes. We're doing this." I breathe the words, needing his lips on mine in the worst way.

"You mean it?" he asks.

"I do."

It must be written all over my face because his mouth is on mine before I can get another word out, and he doesn't stop kissing me and kissing me until I'm light-headed and out of breath. It's the hottest kiss I've ever experienced in my life. I can't get enough of his mouth. It tastes like whiskey, like risk. We're both breathing hard when he finally pulls back.

He pulls me against him, my arms snaking around his neck. His lips brush my ear.

"Fuck," he murmurs. "I don't want to stop, but kissing you like this in public could get us on the front page of every tabloid."

It's a sobering reminder and I reluctantly let go of him and take a step back. I must have lost my freaking mind kissing him like that just feet away from a busy downtown street. I am in over my head. I have zero interest in being the subject of gossip magazine headlines. What had gotten into me? I never lose control like that but with Miles, giving in is all too easy to do. Kissing him is like the high of a drug that hooks you after just one hit. His lips are soft and demanding, his tongue makes you want to beg for more.

I feel my cheeks flush. "I should go," I tell him.

He whispers my name and laughs. The way he says it makes me feel like I'm seeing stars. "You're not going anywhere without me. I'll take you back to your hotel. Give me a second to call my driver."

I open my mouth to protest, but the look on his face makes it clear there is no point in arguing. His phone is already against his ear.

I swallow my smile. Miles is here, with me, standing under a streetlight and looking at me like I'm the only thing in the world that he wants. The only way this can end is with me being broken into a million tiny pieces. Everything about him – his charm, his smile, his lifestyle – has the power to ruin me, and I doubt there's a thing I can do about it.

Against my better judgment, I take his hand when he offers it and I get into the car beside him.

I text Abby to let her know that I left the restaurant, then look out the window at the blur of flashing lights and passing cars against the jet-black sky. Anything to distract me from Miles and how delicious he smells. I want to bathe in his scent, wash my bed sheets in it, bottle it up and make millions.

I don't know where this is going, but I am certain that Miles Bennett could be my demise.

Chapter Nine

Miles

My eyes found her as soon as I walked into the room. Rylee. I couldn't stop staring at her, the curve of her shoulders, the slim band of skin exposed at her midriff whenever she raised her arms a little too high. Wearing a skirt and tank top, she was sexier than any other woman in the place. Certainly sexier than Violet in her barely-there black dress.

Halfway through Jared's party, I couldn't take it anymore. Being in the same room with Rylee but not being able to touch her felt like torture. As the party went on, the spark she lit in me grew into a flame. I had been half-hard, for Christ's sake, all night long. Just from *looking* at her.

I'd behaved myself long enough. Hell, I should have been awarded some kind of trophy for not pulling her into me in front of everyone at the party and kissing her senseless.

And then finding her outside, alone and upset over the stunt Violet pulled, only made me want to convince her that it was her that captivated me, that it would never be a girl like Violet.

Now, standing in front of her hotel room door, I kiss her goodnight. As much as I want to come in and strip her naked on top of her bed, I'm not going to. She's nervous, she's built up walls so high around her heart to protect it. I know I can't rush things. Besides, anticipation is everything. I want her as worked up as I am right now. I want her going to bed and thinking of me.

With self-control I had no idea I possessed I break the kiss. Her vivid green eyes are wide and doe-like, filling me with want. Rylee blinks up at me, her lips parted from the best kiss I've experienced in my life. She's watching me, her eyes blazing, waiting to see what happens next.

"I'm looking forward to tomorrow," I whisper, kissing the side of her jaw. Her hair smells like mangos. *Fuck.* I really don't want to leave her.

"That excited for work, huh?" she teases. Her lips tip up in a small smile and it takes me aback how good her smile makes me feel.

"Excited to see *you.*"

She draws her bottom lip in between her teeth while her eyes do a sweep of me. She wants me just as bad as I want her. I can tell. She's not even trying to hide it. But a goodnight kiss is going to have to do.

"Goodnight, Miles."

She gives me a slow smile and opens the door, stepping inside. I watch it shut behind her then walk away, trying to shake that kiss and everything I am imagining doing to her from my mind. I might be both exhausted and sexually frustrated, but it's clear how much I want her.

That in itself should be terrifying.

It's not.

"Do you have any idea what you're doing to me today in that skirt?" I whisper into her ear.

She stiffens. She doesn't turn to face me, but I know that she heard me when she sucks in a deep breath of air. She keeps her face down, pointed towards the iPad that she carries around everywhere she goes.

I have her cornered just outside of craft services, careful no one is around to see us. From where I'm standing behind her, the scent of her perfume invades my senses. It smells like coconut, a hint of something fruity. She smells like the beach.

I can only see Rylee from the back but it's enough to know she looks hotter than hell and I have to remind myself that she's not yet mine to touch whenever I want. Her hair is down today, the tips of her dark strands brushing against the shoulders of her white blouse. The skirt looks like it was made just for her, the way her slim hips and her ass fill out the fabric. Her long, tan legs taunt me. I wonder if she's left two buttons undone or three. I'm dying to find out.

That feeling I always get whenever I see Rylee invades my chest. It tightens and my heart leaps, threatening to burst from my ribcage. My dick twitches behind the zipper of my jeans, and I haven't even seen the front of her yet.

She finally turns around to face me. Two buttons, not three. I wish she'd undo one more so I could see what she's wearing underneath it. She notices my line of vision is directed squarely on her chest.

"My eyes are up here, M.B."

"I'm aware," I murmur. My eyes raise to meet hers.

"You need to behave." She straightens her shoulders and lifts her chin, trying to look professional. Behaving is the furthest thing from mind at the moment, when all I can think about is this urge to take her back to my trailer and do filthy things to her.

I smile. This is too much fun. The flirting we've fallen into, the sexy back-and-forth – it's the best form of anticipation. Most women would be begging by now to sleep with me. Rylee is not most women, and it's driving me insane. "And what fun would that be?"

"No fun at all, but those are my rules," she says. I usually prefer taking the dominant role but I'm liking this reversal. Waves of arousal wash over me. I've kissed a lot of women, but nothing compares to having Rylee's mouth on mine. I want her so badly I can hardly stand it.

The moment is interrupted when my agent walks past us. "A word. It's important. I'll meet you in your trailer in five," Matthew says to me and I watch Rylee's whole body stiffen. He's been a part of my team for years. A stand-up agent and a damn good one too. Matthew has been with me since the beginning. Before the fame, before the paparazzi waiting outside of coffee shops, before my six-figure contracts. He's good at his job and gives it to me straight. He's exactly what I need in my life. No nonsense, zero bullshit and always 10 steps ahead of the game.

"Catch you on set?" I say to Rylee and she nods.

My phone vibrates in my pocket while I'm on my way to meet Matthew. It's my publicist. I notice a missed call from him too. The text reads: *The internet is going crazy for this story. They've got a photo of you and Violet. It doesn't look good. You need to call me now.*

Fuck. This can't be good. I make a mental note to call him after my meeting with Matthew. He's waiting for me when I open the trailer door, his computer open on his lap. He's on the phone, barking at someone with a scowl on his face.

I open the Twitter app on my phone to see for myself what the hell is going on. And there it is. Photos of Violet and I, my arm around her shoulders, her hand on my forearm, then on my thigh. Her mouth against my ear. It only gets worse. The headline reads: *Miles Bennett and Violet Michelson all over each other in a Vancouver restaurant. Where is Violet's boyfriend?*

"Who the hell's reporting this bullshit?"

My first instinct is to Tweet out a statement, try to put out the fire before it's a full-blown inferno. But I know better than to defend myself online. Twitter always wins. It always has the last word.

Matthew ends his call then looks at me, dragging a hand down one side of his face. "Miles, level with me. Are you fucking Violet?"

I gape at him. "Hell no. This is absolute bullshit."

"Well, these photos sure as hell make it look like you're fucking her. You two are all over the fucking internet. They're digging out photos of you with every woman you've been photographed with in the last two years," he says, flipping the screen on his laptop in my direction. The page is filled with pictures underneath the headline *"Hollywood's player at it again."*

"Look. Let people think what they want. I don't give a shit anymore," I say, taking the seat across from him.

"I'm glad *you* don't, but it's a big fucking part of my job as your agent to give a shit. I just cleaned up your playboy image. This is the biggest role of your life. You cannot fuck it up. The media will crucify you. They're all but waiting to catch you with your pants down. Literally and figuratively."

I agree the photo looks bad, but it's a far stretch from what the tabloids are trying to spin. I'm frustrated that I even have to deal with this bullshit, it's the side of Hollywood I hate the most. If I was banging every woman they report I am, I would never get out of bed.

"Look, Miles. Whether you're sleeping with Violet or not—"

"I just told you, I'm not! Why is that so hard to believe?"

He turns his laptop back around, shutting it. "Let's be clear. Who you do and where you do it is none of my business, but if you like your job and want to keep on working, you need to do whoever you're doing behind closed doors. Capeesh?"

"I don't do women anywhere *but* behind closed doors," I say, whipping off my jacket and chucking it on the chair behind me. "And I haven't done anyone in months."

"Newsflash. It doesn't matter. You're the talk of this town today and you will be tomorrow and the day after that. This is exactly what we agreed you *would not do*," he says, driving home his point. "What do you think the production company is going to say about this?"

"For the millionth time, I didn't *do* anything. Or anyone," I huff. "As for the production company, I guess we're going to find out."

Matthew's fingers begin to furiously type on his phone. There's a vein in his neck that is pulsing. He rambles on and on about me not making his life any harder than it needs to be, about a plan to fix this mess. I've stopped listening. How the hell does a photo get blown this far out of proportion?

This day started out so good, seeing Rylee first thing after somehow dragging myself away from her hotel room door last night. My mind drifts to her ass in that damn skirt, the buttons of that blouse that I wanted to undo one by one. I want to give a shit that my name is all over the media for sleeping with another man's girl, but I can't get

Rylee off of my mind long enough to really care. I shift in my seat and wonder what the hell is wrong with me.

Matthew has finally stopped talking and is glaring at me now with an *Are we clear?* look in his eye.

"Okay," I say. "I get it."

Matthew gets up to leave, pausing with his hand on the door. "I'll speak to PR and see how they want to handle this. In the meantime, stay away from her."

"That won't be an issue."

Chapter Ten

Miles

"This place is sick," my brother Parker says as I tour him through my rental home. Following close behind him is my other brother Liam, his fiancée Ellie and Parker's wife Olivia. They arrived in Vancouver this afternoon for a four-day stay before heading up to Whistler to wind up their trip. I invited them all to stay with me since the house is over 3,500 square feet.

"Yeah man, this place is amazing," Liam agrees. "We may need to extend our trip."

"Mi casa es su casa. Make yourselves at home," I tell them as we end the tour in the kitchen. I dig out five tumbler glasses and a bottle of my favorite whiskey. I grab a bottle of sparkling grape juice for Ellie, who is pregnant.

"Man, they really set you up here. They spared no expense," Ellie says, gazing out the retractable glass doors to the view of the ocean.

"Yeah, well, I'm kind of a big deal," I joke. "Not to mention incredibly good looking." Parker groans and gives me the finger from across the room where he's leaning against the kitchen counter.

"Your head is as big as the whole fucking house," Liam deadpans, reaching for the tumbler of whiskey in my hands.

"I see nothing has changed since I've been gone," I say, sliding two glasses across the counter to Parker and Olivia then turning my attention to my brothers. "You two are still as pleasant as always. A quality you both own so fucking well."

"Geez," Parker laughs, shaking his head.

"What?"

"Nothing. Just busy enjoying the warmth of your welcome," Parker says before tossing back a long sip of his whiskey.

I smile, happy to fall into our familiar routine. My brothers and I like to take the piss out of each other. We always have. The five of us clink our glasses together then move outside, sitting by the pool to enjoy the last of the sun.

"Who's hungry?" I ask. It's 7:30 p.m. and I assume they must be starving after a day of travelling.

Ellie's arm flies into the air, her eyes wide, and we bust out laughing. She loves her food, and the girl can eat. Now that she's eating for two, all bets are off. We wind up ordering Indian food and eating outside by the fireplace. We order extra for Ellie, so she won't dip into ours.

"Have you thought about chartering a boat?" Olivia asks, gazing at the view of the ocean from our deck. "It's so pretty here. It would be nice to see the city from the water. I've heard sometimes they have whale sightings around here. Or is it sharks? I can't remember which one."

"There's a big fucking difference between a whale and

a shark, Livy," Parker says to his wife in between bites of his naan bread. "Where are you getting these facts?"

"I don't remember," she shrugs her shoulders. "Anyways, wouldn't it be nice?"

"I'm with Olivia. I think we should look into it," Ellie says. "We can bring a big charcuterie board, or maybe pick up some sandwiches on the way. Or just keep it simple and barbecue hotdogs on the back of the boat."

We laugh again at Ellie's expense. Always thinking of the next meal. She crosses her arms over her chest, fake glaring at us.

"Ells, you walked right into that one. Even I can't save you," Liam jokes, kissing her cheek. "However, I do think renting a boat is a great fucking idea."

"Hey Miles, you can bring your new girlfriend," Parker says in a mocking tone. I sit up straight in my chair. I haven't told anyone about Rylee, so my brother catches me off guard.

"Your publicist must be pissed that you are sleeping with your *taken* co-star. The media absolutely slaughtered you. It's been kind of entertaining," he adds with a smirk.

Ahh, that's where he's going with this. I guess I should have cleared up the rumors with my family when they hit the gossip rags, but in my defense, they really should know better than to believe everything they read. "I'm not fucking Violet. I barely even talk to her unless we are on set. The whole thing is bullshit."

"Why not? She's more beautiful than a supermodel. Spill the tea. I want to know all the deets on her," Ellie says, rubbing her palms together.

I wipe my mouth with my napkin before answering. "You know how they say you should never meet your celebrity crush? That applies in this case."

Her face scrunches together in disappointment. "Oh no, really? That sucks."

I shrug, stuffing a mouthful of butter chicken in my mouth. Talking about Violet is as appealing as an appendicitis attack. I'm sure her person is somewhere out there – maybe he's driving fast cars in Europe – but that person definitely isn't me. I steer the conversation to something more pleasant. I'd rather drink gasoline than continue talking about my co-star, the one who got me into this media mess in the first place.

"About the boat. I'll have Georgia get you the name of a rental company. Maybe one of you could look into it while I'm on set tomorrow?"

Olivia nods happily. "Leave it to me. Will you come with us if we book a night cruise? You could bring a friend."

"I'll do my best to make it."

There's only one person I'd like to invite, but I worry she'll think it's too soon. And just like that, my mind is back on Rylee. We are the perfect example of how opposites attract, my city to her country. Her cautious to my curious. I have a feeling it would work for us.

After dinner we stay outside a little longer, the four of them catching me up on the news from Reed Point and their plans for their time in Vancouver.

"I rented a Suburban for you guys while you're here, the keys are on the hook by the door," I say. "I'm leaving the house around seven, so I doubt I'll see you in the morning. But why don't we meet here after work for dinner?"

"Works for us," Liam says. "And don't worry, I'll drive. Parker will stay in the back seat."

"I'd appreciate that," I reply with a grin. "Pretty sure Mom never forgave him for that time he drove her car right through the back fence. Almost made it into the pool. Gas pedal, brake pedal. It's a tricky concept, Parker."

"Yup, a shit driver right from the start. At least he's been consistent," Liam adds.

"You two can be total dicks." Parker shakes his head.

"We know, it's a talent," answers Liam.

Man, it's good to have these two assholes here with me.

Chapter Eleven

Rylee

When we arrive at BC Children's Hospital on Wednesday morning, we're greeted by Mary, their media relations manager. Josh asked me to join him since I set up the visit. Miles is here too, as is his agent Matthew, Violet, her publicist and Jared. There's also a camera man here to document the visit.

After introductions, we follow Mary to meet the kids. Their faces light up when they see Miles, Violet, Jared and Josh walk into the room. Miles' expression mirrors theirs, his eyes bright and his smile wide.

"Look who came to visit. I'm excited to introduce you all to some very special visitors. Miles Bennett, Violet Michelson, Josh Lucas and Jared Kennedy are here to spend some time with you," Mary says to the crowd of happy faces. A few of the kids move in closer, crowding around Miles. He bends down so he's at their level, the camera clicking away, capturing images which will be given to the kids.

"I can't believe you're really here." The sweetest little

guy with lightning bolts covering his pajamas beams at Miles. "I've only seen one of your movies that my mom said was appropriate, but my mom has seen them all. Every single one. She says you're the most handsome man on the planet next to my dad."

I swallow back a laugh, and I can tell Miles is doing the same.

"His name is Jackson. He's a cancer patient. He's eight years old," Mary tells me quietly. My heart lurches in my chest as I look at the little boy standing in front of Miles. How can life be so unfair? He's so little. It really puts things into perspective.

I listen to Jackson tell Miles about his pet Pug and his dream to become an astronaut. Miles hands him a Canucks hat, which Jackson immediately flops onto his head. He's thrilled, his adorable grin stretched even wider.

"Thank you. I don't even care that it's not my home team. I'm never taking it off," Jackson says, adjusting the cap on his head.

"You mean you're not from Vancouver, big guy?" Miles asks.

"Nope, but I live here now. I was born in Nashville."

"Really?" Miles nods toward me. "My friend Rylee here is also from Tennessee. I think you'd like her. She says 'y'all' an awful lot. I bet you say it too." Miles teases as I step forward and crouch down to Jackson's eye level. Jackson giggles, bouncing his head up and down in agreement. He's the cutest little thing.

"I thought I heard a little Tennessee in there. I bet you and I could teach this guy a thing or two about how we do it in the south," I say, thumbing towards Miles.

Miles wrinkles his nose. "I'll tell you what," he says to Jackson. "You beat me at a game of rock, paper, scissors and *maybe* I'll admit that your accents aren't funny." Miles does his best to let the 8-year-old win and after the tie-breaker match, Jackson shoves his hands in the air in victory.

Eventually Jared walks over to meet Jackson, so Miles gives the boy a high five and snaps a quick photo with him before moving on to meet a few more kids. He colors with a girl wearing a bright pink ballcap and plays Mario Kart with another little boy. Miles is so good with the kids.

An hour later, we're headed back to the conference room to meet a few of the facility's doctors and nurses. I catch Miles in the hallway before he steps into the room.

"You okay?" I ask.

Miles seemed perfectly at ease in there, taking photos and handing out a pile of merchandise he brought. I could see it in his expression that meeting the kids meant a lot to him. I could also tell by the tension in his jaw when he left how his heart must have been breaking at the same time.

"Yeah, I'm fine," he says, scrubbing a hand over his face. "Bringing smiles to these kids is one of my favorite parts of my job. It's just not always easy. Kids shouldn't have to go through this. They should be happy and healthy and not worried about being sick."

"You were amazing in there. You have a way with kids. They loved you. You really made their day."

"I thought the same about you," he says, reaching for my hand, giving it a squeeze before opening the conference room door.

We are the last ones to arrive. A nurse is taking a photo with Jared while Josh and Violet are speaking to two doctors in front of a window overlooking the hospital grounds. One of the doctors, a good-looking male in scrubs, steps forward with a smile, his hand held out to greet us.

"Miles Bennett," the doctor says, shaking Miles' hand.

"Ethan Moore. Thank you for coming, it's a pleasure to meet you."

"Pleasure is all mine. Thank you for having us. The kids are fantastic," Miles says. "This is Rylee Brookes. She works with Josh Lucas."

The doctor, who looks to be in his thirties, reaches for my hand, and even *I* don't miss the way his eyes focus on mine then sweep down my body. I feel Miles stiffen beside me.

"What do you do, Rylee?" Dr. Moore asks as I slip my hand from his just as Miles is pulled away by Josh to meet some of the other staff.

"I'm Mr. Lucas' personal assistant," I tell him.

"So, does that mean you are also from Los Angeles?"

"It does," I say with a smile. "We all are."

His eyes look over me again, but I try to ignore it. There is only one tall, dark and handsome man I'm interested in, and he is currently standing to my left looking like he wants to bury a body. I cast a sideways glance at Miles, who is looking over at us with a pointed stare.

"So how do you like Vancouver?" the doctor asks, crossing his arms over his chest.

"I love it. The scenery is so beautiful, and the people are very welcoming. We get most weekends off, so I've been able to tour the city." I notice the time, realizing our visit is just about over. "If you'll excuse me, I just need to go check in with Mr. Lucas' driver."

I leave the doctor and step out into the hallway, pulling out my phone. I'm sending a text to the car service when Miles' hand slides across my lower back. "I'm not the only one with a crush on you, it seems."

"Oh, stop. He was just being polite." I tuck my phone back in my bag and adjust the strap on my shoulder. *A crush? Did he really just say that?*

"That wasn't polite. That was flirting," Miles scoffs. "The doctor has the hots for you."

I crack up. "The hots? What are you… 80? Nobody says 'the hots' anymore. And If I didn't know better, I'd think someone was a little jealous. It's actually kind of cute," I say, turning and heading for the door.

Miles is right behind me. "You're hot, Rylee," he says, his mouth at my ear. "Of course he's going to flirt with you. I get it." Then he pulls away, and I immediately want him back. A shiver rolls up my spine as I miss the feeling of his breath on my neck. *I really need to get myself together.*

"I doubt that was it at all," I say, "I'm sure he's busy chatting up Violet as we speak."

"Damn," he says, as I pull open the door. "Violet has nothing on you."

Back at work, today's set mimics a coffee shop with tables and chairs, pastries and espresso machines. Josh explains the scene to Miles and Violet then instructs me to fetch the extras from hair and makeup who are needed on set right away. Like a well-oiled machine, the extras file out ready to shoot and follow me to the sound stage, taking their spots. I stand off to the side, ready if Josh needs me.

While lighting is being adjusted, my eyes are drawn to Miles. He's wearing jeans and a button-down shirt, holding a prop coffee cup in his hand. He spots me eyeing him and smiles a red carpet-worthy smile. I swear my knees go weak. Seeing him on set feels intimate now in a way it didn't used to. Until recently, he was just another actor to me, a movie character. Now everything feels different.

Josh tells Violet to sit at a table while Miles stands over at the counter. She's wearing a slip dress and sandals, her hair swept off of her face, secured by a headband. She's stunning in every way. I swallow down the doubts I feel about myself when I look at her.

We hear "quiet on set," and I stand still, waiting for Miles to do what he does best. The scene starts and I watch intently, something I don't usually do. But with Miles I have trouble looking away.

Eventually the director calls "cut," and everyone in the room relaxes. Background actors need to be filed off set which means it's my job to escort them. I run them to the holding area and minutes later I'm back at Josh's side going over emails he needs written and a meeting he wants set up with media. I notice Miles speaking to a producer. I'm trying to watch him without getting caught, stealing quick glances at him out of the corner of my eye. He's doing the same, it seems. Our eyes meet and he smiles at me. Our little secret. Every nerve in my body feels like it's on fire, a feeling I've never felt before. I finally manage to drag my eyes off of Miles and get back to work.

I'm finishing up with Josh and am about to find a quiet spot outside to work on his emails when Miles appears at my side. "Where are you off to? I hope you're not going far." His voice is hushed, only loud enough for me to hear.

"And why is that? Is there something you need help with? Did your assistant disappear on you?"

He crosses his arms over his chest, giving me a better view of his forearms. They are my weakness – along with every other part of his body. "Oh, I'd prefer your help. I wouldn't object if you ditched whatever it is you're doing for Josh and helped me in my trailer with a few things."

Oh. My. Word.

For a second I forget where we are. The air suddenly feels warmer and I'm praying my cheeks aren't the color of rubies. I'm not sure I'll be able to work this closely with

Miles for the next eight weeks. My body might spontaneously go up in flames.

"Miles," I say, breathy and unlike me.

"Are you considering it?"

I take a look around to see who might be watching. "No. Now hush. You're making me all nervous. Someone is going to hear you."

He changes the subject. Thankfully. "I like it when I know you're on set watching me."

My brows raise. "I like watching you. You know, I could have sworn there really was coffee in your cup," I say, referring to the scene he just shot.

"I'm that good, huh?" he asks, the corners of his mouth tipping up. There's a glint in his eyes. "I do other things really well too."

Does this man ever not flirt?

"Is that so?"

I'm flustered, all hot and bothered. I'm also at my workplace, surrounded by the cast and crew. I'm not cut out for this. When Miles leans in a little closer, I think I might combust.

I swallow hard, glancing around the set again. *What is he thinking?* Miles must catch my drift because he takes a step backwards. Although he clearly enjoys the effect he has on me, he also knows when it's too much.

Before our exchange turns dangerously X-rated, we're interrupted by his PA, Georgia. "Miles, they need you back on set." She has her phone pressed to her ear and a stack of papers in her hand.

"I'll be right there." Miles runs his fingers across the stubble of his beard and smiles another outrageously gorgeous smile, knocking me off kilter. "It's going to be a long one today, then I'll be up late running lines for tomorrow. Can I see you tomorrow night?"

He needs to get back to set, so I answer him quickly. "I can't tomorrow. I promised Abby I would have dinner with her. Another night?"

I'm disappointed I already have plans but I won't cancel on Abby.

"Another night for sure," he says with a wink, before trotting away to set, leaving me in goosebumps.

Miles is different than any man I've ever met. There's something special about him, he has a charisma that not many people possess. He can draw you in, and he always leaves you wanting more.

"This is incredible and why the hell didn't you fill me in on it two weeks ago?" Meg says – make that borderline shouts – into the earpiece of my phone. "You and Miles Bennett. This is *huge*."

There's a muffled sound on the line and I can hear her talking to someone in the room with her. "It's Rylee. Oh shush, I'll tell you later."

I called my best friend after dinner, wanting to tell someone about Miles, needing to share the secret I'm keeping with someone I can trust and who understands me.

"You were in Mexico. Not my fault. And who are you spilling my business to?" I ask, curled up on my hotel bed in my pajamas, a face mask slathered on my face.

"Oh, that's just Adam. Don't worry, he's like a vault. He won't say a thing," she insists about her boyfriend, who has pretty much moved into the apartment we share in Los Angeles. "Ryls, you are dating America's number one bachelor. There is this invention called an iPhone, you know. We both own one. Where was my phone call?"

"I know, but I'm telling you now. But I'm not telling you *everything*," I say, knowing she's rolling her eyes even though I can't see her. Meg is my closest friend, but I don't want to tell her too much. I want to keep my relationship with Miles close, something for only him and I to share. I'm also a bit afraid of what the naysayers will say if they were to find out. *How could a guy like him fall for a girl like her? She doesn't look at all like the supermodels he normally dates. It will never work.*

I cringe at the thought of it. I know full well how crazy this is, I don't need anyone else pointing it out to me. But as foolish as it is to keep seeing Miles, I only want more of him.

"Oh, you are. Now spill," Meg says,

"He's nothing like you would expect. He's fun and easy going and not pretentious at all. And… I'm really enjoying his company."

"Uh-huh, Ry. That is not going to work for me. How's the chemistry? Have you kissed him? I bet you have. I bet it was hot. Was it hot?" Meg is rambling, clearly not ready to let this go.

I sigh. "The chemistry is intense. I don't know how to describe it. Just the eye contact alone feels like magic. And the way he kisses me, Meg… it's incredible."

Meg sighs a long, drawn-out sigh and then lets out a little squeal. I laugh, picturing her trying to process this news.

"Adam!" she hollers at her boyfriend. "Miles Bennett is falling for Rylee. Like, heart-eyes and hot and bothered and shit."

"Are you serious? Stop it," I say, interrupting her. "He is not falling for me. He is not even my boyfriend. I don't know what he is, so you just need to relax."

I exhale. I haven't breathed a word of any of this to

anyone. Not even Abby. I doubt Miles has either. Something about keeping us a secret makes it feel safe.

"Rylee, a guy like Miles Bennett doesn't go out with a girl more than once if he isn't feeling her. Think about it. When have you ever seen him photographed twice with anyone?"

"Exactly my point," I tell her. "I'm the flavor of the month. This is not going to last. And that is why you need to keep it on the DL," I say, my stomach twisting, wondering if what I just said was true. I've tried to avoid the tabloids and gossip about Miles, showing super-human restraint to stop myself from incessantly Googling him. I wanted to get to know him on my own, without the media's skewed perception.

"You are nobody's flavor of the month. Those other girls could never measure up to you. You need to remember that. This is big, Ryls. Speaking of *big*, I need to know how-"

My reaction is immediate. "Not for a second. Nope. Besides, I wouldn't know."

"You're no fun. Geez. You need to get that man naked, and when you do, I want the deets. You get to know everything there is to know about Adam. Fair is fair?"

"I know *way* more than I ever cared to know about Adam, thanks to your love of oversharing. I'm still traumatized over what I know. I can barely even look him in the eye."

"Oh, whatever," she says. "So, are you guys sneaking around Vancouver or what? Who knows about you two?"

"Nobody knows, and it needs to stay that way, Meg. I can't even imagine the shitshow it would be if the media found out. Small-town girl and Hollywood's biggest star. Cliché is an understatement," I say, hating how the words sound.

"It's so romantic. I literally have goosebumps. It's your story. Your love story," she gushes and as she says the words, I wonder if she might be right. I have real feelings for Miles. I like him more than I ever thought possible.

"I gotta run, Megs. Do not breathe a word about this to anyone."

"Never ever, ever. Lock and key, doll," she says. "And Ryls. Go for it. Don't hold back."

Easier said than done.

Chapter Twelve

Miles

"You want to tell me what the fuck is going on with you?" Matthew's voice blares at me through my iPhone. Squeezing my eyes shut, I pull the device from my ear. My agent's underwear is clearly in a knot, but I have no idea why. It's not the first time.

"I'd like to buy a vowel, Matt. I don't have a clue what the fuck you are talking about," I say, slumping onto a bar stool in my rental kitchen. I look around the room – all sleek lines and shiny surfaces. It's top of the line, but it's too cold and too empty. It's not me at all.

"Who's your girlfriend?" he asks.

"Oh my God. If this is still about Violet, I'm hanging up. I already told you-"

"Not Violet, dummy. The girl you almost got pregnant with your eyes today at the hospital. Josh Lucas' PA. The one with the-"

"No." I stop him before he can go any further. "It's not like that. I'm not sleeping with her."

Matthew snickers. "Yet."

"Think what you want, but she's not that kind of girl. Besides, I do know how to have a conversation with a woman, you know. It's not always about sex."

"We'll see. I saw the way you looked at her." He pauses for effect. "*I know* that look, Miles. I know it better than anyone. The press hasn't let up on the *Viles* bullshit yet. The last thing you need is *another* story in the press with *another* new girl. I need you to focus, do your job and keep your eyes and your hands off of her. Don't make my job any harder than it already is. Just behave. Miles. I mean it."

"Yes, boss," I grumble, to get him to stop talking.

I end the call and drop my phone on the counter. As much as I hate to admit it, Matthew is probably right. Lusting over Josh Lucas' PA and risking having it splashed all over the tabloids is not professional. This is the role of my career, and I can't fuck it up. Besides that, I'm aware of the effect all of this could have on Rylee. She's not like the other women I've dated who love the publicity and being in the spotlight. Being with me could make Rylee's life more difficult, and that's the last thing I want.

I lean against the kitchen counter, feeling a tightening in my chest. I know what I should do, but it's very different from what I want to do. Who am I kidding? I've got it bad for this girl, I can't stop thinking about her. When I'm with her, I feel like I can let my guard down, just be myself. That's a feeling I don't have often. Staying away from Rylee will take a level of self-control I know I don't possess.

A few hours later, in the golden hour of evening, I am aboard a sleek white cruiser boat with my brothers, Olivia and Ellie. I sip from a glass of champagne, taking in the view from my seat in the corner of the U-shaped leather bench. My brothers rented the sleek, shiny vessel for the night and although I feel like a third wheel – or a fifth wheel – I'm here. It's not often I get to spend time with my family, so missing this wasn't an option. The sunset float is also giving me the necessary distraction I needed to stop thinking about a sexy brunette for a while. *Right.*

I'm on a million-dollar fucking boat in the Vancouver sunshine and the only thing on my mind is Rylee. The sigh she made when my tongue found hers and the way her body molded to mine.

Olivia snaps a finger in front of my face, catching me stuck in a daydream.

"I was just trying to persuade Parker that a boat like this would be perfect," Olivia tells me, glancing around the boat.

"You like this, Livy?" Parker asks her.

"I do," she says taking a seat next to me. Parker, Liam and Ellie sit across from us.

"Forty feet is a pretty big boat but so is your dock," I say, trying to engage in the conversation going on around me. "Speaking of… how's everything going with the summer house? The photos look killer."

"It's a work in progress. The bones are good, but we'd like to do some upgrades," Parker says of the beach house he and Olivia recently purchased. "I have a contractor writing up a quote for us now on a new kitchen, the bathrooms and the floors."

Another boat glides past us, catching my eye. Two guys are on the bow of the boat drinking beers. There's a girl with them too, reclined on a bench seat, her dark hair a shade that reminds me of Rylee's. She looks nothing like Rylee – she's taller, her hair is longer, her build entirely different. But that doesn't seem to matter to my imagination because now I'm picturing Rylee in my arms, her lips on mine and the feel of her smooth skin under my fingertips.

"Miles!" Olivia claps this time. "Are you seriously not hearing a word of this conversation?"

"I am," I lie.

Parker side-eyes me. He knows me too well. I can tell he's not buying it, but he chooses to leave it.

Minutes into the trip, we get our first look at Granville Island, with its bustling marina and trendy restaurants lining the waterfront. My brothers are holding their girls in their arms as we cross the ocean, taking in the view. I wonder what it would feel like – having someone to be with at the end of a long day, someone to share vacations and special moments with. Someone to share a life with. It makes me think of Rylee. Again. I miss her. Forgetting about her is a lost cause. It just doesn't seem possible for me to give her up entirely.

It's too easy to imagine her here in my arms. If I wasn't so sure she and I would be great together, I'd drop it. But the chemistry between us is too strong. With the rest of the boat preoccupied, I type out a text to Rylee.

> Miles: I miss you like crazy. How do we fix that?

The ocean sparkles like diamonds and the view of the city is incredible, but I barely take it in as I anxiously wait for her reply. It doesn't take long before my phone lights up, along with my smile. I manage to swallow a groan.

> Rylee: I'm not sure, but I bet you can think of something ;)

> Miles: How about that rain check. Can I see you tomorrow? We can start with that.

> Rylee: A good place to start. See you tomorrow.

My face heats.

I can't fucking wait to see her.

The next morning, something comes over me when I spot her walking alone through the circus of trailers. After first making sure there's no one around I follow her, catching up to her behind my trailer. Grabbing her from behind, I pull her around the corner, kissing the side of her neck.

I haven't been able to get our text exchange from last night off of my mind.

I miss you like crazy. How do we fix that?

I'm not sure, but I bet you can think of something.

I've decided to ignore everything Matthew said and go against his advice. Not that I had a real choice in the matter… staying away from Rylee Brookes would be impossible.

"Miles…" she whispers.

"Mmm. You smell so good," I say, smiling into her neck. I kiss the smooth, golden skin of her jaw. Kissing Rylee Brookes has become the thing I look forward to most in life.

"What are you doing? Someone will see us."

We're still a secret but she's at least stopped going out of her way to avoid me on set. She still isn't comfortable with me getting too close to her at work, so I typically don't. I have to fight the urge to touch her on an hourly basis, satisfy myself with only catching her eye whenever I can. The thrill and excitement of knowing our eyes are on each other is usually good enough. But seeing her today after that hotter-than-hell text has me breaking our rules.

"No one is going to come back here," I tell her, flipping her in my arms, pulling her into me by her waist. My fingers dig into her skin. I look into her eyes before kissing her so she can see how badly I need to touch her. Rylee gets to me. Something about her makes me lose all control. I've never been a guy who's enjoyed a lengthy amount of kissing but with Rylee everything is different. The kiss intensifies. It's steamy, sensual. She tastes of mint, something sweet and sexy.

"Oh my gosh." She blinks. "You're crazy."

The taste of her does crazy things to me. Devouring her right here in broad daylight is proof of that. "*You* make me crazy."

I'm not sure how this girl can make me lose all control like this. What I *do* know is she has wound me up in a way no one else has before. I should probably go for a run – burn off some energy, anything to get control of my libido. I need to do something. I want her in every way possible. In my trailer, in my bed and in my life.

"I've wanted to do this all day," I tell her when we pull apart, our breathing shaky.

"That was…" she steps back, tracing a finger over her bottom lip.

"Fucking amazing," I say, finishing off her sentence. "I'm looking forward to our date tonight. I have an idea. Come over?"

"But your family is there."

"So? You will love them. My brothers are easy to get along with and I'm sure Olivia and Ellie will practically adopt you as one of their own." I reach for her hand, lacing her fingers in mine, hoping she'll say yes.

She looks unsure. I'm not surprised. I expected her to take some time to think about it. "I don't know."

"It will be fun. Promise. You can ride with me from here. We'll order take-out and I'll have my driver take you home at the end of the night."

She tilts her head to one side, looking at me. "You're sure about this? It's not too late to change your mind."

"Nothing's changing over here. I want you to come over. I mean it."

"Okay."

I smile then kiss her forehead. She squeezes my hand before letting it go. "I'm happy you are unable to resist my charm," I tease.

"Shut up," she says, with a smile on her face that I want to kiss off. "Maybe I just feel sorry for you. Now let me get back to my job."

Chapter Thirteen

Rylee

"I knew it!" Abby whisper-shrieks from the sink beside me, her wide eyes meeting mine in the mirror.

"Shhh, you have to be quiet," I plead, glancing toward the closed door of the crew bathroom. "Nobody knows about this, and I'd like to keep it that way."

"Fine. But seriously, I don't get you. If Miles Bennett was about to introduce *me* to his family, I'd want it to be front page news."

I hadn't exactly planned on telling Abby about Miles today, but when she pressed me on why I couldn't walk back to the hotel with her after work I got tongue-tied trying to come up with an excuse. After interrogating me like I was a witness on trial, Abby broke me. I ended up spilling it all, from our sushi lunch after Miles found me in the rain, to our first date and our first kiss outside my hotel room.

"You are not helping. I'm already nervous enough," I

say, digging around in my purse for my lip gloss and powder.

Abby pulls out a hairbrush and hairspray and hands them to me. "Here, use these," she says, then tilts her head as she watches me try to fix my hair. "I knew there was something different about you."

I wonder what would make her think that. Miles and I were being so careful. But I don't have time to get into it with her right now. It will have to wait.

"I can't believe I'm meeting his family looking like this." I wince as I look at my reflection in the mirror. I'm wearing a cropped white T-shirt with a pair of black skinny jeans and ankle boots. The hem of my shirt isn't quite long enough to cover my midriff. Thankfully, I did manage to wash and straighten my hair this morning.

"Are you kidding me? You look hot. Those jeans fit you perfectly. Your ass looks amazing," Abby says as I apply a bit of blush to my cheeks then run her brush through my hair for a second time. I finish with a coat of lip gloss and a spritz of body spray.

"It will have to do. This is all I've got to work with," I say, stuffing my beauty supplies back in my bag.

"Don't think we are finished with this conversation. You have been hooking up with Miles Bennett and you haven't said a word. I'm not sure whether to high five you or call this friendship off," Abby huffs with an exaggerated pout.

"Hooking up is an exaggeration. I wouldn't go that far."

"Whatever."

"I'm sorry, Abbs. I don't know… I wasn't really sure what to say. I'm not sure what's going on between the two of us and I didn't want to make it into a big deal and look stupid. I'm sure it will fizzle out soon."

"Or it won't," she interrupts me, holding my gaze in the mirror. "You're a catch, girl, and I'm sure he knows it. Remember that."

"Thanks for the pep talk," I say, as Abby tugs on the hem of my shirt, straightening it. "I better go, he's probably waiting for me."

"Okay, go and have fun tonight. But I want every single dirty detail tomorrow over coffee. And don't do anything I wouldn't do."

"That doesn't leave much," I laugh, as Abby squeals and pulls me into a hug. "You are ridiculous."

I walk out of the restroom not knowing who is more excited about my date: me or Abby.

***

Miles and I walk to the front door of his rental home, a classic Tudor with white shingles and steeply pitched gable roofs. It's the most incredible house I've ever seen. He gives me a brief tour of the main floor, and the *six* bedrooms. *Who needs that many bedrooms?* is the first thing that pops into my mind, but I admit that I'm partial to the massive porch with its outdoor fireplace and flat screen TV. In the grand scheme of things, I'm sure this home pales in comparison to what other wealthy people have – those Hollywood homes you hear about with full-size bowling alleys and 24-karat gold bathtubs – but I've never seen anything quite like it.

"You've got to be kidding me with this house," I gush when we get to the basement. "Somehow it keeps getting better. I've read about houses with movie theaters and wet bars, but I've never actually been in one."

I run the tips of my fingers over the soft, felt surface of

the pool table. "I'm not sure you're going to be able to get me to leave."

As soon as the words fall from my lips I feel like a dummy, but the feeling passes when Miles raises his eyebrows and says, "For the record, I wouldn't object to you staying."

Thankfully he changes the subject before my cheeks have a chance to turn hot pink. "So, how's your pool game?"

"I'm not sure I have one. It's been a while since I've played pool, but I catch on quick if you want to play."

"I'm game." He takes two pool cues down from the rack and hands me one, dusting a kiss to my cheek while he's at it.

Miles still makes me a little nervous, and I sometimes catch myself worrying about saying the wrong thing, but our night is going better than I could hope for. Our conversations are playful and there are never any awkward silences between us. We're able to forget about work and I realize after a while that I haven't thought once about what people might think if they found out we're hanging out. Because that's all that we're doing, I decide. We are two friends who are hanging out. Two friends who some-times like to kiss – not something I normally do, but with Miles I'm happy to roll with it. I want to just live in the moment with him, knowing that soon this time together will end.

Miles stands beside me, watching me as I chalk up my cue. I lean against the pool table and line up my shot. I manage to sink a solid ball into a side pocket, which earns me a high five from Miles and one of his billboard-worthy smiles. His eyes travel my body and even though we've yet to order dinner, he's looking at me like he's ready to have me for dessert. If it wasn't for the fact that his family could walk through the door any second now, I might just let him.

"Look at you go. Do we have a shark on our hands?"

"When you grow up with two older brothers, you learn things."

"How about a wager then? Winner… hmm, let me think," he says, tapping a fingertip against his chin.

"Uh oh, I can already see where this is going."

"I can be good. I swear," he grins. "How about winner gets a massage?"

I was hoping Miles would say something about making out with me if he wins, but a massage will do. "You call that being good?" I ask him, hands on my hips. "I think either way you win. My hands will be on you or your hands will be on me."

I love the way Miles touches me; confidently and sensually and nothing like the way Eric used to. I would happily lose this bet if it weren't for my competitive side.

He flashes me a half-smile, like he has something up his sleeve. The heat in his eyes holds the same expression. "Exactly." he says, cracking his knuckles. "Too late now to back out. Game on."

I shake my head holding my pinky finger out for him to shake and he does. Bringing our intertwined fingers to his mouth, he kisses them. We have a bet.

It's my turn, and I do exactly what I remember my brother Cole teaching me when we were kids. I position myself close to the table, but not too close. I aim for the white ball just slightly off center and take my shot, pocketing another solid ball.

"I'm sorry I ever doubted your skills for a second," he says, rounding the table, gripping my hips with his hands. When he kisses my neck, I breathe in the scent of his aftershave. The whiskers from his jaw tickle my skin and a bolt of excitement rushes through me and heats my core as I meet the desert bronze of his eyes. All I can think about is taking this to his bedroom, feeling his skin against mine. The last thing I want to do is stop. My pulse is racing, and my skin feels like it could melt under his touch.

"Your family will be here any second," I murmur, my breathing shallow.

"Don't care," he says, pulling back momentarily to look at me with hunger in his eyes.

I'm so turned on by the way his fingers are touching me that I almost give in to him. It takes every ounce of willpower to remind myself that his brothers should be back any minute and we really need to stop.

"Meeting your family with your tongue down my throat is not the good first impression I'm trying to make," I say, untangling my body from his arms.

"I guess I can't argue with that," he says, running a hand through his hair and then reaching for his pool cue. He eyes the table. "Where were we before you decided you couldn't keep your hands off me?"

I roll my eyes and laugh. "Very funny."

We're in the middle of our game when we hear voices upstairs. "Sounds like they're here. You ready to meet my brothers?"

I nod, a little anxious.

"Relax, babe. You're going to love them," he whispers as we hear footsteps coming down the stairs.

I meet Liam first, the tallest and broadest of the three Bennett brothers, who politely holds out his hand for me to shake. Next is Parker, who introduces the beautiful blonde at his side as his wife Olivia. Finally, I'm introduced to Ellie, Liam's fiancée, who is very clearly pregnant.

Introductions out of the way, I take a second to appreciate how insanely handsome Miles and his two brothers are, wondering how it is possible that they were all blessed with such incredibly good looks. All over six feet tall with thick dark hair, athletic builds and smiles that you'll never forget. I can't imagine what must happen when they all go out in public together.

"I hope Miles hasn't been too much of a diva on set," Parker says. "We know how he can get when he's hungry or needs a nap."

"It's nothing I can't handle," I answer with a grin. "I just send him to his trailer when he throws a tantrum."

Everyone laughs, including Miles, and it's the icebreaker I needed to relax and enjoy the night.

We order Thai food from a restaurant Miles recommends and while we wait for our food, Parker gets behind the bar, mixing us each a gin and tonic and a grapefruit juice and soda for Ellie.

Drinks in hand, Olivia, Ellie and I sink into one of the plush couches and the two of them take turns asking me questions about where I'm from, and about life in L.A. Ellie tells me that she and Olivia practically grew up together and it's obvious that they're very close, there is such a relaxed and easy banter between them. I like them both instantly.

I steal a glance at Miles, who is sitting at the bar with his brothers. I've been in the room with them for all of 20 minutes, but I can already see that Liam and Parker live to keep their famous little brother's ego in check.

"But seriously," Parker says, holding up his phone to show a recent red carpet photo of Miles. "How long did you have to sit for that spray tan? It must have been hours."

Liam grimaces, swirling the ice in his glass. "Did you specifically ask to look like a walking orange? Because if so, they nailed it."

Parker and Liam laugh at their brother's expense, and even Miles can't resist a sheepish grin as he shakes his head at their ribbing.

"It's crazy, right?" Ellie sighs, catching me looking at Miles with his brothers. "The three of them together? They're way too handsome."

"It *is* kind of overwhelming," I admit with a laugh.

"It can be very annoying, especially when your ankles are swollen to the size of a small elephant's." Ellie rubs a hand over her pregnant belly, rolling her eyes in the direction of the guys.

Olivia swats at her arm. "Stop it, Ells. You have never looked more beautiful."

"And that's why I keep her around," Ellie says with a wink.

A little while later, the Thai food arrives, and we all go upstairs to eat it around the outdoor patio table. The view from the porch is one I've only ever dreamed of, with an unobstructed view of the ocean and the edge of Vancouver Island in the far distance. Dinner is delicious and the conversation flows easily. Miles was right, I had nothing to worry about. It's been a great night.

After dinner, we take the party back downstairs for a game of pool.

"Tell us, Rylee. Just how bad is my brother at pool? He's probably never seen balls that big. I bet he finds them intimidating," Parker jokes from across the pool table and I can't help myself from laughing at Miles' expense.

"Your fascination with my junk is alarming." Miles delivers the comeback as smooth as honey.

Parker scoffs. "Your junk isn't worth mentioning."

I watch Miles shake his head. "Wow, my *much* older brother is bringing it with the sarcasm tonight."

"Pay attention, baby Bennett, maybe you'll learn something. It could even get you an upgrade from the children's table at Christmas dinner."

Rolling his eyes, Miles walks away, and I can't help but watch his perfect ass as he goes.

"Your move, Liam," Miles calls out. "You think you can tear yourself away from Ellie long enough to sink the white ball?"

"It's funny that you're under the impression that I'm *not* going to school you," Liam teases. "Watch how it's done, ladies and gentlemen."

Liam's brows knit together as he studies the table then bends over the edge of the felt, lining up his shot. He skillfully sinks a striped ball into the pocket then strides over to Ellie, settling between her thighs where she sits on a bar stool. "You see that, Ells, I told you I'm good at everything," he jokes, one hand on the nape of her neck, his other on her baby belly.

"Nope. I didn't notice," she says. Liam assesses her with a mock-annoyed grin on his face then kisses the edge of her mouth.

They really are cute together. It's obvious they're both head over heels in love, and it makes me envy their relationship. The way his eyes find hers from across the room and his hands are almost always on her body. And the way she lights up whenever he looks her way. It's what romance novels are made of, and it's exactly what I want to find some day. If I'm being honest with myself, it feels like I'm halfway there.

Miles is up next. He sinks the first shot, then two more after that. "Since when did you become a pool shark, show performer?" Liam taunts him.

"Show performer?" Miles rolls his eyes, mock outrage in his voice. "Try A-list Hollywood action star. That's more like it."

Miles is the furthest thing from a conceited, egotistical actor, but he seems happy to play along with the fun, light-hearted banter. Watching him and his brothers interact is its own form of entertainment. It's like sibling theater. Really hot sibling theater. I'm enjoying myself more than I could have imagined.

The night passes quickly and before I know it Liam and Ellie are saying their goodbyes and heading upstairs to bed. Parker, Olivia and I stay up a little later and chat for a while, but I can't keep my eyes off Miles. He's happy and relaxed and when I smile at him, he returns it with a wink. I manage to tear my gaze away and look over at Olivia, who is watching us with a knowing look.

She gives Parker a look I can't read. When he doesn't react, she clears her throat, interrupting the brothers' conversation.

"Time for bed, Parks," she announces, casting me a quick sideways glance.

Ahh, now I get that look she shot her husband. Parker, on the other hand, doesn't seem to be picking up on her not-so-subtle hint.

"Really?" he asks, looking at his watch with a puzzled look on his face. "It's still early."

"Really, babe?" Olivia answers, this time tilting her head in the direction of Miles and me.

"Oh," Parker smirks, slipping from his barstool with a gleam in his eyes. "I see what you mean. Yes, I'm suddenly very tired."

"Could you be any more obvious?" Olivia teases him, elbowing him in his side.

"Ouch. Like you were any better."

I feel my cheeks turning pink, but I can't help but laugh at the two of them. The grin on my face must be a mile wide.

And then it's just Miles and I. After a long, hungry kiss, I tell him I should probably go. He softly kisses my forehead and I breathe him in.

"I'll call my driver to take you home," Miles murmurs into my hair, then takes a step back and holds his hand out for me to take.

I follow him upstairs to the front door, where he stops to grab his jacket along with mine.

"What are you doing?" I ask.

"I'm coming with you."

"That's not necessary. The car is more than enough."

"I'm not taking no for an answer," he says with a grin on his face, and I can tell there's no sense in arguing.

Twenty minutes later, he's walking me to my hotel room. Once inside Miles wastes no time putting his lips to mine. The kiss is lingering, slow and heart-stoppingly perfect. I'm love-drunk on this kiss.

And then I freeze.

Chapter Fourteen

Miles

We made it two steps into Rylee's hotel room before I lost all control and kissed her. She kissed me back, the intensity between us building. Then suddenly it was over.

"Are you okay?" I ask Rylee when she breaks the kiss. We're nose-to-nose, our breathing still heavy. She's completely unreadable, which is unusual for her.

"Yes and no," she murmurs. "I know what I want. I'm just not sure it's the smart thing to do."

I try to take in what she's saying. "Tell me why."

She pauses for a second and I can see that she's trying to find the words. The room goes quiet while I wait for her to answer. "Because you're you and I'm me and I'm scared to get hurt."

I put my hand on her jaw, cupping her face. I can't stop touching her. I think I know what she's getting at, but I need to be sure. "Whatever you're thinking, whatever doubts you have about the way I feel about you… it's all in your head, Rylee. I can promise you that."

"Miles, I guess I'm just not sure what you see in a girl like me. There's nothing glamorous about me or my life."

"You really don't get it, do you?" I say. "My life is crazy and chaotic and there's always someone who wants a piece of me. When I'm with you, all of the noise quiets. I forget about it all." My hand travels from her jaw down her neck. "And when we kiss, it feels like magic and fireworks and nothing I've ever felt before and I don't want to stop. I like being with you. It's as simple as that."

Looking at her, I realize that simple may have been the wrong word to use. There is nothing simple about the way I feel about her.

"Miles, I had no idea you felt that way. I'm… it's sweet." I can see some of the conflict in her eyes dissolve but she's still not there.

"Look, Rylee. The feelings I have for you won't go away. I can't stop wanting you. Since the day I met you – since the moment I laid eyes on you – I've wanted to be near you. I want to spend every second I can with you. I will always be honest with you and I promise I won't hurt you."

"This feels like a risk."

"It's a risk I'm hoping you take."

The worried crease between her eyebrows eases and I finally feel the last of the tension leave her body. Her long, dark eyelashes flutter closed for a second and when they open, she half smiles. I drink her in. She's beautiful.

Then I kiss her, without warning, pressing my mouth to hers. My heart rate is over the legal limit when she groans into my mouth, her hands sliding down the length of my body.

"I want you more than I've ever wanted anything." The confession slips from my mouth, surprising me. But there's no way I'm taking it back. I mean every word.

She lets out a small breath but doesn't say anything. Instead, her gaze holds mine with an intensity that feels like an electrical current right to my core. The way she's looking at me tells me she feels the exact same way as I do. The back of my neck tingles as blood rushes to my dick.

I lean in, kissing her, showing her that I don't want to wait another day to have her. "Miles," she whispers my name.

"Dammit, Rylee. Tell me you want this too," I say, pressing my forehead against hers, closing my eyes, breathing her in. "I've been fantasizing about you since that day I first saw you outside of Violet's trailer. You are all I think about."

"You have?" she asks. I open my eyes to find her staring at me so intently I can see the flecks of gold in her bright green irises.

"Very much so." All I want to do is kiss her, but I hold off, waiting for her to say the words. "But if you're not ready…if you want to wait. We will."

Her hands softly travel down my chest. We are so close to each other I swear I can hear the beating of her heart. "Miles," she whispers. "I'm ready. More than anything. I want you more than-"

I don't even let her finish the words I am aching to hear. I can't wait another second.

This is happening.

My mouth finds hers and my tongue sweeps inside, slowly and smoothly tangling with hers. Her lips are so soft, and they feel so good pressed up against mine. She whimpers into the kiss, running her fingers through my hair and gripping the back of my head like she wants to hold me there. *I wouldn't end this even if the hotel was on fire.*

She angles her head and I take the opportunity to deepen the kiss. It feels incredible, our tongues teasing each other ferociously. A bolt of lightning flashes through me when her pelvis puts a little pressure on the bulge behind my zipper. Every inch of me is hyper aware of her warm body pressed against mine. I'm high on her, my senses woozy as my tongue flicks against hers. I hear myself moan into the kiss, my body humming and aching to be skin-on-skin with her as soon as fucking possible.

Her fists tighten around the back of my neck, making me even harder. We're talking concrete hard. I wrap my arms around her waist, hauling her into me even closer, gripping her hips in my hands. The beachy scent of her skin is doing crazy things to my senses. I feel dizzy, drunk on her, buzzing with lust.

We keep kissing like we have all the time in the world, sucking and nipping each other's tongues. When I finally pull back from the kiss, I draw her bottom lip between mine, sucking gently. She tastes sweet, intoxicating.

"Can I take this off, Ryls?" I ask, my fingers playing with the edge of her T-shirt.

"Yes," she breathes, and I waste no time lifting the fabric over her head. She's wearing a lace bra that is basically see-through and it's enough to get my dick twitching in my jeans.

There's nothing slow about the way we take the rest of each other's clothes off, dropping them to the floor. We undress one another as quickly as we can until we are down to our underwear. Rylee's gorgeous breasts are hidden behind that sexy lace bra. It goes next. I want to take my time with her lace panties once I get her laid out on the bed.

I watch her eyes travel from my shoulders down to the bulge in my briefs, taking me in, inch by inch. I grow even harder, loving the way she's looking at me. I reach around for her ass, palming each cheek in my hands, squeezing and massaging her over the lace of her panties. She moans and I come undone, unravelling with her every sound.

Slowly, I back her up towards the queen size bed. When the back of her knees hit the edge of the mattress, she sits down, and I work to ease her back to the center of the bed. My body hovers over top of hers, placing a knee on either side of her hips and I rock into her with my erection. I'm painfully hard and even through the two thin layers of clothing separating us, I have to fight to keep myself together. I pause for a minute to regain control.

"Miles, don't stop," she says, an edge of desperation in her voice.

I dip down to kiss her, pushing my tongue into her mouth, licking against her. "I wish I didn't have to," I admit, squeezing my eyes shut and tilting my head towards the ceiling.

She chuckles then reaches for my face, pulling me closer so our mouths are mere millimeters away. "Kiss me."

I give her what she wants.

Then I roll my hips again while my hands cup her breasts, my fingers brushing over her pebbled nipples, watching her shiver. She's gazing up at me through hooded eyes, moving her hips against me in slow, languid circles. I bend down to kiss her mouth, then drag my tongue along her jaw to right below her ear. I nibble on her earlobe and she responds with a shiver.

"Tickles?" I ask, doing it again.

She squirms underneath me. "Yes. Now stop it and make me feel good."

"I promise you, Rylee, no one will ever be able to make you feel better."

Her cheeks flush the palest shade of pink and I slide down her body, leaving a trail of wet kisses over her bare skin. I start at the base of her neck, moving down the center of her chest. I take my time taking each breast in my mouth, sucking and teasing until I move lower, down her abdomen, to the only fabric left on her body. I drag her pale pink lace panties over her hips and down her thighs as her breath catches.

"Fuck, you are perfect."

Her skin is bronze, her legs long and toned. Her jade green eyes are the most beautiful thing I have ever seen.

"So are you." She sits up and meets me in the middle of the bed. We're both on our knees when she runs a finger down the center of my chest down to the waistband of my boxer briefs. "These need to go."

She doesn't move an inch, shamelessly watching me tug my briefs down to my knees, freeing my dick from my boxers. I'm hard and heavy and ready for her when her hand wraps around me, stroking my length with slow, even strokes. I groan and I swear it comes from somewhere deep down in my soul. Her soft hand gliding up and down my shaft is fucking heaven.

"Mmm…" I moan, tipping my head back. "That feels so good."

She adds a second hand, speeding up her rhythm, lighting me up like I'm on fucking fire. Her bottom lip slips under her teeth and my pulse speeds up.

I growl and bite her neck, then I soothe it with my mouth, sucking and tonguing her skin while she groans. It's the hottest sound I've ever heard.

Wanting to make her feel just as good, I reach between her thighs and stroke her. She moans as I trace my fingers over her most sensitive parts. Her eyes float closed when I insert one finger and then another until she's begging in two-word sentences. *Right there. Oh God. Don't stop. God, yes.*

Kissing her shoulder, I watch her skin pebble under my

touch. One of her hands moves to my shoulder, clawing me like she's holding on for dear life. Its pleasure and pain in the most wonderful of ways.

"Oh God," she breathes.

"Not yet, Ryls. Not until I'm inside you. Hang on, baby."

I move my hand away from her center and the grip she has on my dick stills. "You tease," she pouts, and her brows furrow, and I almost feel bad. *Almost.*

"I promise you it will be worth it."

"Promises, promises," she says with a sexy grin.

A minute later, she's lying on her back, cheeks flush, and I'm kneeling between her legs. Right where I've been dying to be for weeks. I'm thanking fuck for the condom I keep in my wallet as I cover up quickly, then hike up one of her knees.

"Rylee. If this isn't okay, you need to tell me now," I tell her, making sure we're on the same page.

"Would you stop talking and fuck me?" I laugh, surprised and thrilled at her response. She reaches for my dick between her legs and softly strokes me, guiding me towards her entrance.

"That's the plan," I say, then line myself up and slowly sink inside, her eyes glued to mine. The feeling is so intense I think I might blackout. When I'm inside of her fully, I pause and exhale the breath I was holding. Everything stills around us. Our gazes are locked deeply on one another, both of us seeming a little in awe that this is really happening.

Bending down, I kiss her, needing to feel the connection of her lips on mine. Then I pump into her in a steady rhythm, not letting up, driving into her harder and deeper each time. She moans and pants with every thrust, then she tightens around me and I swear a jolt of electricity runs up my spine.

I pause, my eyes involuntarily rolling back into my head, groaning against her mouth, trying to hold on. Pulling all of the way out, I slide back inside her and hear her breath hitch. Her eyes go hazy, and her lips stretch into a woozy half-smile. My gaze locks on hers and in this moment I have everything I've ever wanted.

She wraps her legs tightly around my waist, locking her ankles and squeezing tight. She's warm and tight and gripping me as I push into her over and over again.

"Fuck," I groan, closing my eyes, the sensations pulsing, aching, tormenting me as she clenches all around me. I grit my teeth, not ready for this to end.

"Miles…" Rylee starts, her voice drifting off. "You feel incredible."

Beneath me, she pants, her cheeks pink and her eyes heavy with desire. She looks a little gone, like she's love-drunk. I stare at her, certain I've never seen a better view. I've also never felt a connection like this. Sex has never been this meaningful, never feeling anything close to this.

With our bodies still locked together, I can't help myself. I dip down again to take her mouth in a greedy kiss, and she threads her hands into my hair. We moan and breathe heavy into the kiss, every illicit sound we make rumbling through my body. I'm aching for a release and hovering on the edge of that feeling we're both chasing, but I need to get her there first.

I gain momentum, driving her to the edge, determined to get her there, to take her so far over the edge she'll never forget it. I push harder, feeling that pulse that I love move its way up my spine. All the while, our gazes never leave one another's. I'm on the verge, then I'm a goner when Rylee cries out my name, tightening all around me. It's the hottest sound I've ever heard, and I'm done holding on. She shudders and clenches me until I'm pouring myself into her, grunting and gasping.

I hear myself mumble her name, struggling to stay in control. Building, building until I come down from the most glorious high.

Holy.

Hell.

"Yes," she whispers. "Yes." I pump into her one last time, pleasure rolling through me, wracking me and wrecking me in the very best way.

My body settles over top of her, savoring every second. There are no words, just silence. Just the sound of our breathing. Her heart pounds against mine, our sweaty bodies pressed firmly together. I had no idea how good it was going to be with her. Now I know.

Neither of us move, totally exhausted from the most intense connection I've ever felt. Blissed out from the best sex of my life and overwhelmed by the unexpected feelings that have caught me off guard. I want to stay right here with her forever.

When I finally pull back from her, leaning on my elbows, I'm still catching my breath. She stares back at me with such vulnerability, such emotion, that I'm at a loss for words. Forming a sentence might be too much for me at the moment, but what I do know is I want this girl all to myself.

Rylee hasn't moved. She's splayed out on the bed with a smile on her lips. Ridding myself of the condom in the trash, I come back to bed scooping her into my arms, bringing her warm body with me, holding her against my chest. Her cheek rests against my pec while my fingers ever so slowly run through her hair. We lay like this, saying nothing for a long time until eventually I find words to say.

"Full disclosure, Ryls. I've never introduced a girl to my family."

Her head pops off of my chest and she looks at me like she's in shock. "What? Thank goodness you told me this now and not before meeting them. I would have been a mess."

"That's what I thought," I say, rubbing my finger across her bottom lip. For the first time I don't want to get up and leave. I want more. I want to know everything about this girl who is starting to feel a lot like mine. "You're not just some girl, Rylee. I have real feelings for you. I told you I won't hurt you and I meant it."

She buries her cheek against my bare chest. "Do you have to go?" she whispers.

"Do you want me to stay?"

"Yes," she says quietly, her breathing even again.

I sigh in relief. "Good. I'm thinking I stay the night then our morning includes another round."

"You're insatiable."

"Only with you."

She falls asleep minutes later.

I hold her tight.

And I don't let go.

Chapter Fifteen

Rylee

I'm just leaving Josh's trailer when I hear Miles' voice. He catches up with me, his breath against my ear as he falls in step behind me. "You've been driving me mad all day." His voice is low and gravelly as his hands grip my waist from behind me, pulling me around the corner and towards the trailers.

My smile widens, "What are you doing?"

"I need you now, Ryls," he says, guiding me into his trailer and closing the door behind us. He turns the lock and then presses me hard against the door. His mouth hovers so close to mine I can feel his breath.

"Are you crazy? I'm working. What if Josh needs me?"

I tell myself this is a terrible idea. The walls of the trailer are so thin anyone could hear us. But I know I'm powerless to fight the arousal that courses through me whenever I'm with Miles. Hands down, one of the sexiest men in the world. And it's been so long since I've had sex – an embarrassingly long time before last night. I want more.

Since last night, Miles is all I've been able to think

about. I can still feel the weight of him over me. I can still taste his kisses. I can still hear the dreamy things he said. *I want you more than I've ever wanted anything.* Part of me still wondered if last night would turn out to be a single hot night with a man I have to face every day at work. Now here I am, pressed against Miles in his trailer. We all know workplace romances are taboo. We're just asking for shit to blow up on set. But in this moment, all I want is Miles and a repeat of last night.

He takes my face in his hands and drops his lips to mine. I'm instantly woozy with lust when his tongue finds mine, eliciting a hungry moan from both of us. The sound fills the small space. The kiss is hot, possessive – a you-are-mine type of kiss.

"Someone will hear us," I say, the words sounding breathy. But I know it's not going to matter. It feels too good having his hard body pressed against mine. His body that I was up close and personal with last night. I want more of it - the grid of his abs under his shirt, his toned pecs with a light scatter of chest hair and his muscular arms that feel so good wrapped around me. God help me, I can't stop.

He doesn't let go of me, pushing his erection against my center, his tongue licking a line up the side of my neck. My skin tingles as he kisses the edge of my jaw. "I don't give a damn. I can't wait another second."

Apparently that's good enough reason for me, because my mouth finds his in a demanding kiss. My heart is beating wildly in my chest at the thought of Miles taking me up against this door. I can't think straight I'm so needy with desire.

He's showing me how skilled he is with his mouth, kissing my jaw, sucking my bottom lip into his mouth, flicking his tongue over mine.

It's mind-blowing.

He takes my hands, raising them up over my head. Then his hands run down my body to the hem of my shirt, pulling the fabric up over my chest. I moan for what seems like hours when his wet mouth trails open-mouth kisses over my skin. He starts at my navel then heads north until he finds my lace bra, pulling the cups down to lavish each breast. His thumbs brush over my nipples and they stiffen instantly. *Fuck. This is what heaven must feel like.*

He's not gentle and I like him this way, owning me with intensity like he can never get enough. It's sexy as hell watching the color of his eyes turn a vivid, wild, dark charcoal. The moans and sounds he makes. He wants me and I want him too. Bad.

"Fuck, Rylee. You are the sexiest thing I've ever laid eyes on," he growls, the sound of his voice letting me know how turned on he is. Just hearing him say I'm sexy makes me so hot. I feel wanted.

"So are you, Miles," I tell him, hoping to make him feel like he just made me.

His hands leave my body to unbuckle his pants. He pulls them down just over his ass. I look down to admire his perfect dick, long and hard and ready for me. I can't stop watching him as he grips the base of it, fisting his length in one long pull. He notices me shamelessly staring at his goods.

"You like what you see?" he asks, one brow cocked.

"I'd like it better inside of me," I say, surprised at my unabashed choice of words, but then not surprised because he makes it so easy to talk to him. Even if it's something I'm not used to. I've never been into dirty talk but with Miles, I can't help it.

"Fuck Ryls, when you talk like that," he says, kneeling to the ground at my feet, ripping my panties down my legs.

I have to clench my jaw to stifle a moan at the site of Miles Bennett gazing up at me from his knees.

He slips his hand between my thighs, and my already hyperactive libido goes into overdrive. I'm breathless when he asks what we should do about protection.

"Do you have a condom?" I ask.

"Fuck. No," he says. "I forgot to replace the one in my wallet."

"I'm on birth control and I'm okay."

"I'm clean too, but I've never gone bare before."

His confession makes me happier than it should. The idea of getting this first with him makes my heart beat faster. "Me too. But if you're worried, we don't have-"

"Fuck, babe. I want to," he says, slipping his hands under my thighs, lifting me up and holding me against the wall. My legs wrap tightly around him, my ankles lock against his back, and then he's slipping inside me in one swift push. He pauses, glancing at me. His gaze is hooded, pupils dark, and he rumbles a soft, contented sound that curls my toes. I know the feeling. He feels incredible with no barrier between us and for a second I wonder if I'll regret this later. But I push that thought a side enjoying the feeling of him. It feels better than anything I've ever imagined.

"You feel…" He rasps, and he still hasn't moved. "It's never felt as good as this… Feeling you… it's better than anything I've ever felt. I'm already so close."

He takes another minute before thrusting inside of me again and again. Over and over until he hits just the right spot and my orgasm creeps up on me.

I hear myself moan, and suddenly remember how dangerous this is. Anyone could knock on this door – Josh, Violet, Georgia, anyone who works on this set. I need a lobotomy for doing this here and right now.

But I can't stop.

I can't stop when he's fucking me like this, when his tongue finds mine, when he begins to grind against me. Or when he tells me against my ear that we're a perfect fit, that it's never been better. The feeling coursing through me is white hot passion, overwhelming pleasure.

"You're mine, Rylee," he growls. "It's you I want."

"Yours," I whimper. "I'm yours." He wants me; there's no doubt. It's heady to realize that. I feel like I'm floating on air, soaring above the clouds.

"Fuck… Rylee, you feel so good… it's overwhelming." I can feel he's almost there, the tone in his voice giving him away. He's slowly losing all control. His hand cups the nape of my neck, and he's panting and thrusting. "I need to know you're all mine."

"I'm yours…only yours." I just get out the words when he pushes me over the edge. He continues to thrust deep inside of me as I ride out my orgasm, the intensity so strong I need to use his shoulder to muffle my cries. Pleasure explodes out of me, a dreamlike out-of-body experience that makes my eyes roll back in my head.

When he comes seconds after me, I feel every bit of it. He pulses and rocks into me once, twice, three times until he stills. We shudder together before burying our faces into each other's necks, his heart beating rapidly against my chest.

"I love how it feels with you," he manages to say through labored breaths. "It felt so good without a condom. It was-"

"Insanely good."

We both laugh. "It was."

"For me too, Miles."

I'm pinned against the door, my legs wrapped around his back until I start to sag against the wall. What was I thinking, having sex with Miles at work? My brain obviously short-circuits around him.

I feel the loss immediately when he slips out of me and slides me down steadying me. "You're fucking beautiful, Rylee."

Not what I expected, and I'm left speechless. He pulls up his pants, tucking himself back in, then finds my lace panties and slides them up my legs. "You're flushed. I like this look on you."

Running my fingers lightly against my lips, I can feel they're swollen from his kisses. I can still feel the sensation of his mouth on mine.

"Are you going to be okay today?" he asks, smoothing my hair behind my ear.

"I'm a little tired, but I'll be fine."

"That's not what I was referring to," he says, his voice low and soft. His eyes study mine. "I don't want you to feel uncomfortable on set after what we just did."

"I won't be," I say, though I know I totally will be.

"We were quiet. I made sure. I would never do anything to embarrass you." He presses a chaste kiss to my neck, his hands cupping my jaw. My cheeks flame.

"I know."

He straightens himself out then pulls me into him, wrapping his arms tightly around my middle. I relax against his warm body and close my eyes. A minute later, Miles kisses me goodbye, needing to get back to set before anyone notices he's missing. I worry who might be outside when he opens the trailer door. I'm anxious at the idea of getting caught. "Coast is clear, Ryls. You go first."

I slip out the trailer door, hyper-aware that I am the girl who just slept with the lead on set. I can't believe that just happened.

It was exciting and thrilling and incredible. And completely unlike me.

Now for the walk of shame.

"Rylee, I swear… you'd better tell me what's going on. I know something is up."

My brother knows exactly how to read me. He always has, ever since we were kids. He also always cuts right to the chase. With three kids under seven at home, I don't think he has time to drag things out.

My stomach dropped when I saw his name light up my phone screen just before 8 a.m. this morning. It was unlike him to call so early. I answered the phone in a panic. *Are Gran and Gramps okay?* Thankfully, it turns out he was only calling to check in on me. It had been some time and Cara had been on him to see how I was.

We chat for a while about the farm and he gives me an update on my nieces and nephew. I struggle to keep up with the conversation, my mind constantly drifting back to Miles. Would today be the day he would tire of me? Would I show up to work to find him acting like nothing had happened between us? I have to admit he seems genuinely interested in me, but I can't quiet the little voice that tells me to get real. It's not like Miles Bennett is going to make me his girlfriend.

"Come on Ryls…" Cole demands, then the sound is muffled as he talks to someone in the background. "Cara says hello. She also says you might as well spill it because it's only a matter of time before I get it out of you."

"What, are you guys tag-teaming me now?" I ask. I can usually count on my sister-in-law to take my side.

"Call it what you want. Now, are you going to tell me

what's going on with you?" my brother says in his best "dad" voice.

I sigh, realizing he's not going to let it go. "Okay, so there *is* this thing," I say, pushing open the door of my favorite café a few blocks from my hotel. I'm glad I had decided to head out on an early morning coffee run. This conversation is clearly going to require a dose of caffeine.

"I've been sort of seeing someone," I admit. It feels all kinds of strange saying it out loud.

"Okay. That's good. So what's the problem?"

"I met him on the movie I've been working on." I pause to pick up my iced latte from the barista, who looks like she would rather be anywhere else.

"And..." he prods. "I feel like you're about to drop a bomb on me."

"Yeah, I sorta am." I take a seat at an outdoor table, wrapping my jacket around me. It's a typical chilly Vancouver morning and the streets are quiet. "The guy I'm seeing, it's not just anyone."

I pause, then lower my voice so nobody hears me. There is literally no one around but it still feels like I'm about to reveal a huge secret. "It's Miles Bennett. The guy I've been seeing... it's Miles Bennett."

"The guy from *The Back-Up Plan*?" My brother asks, his voice rising three octaves higher.

"Yup, that's the one," I respond nervously, picking at a cuticle on my fingernail.

"Are you for real right now?" he asks.

"Why would I lie about something like that? I know it sounds crazy, but it's the truth."

"Holy shit. My sister is dating an actual movie star. Can you imagine what Mom would say?"

My heart does that flip it does at the mention of my

mother. Cole is right, she would get a kick out of the whole thing. *But am I dating him?* I have no clue.

"Are things serious?" my brother asks. "Do I need Cara to buy me a suit?"

I roll my eyes. What am I supposed to say? That I'm somehow seeing a guy who is completely out of my league? That Miles is sweet and funny and goes out of his way to spend time with me? That I don't know what's going on between us and that really confuses me? I opt for a simpler truth. "He's practically Hollywood royalty at this point, Cole. Really, how far can it go?"

"Well, is he good to you?"

"He is," I say, taking a sip from my coffee now that it's cooled down a bit. *Heaven.* I haven't had much sleep the last two nights, so this is saving my life. "But let's not get ahead of ourselves. I'm not even sure what is happening."

Then why does it feel like he's my boyfriend?

I shut that thought down as quickly as it enters my mind. Since when does Miles Bennett have girlfriends? Never. Anyone who has ever read an *US Weekly* knows that. *Never.* So why would that change now? Whatever it is that is happening between us, it can't possibly mean as much to him as it does to me.

"Listen, he's funny and charming, and I like spending time with him. But I'm being cautious," I say, pulling one knee into my chest.

"In other words, you have your walls up, just like you have for a very long time. At some point, Ryls, you need to let people in."

"I love you, Coley, but since when are you the expert on love?"

"Since meeting Cara, falling in love with her and marrying her. And let's not forget the three kids we made together. I may not know much, but I do know about love.

And I know that it's worth it. I also know that love doesn't stand a chance if you're not open to it."

Everything my big brother just said surprises me. Cole is usually the strong, silent type. But of course, he's right. He's built his life around love. Sometimes I forget that.

"Well, I think my situation might be the exception to the rule. I'm having fun with Miles until it ends. Aren't you always telling me I need to have some fun? The odds of Miles wanting a relationship are slim to none and besides, I'm moving back home soon. The timing is all wrong."

"Whatever you say. Just promise me you'll at least be open to something more. I only want you to be happy."

It's a little scary to like Miles this much, this soon. I'm in over my head. I end the call with Cole, but not before telling him what he wants to hear. It's easier that way.

Chapter Sixteen

Miles

A lifetime of Rylee wouldn't be enough. We've exchanged heated glances every day on set and talked or texted every night before bed, just getting to know each other better. I've already decided that I want as much of her as I can get. But it never seems to be enough. Her quiet confidence and her willingness to open up to me has me captivated and impressed. I am under her spell. She's gotten to me in a way no one else ever has and even though it's only been weeks that I've known Rylee, somehow it feels like years. It's both exciting and scary as hell.

This morning I woke up early and drove my rental car downtown, planning to surprise her at her hotel room with coffee. She answers the door in a towel, and I can hear the shower running in the bathroom. If she's trying to kill me, it's working.

"You keep looking at me like that, and we might never make it to set," she teases, her hand holding her towel against her chest as she steps aside to let me in. Her voice is flirty and laced with innuendo. My heart beats wildly in my chest at the thought of what could come next.

"Look at you how?" I say, setting our coffees on the desk. "Like the sight of you in nothing but a towel might actually give me a heart attack?"

"No, more like you want to join me in the shower instead of drinking your coffee."

And fuck, I'm already hard. My skin seems to crave Rylee's touch. Sex with her is like a drug. I need her nonstop, like a wild addiction, and I want her to know it. I step closer to her, running my nose under her jaw, breathing her in. "Is that an invitation?"

She doesn't answer. Instead, her hands move from her towel to the hem of my hoodie. She lifts the sweatshirt up and over my head while her towel drops to the floor. Then her hands work the button on my jeans. She unzips me, pushing my pants and my briefs over my hips. I kick them off from there.

"Can you be quick? I can't be late for work," she says as I graze my lip over her jaw to her mouth.

"I'm so fucking turned on right now, quick is the way it's going to have to be."

Rylee smiles and my hands grab hold of her ass, pulling her hips into me. I crush my mouth to hers in a hungry kiss. The feel of her bare skin against mine goes straight to my head. She's a high.

And then we're in the shower under a warm spray of water, kissing and touching until I have her pinned against the tile wall and am emptying myself into her.

"You are just what I needed," I whisper once we're done, sliding my soapy hands down her back, kissing her shoulder.

"Turns out, it was just what I needed too. I'm very glad you decided to bring me coffee this morning."

Afterwards we dress and then drink our lukewarm coffees. I drive her to work – almost. She makes me pull over two blocks from set so she can walk the rest of the way. She's still not crazy about the idea of being seen with me. It shouldn't bother me, but it does.

Other than that, my day so far is perfect.

I show up on set quite possibly the happiest man alive. Starting my day with Rylee in the shower then driving to work like we were any other normal couple felt good. It felt right. I want more mornings like this with her. I wonder if she feels the same.

The best parts of my day are the parts I spend with her. I could talk to her for hours and never run out of things to say. The quiet moments, when she's in my arms, her body nestled into mine – I never want them to end. I am learning her body, figuring out where she likes to be touched and how fast or slow she needs me to move to get her there. I listen for cues, like the sounds she makes, and how her body responds when my mouth is on different parts of her. I already know she likes it when I suck on her neck or when I kiss the sensitive pulse point below her ear. Rylee likes to be touched, and that works for me because there's nothing I want more than to have my hands on her.

The day seems to fly by. I manage to focus long enough to shoot a restaurant scene scheduled for this morning. Taking a break for lunch, I'm relieved when I run into Rylee as she's walking past Josh's trailer with a smoothie in one hand and a stack of papers in the other.

"Hey, country girl."

"Hey, you," she says, turning to me. "Have you had lunch?"

"Not yet. You?" I ask her.

"I did. I have a meeting with Josh, so I ate early."

I step closer to her, my eyes on hers. I can't hide my

smile as lust dances down my spine thinking about our shower this morning.

"What's on that mind of yours?" she asks in a quiet voice.

"Our shower together this morning. Have you been thinking about it as much as I've been?"

She smiles, "What do you think?"

"I hope so." And she nods her head not once but twice. *Fuck.* "I want you in my bed tonight," I whisper. "The second I wrap for the day I'm heading back to the house and I want you there when I walk through the door. And pack a bag. I want you to stay."

"What about your family?"

"They went to Whistler for two days. It'll just be us. Say yes."

This time, she doesn't hesitate. She says the only word I want to hear. *Yes.*

When I finally walk through the door later that night, I'm exhausted. It was a long day and I couldn't wait to get home to Rylee. I toss my wallet onto the table in the foyer and toe off one of my shoes.

"Ryls?" I call out. It's almost 9:30 p.m. but after the day I had on set it feels more like three in the morning. I get my second shoe off and walk into the kitchen, desperate to see my girl.

I find Rylee standing at the sink, wearing a pair of very short shorts and a tank top. My dick takes notice of the fact she's not wearing a bra. I instantly need to make an adjustment.

"I thought you might be hungry so I'm making you a little something. I hope you don't mind me messing up your kitchen."

Wrapping my arms around her, I nuzzle my face into her neck. Good Lord, she smells good. I inhale her then kiss the back of her neck. "Mind? You are spoiling me. I like coming home to you."

"You're just excited for my cooking."

"The cooking is a bonus. It's you and these legs and this ass and your mouth that I've been dying to see."

She turns in my arms to face me, rising on her toes to kiss me. I kiss her back, hard. I don't want to stop but she giggles, pulling back.

"Patience, Miles," she says with a sly smile. "I will feed you and *then* I will take you upstairs. I figured you'd be hungry, so I made you chicken and dumplings. It's an old family recipe. As my gran likes to say, you'll be full as a tick by the time you're done."

"Fuck Ryls, when you talk with that sexy drawl of yours, I lose all control." The thought of skipping dinner and taking her straight upstairs crosses my mind. What I really want to do right now is undress her with my teeth. She must notice the heat in my eyes when she gently pushes me away.

"Go wash your hands. Dinner will be ready in less than 10 minutes."

She smirks, then turns her attention to the stove. Dinner smells so fucking good. Watching her, I find myself smiling like a madman. I'm used to coming home to an empty house at the end of the day. Coming home to Rylee is so much better.

Fuck me. What did I do to deserve this girl?

She hands me a tumbler of my favorite whiskey and instructs me to sit on a stool.

"You didn't have to cook. We could have ordered something," I say, taking a sip of the amber liquid.

"When was the last time you had a home-cooked meal?" Rylee looks at me and my chest tightens. She's right, I can't even remember the last time someone cooked for me. We've slipped into these intimate moments so easily. I like that she thinks about what I need, that she recognizes what has been missing in my life.

"It's been a long time," I admit to her.

She continues to move around the kitchen, finding plates and silverware, setting the table. Her hair is pulled back in a headband, her feet are bare, her toes painted a pale shade of pink. She always looks beautiful, but tonight even more so.

"What are you smiling at?" she asks, catching me staring.

"You." I get up from my seat and on my way to the sink I kiss her shoulder. I notice her camera on the counter. "What were you taking photos of?"

"Nothing too exciting, I just thought I might feel inspired, being so close to the ocean. I noticed that Japanese Maple when I was cooking dinner, so I took a few shots. It really is beautiful against the blue of the ocean. I couldn't resist."

I glance out the kitchen window. I've looked at this view countless times and have never even noticed the tree. But somehow, now it's all I see. "Will you show me the photos that you took? I'd love to see them."

"Maybe," she says, blushing. "If you eat all of your dinner, I'll consider it." She winks, and it's cute as hell.

"You're blushing, you know?"

"I am not," she says stubbornly.

"Are too. And I love it when you do."

Rylee grins, and it makes me wish every night could feel this good. I imagine making dinner with Rylee after work, talking about our days, cuddling on the sofa before slipping into our bed together. I come back to reality with a start. *Our bed? What the fuck was that?* Jesus, Miles. You're really getting ahead of yourself.

But I can't deny it. I want more nights like this with Rylee. I'm happy and relaxed and all I want is to be around her. She is… God, she is amazing. And I can't seem to quiet the voice that is telling me to make her mine, to hold onto her and never let her go.

Chapter Seventeen

Rylee

Miles is officially my favorite person on the planet to cook for. He had three helpings of my chicken and dumplings and looked like he had died and gone to heaven with every bite. He sure knows how to make a girl feel good.

"When did you have time to do all this?" Miles holds up one of my homemade chocolate chip cookies. "These are better than… dare I say it… sex."

"Hm. Are you sure about that?" I take one of his feet in my hands and tickle it. We're sprawled out on the couch in his living room, our heads resting on opposite ends of the sofa, our feet a tangled mess in the center. I rub the sole of his foot, tracing the arch with my fingers. The man has seriously sexy feet. For the first time I understand the concept of a foot fetish; who knew I had a kink?

"You're right. But they are close." He laughs. "Stop. You're not playing fair." He pops the last bite of his cookie into his mouth, jerking his foot away from my hand.

"I didn't know there were rules," I joke, reaching for

this other foot, but he's too quick. Next thing I know, Miles has sat up and is straddling my hips, his famous hazel eyes on mine.

"Can I see the photos now?"

A small grin tugs at the corners of my mouth. "Okay."

He moves off me so I can grab my camera from the kitchen. I sit beside him on the sofa and hand it over. He flips through three or four of the photos I took, viewing the images on the small square screen on the back of my mom's old Canon. The maple tree in the yard with the Pacific Ocean in the distance. The light cast over the sea, the thinness of the clouds over the sun, everything tinted in orange.

"These are incredible."

"They need to be edited."

"They don't need a thing."

Miles turns and kisses my temple. "You have a talent, Ryls. I'd love to see more of your photos. Can I keep flipping through?"

"You can," I tell him, dropping back against the couch. He lies down, resting his head in my lap with his legs stretched out across the sofa. We spend the next 30 minutes or so like this, me running my fingers slowly through his hair while he flips through my captures.

"Who's this?" he asks, tilting the screen towards me.

"That's Lainey, my niece. She was eating a slice of my gran's cherry pie and she had it everywhere. It was so cute. My sister-in-law had to strip her out of her clothes and give her a bath she was such a mess."

"She's adorable. The perfect muse. You captured her at just the right moment. I don't know how you take such incredible photos."

"It's not hard with a subject as cute as her. Her brother

and sister too. I've taken hundreds of photos of those three."

Miles flipped through a few more. "You're the best photographer I know."

"I bet I'm the only one you know."

"I could know hundreds of photographers and you'd still be my favorite," he says, looking up at me with a genuine warmth. The compliment zinging straight to my core. "And these are your grandparents?"

"Yes. That's my gran and gramps on the farm." My fingers continue running through the short strands of his hair. My gaze dips down to Miles in my lap, scrolling through photos of my life on the farm. I barely recognize my life. I mean, look at me sitting on the couch with Miles Bennett's beautiful face in my lap. It feels like a dream.

"Is this the farm where you grew up?"

"It is. I was 13 when my brothers and I went to live there."

The room falls silent as Miles moves my camera to the coffee table then turns his head to look at me. "Rylee, you don't have to answer my next question," he says, weaving his fingers through mine. "But I want to ask you because I want to know all of you. Why did you live with your grandparents?"

I knew it was only a matter of time before we got to this part of my life.

It's not something I talk about. It's not something I share. And yet, for some reason I want to share it with Miles. I'm just not sure where to start.

The memories of that day have never faded. All these years later, they remain clear and sharp in my mind. "My parents died when I was 13." My voice shakes, but I continue. "It was devastating. Not only for me, but my brothers and my grandparents. They died instantly. They never suffered. Thank God."

"We don't have to talk about it. I'm sorry if I upset you. I didn't know," he says, softly.

"It's okay. It's been years," I say. "I want you to know. It's taken some time, but it doesn't hurt like it used to." But as I hear the words, they don't seem quite right. It's more like I've learned how to live with the pain. I take a deep breath, remembering the last time I saw my mom and dad.

"What happened?" Miles asks gently.

"They were killed by a drunk driver. Just like that they were… gone." Just saying the words makes my heart ache in my chest as though it could crack into a million tiny pieces at any moment.

"I'm so sorry," he says with sincerity.

"After their deaths it was really hard." I tell him the story that most people have never heard. I tell him how great my parents were, how much fun we used to have together, and the hard times that came for the rest of us when they were gone.

"I wouldn't go to school. Or church. I stayed in my room. I missed them so much I didn't know what to do."

"I can't imagine what it must have been like for you and your family. It's not fair. I hate that you had to go through that."

"I sort of just fell apart. My grandparents were drowning in their own grief and my brothers sort of went off the rails. They got into drinking, started skipping school and getting into trouble. They didn't know any other way to deal with the pain. It was a really dark time, and I wasn't sure how we were going to make it through."

"But you did," he says. "You are one of the strongest people I have ever met." He sits up, gathering me in his arms. I straddle his waist and his strong hands grip my thighs. It's like he knows exactly what to do and say to comfort me.

"I didn't have a choice. I wanted to be strong for my grandparents. I wanted to be there for my brothers. I wanted to live. My parents would have wanted us to keep going. Yes, I was devastated, but after a year of grieving, I told myself I needed to get my joy back."

"You were willing to try to live again."

"I was."

I find it so easy to talk to Miles, even about something as painful as this. I rest my forehead against his, knowing that there is still one thing I haven't shared with him. I need to tell him I'm leaving at the end of filming. I've been avoiding it, trying to convince myself it doesn't really matter. But it does, and now is as good a time as any to let him know. "I need to talk to you about something."

He looks at me with a puzzled expression. "Okay. What is it?"

I take a breath, untangling myself from him and shifting to sit beside him on the couch. I face him, putting a little distance between us to give him the news. He shifts his body to face mine, one hand resting on my knee. "I'm moving back home when we wrap. To… Tennessee. It's been the plan for a while. I knew this was going to be my last film. It's time I go home and take care of my grandparents."

He swallows. "I wasn't expecting that."

"I'm sorry. I feel like you should know. I know this probably changes things between us and I understand if it does."

He places his other hand on my knee, brushing his fingers over my skin. "Rylee, it doesn't change a thing as far as I'm concerned. You're not getting rid of me that easy," he says. "Unless you feel differently, which I'm really fucking hoping isn't the case."

I stumble over my words, trying to find the right ones. "No, that's not it, it's just…" I breathe out. "I like where we're at. I really like being with you."

I can't stop looking at Miles, in awe that this man is mine. Well, sort of mine. We haven't really discussed it, but it really feels that way. I take in his deep hazel eyes, his golden skin, and wonder how I got so lucky. I don't know why our paths crossed, but I'm thankful they did. I also can't help but wonder how someone like him could want someone like me. It's been such an emotional night, and I'm frustrated at not being able to find the right words and exhausted from revisiting the heartache of losing my parents. But I try to put those feeling aside, hoping that we can come to some sort of a conclusion about where we go from here.

"You matter to me. I want to keep seeing you." His eyes soften. Miles gives me a small smile. "How are you feeling about moving back? You've been in L.A. for a while now. Are you ready for the change?"

Truthfully, I am worried. "I'm nervous about starting again – finding my own place and a job in a small town where the film industry doesn't even exist. I worry about that a lot. I worry about my grandparents getting older too. I'll miss my apartment in Los Angeles and living with Meg. And travelling around the world with Josh, which has been pretty amazing."

"Well, now that I know what you're worried about, I hope you'll let me be there for you."

My pulse quickens. I have never been with a man who cares as much as Miles does. "I will," I tell him, and I mean it.

He leans in, threading his hands through my hair,

taking my mouth with his. My whole body melts as his lips brush over mine.

"Fuck, Rylee… what are you doing to me? I know you have to go, but I really wish you didn't."

Miles and I just look at each other. There were no words that will solve this for us. I know that I'm crazy to continue seeing a man when there's no hope for a future. I lick my lips, tasting him, remembering the way he just kissed me, wishing I could kiss him like that forever.

"Want to watch a movie?"

"Only if it's not one of mine."

"But yours are my favorite." I pout and he kisses me again, pulling my bottom lip into his mouth. "Mmm. We can't start, Miles. We need to be good. If we start, we'll never stop."

"I don't see a problem with that," he says, cocking a brow. "Are you as hungry as I am for popcorn?"

"I'm always down for popcorn. But how are you hungry? We just finished dinner a couple of hours ago."

"I can always eat. I may not know how to cook, but I have the number to every take-out restaurant in West Vancouver on speed dial."

I laugh, knowing he's not kidding. I really need to teach this man how to cook. Well, maybe we'll start with boiling water.

While Miles handles the microwave popcorn, I throw together a sad excuse for a charcuterie board. His fridge and his cupboards are practically empty, but I manage to scrape together some cheese, apple slices and a handful of trail mix. We sit on the floor of his living room, our makeshift feast on a tray in front of us, and despite the uncertainty that lies ahead, in this moment I feel purely happy.

We put on a movie – not one of Miles' – and he pulls

me onto the couch. He's shirtless. The muscles in his abs are cut and lean, his pecs defined with a dusting of trimmed chest hair. His skin is warm and soft, and it takes everything in me to pay attention to the movie and not pounce on him like a cat would a mouse. Finally, the movie ends, and Miles takes my hand and leads me upstairs to his bedroom.

We undress each other slowly, then Miles pulls back the comforter and we crawl into bed. He whispers in my ear, a steady stream of sweet and filthy words, as he sinks inside of me. When he's all the way in, he stills and white-hot heat rips through me. We both groan. It's the sexiest sound I've ever heard.

Wild lust.

Wild attraction.

The beginning of falling hard.

I'm still coming down from the most intense, mind-shattering, bone-numbing sex when a realization hits me.

That was so much more than sex and you know it.

The next morning, I wake up on Miles' chest, wrapped around him, his heart beating rhythmically under my ear. I lie that way for a while, enjoying the warmth of his strong body, not wanting this feeling to end. I'm feeling a little… gone. It's like being this close to him is not enough. I would crawl right into him if I could. I want to stay here, draped over him forever.

Miles stirs underneath me, pulling me tighter into his hard, naked body. His fingers run lines from my shoulder to my elbow. Lifting my ear from his chest, I kiss his pec while my fingers drag over the hair on his chest, then along the grid of his abs. Miles' dreamy eyes focus on mine. His hair is tousled, and his eyes are sleepy but somehow he looks like he's just stepped off the set of a photo shoot.

"Hi there," I say, gazing into his eyes, my voice low. A

smile curls his lips, making my heart falter. He can turn me on with just a look, with just that Miles Bennett smile – the one he knows drives me mad. My body lights up like a firecracker, sending a tingling sensation over my skin.

"Good morning," he says in the most heavenly, raspy morning voice.

I think back to last night. Not just the sex – but yes, the sex is definitely part of it. But it's also Miles coming home to me in his kitchen, cooking us dinner. It's the two of us eating together after work like we're a real couple and not just two people in lust who have no chance of a real future together. It's me telling him that I'm leaving, and him still choosing to stay. It's all of it.

My phone vibrates from somewhere on the nightstand, knocking me out of the fantasies running through my head. I reach for it and check the screen to see a text from an unknown number. Swiping the screen to life, I check who it's from. *Hey Rylee, it's Ellie! Oh, and Olivia, she's sitting right beside me. We're having a girls' day in Vancouver tomorrow and would love for you to join us! Let us know xo*

"Who is it, babe?"

"It's Ellie and Olivia. Did you give them my number?"

"Yes. Sorry, I meant to tell you, Ellie asked me for it yesterday when I was on my way home from set. I hope you don't mind I gave it to her."

"Of course not. I'm happy you did. She and Olivia are having a girls' day tomorrow, I guess when they come back from Whistler, and they want to know if I can join them."

"Are you going to go?" Miles asks, tangling his feet with mine.

"Yeah, I'd like to, if it's okay with you?"

"Why wouldn't it be? You should go. It will be fun."

It feels like time is ticking on whatever it is that is happening with Miles and I, and even though I want to say yes, part of me just wants to spend every spare second with him. But I know it would be smart to put a little distance between us. Things seem to be moving so fast.

I quickly text back, telling Ellie I'd love to, and then save her as a contact into my phone.

"Come here," Miles says, motioning for me to kiss him. So I do what he asks. He moves to suck on my neck, and I say a silent prayer that he never stops. Unless he wanted to use his incredible mouth elsewhere. In that case, I wouldn't protest.

When he's finished with my neck, he rolls us over so I'm underneath him, every hard inch of him pressed against my skin. It lights a fire in me to know how quickly I can turn him on. He's rock-hard for me the second we start to kiss.

"Miles," I say against his mouth, running my fingers over the stubble of his jaw.

"I'm a little distracted here, Ryls," he teases, continuing to kiss me like it will kill him if he has to stop. He presses a kiss to my jaw before pulling back and looking me in the eye. "Tell me, babe. What is it?"

"It's been a really great 24 hours with you. That's all."

Miles' hand gently sweeps a strand of hair from my face.

"It's only just the beginning."

Chapter Eighteen

Miles

Parker, Liam and I sit on an outdoor patio at an upscale restaurant overlooking the ocean. We're tucked into a corner, out of sight of paps and fans, my bodyguard standing a few feet away. Olivia, Ellie and Rylee are meeting us here soon, after they're done with their manicures and pedicures. It's my brothers' last few days in Vancouver before they fly back home to Reed Point with Olivia and Ellie. What I wouldn't give to be flying home with them, with Rylee in the seat beside me.

"I'm going to miss you assholes," I say, sipping from my beer.

"I'm going to take that as a compliment," Parker laughs.

"I'm *not* going to miss these damn photographers," Liam complains. "The guy in the parking lot could have gotten himself killed jumping in front of the car like that. Why anyone even wants a picture of your ugly mug is beyond me." He smirks in my direction, pulling my attention away from the patio door, where I've been hoping to see Rylee appear.

"Don't feel bad, Liam," I tell him. "I'm sure Mom still has your photo on the mantle at home."

Parker seems to take notice when my eyes return to the door. "Are you worried she's left town with some other guy? Jesus, Miles, you haven't taken your eyes off that door since we sat down."

"Our little brother has misplaced his balls somewhere," Liam jokes, leaning back in his chair and crossing one knee over the other. "I seem to remember getting shit for that very thing not long ago. Pot meet kettle."

"Fuck both of you very much," I say, slipping on my Ray-Bans to hide the smile in my eyes.

"Things must be pretty serious with Rylee. Admit it, bro. You've got it bad for this girl," Parker says.

I put my hands up in surrender. "I like her. I'm not hiding anything. It's fucked up, right? But there's an expiration date on us. She's on a plane outta here after the movie wraps."

"Who says she has to go back?" Liam says. "Maybe that was her plan before she met you, but plans can change."

"Yeah, they can, but that decision isn't up to me."

Parker clears his throat. "So you're good if she leaves at the end of this? You're totally okay with ending things, or with trying long distance?"

"I don't have a choice. She's going back home, a tiny place called Deer Lake. Try to find it on a map. There's no way I can go with her, unless I want to shit all over my career."

Liam gives me a look over his bottle of beer. "Come on, Miles, I'm not buying it. Why can't you fly back and forth for work? People do it all the time."

"I guess it could work in theory, but it wouldn't be easy. Let's face it, when I'm not halfway around the world shooting, I need to spend my time in Los Angeles. That's where the work is."

I'm trying not to show how bothered I am by the idea of Rylee leaving, but I'm pretty sure I'm failing. My brothers know me too well. If this is what Rylee wants, who am I to try to stand in the way of it? I know all too well what it's like to miss your family. This whole situation sucks.

My shitty mood lifts when I see Rylee walk through the door with Ellie and Olivia by her side. *Finally.* She slips into the chair next to mine and I immediately pull her closer. You'd think we'd been apart for months instead of just a few hours, that's how happy I am to see her.

We place our lunch orders and the girls catch us up on their day out while we wait for our food. After a feast of appies and pasta, we're all stuffed, but Ellie insists on ordering dessert. When it arrives – a towering piece of triple layer chocolate cake – she squeals, then digs in like it's her last meal.

"Are you sure you're not eating for three?" Olivia asks her with a grin.

"Just two," Ellie says, rubbing her pregnant belly. "Olivia, you are such a big bully."

Liam snickers at his soon-to-be wife, draping his arm around the back of her chair.

"What?" Ellie's eyebrows shoot up, the word barely audible with her mouth full of chocolate cake.

"You're not fooling anyone, Ells. Everyone knows how much you like to eat," Liam says. "Personally, I think it's sexy as hell."

"I know you do," Ellie tells him with a wink.

Liam leans over and kisses her on the cheek, resting

one hand on her growing belly. They really are crazy about each other, anyone can see it. Watching them together makes me feel happy, but also envious. I stroke the soft skin of Rylee's knee with my fingertips. Taking a sip of her drink, she turns her gaze to me, placing her small hand over mine.

"Now, speaking of this bean in my belly, Miles, are you coming home for the baby shower?"

"I'm planning on coming home, but you're not really going to make me go to the baby shower, are you?"

"Thanks a lot. Your niece or nephew heard that, by the way," Ellie says, pointing to her baby belly.

"Nephew," Liam quickly chimes in. He's adamant that Ellie is pregnant with a boy. "Don't worry, Miles. The boys are golfing. We're bringing Dad too. There's no fucking way I'd make you go to a baby shower. I'm not that big of an asshole."

"In that case, I'll definitely be there."

We spend the rest of the afternoon laughing and telling stories. Rylee fits in seamlessly with my family, and they're all interested in getting to know her. It's one of the best days I've had in years. When Rylee leaves the table to go to the restroom, Olivia leans in and tells me I should bring Rylee with me when I go back to Reed Point. It's like she's reading my mind. I was going to ask her later today when we are alone.

"Do you think she'll say yes?" Olivia asks.

I pause, considering it. "That's a good question. I'm really not sure. It would be a big step for her."

Olivia looks at me with a smile in her eyes. "We all really like her, if that's not obvious. Don't let this one get away. She's a keeper."

I'm pretty sure a goofy grin takes over my face. "I like

her too, Liv. A lot. Now, if I could only think of a way for us to be together in the same damn city."

"We're here for you, Miles. Whatever you need."

"I know. Thanks, Liv."

Olivia mock fans her face with her hand. "I have goosebumps. This is it, Miles. It's happening."

"Focus on the shower, you're not planning my wedding just yet." I pick up my napkin and swat her arm with it.

"Okay, okay," she snorts, rubbing her arm. "I'll stop, but I'm so, so, so happy for you."

After paying the bill, we decide to walk the seawall. The sun is shining and we're trying to make the most of our last day together in Vancouver. I have my sunglasses on, and my ballcap pulled low, and so far I've managed not to draw the attention of any well-intentioned fans.

I reach for Rylee's hand but she pulls away.

"There's just so many people around, Miles," she says apologetically. "Anyone could see."

"I just want to hold my girlfriend's hand in public like any normal person would," I tell her.

It can be kind of fun, sharing this little secret, keeping our relationship just for ourselves. But on days like today, I want to shout it from the rooftops and tell the whole fucking world that Rylee Brookes is mine. But I know she's scared. The last thing she wants is to be involved in a whole media firestorm, and I get that. Thankfully the internet has moved on from the rumors about Violet and me, turning its attention from the "Viles" bullshit to some other celebrity scandal that doesn't involve me. I've never been happier to be yesterday's news.

Rylee pulls her bottom lip under her teeth, looking like there's something on her mind. There she goes again, making me come undone without even trying. Lust crackles through me. I want her to bite her lip again, preferably while stroking my dick with her soft hands. *I'm so fucking done for this girl.*

"Girlfriend?" she asks, with a grin that looks both nervous and hopeful. Not to mention cute as hell.

"I hope so. That's how I think of you."

I laugh because she looks like she's in a bit of shock. Her bright green eyes sparkle in the sun. "I wasn't sure what we are. I mean…." She stops and takes a deep breath in. "It's just been a while, you know?"

"Since you've dated a guy?" I blurt out, then feel like a dick for it. The rest of the gang are up ahead so I'm not worried about anyone hearing us, but I feel like it came out all wrong.

"Since I've done anything with a guy."

Now it's my turn to be shocked. There's no way. It's not possible, not with a girl as beautiful and funny and sexy as Rylee. How were there not guys lining up for a chance to be with her? I can't wrap my head around it.

"How do you feel about commitment?" I ask her.

She turns her face to the ocean as we walk hand-in-hand and I find myself praying that she's not about to tell me that she's not the relationship type. "Honestly, it's not something I was looking for. But I won't let past experiences stop me from giving my heart to someone."

My heart just about cracks in two. Rylee is open and honest, never afraid to tell me how she feels. It's so damn attractive. Bringing her hand to my lips, I kiss her knuckles. I've never really dated anyone long enough to call them my girlfriend so I'm a little unsure of how this all goes.

The question I'm about to ask her next kind of makes me feel like I'm in high school again, but fuck it, I don't care. I need to be as open as she is, to tell her exactly how I feel. I stop in the middle of the pathway and turn to face her. "I want… I know I really want us to be together. I want to be your boyfriend. I want the label. You and me. Does that sound okay?"

She reaches out and cups my cheek and a slow smile spreads across her face. I swear my heart beats out of my body.

"It sounds more than okay, Miles. I'm good with that."

I fucking smile like I just won an Artist Award. It feels like I'm flying. "Good." I kiss her temple and relief fills my chest. It feels good to know we're both on the same page. But it's just the start. I've decided I want to take her home to Reed Point. I want her to meet my parents. I know it's soon and there's the definite possibility that she'll freak out and say no, but everything with Rylee feels like it's unfolding the way that it's meant to.

I only hope she feels the same.

I'm about to find out.

Rylee

Standing just off set, I watch Miles as he reads through his lines. He's sitting in the black chair with his name printed on the back, his legs stretched out in front of him. I stare a little too long because Miles eventually glances up at me, his expression breaking from total concentration into the smile that I know is only for me. It always makes me weak in the knees. It's sublime. All I can do is smile back and watch as another familiar look takes over his eyes – lust. But that will have to wait. We still haven't told anyone about us, and I'd like to keep it that way for a little while longer. The room is busy, so I do my best to reign in my hormones, which have already started to spin out of control. I move through the crowd of techs to where he's sitting.

"Hey."

"Hi, you. Everything go okay with the tour?" he asks, sitting taller in his chair.

Miles invited his brothers, Olivia and Ellie to set today and I offered to show them around.

"Yes, everything went fine. They are waiting for you in your trailer."

"Great. I should be 15 more minutes. Do you want to-"

He doesn't have a chance to finish his sentence before he's abruptly interrupted by a voice I know all too well.

"Umm," Violet says, looking me up and down like my mere existence is ruining her day. Her PA is right behind her, juggling her iPad and two iced coffees. She looks afraid. I don't have to wonder why. Violet motions with her fingers to the PA to scram, as though she's shooing away a mosquito. I have no doubt I will be next.

"What's up, Violet?" Miles asks, and at the sound of his voice she turns her attention to her co-star.

"I should go," I say to no one in particular. This feels awkward. I don't know where to look. I'm afraid if I make eye contact with Miles, Violet will see the spark that is always smoldering just under the surface with us. But I'm afraid to look at her as well, as much as I hate to admit it. I've never let anyone make me feel inferior, so I'm not sure why I'm starting now. With no good option, I shift my eyes, feigning interest in something happening off set.

"Or you could stay," Miles says to me.

Violet frowns. I inwardly smile. I don't care to stand here and take this woman's crap, yet I can't quite bring myself to leave.

"Listen, Miles," she says with sex in her voice. *Gross.* She looks over at me again like I'm a carrier of the plague. I don't get paid enough for this. Meeting her stare, I part my lips to speak but she beats me to it. "Can I have a second with Miles? Without you around?"

She has no right to talk to me the way she does, to treat me like her human punching bag. It makes me furious, but I don't stop her.

"Whatever you want to talk to me about, it can be done in front of Rylee. Have you two met? Violet, this is Rylee." I could hug Miles on the spot for making me feel important. Forget hugging him, this man deserves to be worshipped with my mouth.

Violet nods at me. I flash her the best fake smile I can muster and wait for whatever it is she has to say.

"Emilio's not happy with me, Miles. He thinks there's something going on between us," she sighs, referring to her race car driver boyfriend. The one she seems to forget all about whenever Miles steps in the room.

"And that would involve me how?" he responds.

"Well, I thought you could talk to him. Just to set him straight. Let him know there's nothing going on with us."

"With all due respect, Violet, that would be a no. This is between you and him. I want no part of it."

Her mouth falls open then closes just as quickly. "I just thought that-"

"Then you thought wrong. I'm sorry, Violet. I won't get involved," he says in a tone that I've never heard him use before. It says *I'm done with this.* This hard-ass side of Miles is a serious turn-on.

"Okay. Forget I asked. I'll figure it out myself. Sorry to interrupt."

Then as quickly as Violet arrived, she turns and walks away.

Before Miles and I can talk about it, he is called to set

for his last scene of the day, and I need to go review Mr. Lucas' calendar for tomorrow.

An hour later, I'm walking by Miles' trailer when the door swings open and Parker, Liam, Olivia and Ellie file out. I stop to say hello, and offer to escort them through security. Miles catches my eye before I go and asks me, quietly, to come back to his trailer when I'm done.

"Thank you for everything today, Rylee. We appreciate the VIP treatment," Parker says as we walk towards the gates. I flash my pass to the security guard and usher them through.

"I was happy to show you around. And I know Miles loved having you all here."

"So will we see you before we leave?" Olivia asks. "Our flight is tomorrow afternoon."

"I'm not sure what Miles has planned, but just in case I don't see you, I'll say goodbye now. I really enjoyed meeting you all. I had so much fun."

Olivia's hand moves to my arm. "We loved meeting you too." I hug each of them, feeling thankful that meeting Miles' family has been so easy and wonderful. He really is lucky to have these amazing people in his life. I can't help but feel a bit sad, knowing I may never see them again.

After saying our goodbyes, I walk back to Miles' trailer with a pang in my chest. It's stupid, to feel this way about people I met just days before. It hadn't taken long for me to grow attached to them.

Miles is waiting for me when I open the door. I know this, because I barely have one foot inside when he says, "I want you to come home with me to Reed Point."

I stare at him. "What?"

Miles leans against the wall, his arms crossed over his hard chest, his biceps flexing. He knows what he's doing to me. He's such a flirt.

"You heard me. I want you to come home with me. It's only three days. You have the weekend off, and there's the holiday on Monday. So there's really no reason you can't come… I already checked." He lays out his case with a sparkle in his eyes to match his cheeky grin.

"I can think of a few reasons, Miles! Meeting your parents is a big deal."

He doesn't hesitate. "I want them to know you. I want to show you Reed Point and take you to my favorite restaurants and introduce you to my friends."

Just thinking about meeting Miles' parents and being inside the home where he grew up makes me nervous. But despite that, part of me really likes the sound of it. It would be nice to see his brothers, Olivia and Ellie again too.

"I'm not sure. What if your parents are looking forward to spending some quality time with you? I don't want to be in the way."

"Not possible. I like having you with me, and my parents will be happy to meet you. Promise." Miles grins. "Besides, Ellie really wants you at her baby shower."

"She said that?"

"She did," he says. "You made an impression on them, Ryls. They all would love to see you again."

"I'd like that, too. Your sisters-in-law are wonderful," I say. "But… you're really sure about this?"

"I'm really sure," he persuades me. "I wouldn't have asked if I wasn't. I want you to come home with me."

How am I supposed to say no to this man?

"Okay then. I'll come."

In three short strides, Miles is across the trailer, scooping me up in his arms. The sound of our laughter fills the small space. I can't wait to see where Miles grew up.

He turns me in his arms, so my back is pressed against

his chest. His soft lips brush over my neck, leaving goose-bumps in their wake. My nervous anticipation at the thought of meeting Miles' parents fades away when his lips find the back of my neck again.

"Relax," he whispers against my skin. "You're going to love my family and they're going to love you."

I listen to the sounds of people moving around outside his trailer, my heart rate starting to settle down with his strong arms around me. "So, tell me about Reed Point and what I should expect."

"Ah, Reed Point is beautiful. If you like the ocean and beaches and great restaurants, you'll love it. We have wineries and breweries, and at night we like to go down to the beach for a bonfire. I'm sure we can stay at my family's beach house, which is about 10 minutes from my parents' place."

I'm instantly relieved to find out we will have our own space. Being with Miles, far away from the distractions of work and his crazy schedule, it sounds like the ultimate fantasy. Just the two of us in a small house on a beach over-looking the ocean.

"That all sounds wonderful. I'm going to go home and start packing tonight," I tease.

"Well, it's still a couple of weeks away, but who am I to tell you what to do?" he says with a shrug. "I'll have Georgia book your ticket. All you'll need to do is be ready to go."

"Just let me know what I owe you for the ticket and I can e-transfer you."

"It's on me. I invited you. Please let me handle it."

He digs his phone from his pocket, and I watch his fingers happily tap the screen. A wrinkle forms in the space between his eyebrows. It's his concentration face and it's the cutest thing. "What are you doing?"

"I'm texting Georgia to book our flights before you change your mind. I've asked her to make sure they're non-transferable and non-refundable."

I laugh. "Don't worry, I'm coming."

Miles looks up at me through his lashes with heat in his eyes, "Oh, you'll be doing that too."

And then he kisses me again

Chapter Nineteen

Rylee

Two weeks later, we arrive in Reed Point just after dinner time, both of us tired after a long week on set followed by a long flight. We pick up our rental car and Miles drives us into town and then down towards the beach.

The beach house is nestled at the end of the street and even though it's dark, I can tell that the coastal style home is beautiful.

It's confirmed when we walk inside. The small home is all blues and whites, with shiplap walls and gauzy curtains leading out to a deck overlooking the ocean. Someone has been here to turn on the lights for us and stock the kitchen with coffee beans and freshly baked cookies. A beautiful vase of peonies sits on the kitchen counter.

"My mom messaged me last night," Miles tells me. "She came over to put a few things in the fridge for us and change the bed linens."

"How sweet of her. Your mom is a saint."

After putting our things in the bedroom, we shower,

rinsing off the long day of travel. Or maybe that's just the excuse we make to get each other's clothes off. Either way, it works for me. We take turns under the spray of hot water. I lather soap over his shoulders and his broad back then turn him around and soap his pecs, his delicious abs and his arms. When it's his turn, he takes his time with my hair, then his hands tour my body. Closing my eyes, I inhale the grapefruit-scented soap and enjoy the closeness of him.

We towel off, both of us feeling refreshed after the shower. By the time I get to the kitchen, having changed into a sports bra and a pair of sleep shorts that leave very little to the imagination, Miles is already busy at the stove.

"What are you up to?" I ask, resting my hand on his warm shoulder and kissing his neck. He's wearing a pair of gym shorts and no shirt, and I feel his bicep flex as he stirs.

"Mmm," he says. "I'm making us hot chocolates."

"Hot chocolates?"

"Yes. Do you not like hot chocolate? Doesn't everybody like hot chocolate?" He turns and leans towards me for a kiss. Happy to. My lips connect with his and even though it's a gentle, relatively chaste kiss, it manages to invade every one of my senses. I take a couple of steps back, putting a little distance between us, to stop myself from blurting out how strongly I feel for him.

I'm falling for you and I'm not sure I'll ever stop. It's at the tip of my tongue. But I can't tell him how strongly I feel for him. It's too soon.

"I guess I didn't take you for a hot chocolate kinda guy."

"Now you know. But only if it has lots of whip cream and a drizzle of chocolate sauce." He dips his finger into the warm liquid and puts it in his mouth, then pulls it back out with a popping sound.

"You are 12 years old."

He flicks off the burner and removes the pot from the stove then turns and pulls me against him, lifting me up onto the counter. My ass lands on the cold, hard marble. "And *you* are beautiful."

I widen my legs so he can stand in between them, then take each of his ass cheeks in my hands with a squeeze. We fit together perfectly, like we were made for each other. I spread my legs even further, greedily wanting him closer to me. His eyes flicker with excitement and I feel it deep down in my bones.

I shiver when he kisses the edge of my jaw. His lips explore me slowly, moving up to my ear while his hand reaches for the cupboard door next to my head. He opens it, reaching for a mug and then a second one and when he pulls back from me I sigh, wanting more.

"Should we take these to the patio? You'll love the view."

"Let's."

Miles fills the two mugs and takes them out to the patio, where we sit in large Adirondack chairs and look out towards the beach. We're all alone, there's no one for miles and it's peaceful and calming listening to the sound of the waves. I carefully take a sip of the steaming, chocolatey drink.

"Mmm. Impressive," I tell him. "You really do know how to make a good hot chocolate."

"Never doubt me. I can be very useful," he says, raising his eyebrows.

I laugh at him. "Thank goodness I have you then. You never know when a craving for a good hot chocolate will hit ya."

Miles chuckles next to me. I look at him stretched out in the chair looking astonishingly content. Still shirtless, he has one arm stretched over his head, a beam of the patio light across his chest. I smile to myself, still not quite believing that he's chosen to bring me here, to introduce me to his family.

"Will we see your family tomorrow?" I ask, a little nervous at the thought of meeting his mom and dad.

"Yes, my parents were hoping that we could all have dinner tomorrow night. Parker and Olivia arrive tomorrow afternoon and Ellie and Liam are free once she closes up Bloom for the day."

"You never told me where Parker and Olivia are staying."

"They're staying at my parents' place. They offered the beach house to us when I called them and told them you were coming with me."

"That was nice of them," I say, appreciating the gesture.

"They thought you might be more comfortable staying here for your first visit," he says, and I still. Thankfully his gaze is towards the water and doesn't notice the look on my face. *First* visit? Was that just a slip of the tongue or is he already envisioning us coming here again? There's so much in that sentence to unwrap, I'm not sure where to start.

"Can I ask you something?"

"Yeah, ask me anything," he says, sitting up in his chair, swivelling his body to face mine.

"Are you sure about introducing me to your parents?"

"Of course I am, Ryls. Why are you asking me that now?" His voice is sincere and gentle, a little uneasy.

I swallow, carefully considering what I want to say. "I would understand if you've decided that this is too big of a deal for you. That's all. I want you to know that."

"Not a chance. I really want them to know you. I want

them to know the girl I can't stop thinking about." His smile feels like a blanket wrapped around me. And although I'm nervous as heck to meet them, I couldn't be happier. My heart thumps wildly in my chest. We're figuring out where we're going. Discovering if we're on the same page. So far, it seems we are.

"I want to keep going places with you, Ryls. I want to have experiences with you and see cool places and try new things."

My heart bites the dust.

I blink once, then again, trying to hold in the emotions that are swirling deep inside me. I'm overwhelmed. I want to do all of that with him too. It sounds perfect. *Too* perfect. But I choose to believe it can happen. That's what I'm going to keep telling myself. It makes me feel happy and scared to death all at once.

"Where would we go first?" I ask him, indulging in the fantasy.

He sips from his mug, his eyes twinkling. "I think the first place we go is Deer Lake."

"Of all the places in the world, you choose Deer Lake? Nothing ever happens there, Miles. If a cow escapes a pasture, it's headline news. I was thinking Hawaii or Italy or Portugal to see the beaches."

He laughs. "Well, now I'm imagining you in a bikini sitting on a beach in Sorrento. I'm trying to be good here, Ryls, and the image isn't helping."

It feels like a future with Miles is possible. Like just maybe, Miles and I could really make this work. I take another sip and Miles does the same, then he rests his mug on the ground. "Kiss me," he says, his voice low and wanton.

I lean over and kiss him, and it tastes like hope and promise and maybe even the beginning of falling in love.

We come together in the warmth of the June summer night, under the stars.

"I want you," I beg, a little embarrassed by the need in my voice. With just a kiss from him, I'm so turned on.

"You have me. I'm yours. I'm not going anywhere."

With a shiver down my spine, I kiss him again. Miles loves to be kissed. The way he kisses me back feels like everything I've ever wanted and everything I didn't know I needed. It feels like what we have is real and ours and never-ending. Now, I just have to figure out a way to hold onto it.

<hr>

The next morning, we stop by a baby boutique to look for a shower gift for Ellie. Miles chooses a ridiculously expensive stroller that he offers to give Ellie from the two of us. But I decline, opting to get her my own gift. A beautiful stroller blanket caught my eye when I first entered the store, so I have the saleswoman wrap it up for me.

After lunch, Miles takes me to Bloom to see Ellie. Bloom is the flower shop she and Olivia own together. It's their first location; the second one is in Cape May, where Olivia and Parker moved for his work not too long ago.

"It's so pretty," I say, walking through the door. A bell chimes over the door and Ellie pokes her head out from underneath a large wooden worktable.

"Did we catch you at a bad time?" Miles jokes. "Please tell me my brother isn't under that table."

She rolls her eyes. "Pullease. Do you think we are a bunch of horny exhibitionists? I dropped a peony and having a stomach the size of a small planet makes it really flipping difficult to pick it up."

Miles chuckles, walking over to the table. "Here Ells, let me help you."

"It's fine now. I got it, but thanks, bro."

Once she's back to standing, we hug and it already feels like we're old friends. She leans a hip against the table and rubs her lower back with her hand.

"I think you've gotten bigger than the last time I saw you. How are you feeling?"

"Like a house! And I can't drink, or eat most sushi, and they say a baby can hear everything from inside the womb so I'm kind of worried our baby's first word is going to be fuck," she groans. "Also, Liam and I watched a birth video at my prenatal class last night and I'm pretty sure he's never going to have sex with me again after witnessing that."

I try to contain my laughter, without much success. Miles drags a chair over and orders her off of her feet.

"How much longer do you have to go?" I ask her.

"Two more months. Honestly, I can't wait to meet this baby. Liam might be even more excited than me."

"It still blows my mind that Liam is the first to give my parents a grandchild," Miles says. "You've turned my serious, brood of a brother into a softie. I don't know how you did it."

"I have my ways, Miles. If I told you, I'd have to kill you."

Ellie is way too much fun. She has the best sense of humor and she doesn't take herself too seriously. She always has an interesting story to tell, and a witty comeback ready. She's someone I could easily be friends with – someone I would miss if things didn't work out with Miles.

It worries me that I'm getting attached to his family already. I told myself in the beginning that I'd keep a safe distance, but that promise went out the window a while ago. I can't assume that Miles wants this relationship to work as much as I do, and I definitely can't make him fall in love with me. I can only hope he feels the same.

That afternoon, we wander around downtown Reed Point, window-shopping and checking out cute boutiques and coffee shops before meeting his family for dinner. Miles booked us all a table at an upscale restaurant on the edge of the ocean. It's a perfect summer night, and when we arrive the warm, golden glow from the setting sun casts rays across the dining room.

"Welcome to Catch 22," the hostess says before taking us to our table, where Miles' entire family is sitting waiting for us. Drawing in a long breath, I follow Miles, my hand tucked possessively in his. They're seated at a round table – Parker and Olivia, Liam and Ellie, his parents and his sister Jules. As soon as she sees us coming, his mom pushes from her seat, striding towards us, pulling her son into a warm embrace and then turning to face me. She clasps her hands together when she sees me, her face beaming as though I'm the First Lady who just stopped by for coffee.

"I'm Miles' mom, Grace," she introduces herself. "I'm so happy to meet you, Rylee. Now, I hope you don't mind, but I'm a hugger." Her slim arms wrap around me in a warm embrace. I like her already. She's elegant, dressed in a cream suit with a soft pink lace camisole, her dark hair neatly styled in a bob at her shoulders. She's wearing a stunning diamond collar necklace and has a diamond on her ring finger the size of a golf ball. I can see where her boys get their good looks.

"Oh my, she's beautiful," Grace says to Miles, and I feel my cheeks heat at the compliment. I look sideways at Miles, self-consciously smoothing the long, pale blue-and-white floral sundress I'd decided on for tonight. She takes his face in her hands and kisses his cheek, and it feels like suddenly the entire room is bursting with love. "And gosh, how I've missed you. You look so handsome, Miles. And happy."

"I am, Mom," he says, glancing at me.

When she lets go of Miles, his dad is next, pulling him into a man-hug, clapping him on his shoulder. He then turns his attention to me. "You must be Rylee. Michael Bennett, Miles' dad. It's a pleasure to meet you," he says, holding out his hand for me to shake. He reminds me so much of Miles. He's tall and broad and handsome, and it's immediately obvious that the Bennett boys inherited their charm from their father.

We make our way around the table. The Bennetts and their significant others are huggers, so it takes a while, but they make me feel right at home. When we finally take our seats, Miles introduces me to his sister Jules, who is sitting to my right.

"I'm embarrassed I'm not cooking for you at the house, but it's all set up for the shower tomorrow," Grace explains, looking at Miles and I from across the table. "I promise to make you a home-cooked meal the next time you visit."

I smile and wave off her apologies, all the while trying not to hang on too tightly to her mention of a next time.

Our glasses are filled – white wine for most of us, with a virgin Mojito for Ellie – and then Jules turns her attention to me.

"You're from Tennessee?" she asks with interest.

"I am, but I moved to Los Angeles almost four years ago for school. It's been a while since I've been back home, but I'll be moving back once we wrap filming in Vancouver."

"That's soon, isn't it? Less than a month?" she says, a wide-eyed look on her face. She looks to Miles with curiosity. I'm not sure what to say. Miles picks up on it and steps in to answer for me.

"Rylee's grandparents live on a farm in Deer Lake, where she's from. They're getting older and could use her help." I feel his warm hand on my knee through the thin cotton of my dress. He keeps it there, calming me.

"Is Deer Lake far from Nashville? I've always wanted to go," Jules asks, holding the stem of her wine glass and swirling the Pinot Grigio in careful circles.

"It's only 'bout an hour and a half away. Nashville is so much fun. Especially if you like country music."

The entire table points at Olivia and Mrs. Bennett, then everyone laughs when the two of them raise their hands. "We do," Olivia says, waving her hand back and forth between herself and Miles' mom. "We love it all, from Reba and Hank to Florida Georgia Line." Olivia goes on to tell me how she's made her mother-in-law a country music fan. Parker's sitting next to her with his arm draped behind her back, giving her I-love-you eyes.

"If y'all ever want to go, I'd be happy to meet you there and show you around."

Olivia eyes Ellie and Jules with a mischievous grin. "Who's in for a girls' trip?"

The show of hands is unanimous. "One condition," Ellie says, pointing her finger to the ceiling. "This trip needs to happen *after* this baby is born."

"You sure about that, Ellie?" Parker asks, eyebrows raised. "I seriously doubt my hotshot lawyer brother can figure out how to change a diaper without you there to talk him through it. Actually, it would make my day to watch him try. Start planning that trip, ladies."

Liam leans back in his chair and folds his arms over his chest.

"Says the guy who acts like an oversized toddler most

of the time. Do you need me to help you cut up your dinner, Parker?"

Mrs. Bennett sighs from across the table. "Don't mind them, Rylee. They've been this way since they were boys. I couldn't stop it if I tried – and I *have* tried."

Jules steers the conversation back towards me. "Okay, Rylee. I have a serious question and I want an honest answer from you."

I nod, my heart suddenly in my throat.

"Are there any hot guys in Nashville? Because I am so done with the men here in Reed Point."

I laugh, relieved. "Oh, I'm sure you could find one or two," I assure her.

While we dine on freshly baked sourdough bread and blue-cheese wedge salads, Miles shares stories from Vancouver, filling them in on the cast and crew, describing the stunning oceanfront home he's been living in for the past almost six weeks. Grace wants to know more about the farm, and how Miles and I met, so we tell them all about that first day in the rain when Miles swooped in like he was some sort of superhero. She also asks me about my photography, which she says Miles has told her all about. I secretly light up inside at the thought of him talking to his mom about me. I wonder what else he has told her.

I soon discover that Jules likes to talk, and she peppers me with nonstop questions while we eat. She's not one of those people who talk just to hear the sound of their own voice – she seems genuinely interested in my answers. When I tell her I have two very protective older brothers, she grabs my hand on the table.

"Nobody understands what my life is like, having three older brothers who have something to say about every single guy I meet," she groans.

"Oh, I do," I tell her. "I'm a part of that same club.

My brothers and I are really close, but they seem to think they should weigh in on who I date. Sometimes it's too much."

"I have a feeling they'll like my brother. Miles is a really good guy and he obviously cares about you. You know he looks at you like you're the only person in the room."

My heart soars. I know it shouldn't, but I can't stop it. I've always felt the heat in Miles' gaze when he looks at me, right from the beginning, and I like knowing that I'm not the only one who sees it.

After dinner, we walk out into the warm night air and say our goodbyes, making plans for tomorrow. Miles and I had walked to the restaurant from the beach house, so we take our time strolling back, stopping at an ice cream shop along the way, where we each order a double scoop. It's a beautiful night and there are people milling around the beach. The shadowy outline of the bluffs up ahead is painted across the skyline. It's a stunning view. Miles is stopped a couple of times by fans politely asking for a photo, but for the most part people leave us alone.

"You look happy, Miles. I think you needed this trip home."

"Are you saying I'm not normally happy?" he asks, wrapping his arms around my middle from behind and kissing the back of my neck. I love being this close to him, his big strong arms and warm chest clasped so tightly around me that it feels like we are one person. My muscles loosen and my mind relaxes. My body melts into his. I want every day to end like this, with Miles.

"No, not at all. You just look content, like you haven't a care in the world. It makes me happy to see you like this. Your job can be so busy and demanding."

His arms squeeze a fraction tighter. "I guess that's what being home does to me."

"I guess so."

"With you, Ryls. Being back home with you here makes me happy. I'm loving every second."

All I can do is smile. Just when I thought I couldn't like him any more than I already do, he goes and makes my heart swell to twice its size. I can't get enough of this man and I'm starting to doubt I ever will.

I'm so close to telling him how he makes me feel. How just the sight of him makes my heart beat a little faster. But instead, I turn in his arms and face him. I go up on my toes, wanting to feel his lips on mine, and I kiss him.

Then I kiss him again with everything in me.

Chapter Twenty

Rylee

The closer we get to Miles' parents' home, the more anxious I become. I've been excited to go to Ellie's baby shower, but now that the day is here I'm a bundle of nerves.

It's just past 1 p.m. when Miles parks his car in front of the most beautiful home I've ever seen. I thought the rental in Vancouver was something, but this puts it to shame.

Miles and I spent a perfect morning together, eating breakfast in bed and then going for a walk on the beach, my hand in his, our feet slipping through the almost white sand. It felt like a dream. Now I'm about to see where Miles grew up, to be included in a huge family moment. I feel lucky. And nervous.

"This is it. This is where I grew up. You ready?" he asks. The early afternoon sun slices through the driver's side window, making his hair appear golden.

"I think I am. Meeting everyone last night helped."

"Good. I'll stay with you as long as you want me to." Miles kisses me softly before opening his door and rounding the front of the car to open mine. We walk the stone pathway to the large door, his hand pressed possessively against my lower back. His mother greets us as soon as we step through the threshold like she's been waiting all day for us. She opens her arms to the two of us.

"Hi, Mom." Miles greets her with a tight hug. There are servers dressed in black milling around and the sounds of women talking and laughing drift from the other room. "Looks like you've got your hands full today."

"I do. Isn't it great? It's so good to see you two. Miles, having you back home makes me so happy." His mom wraps her arms around me next then pulls back with a smile. She looks lovely in a simple, off-white pant suit and heels. The stunning diamond necklace she wore last night is around her neck again today. "We are so happy you can join us, Rylee. The girls are all excited to see you. Thank you for coming."

"Now," she says, turning her gaze to Miles. "You should go on in and save your brother. He's been waiting for you. You know how Liam gets about these types of things."

Miles chuckles. "I'll do you all a favor and get him out of here. Where's Dad?"

"Probably in his study. I bet you'll find your brothers hiding out in there too."

Miles takes me by the hand, and we head into the kitchen. It's large and spacious with a giant island running straight through the center of it. A wall of retractable glass doors leads from the kitchen to the backyard and from where I'm standing I can see the pool and manicured lawn. The house couldn't be more different from the one I grew up in. Everything looks new and modern, but it still manages to be so warm and inviting. I can imagine Miles and his siblings here when they were kids, what a happy place it must have been to grow up in.

I look around at the other guests, a group of perfectly put together women in designer dresses and pant suits. I look down at my own dress, which I picked up on clearance back in L.A., and suddenly hope it was the right choice for today. Miles must notice my apprehension because he kisses me on my temple and tells me I look beautiful.

"What can I help you with?" I ask Grace, handing her the flowers I picked up at Bloom before coming here.

"These are gorgeous, sweetheart. Thank you. And how sweet of you to ask, but I have everything under control."

It does seem utterly impossible that there was something I could help with – Miles' mom seems completely in charge and at ease hosting such a big group – but I want to be polite.

"You're here!" Ellie squeals as she enters the kitchen from the back yard. She's wearing a fuchsia pink dress that shows off her baby bump and a pair of matching heels. I'm amazed she is able to balance in them with her belly the size of a small watermelon.

"I'm so happy you came," she says with a big smile, grabbing my hand. "Miles, you can go now, she's coming with me. Skedaddle. She'll be just fine."

Miles looks at me with an *are-you-sure-you're-okay* look on his face and I nod. "I'll call you after our round of golf. Have fun." He kisses me chastely on my lips, his gaze holding my own for just a second more before leaving, and even though I know he will only be gone for a few hours my silly heart already misses him. It's ridiculous, I know.

"He looks at you like you're chocolate cake."

I turn to face Ellie, and scrunch up my nose at her, confused. "Is that a good thing?"

"Of course! Is there anything better than chocolate cake?"

I smile and drop my head, hoping she doesn't notice the blush I can feel spreading across my cheeks. "Nope, you're right. Only really weird people don't appreciate chocolate cake."

After Grace introduces me to a few of her friends in the kitchen, Ellie pulls me away, into the backyard. It is dreamy, with elaborate floral centerpieces decorating the round tables that are scattered around the pool. There is a giant mound of beautifully wrapped baby gifts by the outdoor fireplace.

"Grace throws the most amazing parties. She does almost everything herself. Parker and Olivia's engagement party and wedding were both held in this backyard and she's trying to convince Liam and I to get married here too."

I'm surprised Ellie wouldn't jump at the chance to marry Liam in the most spectacular home I have ever seen. "Why wouldn't you? This looks like a dream."

She shrugs. "I've never wanted a big wedding and neither has Liam. We would both rather just run off and get married in Vegas. Some days I think the courthouse sounds good too. We'll see once the baby is born. This baby shower is a lot for me, but I know how much Grace wanted to do it."

"Rylee!" my head turns when I hear my name and I spot Olivia and Jules sitting in one of the outdoor patio areas with three other girls. Olivia stands, champagne glass in hand, and comes over to pull me in for a hug. "I'm so excited you made it. You look beautiful. I love your dress. Let me introduce you to everyone."

And just like that, I feel like I'm a part of something.

Like I belong in Miles' world. Like I could be happy here with him for a very long time.

After the party ends, it's just Olivia, Ellie, Grace and I who are left. We are sitting around the island in the kitchen listening to Ellie tell us about their plans for the baby's room. Even though they haven't found out the gender, Liam is convinced it's a boy and wants to paint the nursery blue. Grace laughs like it's the cutest thing she's ever heard while Ellie just shakes her head.

Today has been as close to perfect as it gets. Being with the Bennett women is better than I could have imagined. It all feels so wonderful. They're so close, and they all genuinely love each other, and the conversation is always fun and easy. Still, I can't help but feel a little heartsick knowing that this may be the last time I see them. Leaving L.A. and moving back home means leaving Miles too.

My phone rings and when I look at the screen, I smile. I apologize to the girls and slip off the stool, walking towards the foyer.

"Hi, you."

"Hey babe," Miles says. "How's everything going over there?"

"It's great. Everything was so beautiful, and Ellie's friends and your family are all so nice."

"I knew you'd have a good time. Is everything wrapped up?"

"Yes. It's just me and your family left. We're chatting in the kitchen, but I feel like I should be helping your mom clean up."

"I'm sure she'll argue with you over that. She'll have the rental and catering company come pick everything up. Then her cleaners will be there in the morning to do the rest. Trust me. It's a well-oiled machine over there."

"Okay. I won't argue. I just feel bad."

"I miss you," he says. I can hear his brothers in the background.

"I just saw you five hours ago."

Miles laughs. "Too long. We're on our way. There's somewhere I want to take you tonight so don't make any plans before I get there."

"Okay. I'll see you soon." We end the call and I return to the kitchen.

"Let me guess who that was," Grace teases, and I feel my cheeks heat.

I sit down and reach for my glass of water. "The boys are on their way," I tell them.

"I'm sure Miles was counting the hours," Grace says through a smile. "Michael and I are really happy you came, Rylee. It has been so lovely to meet the girl our boy talks so much about."

"Thank you for having me. I've really had the best time getting to know y'all."

We chat some more about the shower and all of the incredible baby gifts. And then Miles is back. I know he's in the room before I see him. I can feel his eyes on me. I can feel the tingle that zips down my spine and the current of electricity that courses through the air.

"Hey, you," he says quietly, taking the stool beside me, pressing a kiss to my shoulder.

I'm thrilled to see him but am also hyper-aware that his parents are right there with us. "Hey," I say softly with a smile. He grabs my hand underneath the counter and rests our joined hands on his thigh.

Ellie takes Liam into the living room to show him all of the gifts while Parker joins Olivia at the island with us. Mr. Bennett passes the island and walks straight to where his wife is standing. He bends to kiss her on her cheek, and she glows. There's little doubt they are just in love as they were when they got married and it makes me think of my own parents. They were always the happiest when they were together. When my father loved, he did it with everything he had. He loved my brothers and I the same way. I'm sure their marriage today would be just as joyful and strong as the Bennetts'.

"I bet you're hungry after golfing with the boys," Grace says to her husband then turns her attention to the leftover lemon cake, cutting him a slice. She slices three more for Liam, Parker and Miles.

"We should get going," Miles announces after scarfing down the delicious cake. "Can we help load the presents into Ellie's car?"

"I'm sure your brother would appreciate that," Grace says.

After too many trips to count, we manage to get most of the gifts into Ellie's SUV and we all head out. Miles drives, his hand holding mine in my lap. The scenery passes us by like we are in a dream, moving further and further away from the city and the noise. I sneak glances at Miles as he drives, studying his strong profile, and his muscular, strong forearms. His big hand on the steering wheel. I could live a very happy life if I was able to stare at this man every day.

"Where are we going?" I ask.

"Somewhere I want you to see. And where we can be alone."

"Sounds perfect."

After a short drive, we park at a lookout overlooking a stunning view of Reed Point. Miles is quiet as he pulls a blanket from the trunk, spreading it out over the grass. We sit, both leaning back and stretching our legs out in front of us, staring at the city below us. He turns his ballcap so it's backwards on his head. I swoon beside him.

I inhale the warm, summer air and let the breeze cool my skin. "This is beautiful. I can't get over the view," I say, wondering how I got so lucky to be experiencing this with him.

"I haven't been up here in forever, but no matter where I go it's always one of my favorite views."

"I can't imagine what it's like to travel so much. Do you ever get tired of it?"

"All the time. I miss my family. I miss seeing my friends on a regular basis. I hate that I never really get to know their wives and girlfriends. It's going to be even harder when my niece or nephew is born, but it's the way my job goes. I guess you have to take the good with the bad."

This isn't the flirty, funny side of Miles that I'm used to, and I'm grateful that he's letting me in. He's typically a glass-half-full type of guy, never letting much get the better of him, so seeing this new, vulnerable, soft side of him is nice.

Miles moves his hand so that it covers mine and I lean my head against his shoulder. I cast a sideways look at him. My heart is racing being here with him in one of his favorite spots. It's also racing because I really want to kiss him.

"I try to come home whenever I can," he says. "Georgia is good about clearing my schedule every few months so I can make the trip. It helps."

"I'm glad you have Georgia. She seems to take good care of you."

"She does. I would be lost without her."

As we sit overlooking the view, Miles fills me in on his day with his dad and brothers. He laughs, telling me that his dad is having a treehouse built in the yard for Liam and Ellie's baby. Liam thinks he's crazy, seeing as the baby won't be able to use it for years, but his dad doesn't care. I hear about the summer house that Parker surprised Olivia with last month, about their plans to buy a boat and spend more time on the water. I smile and nuzzle my ear a little closer into his shoulder. It all feels so good, and I almost manage to forget that Miles and I are only temporary.

"I'm glad you're here," he says, causing butterflies to dance around in my belly.

"Me too."

"I missed you today. I thought I'd be able to go a whole day without you, but I was wrong. I couldn't stop thinking about you."

My heart might have stopped beating. "I know the feeling."

"I knew, Rylee. From the first second I saw you, I knew that you were special. I had never seen anyone more beautiful in my life. You took my breath away. I'm not joking," he says, twirling a piece of grass between his fingers. "It scares me that I feel this strongly about you. I don't know how I'm going to be able to watch you go. I don't want you to leave."

"I feel the same way. I don't want to leave you either. Let's not ruin the night by talking about it. I want to remember this night as one of my favorites with you."

Miles looks so handsome in the late day sun. He looks good anytime of the day in any type of lighting, but right now he looks like the best thing to ever happen to me. He tosses the blade of grass and looks at me. He looks like he's trying to find an answer to our problem, an answer that I know doesn't exist. It feels like there's so much uncertainty surrounding us right now, but one thing I know for sure is the way he feels about me. I don't have to doubt that.

I move closer to him, needing to touch him. Miles smiles a mischievous grin, then pulls me into his lap. I wind my arms around his neck, enjoying his athletic body pushed against mine. His hands slide up my spine, warm and hard. My mouth is on his a second later, throwing caution to the wind. Someone could walk by and sees us at any time, but I don't care. I lightly rock my pelvis over the bulge in his pants and he sighs against my lips.

"Should we do something about this?" I ask him, looking down at his lap.

"I think we should." He gives me a look so hot it could melt butter. It's a laser gaze that makes me feel like he's looking deep into my soul. My pulse races and my heart beats so loudly in my chest I swear he can hear it. It's a total rush and I can't look away. He knows what he does to me, and he knows I know it too.

I close my eyes, perfectly lost in him as he whispers in a silky voice against my mouth. "Should we go back to the beach house?"

I feel my neck heat up at the mention of the beach house and all the places we've christened in it. A couple of weeks ago, having sex multiple times a day in any room and on any surface would have sounded like someone else's life and not mine. Now it's me who loses all control and can never get enough. I'm addicted to Miles Bennett.

"I...." I slip my hand under his shirt. "What was the question?"

Miles laughs. "It doesn't matter anymore."

"No, it doesn't." Nothing else matters when it's just the two of us.

Miles sets a warm, strong hand on my thigh. I close my eyes for a second. It's like his fingers are lighting a fire to every nerve in my body. This intense contact feels posses-sive, sending heat barreling through me. Being here, where anyone could see us, it feels sexy and taboo. Libido circuit overload.

A moment later, in an unspoken agreement, we get up

from the blanket and get into the car. We breeze towards the city and our last night in Reed Point. This trip has been a dream. I love Miles' family, how close they are and how welcoming. I'm envious of Olivia and Ellie for being able to call Mrs. Bennett their mother-in-law. I imagine what it would be like to share Christmas dinners with them all, to make new memories together. It's only a fantasy, all of it too good to be true, and I need to remember that.

I need to stop thinking about a future with Miles.

The problem is, it's way too easy to imagine a life with him.

Chapter Twenty-One

M iles

"What's with you today?" I tap my fingers on the table between us, tilting my head at Matthew. We're sitting in a coffee shop 10 minutes from my rental in West Vancouver. A quick meetup to discuss a project I'm hoping to land, among other things. When I'm done there, I have a date with my girlfriend.

"Well, it might be Justin Teller, whose career has just taken a nose-dive, or maybe it's my wife, who has made it clear she is sick of being married to an apparition. So, if I look a little crazy, now you know why."

"Shit, man," I say sympathetically. Justin is an actor who's been Hollywood's biggest bad boy for the past few years. He's a nice enough guy, but his drug addiction has gotten the best of him lately and he's been stumbling out of bars and starting fights with paparazzi. He's also one of Matthew's clients.

"All right, enough about me. The reason we're here. What's happening, Miles? This will be easier on both of us if you just fill me in."

I give him a *what-the-fuck-are-you-talking-about* look.

He laughs. "Rylee. How serious are things with her? Did you see the photo on the internet this morning?"

"What? No," I say, sitting up in my chair. "What the hell is it this time?"

Matthew tells me to check my phone, so I do, Googling my name. The photo pops up right away. It's of Rylee and I walking the beach in Reed Point on the night we met my family for dinner at Catch 22. The photo is dark and a little blurry and if you didn't know Rylee personally, you wouldn't be able to tell it was her. The photo is nothing. Thankfully I have nothing to worry about.

"This is it?" I ask, shoving my phone at Matthew.

"Yup," he says, sitting back in his chair, crossing one knee over the over. He takes a sip of his coffee then rests the cup on his thigh.

"And this photo is a problem, why? You can barely make out who's in it. They didn't list her name. It's impossible to even tell that it's Rylee."

"That's all true," Matthew agrees. "This time. But I'm going to need you to keep me in the loop from now on so I can control what the media is reporting. I can't do my job if you're not upfront with me. How serious is this thing with the two of you?"

I don't bother asking him how he knows I'm seeing her. The guy is always two steps ahead of me. It's part of his job. It's one of the reasons Matthew is so good at what he does.

"It's serious," I say.

Matthew says nothing. He only leans forward in his chair, sizing me up. "You don't do serious."

"Then why'd you bother asking the question?" I grumble.

"You know how this goes. You know this business.

You're at the top right now and it's my job to keep you there. I ask the questions and then I decide how much of the real story you are giving me."

I narrow my eyes at him. "It's serious," I say again. "I won't stop seeing her. End of story."

"Jesus, Miles. You really like this girl."

"I do. There's something else you should probably know."

Matthew blows out a breath, running his fingers through his thick hair, bracing himself. "Okay, what is it? You know you can talk to me."

"It's nothing dramatic," I say. "But I'm going to Tennessee with her to meet her family. She doesn't know yet. I'm surprising her. I'm leaving next week and I'm not bringing security. She's from a small town. Her family lives on a farm. I'm not bringing a bodyguard and freaking everyone out."

I need to keep my relationship with Rylee out of the press and arriving in small-town Tennessee with an entourage will only draw attention. Attention I don't need.

"Fuck no. I'm not letting you go without security. Neither will Georgia. It's not safe, Miles, and you know it."

"She lives out in the country, literally surrounded by fields. I'll fly private and wear a disguise," I argue. "Besides, showing up with a six-foot-four dude in a dark suit will cause more attention than if I just show up on my own."

Matthew pinches the bridge of his nose with his fingers. "Dammit, Miles. I'll talk to Georgia and get back to you on this. But I'm not making any promises."

"Fine. Let me know what she says, but I'm not backing down. And don't let this get back to Rylee," I remind him. "Now I've gotta run, I have plans. Forget about me and go home to your wife. Do whatever it is that married guys do."

Heading out into the sunshine, I throw on my ballcap, put on my shades and walk to my car. I fish my phone from my pocket and tap out a text.

I'm on my way, country girl. See you soon.

I add a heart emoji at the end.

I can't fucking wait to see her.

By some miracle, Rylee and I have managed to avoid the paparazzi for a month now. Besides our family and a few in our inner circle, no one suspects a thing.

We spend every second we can together. I admit that in the beginning I assumed it would be a one-time thing, like my usual hookups. In the past, the attraction has always fizzled out quickly. But that couldn't be more different from what's happening with Rylee. She is like an obsession I can't ever seem to get enough of. I can't stop thinking about her, dreaming about everything I want to do to her. I even found myself yesterday wondering if our children would have her emerald green eyes. I must be temporarily insane.

Sex has always been pretty good, but with Rylee it's completely different. I get lost in her. I fantasize about having my hands on her, my mouth on her, all day long. But it's not just the sex. It's everything about her. I want to know what she likes, what makes her happy. I want to be able to bring her a cup of her favorite coffee or rub the nape of her neck, which I've learned is one of the places she loves to be touched. Her family and the farm are what she loves most in the world. She talks about her grandparents like they hung the moon, she misses her brothers, and she worries that her nieces and nephew are going to forget her.

How could they? Rylee Brookes is impossible to forget.

I'm not sure I've ever been happier. I'm too happy, hiding away from the rest of the world with her, sneaking around, our relationship under wraps.

And that's the problem. This is going to end and there's nothing I can do about it. Rylee is flying back home to Tennessee in three weeks, our relationship hitting its expiry date. We both know it but refuse to acknowledge it. It's a fact that is looming silently and heavily over both of us.

I'm meeting up with Rylee for some window shopping at an outdoor mall this afternoon and by the time I see her I'm in a fucking incredible mood. There's something I've been wanting to ask her for a while now, and today's the day. I'm tired of mulling it over.

I move closer to her as we stroll the sidewalk under the warm Vancouver sun, the rays warming my skin. "I want you to be my date for The Artist Awards," I blurt out, despite knowing how Rylee feels about taking our relationship public.

I feel her body tense next to mine. "Miles, you know how I feel about that. I don't think I'm ready."

"Why not?" I ask, looking at her, my head cocked slightly to one side. I rearrange the look on my face, trying to mask my disappointment. I won't push her, but eventually I hope she can get to a place where she's comfortable being out with me. "I want the world to know that you're mine."

She can't hide the grin that is tipping up the corners of

her mouth. "Let me think about it. I'm not saying no. I promise I will consider it."

"That's all I ask," I tell her, adding, "I want to kiss you."

"Here?"

"Yes, here. I'm dying over here. It's been… what… three hours and my hands, my mouth or my dick haven't made contact with you. Ryls, I can only take so much."

"You are incorrigible."

"I think obsessed is more accurate."

"We could be caught," she says, the grin she's been fighting returning to her lips. She wants me to kiss her. I know she does, she's just too scared.

"We haven't been caught yet," I reassure her, looking around us. "Walk around to the back of that building. I'll follow you."

"Are you insane? We've been lucky. Our luck is bound to run out," she says, but then walks slowly in that direction anyway. I follow a few seconds later.

She's right, this is insane. I've caught shoppers side-eying me all day. I've also seen a few iPhones casually aimed in our direction. Canadians are typically too polite to come up and ask for an autograph or a photo, so we've managed to be left alone. But it only takes one photo leaked to the media.

I don't give a shit.

Joining her behind the store, I don't hesitate. I don't waste a second. I kiss her hard on the lips, threading my hand into her hair. One hand on her lower back, the other cupping the back of her head. She moans into the kiss. It's a feel-it-all-over-your-body kiss, one I feel under my skin, in my toes, behind my zipper.

She breaks the kiss. "Miles…" she whispers softly.

"Have I told you how much I love hearing you whisper

my name?" I kiss her jaw, her neck, then her lips. My heart is beating so fucking fast. My feelings for this girl are out of control. All I want is Rylee.

Cupping her jaw in my hand, I trace her lower lip with my thumb, trying not to dwell on the intense feeling in my gut that is telling me this girl is the one. Every second with Rylee is off-the-charts, every kiss with her lights a fire in my soul. I know. I just know that there's no one on this planet who can make me feel the way she does.

"Have I told you how much I love it when you kiss me there?" she asks, running her fingers over the curve of her neck.

"Noted," I smile. "Dammit Ryls, I've wanted to hold your hand, to kiss you, all day. Anything to touch you."

She runs her finger down the center of my chest. "I'm really happy you did."

I'm really happy I did too.

Chapter Twenty-Two

R ylee

I'm sitting in my hotel room thinking about Miles – surprise, surprise. Not just about our amazing afternoon together, or *that* kiss. I'm thinking about the way I can't stop obsessing over him. The way I can't stop wanting to be around him. I'm thinking about all the ways this feels different from my previous relationships. Well, make that relationship. Singular.

I dated Eric for two years, but for the last several months I knew it wasn't going to last. Honestly, I should have known even earlier than that. When I chose to stay home instead of hanging out at his house, when I spent my weekends working extra hours instead of hanging out with him. I should have seen the signs, but I didn't. I was 22 and too naïve to know we were headed for the end.

Eric and I had planned to move in together. It seemed like the right thing to do after we had been dating for so long. He was 24 and in a rush to get married and have kids. I never stopped to think about what I wanted. Being with Eric was safe and easy. We had mutual friends, we knew each other's families. Everything was *fine*. Our sex life was *fine*. I could take it or leave it. It's clear now we had zero chemistry. The way I felt with Eric, it wasn't even in the same galaxy as the way I feel when I'm with Miles.

Leaving Eric was far too easy and that's when I knew it was never love. Love shouldn't be so easy to walk away from. It should hurt like hell when you do. It should feel the way it does right now when I think about having to leave Miles.

My thoughts are interrupted by a knock on my hotel room door.

I answer it to find Abby on the other side, a bag of potato chips in one hand and a bottle of wine in the other. It's our weekly get-together to watch *YOU* and objectify Joe Goldberg, aka Penn Badgley.

She bursts through the door. "I'm here and I brought the good stuff."

"Did you go visit the creepy bartender at the bar across the street again?"

"You know I only go there for the cheap wine."

"I don't blame you. Now, get in here," I say, closing the door as she kicks off her flip flops and cracks the bottle. She fills two plastic cups, then hands me one. Abby crawls onto the far side of the bed and gets comfortable. I settle in as well, my cup of wine in one hand, and then prop my laptop on a pillow and find our show.

"Shall we?" I ask, my finger hovering over the play button.

"We shall."

We watch two episodes of *YOU* and polish off the bottle of wine. Another wild Wednesday night in the books. When I turn off the laptop, Abby asks the question I know she's been dying to ask ever since she got here.

"So, how's Miles? Tell me the latest. You still need to

fill me in on your trip." She sits up on the bed crossed-legged, facing me.

Rolling up the sleeves of Miles' sweatshirt I'm wearing, the one he gave me on that rainy day and the same one I find myself wearing most nights, I turn my gaze to her. "It went great. His family are the nicest and Reed Point is beautiful. It's right on the edge of the ocean."

She makes a snoring sound. "Yada yada. Get to the good stuff, like what happened in the beach house. I bet you had sex all over the place. Speaking of… how is the man in bed?"

I roll my eyes. "I don't have to answer that."

"You don't have to, but you should. The man looks like a fucking God. He must be one in the sheets too."

"You'll never know," I say, waggling my brows.

"I hate you. You're busy going to the bone zone with Miles Bennett while I've exhausted every single loser on Bumble."

"I'm sure you'll take a trip to the bone zone too, as you so eloquently put it."

"Here's hoping. I'm not letting this go, you know."

"Can't you just discuss my love life behind my back like a normal person?" I tease, shutting my laptop and placing it on the bedside table.

"I'm living vicariously through you. I'm painfully single and jaded from the *asshole*."

"Are we still referring to Tyler as the asshole?"

"Until the end of time. He deserves to be drop-kicked in the balls. He's lucky he's still living."

Abby has a complicated history when it comes to dating and relationships and falling in love. While she worked her way up the production ladder, Tyler, her ex, worked his way through the entire staff at The Buddha Bar, where he works.

"Love hurts, Rylee. Well, not for you. In your case a smoking hot sex symbol has fallen head over heels for you."

"Okay, let's not get ahead of ourselves," I say, fiddling with the hem of my T-shirt.

"And let's not discount what is happening either. You make him happy, you know? Even I can see it."

I shrug, but then decide to be honest about my feelings. "He makes me happy too. You know, he asked me to go to the Artist Awards with him."

"And you said yes, right?"

"I told him I would think about it, and I have, but it all seems really overwhelming. I don't want the attention it would bring. I definitely don't want my face in any magazines."

I've always been a private person, knowing first-hand what it feels like to have an entire town talk about you. I didn't like the attention then and I've tried to stay away from it since.

"Rylee, you're dating a celebrity. A really big celebrity. One day, the world is going to find out about you and Miles and you're not going to have a choice. It's inevitable. Have you thought about that?"

"I have, and it makes me uncomfortable."

"Then maybe you're dating the wrong person," she says. "Listen, I don't think that's the case, but you are going to have to find a way to deal with the attention if you want to be with him. You can't stay a secret forever. For what it's worth, I think you should go to the awards."

She's right. I've known that Miles and I can't stay in this bubble forever. It's only a matter of time before we are outed, and I need to come to terms with that. I need to take a leap of faith and go for it.

I know all of this, but I still feel terrified.

"I don't have a clue how people aren't on to the two of

you," Abby admits. "You both go all googly-eyed around each other. It's… cute."

"Stop. I do not," I say, leaning back against the headboard. "And if I do, it's only because of how great he is to look at."

"I'll give you that. The man is a walking orgasm."

"Really, Abbs? You're talking about the man I'm dating," I laugh.

"It's harmless. But I'm serious, you and Miles are good together. You care about him and not what he does for a living. And he cares about you. It's sweet. And on that note, I'm heading back to my room. I'll see you in the morning. Meet me in the lobby for seven?"

"I'll see you then."

I get ready for bed and hop in between the sheets, thinking about what Abby said. She isn't wrong. The fact that Miles is a famous actor is exciting, but it's not the reason I'm crazy about him. I would feel the same way about him if he was working in a bank. It's our chemistry. It's undeniable. I feel it in my bones.

It's always hot between us, always intense. Earth-shattering. An image of Miles on top of me, his arms flexing while he drives into me, flashes through my mind. Just the thought of him, of his toned, hard chest and abs, is enough to send a rush of heat through my body.

I turn off the light and sink into the warmth of the bed, smiling into my pillow. It could be fun, going as Miles' date to the awards show. I could walk the red carpet on his arm and maybe the press would print a quick story and then forget all about us. Or maybe they'd blow it up into something crazy, hound us relentlessly and his fans would decide they hate me.

I guess there is only one way to find out.

Chapter Twenty-Three

Rylee

The days are suddenly rushing by in a blur. Miles and I are trying to make the most of the time that's left, and we spend every night in bed together. We can't seem to keep our hands off of each other. We have a lot of sex – *a lot* of sex – but we do other things too. We watch movies in the theater room at his place, skinny dip in his pool late at night. I even teach him how to cook my Gran's famous chicken. We spend most nights at home, still trying to keep our relationship out of the public eye. I still haven't given Miles an official answer about the Artist Awards, and he hasn't pressured me for one.

It's weighed heavily on my mind. I want to make him happy and accept his invitation, but I still worry about the fall-out. I'm still too afraid of what America might think of me. There's something else that's worrying me even more: the fact that I may not survive losing Miles when I leave him at the end of the month. I've grown so used to being with him every day and every night. Staying at his home, surrounded by his stuff, sleeping in his bed – none of that is going to make saying goodbye any easier. Going public with our relationship weeks before it ends also seemed foolish. I need to start putting some space between us.

That would be the smart thing to do. But I don't have the strength to pull away from him. Instead, I just want to be with him every chance I can. I just want to make him happy.

"I've been thinking," I say, my head resting on the side of the hot tub at his rental house, enjoying the feeling of the jets massaging my back.

"Okay," Miles asks cautiously. "You've got me curious."

I cut to the chase. "About being your date for the Artist Awards."

"And..." he asks, his eyes hopeful. He looks like a dream, all tanned and wet, but what really gets me is the way he's looking at me. He really wants me to say yes.

"I would like to go with you if the invite still stands."

His eyes go wide, and he breaks into a huge smile. "Of course it still stands! Really? You're going to come? Because I'm going to be really fucking sad if I heard you wrong."

"Yes," I tell him, nervous and excited at the same time.

"Fuck, Ry. I'm so happy right now," he says, moving towards me through the water. He grabs me by my hips and pulls me onto his lap. My legs straddle his waist while he kisses me chastely then pulls back just a few inches meeting my gaze.

"You know what this means, right? There's no more hiding it after this. People will know we are together."

"Yeah, I know. It's going to be a lot, but I'm tired of hiding our relationship. I've thought about it and if it's something that matters to you, then I think I can handle it. I'm only nervous about them digging through my past."

I didn't have to elaborate. I can see in Miles' eyes that

he knows I'm referring to my parents' accident. "I won't let it happen."

I nod, knowing he will protect me in any way he can.

"I'm so damn excited to show you off to the world."

Excitement surges through me. As terrifying as it sounds, I would be proud to be photographed on Miles' arm.

My hands run up over his pecs to the back of his neck, where I clasp my fingers together. He lowers his mouth to my neck, gently sucking on my skin, then nudges his nose under my jaw. I tilt my head back so he can continue his trail of kisses down the column of my throat. It feels so good. The night's crisp air against the hot water of the jacuzzi, and Miles' cool, wet kisses on my skin.

He fiddles with the strings of my bikini and I get the feeling he wants to rip it right off of my body. He's already hard. I can feel him against my belly.

I playfully roll my hips over the bulge in his swim shorts, earning a low groan from his lips, his eyes rolling to the back of his head.

Miles runs the tips of his fingers up the sides of my body. "We won't have to hide anymore. I can hold your hand in public. Or kiss you," he says. "Or I can push you up against a wall and devour you at the grocery store."

I shake my head. He's ridiculous. He leans in, capturing my mouth with his. The kiss starts off slow and controlled but turns sloppy and feral. His tongue moves over mine in slow, soft strokes. His mouth on mine, his erection grinding into my center. Being this close to him, our bodies touching everywhere, feels incredible and I never want him to stop.

But he does, lifting me from his lap, putting me on my knees on the seat beside him. His hard chest against my back. He sucks on my neck from behind me as he gently pushes my chest into the edge of the tub. His hands on my hips. He slides off my bikini bottoms, and his swim shorts go next.

"Mmm," I moan as he pushes inside of me. I feel my eyes flutter closed and my entire body shudder. He gives it to me slow, and hard. "Oh, Miles. You make me crazy. Keep going. Just like that."

"Incredible. I know. So good," he says through kisses against my shoulders. He moans my name as he pushes further into me. The sound makes me ache all over. "Perfect. So perfect," he murmurs, controlling my body with every thrust.

His hands wander down my back to my ass, squeezing, as he uses the hold he has on me to rock his body into mine from behind. Then he tortures me with a spot so sensitive, I tremble everywhere and soon I'm headed for the finish line. From the sounds he's making and the pace he's moving, I can tell he's on his way too. I rock back into him and that's all it takes for him to cry out my name. I look at him over my shoulder, watching him unravel and my heart nearly stops. It's the most beautiful thing I've ever seen watching him come undone because of me. He turns me into his lap, where we collapse together in the warmth of the water.

I cup the back of his head in my hand and kiss him hard. He kisses me back with the same intensity, controlling the kiss, stroking my tongue. It's bliss, it's heaven. Miles Bennett knows how to kiss a woman. He also knows how to set my heart on fire.

He can't know how much his desire means to me. I have never felt so wanted in my life. I know that tonight is a memory I will never forget, because there's no way I could.

"Want you so bad, Ry," he moans against my lips.

"You've got me, baby. I'm yours."

"You're everything. You know that, right?"

I kiss him, because I want the words to be true, not just something said in the heat of the moment. He opens for me, his tongue welcoming mine, then my shaky hands grip the back of his neck and I see stars.

When it's over, he hoists himself out of the tub and grabs our towels. Minutes later we're in bed, both sleepy and sated, falling asleep in each other's arms.

Sometime later, in the middle of the night, I'm woken by sounds in the bedroom. I see Miles across the room. He sets a script down on the dresser, then slips between the sheets and slides his arm around my waist, pulling me to him. It dawns on me that when my workday is over, it's over. I can go out with friends or spend the night reading and relaxing in a warm bath. Miles never seems to stop. He finishes a long day on set then needs to memorize lines, meet fans, sit for interviews and always be *on*.

He feels warm and heavy pressed against my naked body. His hand cups my breast as he softly kisses the edge of my shoulder. The scruff of his five-o'clock shadow sending goosebumps over my skin.

"Go back to sleep, baby. I didn't mean to wake you," he says, holding me tight. His arms feeling like home.

My body feels serene in the best of ways. I'm exactly where I want to be.

My eyes heavy, sleep takes hold.

Three days later, I have a date with Georgia to find me a dress for the Artist Awards. I can hear her downstairs talking to Miles while I finish getting ready. When I'm finished, I join them in the kitchen.

I take a seat next to Miles, who is eating a slice of banana bread I made yesterday. He sips his coffee while Georgia talks about something in a serious tone. "This needs to be discussed, Miles."

"I don't need you scaring her." Miles gives Georgia a death glare, making my nerves go haywire.

"What needs to be discussed? And why do I not like the sound of this?" I ask. It's clear that their conversation was about me.

"We need to talk about the press and what to expect after you and Miles go public," Georgia says and after a moment I nod.

"Are your social media accounts private?" Georgia asks.

"Yes."

"Good. They're going to try and dig up photos of you. They'll want to know who Rylee Brookes is. And what they publish won't all be accurate."

Miles puts down his coffee cup and frowns. "I told you to stop scaring her."

"I'm not trying to scare her, but she needs to be ready for a media circus," she says, giving Miles a pointed look. "They're going to be talking and not all of it will be nice."

My nervous gaze finds Miles'. I can handle what they say about me. I'm prepared to be referred to as a star chaser and be accused of only being with him for his money and fame, but what I'll never be okay with is seeing the details of my parents' accident in print.

Miles sighs. He can read me like a book. "I won't let them, Ryls. I'll threaten every single one of them if they try."

"Okay," I say quietly. Thankfully Georgia doesn't question it.

"I'll set up a Google alert for her name and she's going

to need a bodyguard when you go back to L.A.," she notes. "I think she'll be fine in Vancouver."

My forehead creases at the thought of how my life is going to change soon. I begin to second guess my decision to go with him. Miles notices. But I know how much this means to him. He lives his life publicly. He likes the limelight. I'm not that way, but I can do this for him.

"It won't be like that for long. Eventually they'll move on to someone else. It won't always be crazy," he rambles. "Some celebrity couple will get a divorce and the attention will move to them. Trust me, Ryls, I know how they work."

"I trust you."

"Are you okay?" he asks. His famous hazels looking deep into my greens.

"I'm okay."

Georgia flashes me a gentle smile. "Then let's go find you a dress."

———

"That has to be the one. You are giving me major Scarlett Johansson vibes."

Georgia is standing behind me, eyeing me in a gown that must cost more than my annual salary. I wouldn't know for sure, though – Miles gave the boutique and Georgia strict instructions not to share the price tags with me, knowing I wouldn't feel okay about spending much money on a dress I'll probably only wear once. A girl doesn't often need a gown on the farm.

"I'm pretty sure Ms. Johansson would take offense to that," I tell her, catching her eye in the mirror.

"I'm not kidding. It looks like it was made for you. We would only have to hem the length. The bodice fits you like a glove."

"Do you think Miles will like it?"

"Are you kidding me? I will be picking him up off the floor. I think it's perfect, but we can try on a few more."

Right after I told Miles I would be his date for the Artist Awards, he was on the phone with Georgia asking her to book me a private shopping appointment at an exclusive boutique. I argued with him, insisting that I could find a dress myself at The Grove, but he just smiled and said, "Let me do this for you. I want to spoil you."

So here I am, standing on a pedestal wearing a high-necked emerald green gown with a fitted bodice and a long, flowy silk crepe skirt. The dress is nicer than anything I've ever seen in my life, but I can't help but feel like an imposter wearing it.

"I don't think I need to see any more. I really like this one."

"Perfect. I'll have the sales lady come over here and fit you."

An older woman with an Italian accent starts pinning the hem of the gown while Georgia works on her laptop, taking occasional breaks to fuss with my hair.

"I think you should wear your hair down. I don't think it's long enough to put up. I'm thinking a side part and waves. Maybe one side behind your ear," she says, tapping a finger to her chin. "I'll have a stylist come to the house. You should also go for a manicure and a pedicure. I'll set that up for you too."

"That's really not necessary. I can do my own hair. I can paint my nails myself too."

Georgia walks around me so she's in front of me with a thoughtful look in her eye. "You could, but Miles would kill me. He wants to do this for you. Can I give you some advice?"

"Yes."

"I've known Miles a long time and he's never asked me to set up a dress fitting, or even asked a girl to be his date for an event. The girls you see him with in photos at these events are usually dates that have been set up to benefit both parties, if you know what I mean. This is making him happy, trust me. Let him do this for you."

"Okay. I won't argue. This is just a lot for me to get used to."

Georgia nods. "I can only imagine. Miles' life is a lot to get used to, but if it's what you two want, you will figure it out in time."

Chapter Twenty-Four

Rylee

A week later, we've arrived in L.A. Miles lives in the Bird Streets, a prestigious and expensive area up in the hills that overlooks West Hollywood. It's home to the celebrity elite, the who's who of La La Land. The homes are all hidden behind mechanical gates, the winding roads marked with palm trees.

I'm not exactly sure what I expected, but everything about his house is a surprise. It's warm and inviting, with a gallery of black-and-white family photos hung on the entryway wall.

"Your sister?" I ask, pointing out a photo of a little girl with a gap-toothed grin.

"Yep, that's Jules," he says.

"And your parents," I say, stopping at another picture of the Bennetts sitting together at a black-tie event, Miles' mom resting her head against his dad's shoulder. "They always look so in love." I try to take in as much as I can in the few seconds we spend gazing at the memory wall.

Miles pulls me further into his home. The house itself

isn't overly large, a modern rancher with a view of the city below. The floors are polished concrete, and the kitchen is open concept with sleek, dark cabinets and glass windows overlooking a large deck, a pool and hot tub. There is no question that a man lives here. The walls are painted gray, the furniture is all rich leather, and a huge TV is mounted on the wall in the family room. There are three bedrooms, including Miles', which opens out onto the deck. It couldn't be more different from the tiny apartment I share with Meg in Burbank. Or the farm where I grew up for that matter. It reminds me just how different our lives are.

When we reach his bedroom, he sets our bags down on the bed. I scan the room quickly before he turns around, noticing the California King bed in the middle of the room with its dark navy duvet and crisp white sheets. A large black-and-white photo of a Los Angeles street lined with palm trees hangs on the wall across from the bed. It all feels like Miles.

He turns around, gesturing for me to come closer.

"Your dress arrived," he says, nodding at a garment bag hanging from a rack in the corner of the room. A second bag is hung next to it, which I assume is his tux. My stomach twists in a knot. This is all too much. I feel like I must be dreaming. In less than 24 hours, we will walk the red carpet together. Our secret will no longer be just ours.

"Do I get a sneak peek?" he asks, sitting on the edge of the bed, pulling me between his spread legs by my hips.

"Absolutely not," I say, ruffling my hands through his hair.

He sighs. "I'm so happy, babe. I can't wait to show you off to the world. I'm so glad you said yes."

Miles is ready. I'm a ball of nerves. But his faith in our relationship means everything to me.

"You look beautiful."

Miles' eyes tour my body, taking me in, from my sleek, straight hair to my Jimmy Choo heels. Tonight is the Artist Awards and Miles left me to get ready in the master bedroom with a full team of stylists while he got changed in one of the spare bedrooms.

"Is it okay?"

"It's so much more than okay," he says, taking my hand and twirling me in a circle. "I won't be able to let you out of my sight."

My breath hitches when I take Miles in. He looks incredible in his black tux and bowtie, his hair styled back, and his usual stubble trimmed close to his face. It should be a crime to look as good as he does. The man knows how to dress for any occasion.

"You look so handsome." I stare at this gorgeous man who is all mine and can barely believe this is really my life. He looks like Hollywood royalty. Probably because he is. My fingers tremble a little straightening his bowtie.

"How are you feeling?" he asks, grasping my hands in his.

"I'm nervous. I can't lie."

"You're going to be fine. I've got you. It's you and me tonight. Okay?"

"Okay."

"The car is here. We should get going." He offers me his arm and we head out to the limo.

An hour later, the driver opens the door, and flashes of light go off all around us, cameras and iPhones held up high trying to capture a photo of us. A photo that will be in every tabloid across the country. My heart pounds in my chest. Fans and reporters scream all around us.

The crowds, mostly women and paparazzi, wave and shout Miles' name, wanting a piece of America's number one bachelor. I watch them push and shove one another to get a better shot. Miles handles it all effortlessly with his Hollywood smile and a wave to the crowd.

He doesn't let go of my hand until he's asked to take a few photos by himself. Once he's finished, his hand laces through mine again. We continue down the red carpet, stopping for photos as we go. Miles is at ease, completely in his element.

A beautiful blonde in a strapless sequined dress pushes her way over to us, microphone in hand. She introduces herself then asks Miles the usual questions: *who are you wearing?* and *what is it like to work with Violet Michelson?* "One more question, Miles," she asks. "Who is your date tonight?" He looks at me with a twinkle in his eye and pulls me into his side. "My girlfriend, Rylee. Doesn't she look beautiful this evening?"

I feel like I'm blushing all over.

"Who are you wearing?" The pretty blonde leans the microphone towards me. Miles lightly squeezes my hip in a display of support while I silently thank the Lord that I actually remember the designer's name.

"My dress is Valentino."

"Stunning," she says and then thanks us for our time.

We continue to make our way down the carpet. I watch Miles with pride as he shakes a few hands along the way. The bright lights and snaps of cameras follow him. How could they not? The man radiates charm like the sun.

"Miles Bennett, my man." Zach Miller claps Miles' shoulder then brings him in for a bro hug. I recognize Zach from his countless movies. He's famous for his boyish looks and Australian accent. He's ridiculously attractive – everything he seems on the big screen and then some. After greeting Miles, he shakes my hand and introduces himself. Like there's any woman on the planet who doesn't know exactly who this man is.

"It's nice to meet you."

"Pleasure is all mine," he says with a cheeky grin. Miles laughs, removing my hand from Zach's.

"You may want to think about getting your own date. Did you bring Maya with you?" Miles asks.

"Maya who? She broke up with me for some rock star. She'll realize the mistake she made soon enough."

"I would imagine so," Miles jokes. "Doesn't she know who you are? I mean, doesn't everyone?"

"If they don't, they should. My mom says I'm a big fucking deal." Zach winks and shakes Miles' hand then kisses my knuckle. "If you tire of this guy, slip into my DMs."

We continue our walk along the red carpet, my hand in his and his lips at my ear. "You are a natural, babe." I know there are a million photos being taken of me right now but all I can see is Miles. "All I want to do is get this over with and take you home and fuck you," he whispers in my ear and my face heats. "Smile, babe. There are people taking our picture."

Cheeky boy.

He's looking at me with a devilish grin while I plaster a smile on my face. He dips his head down and kisses my temple and lights flash from every direction. Photographers shout his name, and the fans go wild.

He laughs and whispers into my ear again. "Told you they'd love you."

And I can't help but wonder if he's right.

The dinner is held in the grand ballroom of the Beverly Hilton hotel. We make our way to our table to find Violet already seated when we reach the table. Even if I didn't see her sitting there with my own two eyes, I would have felt her glaring at me.

"Hi Violet," Miles says, pulling out my seat and then taking the one beside me. He introduces himself to Violet's date, who turns out to be her brother, Max.

Violet smiles tightly, which seems to be her normal expression. I take a sip from my water glass, choosing to ignore her.

For three hours, we dine on Kobe beef and lobster tails, Miles' hand on my thigh under the table for most of the night. We make small talk with our table and other celebrities who approach Miles. He never forgets to introduce me. And when I say I'm starstruck it's an understatement.

Once dinner is over, I excuse myself to go to the washroom while Miles chats with a director he knows.

I'm washing my hands when Violet walks in, looking both unamused and unimpressed that I'm breathing the same air as her.

Holding my shoulders back, I refuse to let her know how much she gets to me. Her confidence typically unnerves me, but not this time. I'm not hiding. I refuse to allow her to let me feel less than her.

"I had no idea you and Miles are dating," she purrs. "I hope things won't be awkward on set when you aren't anymore."

"Excuse me?" I say, meeting her eyes. *How does this woman have the nerve?*

Violet snickers under her breath. "I'm being candid, which I hope you can appreciate. Miles doesn't do relationships, so save yourself the heartbreak by not getting too attached. You'll thank me later."

I've never hated anything more. Not mosquitos, not traffic jams, not even the dentist. I'd rather lose one of my fingers than stand here and chat with her for five more seconds.

"I'm just telling you the truth. Miles will bore of you soon and go back to his womanizing ways."

"Thank you for clarifying, but I heard you perfectly fine the first time."

She smirks, her expression chilly. I can't figure out why she goes out of her way to torment me. The world is her oyster. Why does she even care about Miles and me?

I'm on the verge of saying something I'll regret, but then I compose myself. The last thing I need is to be a part of a public scandal. I try to conceal the glare in my eyes. "Enjoy your night, Violet." And then I walk out.

"There you are." Miles' lips caress the back of my neck, his breath on my skin causing a shiver when I enter the ballroom. "This is for you." He passes me a flute of champagne. *Lord knows I need it.*

With his hand settled against my lower back, we walk towards the bar. Violet walks past us with a curt grin on her face. "Everything okay with her?"

"Everything is fine," I respond stiffly.

The night has gone so well, Miles is happy and in his element, and I would like him to stay that way. But everything Violet said to me in the washroom sticks with me. Am I being naïve to think he cares about me the same way I do for him? Am I only setting myself up to be crushed?

Then Miles turns his dreamy eyes to mine and my worries all but disappear. He looks at me like he wants me. Right here and right now. His lips tip up into that Hollywood smile that I'm sure gets him anything he wants. I know it works every time with me.

"It looks like it's time for dessert," I say, watching waiters move throughout the ballroom placing crystal footed ice-cream bowls on tables.

"Or we could go back to the house?" he says, raising an eyebrow at me.

"You need to get one thing straight if you're going to date me."

"I'm listening."

"It's quite simple. I never say no to dessert. And if it's chocolate, I might want seconds."

He taps his finger to his temple twice and grins. "Noted. Let's get the girl what she wants."

The dessert was worth sticking around for. I scrape the last bite from the bowl and then we start to say our good-byes. We fall into bed way past midnight, exhausted and bleary-eyed, and ignoring our phones. Whatever they're saying about me, whether it's good or bad, I don't want to know.

Miles raises my tank over my head. His eyes dip to my breasts for just a second, then they're back up to mine.

"I didn't expect you."

Confused, I ask. "What do you mean?"

"I mean that I wasn't looking for someone," he starts to say. "But then I met you and you took over some major real estate in my mind."

"I'm happy you met me."

"Rylee, I don't want to talk anymore. Give me your mouth."

I do exactly that.

Chapter Twenty-Five

Rylee

I wake up the next morning in Miles' bed alone. Missing his warm body next to mine, I swap my pillow for his, inhaling his scent, and smile a ridiculously sappy smile, remembering everything that happened last night. Is this really my life? Walking a red carpet, wearing a designer gown, shaking hands with the who's who of Hollywood. I roll onto my side, pulling the bed sheet across my bare skin, and take in the sight of my gown next to Miles' tux draped over a chair. *It really did happen.*

He let me sleep in this morning while he headed to a read-through, so I made plans to visit Meg at my apartment. It's been months since I've been home, so I'm excited to get there.

An hour later, Meg and I are enjoying smoothie bowls on the couch in our apartment.

"Beautiful brunette hand-in-hand with Hollywood's leading man, Miles Bennett," Meg says, staring at her phone. "Who is Rylee Brookes and can she tame the infamous heartthrob?"

I can only laugh. "Why are you reading that crap?"

"Because my best friend is on every gossip site in America. How are you *not* reading it?"

"I don't know why anyone would care about me. It makes no sense." At least the headlines aren't mean. That is a blessing.

I didn't open any of my social media apps this morning on purpose, choosing to ignore whatever was happening online. I've never cared much about what people think of me, so it isn't that hard to ignore the articles and photos that I know are circulating. Meg has filled me in on a few things that are being reported. Apparently they've dug up a photo of me from high school and although it isn't flattering, it could be worse.

Meg insists on showing me one photo of Miles and I on the red carpet. I'm relieved to see I don't have three chins and both of my eyes are open. The short train of my gown trails behind me and I'm pressed firmly into Miles' side. My gaze is to the camera while Miles stares down at me. The photo is a good one, but it's the expression on his face that makes me pause. Anyone looking at this photo would think he was head over heels in love with me.

"They know your name, Ry. Your photo is going to be plastered everywhere. I hope you're ready for what's to come," Meg says, her finger scrolling through articles and images.

"As ready as I can be. Miles is insisting I have security now wherever I go." We talked about that again last night. He's not willing to take any chances, hence the car he had waiting for me in the driveway this morning to bring me to my apartment and the bodyguard he insisted escort me to my own front door.

"And you're okay with that?"

"I'm honestly not sure. I said I would try, because it's important to him. Anyways, enough about me, Megs. What's going on with you? How are things with Adam?"

Meg taps her chin, "Hmm, let me see. Ah-mazing. He's the one, Ry. I know it."

But Meg refuses to let me change the subject for long, steering the conversation back to Miles and me. "So, what happens next for you two? Are you still planning on moving back to the farm?"

"I am," I say.

"Miles will stay in L.A.?"

"That's the plan." I shrug, realizing how it must sound to her. But how can I convince Meg we'll find a way to make it work when I'm having trouble believing it myself?

***

Later in the day, it happens.

Miles called me as I was leaving Meg and my apartment and asked me to meet him for a late lunch. The driver took me to Sunset Boulevard and a cute little restaurant not known for celebrity sightings. Miles was waiting for me when I arrived.

Lunch went smoothly. We ate grilled chicken salads while I filled him in on my morning with my closest friend. He told me about his meeting and the project he'll be working on in the fall.

It wasn't until we were leaving that the day went sideways. Someone must have tipped the paps off because we didn't make it more than 15 feet before it felt like we were being swarmed.

It began with one, then escalated to around fifty or so. There were cell phones pointed at us from all different directions. Miles slid his arm around my waist, drawing me to him. A few were obviously paparazzi, shouting questions at us. A lady with a small child followed beside us, pointing her camera in our direction. I leaned against Miles while he steered us towards the buildings.

Now, hiding out in the back of a Starbucks, I try to pull myself together.

"Are you okay?" His hands grip my shoulders as he kisses my forehead.

"I'm fine. That was… that was just a lot."

"Relax, babe. I've got you. Nathan will handle the crowd." Nathan is one of the four bodyguards on rotation for Miles. He must be six-foot-four, with a broad chest and bulging biceps. I wouldn't want to be the one to piss him off.

A group of teenagers sitting at a table are now paying attention to us while I try to calm down my racing heart. I had wondered what this moment was going to feel like when it finally happened and now I know. It's frightening. It feels strange having people stare at us and take pictures. It's hard to believe that Miles deals with this on a daily basis.

"I'm sorry," he says, pulling me into his chest, kissing the crown of my head. Miles has a way of knowing exactly what I need in every moment. The safe, warm place in his arms and his gentle kiss were everything I needed to relax me and calm my nerves.

"It's not your fault," I say through a shaky breath.

"It kinda is. You wouldn't be having to deal with this if it weren't for me," he sighs. "I'm sorry this ruined our day."

"It's fine, Miles. And it didn't ruin anything. It had to happen sometime."

"Are you sure you're okay?"

"I promise." I force a smile onto my face. "But I feel like we are sort of trapped in here. Is there another way out?" I ask, trying to make light of our situation.

He smiles. "Let's see what we can do."

Nathan arrives and after a quick chat with the manager of the coffee shop, we're ushered out the back, where a car is waiting for us.

Paps - 0

Miles and Rylee - 1

Chapter Twenty-Six

Miles

"If they fuck with you, Ryls, they fuck with me."

We're sprawled across the outdoor sectional on my patio, admiring the view of L.A. We have to catch a plane back to Vancouver in two hours, but right now her head is on my chest and my fingers are running through her hair.

"I'm fine, Miles. It was scary in the moment, but nothing happened. I'll be better prepared next time." She seems to be handling the paparazzi disaster from yesterday better than I am, which is surprising.

"Will you stop fighting me on the bodyguard? If anything were to ever happen to you I would never forgive myself."

I know that I'm right to be upset about what happened. It's not just the paparazzi that worry me; there are people out there who cross the line when it comes to celebrities. If I'm honest with myself, though, I also know I'm probably overreacting.

"You've made your point. I'll make sure I have one of

your bodyguards with me when I go out. I'll be careful," she says, kissing my bare chest. "This really is a gorgeous view. I'm not sure if I prefer it in the daylight or when the city is all lit up at night."

"I really need to take you to Malibu. I think you'd like the view there too," I tell her, my fingers travelling up and down her arm. "There's this restaurant that I really like. It's farm-to-table, the food is amazing. And it's perched high up on the bluff overlooking the beach and the Pacific Ocean. I'll take you there next time."

"I would like that."

I still haven't told her about the surprise trip back to Deer Lake I've planned, but something about this moment feels right. I decide to bite the bullet and go for it, hoping she doesn't think I overstepped.

"There's something I want to ask you, but I'm scared that it might freak you out," I say, hesitating for a second. Lifting her head from my chest, she sits up to face me with a nervous expression on her face. I didn't mean for it to sound so serious, like I was about to ask her to marry me or star opposite me in my next film. "I'd like to fly you out to see your family next weekend. I'd also like to go with you."

Rylee's eyes go wide, and I immediately worry that it's too much, too soon for her.

"Are you freaking out right now?" I ask her. I desperately want her to say yes to this trip. I want more time with her before she moves back home for good. I also know how happy it would make her to see her family. And maybe it's selfish, but I want to be the one who gives her that, who puts that smile on her face. "I wasn't kidding when I told you I'd like to see Deer Lake. I'd love to meet your family too," I say.

"You want to meet my grandparents?" Rylee asks softly.

"You talk so much about them. I feel like I already sort of know them. I should confess that I already bought the tickets. I'm really hoping you'll say yes, but I can-"

"Miles, I don't know what to say. I think that's the nicest thing anyone has ever done for me. When do we leave?"

"Friday. It's the long weekend so I wanted to take advantage of having three days off. You're sure you're good with this?"

"More than good, Miles. I'm so happy. Thank you."

I feel a rush of relief. Her arms snake around my neck and I pull her to me. There's no doubt in my mind that Rylee is exactly where she belongs. I am starting to not be able to imagine my life without her.

It was after 9 p.m. when our plane touched down in Vancouver. I had my driver take us straight to Rylee's hotel. We both had to be at work the next day and she said she needed a change of clothes for the morning, so we agreed to stay there.

"I'm not sure I'm going to be able to sleep tonight," she says as we roll our suitcases through the door of her hotel room. "I'm still riding the high of being in L.A. with you and now I get to look forward to seeing my family."

"I can head to my place if you think it will help?"

"No," Rylee turns to face me. "I want you here with me. If that's okay?"

"I was hoping you'd say that. Let's have a quick shower and get into bed."

And that's what we do, except we don't fall asleep right

away. We lie on our sides facing one another, talking about Deer Lake and her childhood and her favorite memories. We talk about her brothers and her nieces and nephew and all the places she wants to show me.

It's after midnight when Rylee's breathing slows, and her body settles, and I know she's fallen asleep. I watch her in the dark wondering how I will ever be able to go to bed without her.

Chapter Twenty-Seven

Rylee

Word travels fast in a small town. I predict it will take about 5 minutes before all 7,300 residents of Deer Lake know that Miles Bennett is here. Thankfully he is used to attention, because Miles is about to become the town's sole source of entertainment.

But for now it's just us, driving in the direction of the countryside, me tucked closely against his side.

I watch him gaze out the window like he's in awe of the fields going by in a blur, tall oak trees and brightly colored mailboxes lining the dirt roads. I wonder what he's thinking. Will he like it here? It's about as different from L.A. as you can get: Quiet country roads, diners by the dozen, mom-and-pop shops and neighbors who always know your business.

Miles is wearing his baseball cap, but instead of pulling it low on his head like he usually does when he doesn't want to be noticed, he has it flipped backwards. It's quite possible I'm seconds away from cardiac arrest because Miles in a backwards hat is the best thing I've ever seen.

He's wearing jeans and a black T-shirt, looking casual and effortless. The look suits him perfectly. He's laid back, at ease, always up for a good time.

He's still looking out the window when I tell our driver to turn right at the next mailbox, my stomach doing that fluttery thing it does whenever I get excited. "We're here."

The white and gray farmhouse comes into view as we drive the dirt road that leads to it. Its white clapboards gleam in the June sunshine, and the wooden porch swing my gramps made for my gran hangs proudly. I scan the old house, seeing it anew after being gone for so long. It looks to be in good shape right now, but something was always breaking down or in need of repair when you lived on a farm. It's one of the reasons I need to move back home. The farmhouse is getting to be more work than my grandparents can handle.

As the car slows to a stop, the familiar flash of love that I feel every time I look up at this house charges through my chest.

I pull open the big wood door, its hinges groaning a welcome. A second later a Jack Russell Terrier charges out to greet us. "Hey Maisy girl, you pretty thing," I say, scratching the brown-and-white dog behind her ear. "I've missed you too."

Miles also bends down to pet Maisy, receiving a big sloppy kiss in return. He doesn't seem to mind at all.

We toe off our shoes, making our way into the kitchen where I know I'll find my grandparents sitting around the table drinking sweet tea, reading the newspaper.

The house is exactly like I left it. Floral wallpaper marked with family photos in mismatched frames and sizes. Weathered wood floors and bathrooms with bubble gum pink sinks and matching toilets.

"Rylee-Jay, is that you?"

"It's me, Gran, and I brought you some company."

"You bring that boy in here straight away."

Miles looks at me, one eyebrow raised, with a lopsided smile. Taking him by the hand, we step into the kitchen. I couldn't wait to see them. Gran is in front of the stove cooking something that smelled amazing. She puts down her wooden spoon when she sees me.

"You come on over here, Rylee. Your Gran has missed you like crazy." She opens her arms, which are a little skinnier than the last time I saw her, and I step into her embrace.

"It's so good to see you. I've missed you too."

"Let me get a good look at you," she says, taking a step backwards, giving me a once-over. "A little too skinny, but nothing I can't fix in a couple of days. Now, who is this handsome man?" she asks, turning her attention to Miles beside me.

"I want you to meet Miles. Miles, this is my grandma, Audrey."

I watch him give my gran a hug. She looks so small in his arms. "Wow, you really are a looker," Gran says, when they pull back from their embrace. "You are finer than a frog's hair."

"Gran," I laugh, interrupting her. "What smells so good in here?"

"Yes, it smells like heaven," Miles agrees. "And you'll have to tell me later if being finer than a frog's hair is a good thing or a bad thing."

"She's got all your favorite things cooking. She's been talking about this visit all week," Gramps says, from his chair at the kitchen table. Using the table for leverage, he pushes to standing. With open arms, he pulls me into him. "Gosh, I've missed my girl."

"You look so good, Gramps. How are you feeling?"

"I'm feeling just fine," he replies before extending a hand to Miles. "Thank you for bringing my girl home and making this old man happy."

Miles shakes his hand. "It's my pleasure. You have a beautiful home. Thank you for having me."

It feels surreal and sublime all at once being back in my childhood home. Watching Miles talk to my gramps, I still can't quite believe this isn't a dream. I am so happy to have him here with me I feel like my chest might just burst. Miles seems really happy too, which makes it very difficult to wipe the silly smile from my face.

"Cut the stove for me, Rylee. I don't want the pies to burn," my gran says, breaking me from my thoughts.

"I'm fixin' to have dinner for seven tonight. Will that be okay?"

"That works for us."

"In the meantime, you two must be starving. Let me make you a steak sandwich. And not like the ones they make at the diner. Those darn things are tougher than a two-dollar steak."

Miles laughs a deep, happy laugh that spreads warmth right through me. I smile at him, and he winks. God, I love it when he does that. I love so many things about Miles Bennett. I still sometimes wonder how I got so lucky to call him mine.

"Let me get that, Gran. Go sit. I know my way around this kitchen."

"As do I. It's not often I get to cook for you, so I'm going to do it." She looks to Miles. "Ignore my grand-daughter. She thinks her Gramps and I are old folks. She's decided to fuss over us until she's an old maid herself, leaving us great-grandchildless. I'm not sure she's aware that grandbabies don't fall from trees."

Mile laughs and his gaze moves to meet mine. His

smile is a country-mile wide. It's not his Hollywood smile, but the real one – the one he saves for the ones he loves. The Miles sitting here in my gran's kitchen is the boy from Reed Point, not the motion picture star. Having him here feels right. Like it's right where he belongs.

We spend the next hour sitting around the old kitchen table telling stories. My heart feels like it could beat right out of my chest, and I wonder to myself how it could possibly get better than this.

Chapter Twenty-Eight

Miles

So, this is Rylee's home. This is Deer Lake. We're standing on her grandparents' porch admiring the land. Their farm looks like it stretches on for miles, rolling hills painted green against the blue midday sky. The fresh, crisp air feels like a balm to my lungs. There's a large red barn that looks like it's directly from an old movie set and the scent of apples drifts through the air from the orchard. I've heard her describe the farm a hundred different times before but being here and seeing it up close is another story. I take it all in, picturing Rylee as a little girl running through the rows of apple trees. This place feels familiar, comfortable, carefree, full of life and beauty. It couldn't be more her.

After lunch, Rylee took me out to the porch. She told me all about the orchard and explained the harvest season, pointed out the stable and the path that leads to her favorite lake.

"This place is so you, Rylee."

"It's home. I love it here. "

"Have you brought many of your boyfriends here?" I ask even though I know it's none of my business.

"Actually, you are the first," she answers, looking sexy as hell, a breeze brushing her hair across her face. "I've never wanted to bring anyone home until now. There hasn't been anyone who's mattered as much as you."

"There isn't anyone here who… mattered?" I know I'm being nosy, but I want to know.

"Not really," she says. "I've never felt that deep, intimate connection with anyone. The kind that feeds your soul. The closest I've come was with a guy named Eric. I met him at film school, we were together for two years."

"Two years is a long time. You never wanted to bring him here, introduce him to your family?"

"No. He never seemed all that interested and deep down I think I knew there wasn't a point. I wasn't in love with him."

Her admission makes me happy. I want to be the first person she's brought home to meet her family. I want to be the first person she's given her heart to.

"I feel pretty lucky all of a sudden."

"I guess you should," she says, reaching for my hand. "Come on, I'll show you where we're staying." We head towards the stairs, stopping in the hallway to look at the wall of family photos. There are candid pictures of Rylee when she was young, with her parents and her brothers. Other family photos look like they were taken by a professional photographer. I wonder if they are hers. "These are your nieces and nephew?" I ask, pointing to a photo of three adorable kids running through a field.

"They are. This one is Belle. That one is Lainey, and the little guy is Noah," she says, pointing them out, her face lighting up.

"Did you take any of these?" I ask her, looking over the wall of memories that obviously mean so much to her.

"I did," she says shyly, leaving it at that. But I'm not letting her off the hook that easy.

"Which ones?"

I'm blown away as she shows me the photos she took. Each one tells a story. "These are incredible," I tell her honestly. "I know you love to take photos, but I've never asked you how long you've been doing it."

"Oh gosh, as long as I can remember. My mother always had a camera in her hands. She never went to school or anything, but she had an eye for it, I guess. She taught me everything she knew. Then it became a thing that my mother and I did together. After she died, I stopped taking photos for a while."

"What made you want to start again?"

"Belle," she says, touching the tip of her finger to her niece in a picture. "When Belle was born, I wanted to capture every memory I could. I knew if my mother was with us she would be snapping photos of every single milestone. It was Belle that got me back at it."

She takes a step up the stairs, a melancholy look in her eyes. "Come on, I'll show you my room, that's where we'll be staying."

I follow her up the worn wooden stairs to her childhood bedroom. It's small, with a double bed and an old dresser. A bench seat beneath the window overlooks the back of the house. I pick up a framed photo from her dresser. "Your parents?" I ask her gently, turning to face her.

"Yes. That was taken at church. I love this photo the most because of my mom's big smile. She was extra happy that day, it was my first time reading a scripture in front of everyone and she was so proud."

"You have her smile. And your dad's dark hair. I can see them both in you."

"So I've been told." She smiles as I set the frame back where it belongs. "The bed is a little smaller than you're used to," she says, changing the subject.

"I personally think in this case that smaller works to my advantage." I tease, sweeping her hair over her shoulder, pressing a kiss to the back of her neck. My lips linger over her skin.

"Miles Bennett, don't you dare start that now. The walls are thin in this old house. Everyone will hear us," she squeals, turning to face me. I can't resist her, backing her up towards the bed then turning us around. Sitting on the edge of the bed, I pull her in between my spread legs, and she giggles as I kiss her, her hand against my chest.

"I'm excited to be here with you," she says. "Thank for your bringing me home."

My heart expands in my chest as she smiles like I've given her the world.

You are my world.

I can't believe that you're mine.

She smiles then kisses my forehead. "Come on city boy, let me show you around the farm."

I follow her through the tiny kitchen and out to the back porch. Our walk takes us past a stone fire pit and down a path to a pen where a giant sheep appears to be taking a nap. We carry on, eventually meeting Rylee's grandpa at the far side of the farm.

"Well, there you two kids are," he says when he sees us. "Are you out here to help me feed the goats?"

"I don't know, Gramps, what do you think? You think this city boy can handle it?"

"I think we're about to find out," he says, handing me a bucket full of what is apparently goat food. "Come on, now." Rylee stays put as I follow him, but she gives me a playful smack on the ass on my way by. "We really need to take this boy to Walmart and get him some clothes he won't be afraid to get dirty in."

I look down at my tennis shoes, already dirty after our walk across the farm. Maybe a trip to Walmart isn't such a bad idea. Her grandpa leads me over to an old tire and instructs me to set the bucket in the middle of it, explaining that the grain feed needs to be placed off the ground. Then he walks me over to a wheelbarrow filled with hay.

"Take these," he says, handing me a pair of black work gloves. "You need to fill those mangers over there with hay." He points to three wooden troughs around the perimeter of the pen. "Can you do that for me?"

"I can, sir."

Looking at me under his unruly, silver eyebrows, he says, "Everyone here in Deer Lake calls me Gramps," he says, "You can do the same."

"Okay, Gramps it is."

I slide on the gloves, reach down, and grab a handful of hay. I begin to fill the troughs while Gramps exits the pen carrying buckets for water.

"You need a name," I say, holding out a handful of feed while the goat eats from my hand. "You look like a Darla. Don't cha, girl?" I notice Rylee inspecting my work out of the corner of my eye.

"How am I doing?" I ask her.

"It might be easier with your shirt off." Her eyes rake over me. My country girl is sitting on the fence, her dark hair gleaming in the late-day sun. The sunlight worshiping her. She's killing me in cowboy boots and a pair of jean shorts, swinging her legs back and forth.

"You would like that," I call back.

"That's right, I would."

I walk in her direction, dusting my hands off on the back of my jeans. When I reach her, I part her golden legs and stand in between them, gripping both sides of her hips in my hands. She squeals as I cage her in, my mouth on her neck. "You know that I'm losing it looking at you dressed like that," I whisper.

"Is that so?"

"Painfully." At this rate I am going to be in need of medical attention if I don't get my hands on her. Her in those boots. Being this close to her. It's all too much. "Just *how* thin are those bedroom walls of yours?"

"The house is over 60 years old. What do you think?"

"I think I might die."

"And you must be Belle," I say to the adorable little pigtailed girl. The splatter of freckles across her nose reminds me of her aunt's. I'm crouched down to her level in the family room that's packed with the rest of Rylee's family.

"Yes, I am. And you must be the actor who my daddy says Aunt Rylee is all woozy over."

I laugh, looking up to see Rylee smiling at us. The happiness in her eyes is priceless. "That is definitely me. It's nice to meet you. Will you introduce me to your brother and sister?"

"Of course. This is Lainey and my brother's name is Noah. I'm the oldest so I know the most. My brain..." she says, tapping her skull with her tiny pointer finger, "is full of things."

The kid is fucking adorable.

"Okay you three, I'm going to need you to take the dog outside," a woman who must be Rylee's sister-in-law says.

"I'm Cara and this is my husband Cole, Rylee's oldest brother. We've heard so much about you. It's a pleasure to finally meet you," she says, holding out her hand.

"It's good to meet you," Cole says next, giving me the older brother once-over. "Let's get a beer and chat on the porch?"

"Sure. Let's do it," I answer.

"You be nice to him, Cole," Gran hollers from somewhere in the kitchen. "Leave him alone."

"Should I be worried?" I whisper in Rylee's ear.

"He shouldn't give it to ya *too* bad." She winks.

I follow Cole into the kitchen, where he grabs two cans of beer from the fridge. He hands one to me and we head out to the porch. I take the chair next to Cole's and we sit in silence for a moment, both taking a swig from our beers. Wiping his mouth with the back of his hand, he eyes me as he sets the can on the arm of his chair.

"It's good to finally meet you, man. You have a beautiful family," I say, popping the tab on my beer.

"Thanks. Some days it feels like I'm living in a frat house, but I wouldn't trade it for the world. They're good kids."

"I don't have any experience, but my brother is having a baby in the fall."

"So, you're going to be an uncle."

I smile. "Yeah, I'm going to be the best damn uncle. I can't wait."

He laughs, then takes another sip from his beer. We make small talk, chatting about my family, his auto repair shop. We have more in common than one might think – both from small towns, both very close with our families, both big into baseball.

Then the tougher questions come. "You met my sister on set?"

"I did. I, um… saw her from across the room and I know this is going to sound crazy, but I just felt like I needed to know who she was. To know her name. There was something about her."

She's been making my heart crazy ever since.

"You really like her, huh?"

"I do."

"I can tell you make her happy," Cole says. "She hasn't stopped smiling since I've been here. And there's nothing I want more than for my sister to be happy. But I'll be honest with you… I have my concerns. She's moving back home. I have mixed feelings about that, which Rylee knows, but she's stubborn. So what will happen then? Have you two talked about that?"

"We have. It won't be easy, but we don't want to stop seeing each other. I don't think I could if I tried," I say, looking him dead in the eye. "So I'll visit when I can. We'll take it one day at a time."

"You think you can do the long-distance thing? That sounds tough."

I frown. "I'm willing to try. I don't know what else to do. She wants to be here. It's important to her."

"Yeah, it is. She always puts herself second to others. It's just the way that she's wired."

This could be going a lot worse. Cole is level-headed and understanding and it seems like he genuinely wants to get to know me. I completely understand his concern for his sister, I feel the same way about Jules.

"I'll miss her," I say, trying to ignore the sadness squeezing at my chest at the thought of not seeing Rylee every day.

He's quiet for a second and it makes me wonder what he's thinking.

"I'm always on her side, and I'll always be here to support her. I hope you two can find a way to work it out. Just be careful with her heart. She's been through enough."

I look him in the eye and nod. Cole is cool and calm and seems like a genuinely good guy. I can see why Rylee is so close to him. I'm glad she has him looking out for her.

He stands then, and I do too, both having said what we needed to say.

"When you're around next time, you should stop by my shop for a beer. Or if you like fishing there are some great rivers around here I could show you."

I smile. "Yeah, I'd like that. Let's do it," I say, and I mean it.

Back in the house, I offer to help Rylee's Gran with dinner. She hands me an apron and a masher and directs me to the pot of steaming potatoes. I don't exactly know my way around a kitchen, but I'm hoping even I can't screw up mashing potatoes too badly.

I'm midway through mashing when Rylee walks in with her camera. She grins like she's caught me with my hand in the cookie jar.

"That apron looks good on you," she says, with one eyebrow raised. And fuck, if it doesn't come out as sexy. Why does everything she say sound so fucking sexy to me? She snaps a photo, smiling.

Gran comes over to inspect my work, peeking into the bowl of potatoes. She makes a face. "You can do better than that," she says. "Look at all those lumps."

I hear Rylee snicker from somewhere behind me. "I'll leave you to it," she says, abandoning me.

"You know, my granddaughter is an awfully good cook.

She used to spend hours with me in this kitchen when she was a kid."

"I've been the lucky recipient of her cooking *and* her baking," I reply. "Everything she makes is incredible. She must have learned from the best."

Gran chuckles. "Her secret is that big ole' heart in her chest. She does everything with love. You can't go wrong when you're cooking with love."

Gran is right. Rylee wears her heart on her sleeve. She puts others' happiness before her own and goes out of her way to make people feel special. I've never met anyone like her. And now she has my damn heart in the palm of her hand.

"And she's prettier than a peach," Gran adds with a wink.

"Never seen anything more beautiful in my life."

I'm in love with your granddaughter.

She's become my whole world.

"You two are cute as pie. I'm rooting for you." She gives my wrist an affectionate squeeze. "Now, you give those potatoes a little extra love and then help me take this all to the table."

Eventually we all take our seats around the dining room table. The house smells delicious thanks to the feast of buttermilk biscuits and gravy, garlicky skillet greens, mashed potatoes and fried chicken. I take heaping servings of everything, savoring every delicious bite. For dessert there is an apple pecan pie that Rylee baked this afternoon with her grandma.

"I can't believe you made this," I say before taking my last bite, holding back a moan. "Are the apples from the farm?"

"Hand-picked by me," Gran says.

The evening flies by and soon Cole and Cara and the

kids say their goodbyes. Rylee and I help Gran with the clean-up and then head upstairs to bed, both exhausted from the busy day.

We slip into her small bed, me in my boxers and Rylee in a thin tank top and shorts. I lean back against the pillow, one arm around Rylee, her head on my chest.

"I had a great time tonight. Thank you for allowing me to join you."

"You did?" she asks, looking up at me.

"I absolutely did. But I ate too much. Your Gran is some cook."

"She likes you."

"I'm not surprised. I'm hard to resist."

"Stop flirting with me when we're talking about my grandma," Rylee teases, resting her cheek back against my chest.

"She's barely five feet tall, but she's a force to be reckoned with. I would be lost without her," she says with a small sigh. "I don't think anyone expects their children to go before them."

"I see a lot of you in her, you know."

"You do?"

"I do. Her strength, her warmth. She's empathetic and kind just like you. And you're both a little stubborn."

"Is that so?"

"Definitely. I've never had to work harder in my life to win a girl over."

"Then you were flirting up the wrong girls," Rylee teases, her voice low and silky.

"You know how important you are to me, right?" I ask her.

"I think I do, but maybe you should show me," she says. "Quietly."

I shift behind her, my breath against my neck. "Very," I whisper.

Chapter Twenty-Nine

Miles

The next morning after breakfast, Rylee's Gramps heads out to the farm and Cara stops by to pick up Gran and take her to a hair appointment.

Alone in the old farmhouse, Rylee and I take our second cups of coffee out to the porch and sit together on the swing, looking out over the countryside. The trees are so full and green they look like a movie set. Everything out here feels more alive, more vibrant. We sit quietly, the morning sun warming our skin. I'll miss this on Tuesday when I'm back in Los Angeles inhaling the smog, sitting in traffic, dealing with the ever-present paparazzi. Fresh country air, pecan pies and good people. I think I could get used to this.

"You're killing me in that sweatshirt right now." She's wearing my hoodie, the one I gave her the day she was soaked from the rain. *Fuck.* There's something about seeing her in my clothes that does something to me.

Rylee eyes me over her coffee cup with that look in her

eyes she gets when she catches me staring at her. "I am, am I?"

"You know you are, country girl," I say with a flirty look in my eyes then decide to change the subject before things get too heated. It's the way it's always been with her. Things go from zero to sixty in seconds. "This is a pretty great place for a child to grow up. I can see why you love it so much," I say, pushing the swing back and forth with the tip of my toe.

"Over there is where my brothers and I would play capture the flag. And see that rope swing on that tree? That's where I broke my arm. This farm is where I've made most of my memories."

She points to a narrow, dirt path that disappears into the field. "That path right there is where my brothers would sneak off with their girlfriends. I used to bust them from my bedroom window."

"And what about you… did you sneak out to meet your boyfriends too?"

"No. I was too afraid to get caught. I never wanted to upset my grandparents. They were busy enough trying to keep my brothers in line. Besides, I didn't date much."

"Why is that?" I ask because it's her and everything about her fascinates me.

"A whole bunch of reasons," she says, nuzzling her head against my shoulder. I kiss the top of her head.

"Tell me just one."

"Hmm… okay." It's quiet for a moment while she ponders the question. "I think I felt like it would be a distraction. I wanted to keep my grades up. I wanted to spend my weekend on the farm harvesting or helping with the animals. And Gran always needed help in the kitchen."

"I'm guessing you'll be doing a lot of that when you move back. Helping in the kitchen?"

"Yeah, there will be a lot of that."

I want to ask her what makes her happy. I want to tell her that she doesn't *have* to move back to the farm. I have other questions too: What are your dreams? If you could do absolutely anything, what would it be? But what I really want to say to her is *stay with me*.

"It's bittersweet," she says, looking up at me, making me want to brush the tips of my fingers over the freckles on her nose.

I think I know what she means. This farm *was* the perfect place to grow up, until that fateful day when her parents were killed. I'm not sure anything I say can make that kind of pain go away so I instead pull her body against mine. She leans into my arms.

Later that night, she takes me to the Sunny Side Up, a diner not far from the farm. It's one of three restaurants in Deer Lake – there are far more churches in town than there are places to eat. In addition to the Sunny Side Up, there's a pub and a fish and chips place, which I find odd for a small town in Tennessee. As soon as we pull into the parking lot it's pretty clear that word has gotten around that I'm in town. I can feel the eyes on us, hear the hushed chatter as we get out of Rylee's Gramps' truck. It doesn't bother me. We may as well give them what they're hoping to see.

Holding her hand, I walk with Rylee into the family-owned restaurant. It looks like a flashback to the 1950s, with a long, sit-down counter and a row of avocado green, leather barstools. There's a galley kitchen behind the counter and the walls are decorated with black-and-white photos and memorabilia. We're greeted immediately by an older woman in a pale blue dress and a white apron.

"Rylee Brookes, is that you? I heard you were back in town! I was hoping you'd come for a visit."

"Hi Linda. It's good to see you. I see some things never change, it's always busy here."

"It rarely slows down." Linda is speaking to Rylee but her gaze rests on me. "Table for two?"

She grabs a couple of menus and shows us to our table. I slide into the booth against the window and Rylee takes the bench opposite me. Linda places a menu in front of each of us. "Rylee, are you going to introduce me to your friend?"

"Of course, this is Miles. Miles, this is Linda Baker, she owns the diner."

"It's a pleasure to meet you," I say, holding out my hand. "I'm Rylee's boyfriend."

"The pleasure is all mine. I've seen all of your movies." She glances towards the kitchen for a moment, then decides to continue. "My favorite is *A Long Way Home*. I must have seen it a hundred times."

"You don't say? I appreciate that." I can almost hear Rylee roll her eyes from where I'm sitting.

"Let me take your drink order. What will it be?"

We order our drinks and Linda saunters away. I look at Rylee, her head slightly tilted to the left with a smirk on her face. "I swear she's going to have you autograph her chest."

I laugh. "I've been asked worse."

"Ew, gross. I do not want to know."

We order our meals. I get the patty melt and Rylee orders chicken strips and fries.

"A patty melt?" Rylee questions me. "Isn't that a lunchy type of food?"

"Says the girl who just ordered from the kids' menu."

"What's wrong with chicken fingers?" she demands.

"Nothing, if you're seven," I tease.

Linda comes back with our orders a short while later,

lingering several seconds longer than she needs to. I get the sense that when it comes to small town gossip in Deer Lake, Linda is the queen bee. I ask Rylee about her and she confirms that Linda knows everyone in Deer Lake and everything about them.

"It can get pretty cliquey here. The ones who've been here their entire lives tend to stick together, which leaves the newcomers to form their own social circles. First impressions are based on who your family is and what they've done for this town."

"Where does that leave me, then?" I smirk.

"With me. And the subject of *a lot* of talk." Glancing around the diner I can tell she's not wrong. There are plenty of eyes on us, but it beats paparazzi hiding behind plants any day of the week.

"What do you think they're talking about?"

"Oh, I don't know," she says, leaning her elbows on the table. "I'm sure they don't believe we're really a thing."

I smile, grabbing her hand from across the table. She's going to kill me for this, but I do it anyway. I lace our fingers together and before she has the time to process what's happening, I lean over the table and take her chin in my other hand. I pull her face towards mine and press my lips to hers. Breaking the kiss, I whisper into her ear, "Let's make sure this whole town knows how crazy I am for you." She giggles against my cheek and I kiss her once more, this time taking my time so everyone in the restaurant sees it.

"Okay, okay," she says, blushing. "You made your point."

I sit back in the leather booth, keeping her hand in mine and my eyes on hers. "I'm just getting started, Ryls."

She just shakes her head at me with cheeks the color of roses. Linda chooses now to check in on our table with a smile so big, I swear it must hurt. "Looks like you two are enjoying yourselves. I'll leave ya to it."

If we aren't small town gossip tomorrow, I'll be really fucking surprised.

I wake up in Deer Lake in a great fucking mood. I'm right where I want to be, with Rylee asleep on my chest, her body snug against my side. I can't seem to ever get enough of her, the morning wood that I'm sporting right now is proof of that.

It's mornings like this, when it's quiet and it's just us, that I'm going to miss most when she leaves. Normally, we would both have to get up right away to get to work but today we can take our time. I want to wake up this way for the rest of my life.

"Good morning," Rylee says in a raspy morning voice.

"Mmm… morning," I say, kissing the top of her head before she turns so that her chin rests on my pec. She looks gorgeous and sleepy, her cheeks rosy and her eyes heavy-lidded.

"How'd you sleep?"

"Great," I answer, tucking her hair behind her ear. Any excuse to touch her. "We have the entire day together. What should we do?"

"I have plans for us," she says, smiling against my chest.

"You do?"

"I do," her eyes drop to my abs while her fingers roam in lazy lines across them.

"Are you going to tell me what they are?" I ask, running my fingers down her arm, watching her skin pebble under my touch.

"Nope."

"That's it? Just 'nope.'"

"That's it," she says, as I lift her hand to my mouth and kiss each one of her fingers.

"Does it involve you naked and underneath me? Because if it does, I'm definitely in," I say, giving her ass a squeeze. She squeals.

"It doesn't, but I think that might be a great way to end our date."

"So you're taking me on a date?"

"I am. As much as I would love to stay here in bed with you all day, I have things to do," she says, pressing a wet kiss to my chest. "You can take your time. I need an hour or so and then we'll be ready to go."

She drops a kiss on the corner of my mouth and then pushes up from the bed. I watch her as she goes. I can't look away, from the golden glow of her smooth skin to her body, perfectly toned in all the right ways. Her tank has risen up, showing her stomach, which I'm aching to touch; the shape of her hips in her sleep shorts make my mouth water. She disappears from the room and I roll over onto my stomach, smiling into the pillow. I'm dizzy with happiness. Seconds later, I close my eyes and doze off back to sleep.

After breakfast, Rylee tells me it's time to leave for our date.

"Do I get a hint where we're going?" I ask. "What should I wear?"

"Just your swim trunks," she replies with a mischievous grin.

We leave out the back door and walk hand-in-hand through the fields, passing the barn and the apple trees. When we reach the path she finally shares her plans for the day.

"I thought we'd spend the day swimming. The water warms up this time of year, but it will still be really... refreshing."

"Just *how* refreshing are we talking about here?"

She scoffs. "Silly me. I forgot for a second I'm dating a city boy. You might not be able to handle it."

"Is that a dare, Rylee-Jay?" I tease as the lake comes into view up ahead. She narrows her eyes at me. She really does hate that nickname. "Because I'll have you know, I am famous for never backing down from one."

"I thought you are famous for your ability to make grown women scream?" she grins.

"Well, that too," I say.

She's kicks off her shoes, holding them dangling from one hand. The sun against her airy dress shows a silhouette of what's underneath. She makes me harder than I think I've ever been. She catches me staring and a slow smile spreads across her face like she's very pleased with herself.

She stops then and peels off her sundress, drops it to the ground and heads towards the lake, flashing me an *are-you-coming* glance. She's wearing a white string bikini, my hungry eyes getting my fill of her before she disappears under the water.

I don't think twice. *Fuck yeah* I'm coming. Hauling my T-shirt over my head, I kick off my shoes, following her into the water.

I gasp as I wade deeper, the cold water momentarily taking my breath away. Rylee looks back at me over her shoulder and laughs when she sees the expression on my face.

"*Such* a city boy," she teases.

I catch up to her and pull her against me, sliding my arms under her thighs to her incredible ass. The water is still shallow enough for me to stand. "Killing me in that swimsuit."

Wrapping her hands around me, Rylee locks her feet behind my back. "Good," she whispers against my mouth. "That was the plan." She kisses me and I kiss her back, pushing my tongue past her lips. I can't stop touching her. Her chest is pressed against mine, her arms tangled around my neck. When I finally manage to pull my mouth from hers, she shivers and turns her face toward the sun.

"You," I say, squeezing the two globes of her ass in my hands. "You are every one of my fantasies come true."

And that's exactly what this feels like. I have the most beautiful girl in the world in my arms. It's monastery quiet, only the sound of the breeze whispering through the trees breaking the silence. A broad span of turquoise blue sky stretches above us and the lake around us shimmers beneath the sun's rays. It's peaceful and still. It's paradise.

We spend the afternoon at the lake. When we start to get hungry, we towel off and walk up the hill to a tall oak tree. A blanket is spread out underneath it, a picnic basket sitting on it.

"What's all this?" I ask her as Rylee sits down, twirling her wet hair up into a knot at the nape of her neck.

"It's lunch," she says matter-of-factly. "Come sit."

"When did you have time to do all this?" I ask her, watching her pull two glasses from the basket along with a bottle of sparkling water.

"When you were sleeping like a log this morning."

"You did all this for me?"

"It's really nothing. I just wanted to show you what I like to do when I'm back home." I sit beside her, taking her in. I love seeing this side of Rylee. She's in her element here on the farm. It's easy to see how happy this place makes her.

Rylee goes back into the basket, pulling out a Tupperware full of pasta salad and another full of fruit and cheeses. Napkins and cutlery are next.

"This is definitely not nothing, babe. You planned a date for us. You cooked for me. It's perfect."

It's the best date I've ever been on.

"I'm happy you think so," she says with a sexy grin.

I love that grin. I do. I love the way her eyes sparkle when they find mine. I love how she's open and vulnerable and says what she feels, so I never have to guess. I love the sounds she makes when I'm inside her and the way her body fits mine like we are two pieces of a puzzle. She is so much more than just my girlfriend. She is everything I've ever wanted, and I'm starting to realize I will never find another woman that compares to her.

She scoops the pasta onto two plates and hands me one. It looks incredible, and I'm not surprised.

"Did you always want to be an actor?" she asks out of nowhere.

"I didn't spend my childhood dreaming of it, if that's what you're asking."

"So, how did it all happen then?"

"I fell into acting in high school and sort of just took to it. I was a sophomore and the girl I had a crush on joined drama class, so I joined too. The drama teacher thought I was good and recommended some acting classes outside of school. I started taking the classes at 16 and by 19 I was discovered by an agent who saw one of the casting tapes I had made. She was looking for talent for a teen sitcom and thought I'd be perfect for the leading part. I won the role and the sitcom was a big hit. That turned into a small part in a movie, which turned into another movie and the rest is history."

"You mean the rest is the beginning of Miles Bennett becoming a star."

I laugh. "If you say so."

"Why are you laughing? It's true. The whole world adores you."

"I adore *you*," I tell her, not able to hold it in any longer. "You're funny and selfless and one the strongest people I've ever met. You're good for me, Ryls."

"We're good together," she says, looking down at her hands.

I take her hand in mine and kiss her knuckles. Her eyes are back on mine, those emerald eyes rimmed in gold in the sunlight.

"We are. I like you a lot, Rylee-Jay."

Her smile twists into a frown. "Ditto, M.B. But a new nickname would work much better for me."

"What? You don't like Rylee-Jay?"

"I'm not 12."

A laugh escapes me. "Well then, how about Princess? Or Buttercup?"

She grimaces. "Those are even worse. And if you suggest Muffin or Sweet Cheeks next, I will hurt you."

"Oh, Sweet Cheeks. That one I like," I tell her with a wink, dodging the napkin she throws at me.

The two of us lie together under the Deer Lake sun, her head on my chest. I listen to her breathing and wish that we could freeze this moment in time when everything is easy and a life with Rylee seems possible. Filming in Vancouver will wrap in a few weeks and everything will change. Rylee will come back here to the farm, and I will go back to Los Angeles. And what it looks like from there, we'll just have to wait and see.

So for now, I try to memorize the scent of her skin, the

feel of her hair beneath my fingers, the way she fits perfectly against my side. Right now, I want to remember every inch of her and never, ever forget.

Chapter Thirty

R ylee

"You need to stop that. They're going to come looking for us soon," I giggle. We're in my childhood bedroom. Miles' arms are wrapped around my middle, my back pulled into his front and he's kissing my neck over and over again.

He laughs into my shoulder. "Five more minutes."

This guy. I swear.

"We are the only ones missing at our own farewell brunch. I can hear my brother and the kids downstairs."

I close my eyes, leaning back into him, enjoying our last few minutes alone together in this little room. For four days it's been our little oasis. Falling asleep together every night, and then waking up in Miles' arms every morning. It's been magic; maybe the best four days of my life.

That's why even though I know we should go downstairs, I'm not moving. Instead I breathe him in, ignoring the sounds of my family who I know are all wondering what we're doing up here.

"I wish we could stay here in this room for three more weeks," he says, like he's reading my mind.

"Did you like it here?"

Miles turns me in his arms, cradling my face in his hands, kissing me on the mouth, then the tip of my nose, then my forehead. He pulls back to face me with a look in his eyes that makes my skin begin to tingle. "I love it here. I hope you'll invite me back someday."

I shiver. Only Miles has ever made me shiver with just a few words. "What was your favorite part?"

"You naked underneath me in your childhood bed."

"Miles," I say, stretching his name into two syllables. "Did you really just say that?"

"What?" he asks playfully. "Okay, I change my mind. I think it was when you gave me that hand job in the lake."

I burst out laughing, putting my hand onto his hard chest and pushing him backwards. I stand with one hand on my hip, the other pointing to the door. "Out," I tell him. "Downstairs you go."

He laughs, flashing me that Miles Bennet smile I love, completely enjoying the rise he just got out of me.

"Now," I say, shaking my head at him with my arms crossed over my chest, mock- chastising him for his coarseness.

He turns to leave, but pauses at the door, turning to look at me.

"It wasn't either of those times, although I loved the shit out both of them. It was sitting on the porch swing with you looking at the sky, the fireflies brighter than the moon. It was sitting around the dining room table with your family eating homemade corn bread and casseroles and listening to stories of what a do-gooder you were. And I want to do it all again with you soon."

He disappears down the hall and I swear he takes my heart with him.

After lunch, we say our goodbyes to my grandparents, Cole, Cara and the kids. I already miss them, and I know they'll miss me too. And then there's Miles. He's the most charismatic man I've ever met. I have no doubt that my grandparents adored him, especially my gran. As soon as I walked into the kitchen and saw him mashing that pot of potatoes, I knew he'd won her over. She rarely accepts help in the kitchen, but she seemed to make an exception for Miles. Seeing the two of them together made my heart so happy.

It won't be long before I'm back in Deer Lake for good. The thought of being back on the farm with my family fills me with warmth. Except that also means that Miles and I will be going our separate ways. I know that an A-list movie star and a country girl from Tennessee don't belong together – I'm not *that* naïve. I have always known that things with him would come to an end, but that doesn't make it any easier.

I'm not ready to let him go.

Chapter Thirty-One

Miles

Rylee is leaving Vancouver tomorrow, catching a flight home to Tennessee. I head back to L.A. on Sunday. We decide to spend our last night together at the rental house with some take-out Thai food.

Since arriving home from Deer Lake, we've managed to make the most of our last few weeks together in Vancouver. The movie wrapped three days ago, and we celebrated over thin crust pizza and beer with the cast at an Italian restaurant. We went together as a couple, and it felt good being out in public with Rylee. She's getting a little more comfortable being in public with me, getting used to tuning out the cameras and noise. Most of my cast-mates were surprised to find out Rylee and I are a couple – proof that we did a good job keeping it under wraps. Everyone seemed genuinely happy for us. Everyone except Violet, that is. Something seemed to be stuck up her ass all night. *Hashtag-not-my-problem.*

Rylee checked out of her hotel a few days after we returned from Deer Lake and has been staying at my rental house since then. We've basically hidden ourselves away from the rest of the world, only leaving to go to work or pick up food. We've had an incredible amount of sex – whenever and wherever we can, usually unable to stop long enough to make it to the bedroom. She's become my addiction. It's going to crush me to watch her leave.

We've talked a lot too. About life after Vancouver. The movie I'm working on next. Her search for somewhere to live in Deer Lake. She hopes to buy a place instead of renting. She also needs to buy a car and furniture and find a job. I want to help her with all of those things, because I can, but she won't hear of it.

I've tried not to count down the days, wanting instead to focus on the time we have left together. There's no point watching the clock. Tomorrow is going to come and she's going to get on that plane and there's nothing I can do to stop it. So for tonight, we've decided not to talk about it. We can do more of that tomorrow.

We're sitting on the deck off of the master bedroom, taking in the ocean view and eating our Thai food. It's a perfect Vancouver summer night, the stunning ombre sky a swath of red, pink and orange.

"Are you going to let me see them?" I ask, the sound of her camera click, click, clicking as she focuses on the sunset and then back to me.

She looks at me over her camera. "I will one day."

"One day when? I want to see them now."

"I need to edit them first, but I promise I will. Have you heard from Matthew?"

"Nothing," I say, picking up my phone and checking it again. No messages or missed calls from him. I'm waiting to hear on a project I'm being considered for and am trying not to get my hopes up. It's something I've never done, a recurring role on a series airing on a top streaming service.

She sets her camera down and reaches for my hand. We slide our fingers together. "You'll get the part. They'd be crazy not to give it to you."

My heart hurts a little more in my chest. Knowing this is our last night together is slowly breaking my heart. It also feels really fucking good because having her support is something I didn't know I was missing.

"I'm going to miss this house," I tell her, taking a bite of my green curry.

"I'm going to miss Vancouver. It will always be ours," she says, her voice breaking at the end of her sentence.

I brush my thumb over her knuckles. Her skin breaks out in goosebumps. Her gaze drops to our joined hands and I can see the tangle of emotions threatening to take her under. "Ryls, baby, we're going to be okay."

Her wet eyes flicker up to mine. "I don't want to do this on our last night together. I'm sorry."

"So, let's not. Let's talk about something else." This would all be a little easier if we knew when we could see each other again. If we had a date on the calendar to look forward to. But we don't, so for now we are forced to take it one day at a time.

She stares at the horizon, pulling her knees into her chest, then looks at me. "I better be the first person you call when Ellie has her baby."

I laugh. "There's a good chance she'll call you before me."

"Are you excited to become an uncle soon?"

"Hell yeah. I'm going to make sure that kid's first word is Miles."

She laughs, staring out at the boats sailing by. I knew tomorrow would eventually come, and I knew it was going to be hard, but nothing could have prepared me for what this would feel like. It's like a fastball hitting me square in the chest. I desperately want her to stay.

"Being an uncle will be your best role yet, I'm sure." The look in her eyes levels me. It's an *I-miss-you-already* look.

My chest tightens.

My throat aches.

Rylee is leaving me tomorrow.

I pull her up from the chair, grabbing her face in my palms. I kiss her lips, her chin, her jaw. She leans her head to the side so I can kiss her neck. "I'll visit the first chance I get. I promise," I say, wrapping my hand around the back of her head, fusing my lips to hers. "Now let's get in bed. Tonight is our last night in this house and I plan on making the most of it. I might not let you leave."

"I might be okay with that," Rylee replies, then wraps her arms around my waist, kissing me.

I back her into the bedroom without breaking the kiss. We stop at the foot of the bed and undress each other slowly. Taking our time like we have an abundance of it when really the clock is ticking. Soon, we're naked and needy, hands all over each other. It's sexy, it's hot and we're desperate for more. Both painfully aware that this could be our last time together.

She'll be gone tomorrow.

And somehow life will go on.

I'm going to miss this.

Rylee made us breakfast this morning – scrambled egg sandwiches with a bowl of mixed berries on the side – and my stomach is happy.

We're sitting on the deck, the morning air still chilly but not cool enough to force us back inside. Her long, bronze legs are stretched out, resting on the chair beside her. She's in nothing but my T-shirt. I've decided it's the look I like best on her.

"You never did teach me how to make these," I say, referring to her famous breakfast sandwiches.

She arches a brow, setting her coffee cup down on the table, "They are scrambled eggs. Miles, how are you 26 years old and you still don't know how to scramble an egg?"

I laugh. "You may not have realized, but I'm a momma's boy and this boy's momma enjoys cooking for her kids. I've never had to learn."

She smirks. "I don't know what I'm supposed to do with you."

All I hear is innuendo because I'm a guy and I'm rarely not thinking about sex. "I know exactly what you could do with me," I say, leaning in close to her, kissing the sensitive skin under her ear. This is my last chance to get my fill of her and I don't plan on wasting a second.

"Mmm. Do that again," she says, tipping her neck to give me better access. I'm only too happy to give her what she wants.

"But Miles?" she sighs. "There's just one problem."

"What's that?" I ask her, my voice low and gravelly. "I don't see how me being inside of you could ever be considered a problem."

She turns her head to face me. "That's because you are insatiable."

"When it comes to you, I can never get enough. I seem to recall you wanting me again and again last night too."

Rylee taps her finger to her temple pretending to consider this. "Really? What *exactly* do you recall?"

"Every single second," I say in between kisses down the slope of her neck. "Fuck, Ryls, it was so hot." And it was. It always seems to surprise me how badly I want her. Once is never enough with her. But I don't think it's just the sex. In fact, I know it's not. It's everything that comes afterwards too. Having her in my arms, savoring every second with her.

Rylee swallows, her eyes darkening, locking with mine. "It's always amazing with you. It always feels incredible."

"So, we should do it again. Right now. And maybe not just once."

"We should…" she says, so I immediately lean in to kiss her, before she stops me with her finger to my chest. "The problem, Miles. Remember? We have one problem."

"I already forgot," I mumble the words, my mouth hot on her neck again.

She giggles and I want to record that sound so I can play it back on repeat after she goes. *After she goes.* How am I ever going to be able to say goodbye to her?

"You have a meeting to get to and you can't be late."

"Then I'll cancel it. I don't care about the meeting. I only care about you."

"I also need to go and pack. Someone kept me very bust last night. So busy that I didn't have time to pack for my flight."

"I'll cancel my meeting *and* your flight then," I tease, with a wicked grin. *If only that was a possibility.*

She sighs. The sound hits me in my core, reminding me of the 2,000 miles that will be between us after today. But I know I can't only think about myself and my feelings right now. She wants to be with her family, and I need to man up and support her.

"What can I do to help?" I ask her, brushing an errant strand of hair away from her face.

"You're sweet, but I'll be fine."

"Let me at least take you to the airport then."

"Miles, we talked about this. You'll be in your meeting. I can take an Uber," she answers, her voice taking on a more serious tone. She's referring to our conversation at lunch yesterday. Despite my best efforts to persuade her to let me drive her, Rylee was adamant that she would go to the airport alone. I think she might be scared of goodbyes. After everything she's been through, I can't say I blame her.

I scratch my jaw, trying to make sense of it all. Her leaving. Me staying. Our last morning together. Sleeping all alone tonight. I want her to stay. I don't want to do the long-distance thing. But I also don't want to stand in her way. So if long-distance is the only way to keep her, so be it. I want her to be happy, but for me happiness is being with her 100 percent of the time.

I wish we could figure it all out. I kiss her lips softly, wishing I could find the right words to say. My head is a mess. My stomach is in a knot. I pull back, trying to remain calm, but I need to tell her how I feel. I want her to know that I'm all in with her. I want to ask her to stay.

I clear my throat. "I admire you, Ryls," I begin. "So fucking much. I know how much your family means to you. Your grandparents are damn lucky to have you," I tell her, running my fingers over her cheek.

"I see it so differently," she says with warmth in her emerald eyes. "I'm lucky to have them. They saved me, Miles."

It feels like I've been sucker punched. No matter how badly I want her to stay, I know I can't ask that of her. The look in her eyes makes it obvious that Deer Lake and the people who live there mean everything to her. I can't make this more difficult on her than it needs to be. I have to let her go.

"I'm going to miss you. You know that right?"

She offers me a small smile. "I know. I'm going to miss you too."

"We're going to talk every day," I tell her. "We can FaceTime. We can also FaceTime naked. You'll be sick of me in no time."

She presses a chaste kiss to my lips.

"Insatiable… that's what you are," she says, holding my face. "And I look forward to it." She kisses me again, but this time it feels laced with desperation.

I groan. "You realize this is not helping my situation right now." She looks down at my lap and my joggers that are severely tented. She covers her eyes with her hand, shaking her head.

"It's only you. You know that right?" I confess, needing to tell her, hoping she feels the same way I do. "I'm not going to be with anyone else."

"Miles…" she whispers. "I can't-"

"I mean it, Ryls. I couldn't be with anyone else. This is me telling you that I've fallen for you. So fucking hard."

It feels like the right time to tell her that I love her, because I do. I feel it deep down to my core. I want her to know, but it would only make it harder for her to leave. I can't do that to her.

"I wouldn't be able to be with anyone else either." *Fuck.* I love this woman. I love her so damn much.

Neither one of us saw *us* coming. We weren't looking for love or a relationship, but we happened anyways. A wildly, unlikely chance encounter that we both couldn't ignore. We will always remember Vancouver as our beginning. The city I fell in love with Rylee Brookes. I'll do everything I can to make sure it won't be our ending.

I smile, finally letting out the breath I didn't know I was holding. We're doing this. We'll make long distance work. It's everything I needed to hear to let her get on that plane.

"We'll figure this out," I tell her. "One day at a time. I'm promising you right now we'll figure things out."

The conversation ends when I kiss her. It starts out slow and gentle, then turns hungry and full of heat. I fall more in love with this woman with every brush of her lips.

I kiss her like it's the last time. Her lips press against mine and I pull her as close to me as I can. I've fallen hard for her. Everything I thought I wanted out of life is changing, and Rylee is the reason for that.

Chapter Thirty-Two

Miles

My heart is aching more than I thought possible.

I just spent the best two months of my life with a woman who is incredible in every way. She's smart, courageous and genuine, and she has a heart as big as the sky. Most importantly, she saw me for me. She walked into my life and stole my heart. The only woman I have ever loved. No one has ever come close to making me feel the way she has. No one. Ever. *And she's gone.*

Rylee boarded a flight to Nashville today while I was stuck in my meeting – a meeting I would have cancelled without a second thought if it meant I could have more time with her. But she wouldn't hear of it.

Instead, I'm standing in front of the refrigerator looking for something to eat. Nothing looks appealing, so I grab a beer and an apple and flop myself down on the sofa. I turn my gaze to the clock on the wall for the 50th time in the last half hour, waiting for it to be 8:30 p.m.

That's when Rylee's flight lands, which means that's when I can call her. *Fantastic.* I've turned into one of those guys who can't live a day without his girlfriend. I've officially hit a new level of pathetic.

I stretch out on the couch, wishing Rylee was sliding in next to me. I turn on the television hoping for a distraction and flip through the channels, stopping at a sitcom I've been hearing about. In the scene, the two main characters are on a date. I watch as they hold hands and walk down the street. And all I can think of is Rylee. And as ridiculous as it is, it pisses me off. I'm envious over two actors in a fake dating scene. I flick the TV off. I've absolutely lost my mind.

In need of a distraction, I pick up my phone and search for a podcast. I scroll through at least a dozen before deciding I hate them all. I also hate everything about this house without Rylee in it. It's too quiet without the sound of her voice. It feels empty without the scent of her body lotion, without her camera on the kitchen counter or the pair of sandals she'd always leave just inside the patio door.

With a dull ache in my chest, I push up from the sofa and dial my brother Liam's number. He answers on the second ring.

"Miles. What's up?"

"Not much, man. How ya doing? How's Ellie?" I ask, walking over to the windows that leads to the yard.

"No baby yet, if that's what you're asking."

"I'd be pretty pissed if there was one and this was how I was finding out," I say. "How's Mom and Dad?"

"They're good. Dad's been busy at the office working out the logistics to get Parker moved back home. I think he's found a replacement for him out in Cape May and a new position for Parks in Reed Point. He's keeping it all under wraps, though. And mom, well… she's freaking out that we don't know what the sex of the baby is. She wanted to have one of those stupid gender reveal parties."

"Why am I not surprised?"

"How's Rylee?" Liam asks, and I realize that he doesn't know about her heading home.

"I guess I haven't told you. She's gone. She went back to Tennessee." So much for not thinking about Rylee. I think I made it all of two and a half minutes.

Memories of us together flash through my mind like a slideshow. The way she tilts her neck to the side so I can kiss her favorite spot under her ear. The freckles across the bridge of her nose. When she said she could never be with anyone else after I told her I was falling for her.

"And you let her?" My brother interrupts my thoughts.

"What the fuck was I supposed to do, Liam? That was always her plan. She wants to take care of her grandparents."

"Is that what she *really* wants?"

I'm pacing the floor. It's a habit when I'm agitated.

"What do you mean? Of course it is." I picture Rylee sitting right this second on the plane that's taking her back home. Is she excited? Or is she sad because she misses me too? Does it make me a horrible person that I hope she's as miserable as me? *Shut the fuck up, Miles. You don't really mean that.*

"Huh. I didn't think you were that dense," Liam says.

"And I didn't call you so you could make an already bad day worse."

Liam clears his throat. "Wasn't my intention. Look, just make sure you've thought about this from all sides. Maybe there's another way. I know what she means to you."

It's quiet for a moment while I let his words sink in.

There has got to be a way for us to be together. I drag my hand over my face, trying again to shake the images of her from my mind.

After I say goodbye to Liam, I strip down to my briefs and crawl into bed. I'm tempted to text Rylee, but it's pointless. She's at least an hour from her plane landing. Instead, I scroll through our old texts, reading and re-reading our last string of messages.

I lock my screen and let my phone fall to the mattress. I've officially made it eight hours without her. How the hell am I expected to make long distance work?

Saying goodbye is fucking hard.

I fell in love with her.

Now I have to figure out a way to live life without her.

Rylee

I hate the way I left Vancouver. After we had breakfast on his patio I made sure Miles left for his meeting. But once he was gone I couldn't bear the thought of staying one more minute in that house. It took me all of 10 minutes to change out of his T-shirt and into my own clothes and call an Uber to take me to the airport.

That was five days ago.

I walk to my grandparents' kitchen in my bathrobe, my hair wrapped up in a towel. My gran is at the stove making lunch.

"For you," she says, handing me a glass of sweet tea. "Have a seat at the table. I'm making pan-fried chicken and field beans. You need to eat."

A few minutes later, she joins me at the table with a heaping plate of food that she sets down in front of me.

"Now," she says. "Are you going to tell me what is going on with you because I can't take one more second of your moping."

I don't answer right away, instead reaching for my napkin and folding the corners into little triangles. I'm afraid that once I start talking, I won't be able to stop the tears that have been threatening to fall for days. It's only been days but my whole world feels off kilter. They say it's the first couple of days that are the hardest but that's a lie. Every day since leaving Miles has been excruciating.

"Spill it, Rylee-Jay. I've raised you since you were 13 and I know you better than anyone."

"Gran, I'm fine," I say, trying to convince her.

"How about you tell me why you're here in Tennessee with us and that gorgeous man who gets stars in his eyes every time he looks at you is in Los Angeles?"

Stars?

My heart swells hearing that, hoping it's true. But I still can't find the words to answer her.

"It's true. He loves you from here to hereafter and five miles past that. Anyone can see that."

I feel my heart crack in two.

I'm in love with Miles.

That's what this feeling is, the one deep down in my chest. I love him. I love how he makes me feel like I'm the only person in the world when we're together. I love his smile that lights up an entire room, and how he loves his family more than anything. I love the way he makes me laugh.

I know that I'm in love with Miles, but there is still just so much left to figure out. Being with him feels like an impossible dream.

"It's not enough, Gran. Sometimes all the love in the world isn't enough."

Besides, he never asked me to stay.

"Now that's as crazy as a betsy bug," my gran blurts. "I've never seen you as happy as you are when you're with Miles. He makes you all weak in the knees, which makes me happy because that's all I've ever wanted for you. To find someone who loves you like your daddy loved your momma."

She sets her hand on top of mine, her eyes wet with unshed tears.

My eyes well up too. I would love to have what my parents had, and with Miles that actually feels possible. At least it did. But I'm a realist. The fact that a guy like Miles Bennett ended up with a girl like me is hard to believe. Now throw in the fact that our relationship has to be long distance? Even I can see that the odds of it lasting are pretty terrible.

"You're miserable here and your Gramps and I can't take it for too much longer," she says. "You should go back to him."

"I'm scared. He's Hollywood royalty. He could have anyone he wants. My heart couldn't take it if he didn't love me back."

"Now you're just talking crazy. I saw the way that boy looks at *you*. He wants you." She raises her eyebrows. "The Rylee I know is brave. Tell him you want to be with him, sweetheart."

I want him too.

"And what if he doesn't feel the same way?"

"And what if he does?" she replies, her hand squeezing mine. "You'll never know unless you talk to him. You deserve love, baby. That big kind of love that's meant for romance novels. Tell him how you feel and then be brave enough to walk away if you have to."

I could tell Miles that I love him.

I could put my heart on the line.

I could take the leap and have faith that my poor heart won't crack in two.

I could be brave.

Chapter Thirty-Three

Rylee

The Sunny Side Up diner is full, with a line-up of people forming at the door.

Thankfully Cole and I scored the last booth in the restaurant. Having lunch with my brother is exactly what I need to distract me from the thoughts of Miles that are constantly spinning through my head. Spending time with my nieces and nephew is the only other thing that has worked.

It's been one week since I've seen him, and I feel like I deserve some sort of damn medal for getting through it.

"You're a saint, Rylee. You know that, right?" Cole says before biting into his BLT.

"Obviously, I know," I sass back. "But wanna tell me why you're stating the obvious?"

"You are living under the same roof as your 70-something year old grandparents, you cook and clean all day and all night, you garden, you make sure they're taking their medications and you never do anything for yourself.

If your picture isn't beside the definition of saint in the dictionary, I'd be shocked."

"You make it sound like a prison. I want to take care of them. I wouldn't do it if I didn't enjoy spending time with them."

"I hope so."

"Is that why you invited me out to lunch today? You think I need more of a life?" I ask, straightening my cutlery.

"Maybe. When's the last time you went out?"

I haven't been out since I got back to Deer Lake. I've been busy on the farm, trying to make things easier for my grandparents. And honestly, I just can't find the motivation to focus on my non-existent social life.

"You are going to lose your mind if you don't get out and start talking to people your own age," Cole warns.

"Awesome." I roll my eyes. "Happy to know I've become your charity case."

Cole swallows a mouthful of lemonade. "It's not like that. If staying here in Deer Lake is what you've decided to do, I just want to make sure that you're happy. We all want you to be happy. And from where I'm sitting, it doesn't look like you are."

"I'm happy, Coley. Honestly. I've been away for too long. They need me. Gran can barely do the stairs anymore with her knee as bad as it is, and Gramps is tired. I'm sure you've noticed."

"I have," he admits. "I get that you want to help, but you can't live there forever. You need a life of your own. Don't you want to get married? Have kids? I'm not sure how that works when you're living in your childhood bedroom."

If lunch with Cole was supposed to distract me from

my situation with Miles, that plan is officially failing miserably. Because now he is all I can think about. A life with him. A little boy or girl with his smile and my dark hair. My heart clenches and the familiar ache in my chest returns.

"Where'd you just go?" my brother asks, though I'm sure he already knows exactly where my mind has drifted off to.

I focus on my fingernails like they're the most interesting thing I've ever seen, a pained smile crossing my face. "I'm sorry. I'm good. I'm adjusting to life back home on the farm, that's all," I lie.

"Whatever you say, Rylee." He gives me a half-grin. "I'm sure he's just as miserable as you are, you know."

Cole's words send a waterfall of tingles down my spine-that my brother could be right. Tears prick my eyes for what feels like the hundredth time this week. The last thing I want is for Miles to be miserable, but the thought that maybe he is in L.A. missing me just as much as I miss him offers some strange comfort. Maybe being so far away from me causes him the same kind of pain I'm feeling. Maybe he even loves me, just as much as I love him. I close my eyes, rubbing a hand across my forehead. I can't let myself go down that road. I am in Deer Lake and Miles is hundreds of miles away in Los Angeles. That's not going to change.

I look up to find my brother staring at me, the concern clear in his eyes. He shakes his head, running his thumb around the edge of his water glass. "Cara asked me to invite you for dinner tomorrow night. Can you make it? The kids won't stop asking when they're going to see you next."

"Of course I'll be there."

Being with my family is the reason why I quit my job and returned home to Tennessee. I've already missed so much. Spending time with them is the distraction I need to make staying here in Deer Lake feel a little bit easier. With time, maybe I can actually do this.

When we finish up lunch, Cole heads back to work and I slip into the old pickup truck I've been borrowing from my gramps and call Miles. He answers on the first ring.

"Hey, baby." The sound of his voice sends goosebumps over my skin.

"Hi. Is it a good time?"

"It's always a good time to hear your voice, Ryls. I miss you. I miss you so fucking much. I wish you could see the smile on my face."

It feels like there are butterflies fluttering around in my stomach. I lean my head back against the old seat and close my eyes, steadying myself against the rush of emotions bursting through my body. "I miss you, too. So much. Hearing your voice is helping. I feel happy again."

"Me too," he says, his voice quiet. "I feel the same."

"So how was your day? Have you booked your flight to New York yet?" I ask, changing the subject to something less heart-wrenching. Miles is shooting a campaign for a high-end watch company.

"Georgia booked it for me this morning. I'm leaving next week, then I thought I could come visit you the weekend after."

"I would love that. I know everyone misses you around here."

"I miss them all too. But it's you I'm really dying to see. You better be ready for what I'm going to do to you."

"Promise?" I ask, knowing what that single word will do to him.

He growls. His voice is rough and low. "You're killing me, Ryls. Do you know what it does to me when you talk like that?"

"I have a pretty good idea, but you could tell me yourself."

"I am so turned on right now. I wish you were here with me. I'm going to have to take matters into my own hands."

I can hear the smile in his voice. My body feels like it it's vibrating from the sound. "We could FaceTime when you do. I'll be home in 10."

As soon as I utter the words, my hand flies to my mouth. I can't believe I said that.

"Dammit, Rylee."

Twenty minutes later I'm looking at Miles sprawled out on his L.A. bed, shirtless and wearing gray sweatpants. Gorgeous and driving me wild. I swallow hard.

My gaze is stuck on his abs, which are flexed with a happy trail right below them leading me to another part of his body that I also like a lot. I can see the imprint of him faintly against the fabric. *Find the will, Rylee.* You can't touch, but you can still look.

"You didn't tell me what you did today. I want to hear about it all," he says, absently bushing his fingers over his abs. I recognize the bedsheets; the same ones we slept in when I stayed there after the Artist Awards. My pulse spikes at the memory.

"You do, do ya?"

"Yes." He raises one arm behind his head and it's sexy as hell. My thoughts turn obscene knowing how good his muscles feel under my touch. How good he is with his mouth.

I snap out of it, focusing on his question. "I went out on a lunch date. You'd be jealous. We went to the Sunny Side Up and I had the patty melt. I think it was the best one I've ever had there."

"Killing me. You know I could eat three of those."

I swear there's a jealous undertone to his voice when he asks, "Who was your lucky lunch date?"

I decide to tease him. "A guy I know."

"Really?" he asks. "A guy. Hmm… I'm glad you made a friend but now I'm going to have to knock him out."

I laugh, knowing I've worked him up. Getting a reaction out of Miles is fun. "My brother, you dummy. I went out with Cole."

I watch the grid of his abs tighten and flex as he laughs. "Thank God. I won't have to kill someone. Did you see Cara?" he asks. "And the kids?"

"Not today. It was just me and my brother. It was nice. I get the feeling he thinks I'm turning into some crazy old cat lady living at Gran's. He's already foreseeing having to watch my two dozen cats one day."

"He's probably right."

"Oh, thanks. I appreciate your vote of confidence," I joke, sitting up on my bed, shifting to cross-legged. "I'll have you know I don't even like cats."

"Whatever you do, do not tell Ellie that."

"Why not?"

"She has a crazy, unhealthy obsession with everything cats," he says with a shrug, dragging his hand through his thick brown hair.

"That must go over well with Liam."

"It's Ellie, so he deals. She has him wrapped around her little finger."

I watch Miles cover a yawn with his hand. His hair is sticking up in a million different directions. His hazel eyes shift from playful to sleepy. And then he smiles, a lazy smile that I've seen so many times before. It's so unmistakably Miles. "You look tired."

"I am. It's been a long week. Too many early mornings. Georgia has me working like a dog. I think I've slept a total of eight hours over the past two days. Exhibit A: it's 2 p.m. here and I've already been hard at work for nine hours."

Innuendo is all my brain takes from that. Honest to God.

"You should get some sleep. I need to go anyways. Cole and Cara and the kids are probably here already."

Miles shifts on the bed, settling in under the duvet, his cheek resting on the pillow. His eyelids flutter closed for a moment and I admire his full, dark eyelashes fanning over his cheeks. "Talk to me for a minute," he says sleepily. "I don't want to say goodbye."

I smile. "You are going to fall asleep."

"Most likely. That's the point. Then I really won't have to say goodbye. I like hearing your voice. Keep talking."

"What am I going to do with you, city boy?"

"I could think of a million different things you could do with me."

Two minutes later, as I'm telling him about the photos I took for a neighbor, he falls asleep to the sound of my voice.

Chapter Thirty-Four

Miles

Georgia is trying to kill me. Over the next few days she has me scheduled for two photoshoots, a meet-and-greet and a quick trip to New York for a watch campaign I've been asked to rep. I don't remember what it's like to sleep in. Hell, I don't remember what it's like to get more than 6 hours of sleep a night. Although I'm exhausted, both mentally and physically, the upside of being this busy is that I don't have time to obsess about missing Rylee. Sort of.

We talk and text as much as we can, usually at night when we have a better chance of not being interrupted. She talks about looking for her own place, but I didn't think she's really looking. She enjoys living on the farm and spending her days with her grandparents. At some point I know she'll find her own place, and that will make her move feel more permanent. That's not something I like to think about. As long as Rylee is staying at her grandparents' place I can tell myself she might change her mind about staying in Deer Lake.

"I think it will work," Georgia says, looking at my schedule.

It's 7 p.m., the end of another very long day, and the two of us are in my hotel room not too far from Central Park. I suggested that we order room service, too tired to go out. I'm flopped on the couch in jeans and a T-shirt while Georgia sits in the armchair beside me in her usual business attire. Dress pants, a white silk blouse and a pair of modest heels. For as long as I've known her, she's never not in work mode.

"It will only work if it doesn't get in the way of my trip to see Rylee. You have those dates blocked out, right?" I sound like a dick. Those dates are months away but it's her gran's birthday and I would like to be there for it. Georgia is incredible at her job. She absolutely has the dates blocked off.

"Yes, Miles," she says, giving me her best *do-you-think-I'm-a-total-idiot* face. "Do I need to remind you this isn't my first rodeo?"

"I'm sorry. I know you're on it. Ignore me, it's been a long day. Any word from ActionFlix?" I'm still waiting to hear about the role I auditioned for.

"Not yet. You know I will call you as soon as I hear anything." I force a half-hearted smile while removing my new watch, dropping it on the side table. I rub the red mark on my arm that it leaves in its place and try to stifle a yawn.

I love being an actor and I plan on doing it for as long as I can. At this point I honestly can't imagine doing anything else. I've made over 15 motion pictures, always eager to start filming, never dreading the long days on set. But lately all I feel is exhausted. I feel like I'm a million miles away watching as Georgia fills my calendar like a giant game of Tetris.

I do my best to answer her questions, albeit not well, and we finally finish my schedule. I have a fitting for a new designer that wants to work with me, a bunch of interviews and my personal trainer is booked every Monday, Wednesday and Friday for the next three lifetimes.

It's been one month of missing Rylee. One month of phone calls, texts and video chats, wishing I could feel her skin against mine and inhale her summer scent.

I look up to find Georgia staring at me, clearly waiting for a response to something I missed entirely.

"What…?" I scratch my fingers through the scruff on my jaw, missing what she said. I know it's not Georgia's fault, but I still feel aggravated at all the things I have to do instead of the things I want to be doing. Like Rylee.

"I said you haven't touched your chicken. Is it not okay? Do you want me to ring room service and ask them to send you something else?"

"No, no, it's fine. I'm just not that hungry."

"*You're* not hungry?" She frowns, removing her reading glasses from her face, then makes a show of peering around the hotel room. "Are pigs flying?"

I smile. If anyone can shake me out of this funk I'm in, it's Georgia. She's always known how to handle me.

"You sure you're okay?" she asks, squinting at me over her computer screen.

"I'm fine. It's just been a long day."

"Okay, but if something is bothering you, you need to tell me, Miles. I can try and fix it."

"I'm fine."

You see, the thing no one tells you about long-distance relationships is that they're not just hard, they're fucking impossible. I'm only four weeks into this and I'm not sure how I will survive. I'm tired of missing her. I'm tired of counting down days on a calendar until I can see her again. I'm tired of not being able to focus because of the reel of images of her that are constantly replaying in my mind.

I also worry about her, and how she's handling the distance between us and being back in Deer Lake. This move is what she wanted, but that doesn't mean it's an easy transition after living in L.A. for so many years. I hope she's taking care of herself. I know Rylee well enough to know she puts everyone else's needs first.

"Okay, well, we're done here," Georgia says, closing her computer. "I'm meeting some friends for drinks at Dream Terrace if you want to join. It will be fun. You should come."

"Thanks G, but I don't know that I'm up for it tonight."

Truthfully, I'm not up for much of anything these days. There was a time not that long ago that I would never had said no. I was always up for going out. But tonight… I just can't. I have nothing left in the tank.

"Another time," she says, shoving her laptop in her bag. "I'll be at your door at 6:30 a.m. tomorrow so we can catch our flight back to L.A. Get some rest."

A couple of hours later, I'm lying in bed staring at the ceiling with a heavy feeling in my chest. I called Rylee after Georgia left, but she didn't pick up. She's been taking photos for people she knows to pass the time until she finds a job and I know she had a session scheduled for today. It must have gone longer than expected.

I reach for my phone, hoping by some chance I missed a text from her. *Nothing.* So I open her socials account and check her stories for a glimpse of her. I'll take anything I can get. She's posted a video of a field of flowers at sunset. Another of two little girls on a swing under a large tree. And another of a family holding hands, standing on a dirt road. The images come to life on my screen and I can't help but be so damn proud of her. She's incredible with her camera. The photos are fantastic.

I scroll her feed, needing to see her face. There are photos she's taken of the farm. Others of her and her friends. She's smiling, laughing. She's so damn beautiful and I find myself wanting to know the story behind every shot.

I type out a quick message to her before setting my phone on the nightstand and turning off the light.

Stalked your socials account. The photos are as beautiful as you. Miss you like crazy. M. xo

Then I stretch one arm over my head, resting it on the pillow, and realize yet again just how much I feel for this woman.

I wake up the next morning to a missed call from Rylee and a text.

I'd do anything to see you right now. Ry

Sitting up in bed, I video call her. I'm desperate to hear her voice. When she answers, I smile. She's wearing my sweatshirt and it makes me stupidly happily. I lean back against the headboard and she smiles back at me, her green eyes shining. I've missed those eyes.

"Hey you," I say. "How's my girl?" I run my hand through my bed-tousled hair.

"I'm good. Better now. Sorry I missed your call last night."

"It's okay. I knew you had the photo shoot. How did it go?"

"It went great. The family was so sweet. She's the daughter of a friend of Gran's at church. I guess Gran has been telling everyone she knows all about me. Word travels fast around here. I have two more bookings this week."

"Oh yeah? That's amazing. I'm really proud of you,

Ryls," I tell her, because I really fucking am. "Have you thought about starting your own photography business instead of looking for a job?" I ask her, watching her eyes roam over my naked chest.

"I guess I've considered it. But I don't know. I don't have any formal training. I'm not sure how much work I could really get."

"That's crazy. You have talent. Your photography is creative and beautiful. Every picture you take tells a story. I could go on and on."

"Could you?"

"I can."

"I'm sorry, I actually wasn't listening to what you were saying. I'm distracted," she says, her eyes on my pecs. "You without a shirt means I can't think straight."

I laugh, running my hand across my abs, teasing her, making her want me as badly as I want her right now. Wearing my sweatshirt, her hair pulled off her face, and she's not wearing any makeup. She's fucking breathtaking.

"Why is that?" I ask with a smug look on my face.

Rylee's lips curve up. "You know why."

"Remind me. I haven't seen you in a while."

"Isn't it obvious?" she asks, clearly trying to hide her smile.

"I still want to hear it."

"Because…" her voice changes to a more seductive tone. She blushes. "Your body is too much. It's perfect. It does crazy things to me. Are you happy now?"

"Almost. So, what you're saying is that you think I'm sexy."

"Oh, enough already. You're hot, Miles. I love your shoulders and how broad they are, and your chest and your arms and your hands... I especially love it when your hands are all over me. Not being able to touch you right now is torture."

I groan. I know exactly what I would do to her if I could. "I want you so bad right now. You have no idea." I get hot all over, thinking about sex with Rylee.

"I want you too."

"Maybe there's a way I can see you. I have an idea." I sit up in bed, feeling like a light bulb just went off in my mind. Why didn't I think of this sooner? "I'll shave a day off my trip home and fly to Tennessee. It would only be one night but it's better than nothing." It's my buddy's 30th birthday and I'm flying home to Reed Point for the surprise party.

"Miles, that seems crazy. You're already exhausted from work and flying across the country. You can't keep going like this."

"I don't care, Ry," I say, interrupting her. I *am* tired and it *is* a long flight just to spend 24 hours with her, but I will gladly do it. "I'm dying over here. I'll take whatever I can get. I'll have Georgia look into flights."

Her face lights up in the smile that gets me every time. "Okay. Let me know what she finds. I'm not going to get my hopes up just yet."

"I'll find a way. This is happening." I check the time on my phone, knowing I'm cutting things close. "I don't want to go but I have to. Georgia is going to be knocking on my door soon. We need to catch our flight."

"Okay," she says in a voice just above a whisper. "Safe flight today. Call me when you land."

"I will."

There's a pause. It feels like I should tell her I love her because I know without a doubt that I do. More than anything. I'm so fucking in love with this girl it feels like my heart might burst sometimes. But this isn't how I want to tell her for the first time. I want to be able to say those three words to her in person.

"Ryls," I say her name before she ends the call. "I forgot to tell you how beautiful you look."

I watch as her breath hitches and her eyes are sparkling with something that looks a lot like love. Then they go teary. "I'm not sure how we are going to do this. I miss you so damn much. I want to kiss you so bad it hurts."

"I know the feeling. It's the same for me, Ryls."

"You better go," she says, wiping the corners of her eyes with the backs of her hands.

"I'm sorry. I'll call you tonight."

I hop out of bed with a newfound burst of energy and a smile on my face that I'm pretty sure is impossible to erase.

I know 24 hours with Rylee will never be enough with her, but I'll take it.

I can't fucking wait.

Chapter Thirty-Five

R ylee

My niece Belle is perched on a pony at my grandparents' farm. She's wearing faded jean overalls and cowboy boots, her long, wavy ponytail floating behind her. It's possibly the sweetest thing I've ever seen. I get a little closer to snap a photo with my iPhone and then send it to Miles. He's always the first person I think of when I want to share moments like these.

> Rylee: Belle on a horse. I dare you to find something cuter.

> Miles: She wins. Not even a baby duck in a bowtie could beat that.

> Rylee: I've never seen a baby duck in a bowtie, but you're right; definitely not even close.

I return my gaze to Belle and my brother Cole, who is leading the pony in a circle. Cara will be here soon with

Lainey and Noah, who were napping when my brother left the house. Seeing my niece learning to ride brings back old memories of me and my daddy. I remember being her age and begging him to take me riding. He rarely said no.

> Miles: She looks like a pro up there on that horse. Now I need a picture of you <3

Flipping my screen to selfie mode, I snap a photo. My hair is pulled back into a messy bun and the only bit of makeup I'm wearing is clear lip gloss. It won't matter to Miles. I already know what he'll say. *You look beautiful.*

He texts back right away, and it's exactly the response I predicted. I laugh.

> Rylee: Are you just saying that because I'm seeing you soon and you want me to give you multiple, brain-numbing orgasms? I'm a sure bet, Miles. No sweet talking necessary.

> Miles: I never lie. But YES, that's exactly what I want you to do!!! I added the exclamation points to show you how much.

I laugh again, about to ask him what he's up to, when Cara appears beside me. "What's so funny over here?"

I turn, happy to see her. She has a sleepy-looking Noah in her arms, and Lainey is following close behind holding Gran's hand. My sister-in-law catches Cole's eye and his face lights up. They've been giving each other these looks since they were teenagers. I can't help but feel envious at how easy their relationship has been.

"Hello my sweet Lainey-girl. How was your nap?" I ask her, tickling her side. She squirms against my hand and giggles.

"This girl loves her sleep. She takes after her momma," Cara says, ruffling her hair.

"We're all so happy you're here, Rylee," Cara says. "I know Cole likes having you closer and the kids think their auntie Ry is the coolest. Not to mention what a help you are to Gran and Gramps." She slowly rocks back and forth on her heels with Noah still in her arms. "I know your brother isn't always the best at expressing his thoughts, but he really appreciates you being there for them. He sleeps better at night knowing you're there. We just really appreciate everything you do for them. I hope you know that."

"I do. Thanks, Cara. I really like being back home too."

"But-"

"No buts," I interrupt her, shaking my head. "I was gone a long time and it feels good to be back. I like being able to see the kids whenever I want. I like spending time with you and my brother. The movies were wearing on me. It was time to come home."

"Right," she says, but something in her voice makes me think she doesn't believe me. "Do you think you'll stay permanently?"

"I have no plans to leave." I pause, clearing my throat. What I told Cara is the truth. I am happy to be back in Deer Lake, and it feels good to be near my family again. What I didn't tell her is that I miss Miles every single day, and that part of me worries that by being here I am missing out on a real shot with him.

"You miss him like crazy, Rylee," she says, reading my mind. "It's okay to admit."

I nod, a lump forming in my throat. All I want is for him to be here with me. "I've been missing him a little harder lately."

"I know. I can tell. Was it him you were texting when I

got here earlier?" She asks, shifting Noah onto her opposite hip.

"That obvious?"

"Well, it was hard to miss that love-struck look on your face," she says, making me blush. "He's a great guy. Your brother even thinks so and that's saying something. He's damn easy on the eyes too."

She gives me a wink, and I laugh, thankful to her for lightening the mood a little. "I guess I haven't told you yet. Miles is coming for a visit next week. He's only here for 24 hours but it's better than nothing. I need it. We both do."

She smiles, grasping my wrist in her hand. "I'm so happy for you. I'm guessing we won't be seeing him? I'm assuming you're going to want him all to yourself."

She's right, I do. "You guys will understand if we don't have time for a visit this time?"

"We absolutely will understand. I'll make sure to talk to your brother."

I scrunch up my nose. "That will be a cringey conversation."

"I'm not going to tell Cole that there won't be time for a visit with Miles because his sister wants to bang him into next year, if that's what you're worried about."

My jaw drops and I look over my shoulder to see Gran and Lainey busy filling the watering trough. "If Gran just heard that I will hurt you. You're going to give the poor woman a heart attack."

I spend the next couple of hours chasing after the kids, taking them for turns on the pony and pushing them on my old rope swing. Belle, Lainey and Noah are exactly the distraction I need.

When the three of them are finally worn out, Cole piles them into the truck to head home for baths and bedtime.

"I could use a break," Cara announces, and I don't miss the sideways glance she gives to my brother. "Rylee, let's go into town for a drink. Come keep me company."

I have a feeling it's just an excuse that Cara and my brother concocted to get me out of Gran's house and around people my own age, but I don't argue with her.

The night life options in Deer Lake are pretty limited, so we end up at The Golden Boot for a drink. It's Friday night, so the place is pretty packed, but we manage to find a table. As we weave through the crowd, we pass a group of girls I recognize from high school. Cara says a quick hello, while I nod and smile. It's been so long since I've seen most of them, I'm not sure what to say. Small towns are welcoming and warm, but they can also be small-minded. Some folks don't forgive you very easily when you leave.

Cara and I slip into our booth, ordering a beer each. I'm aware some folks are staring, I can feel their eyes on me, but I do my best to ignore them. Cara needs this night out just as much as I do so I'm determined to give her my full attention.

"You remember Brenna, Emily and Taylor, right?" she asks, referring to the table of girls we just passed. "They're the same age as Walker. Between you and me, I swear Brenna is waiting for him to come home from the Marines. She's always asking Cole and I about him with this dreamy, hopeful look in her eyes. I bet she comes over here and tries to strike up a conversation with you."

Brenna dated my brother Walker in senior year. I'm not sure why they broke up, but I know she took it hard. I hope Cara is wrong, and Brenna's not actually still hung up on him. Waiting for someone for over five years – someone you haven't seen or talked to, who's living hundreds of miles away – sounds like a form of punishment. But then again, I guess I'm not that far off.

I try to brush that sad and depressing thought away and take a sip of the beer that the waitress just set down.

"And what about the other two? Are they married? Kids?" I ask.

"Emily is married with two kids. She married Casey Austin, he's a mortgage broker now. Do you remember him? Taylor was married to a guy she met from Nashville, but he cheated on her and then left her for the other woman. It was a big scandal around here. People were talking about it for months. I felt really bad for her. She barely left her house when it first happened, but eventually the talk died down."

"That's awful. Poor girl. Is she dating again?"

"I'm not sure. I doubt it's easy living in this town after something like that. By the time you're ready to meet someone again, the good ones have all been taken."

Cara's right. I hate to even go down this path, but what if things don't work out with Miles? If I'm being painfully honest with myself, the chances are high that they won't. Long distance dating is impossible at the best of times, but throw in two people who are obviously mismatched and it becomes a disaster just waiting to happen. Where would I go to meet a guy around here? And between taking care of my grandparents and working, where would I find the time to date? I take a deep breath, trying to clear my head. There's no point getting ahead of myself. What I really need to focus on now is finding a job.

"The good guys aren't the only things that are taken. Seems like the good jobs are as well." I sigh.

"Haven't found anything that interests you?"

"Not one," I reply, picking at the edge of the label on my beer bottle. "Although to be fair, I haven't spent a ton of time looking. I don't know what I want to do. The movie industry is all I've ever done, and that's not something I'll find around here."

"No, you won't," Cara agrees. "I'll ask around and see what I can find for you. You never know, your dream job just might be waiting for you."

Before I can answer her, Brenna and Taylor – the girl who might still be into my brother and the girl who was cheated on, in that order – are standing at the end of our table. "We hope we're not interrupting," Brenna says with a huge smile. "Rylee, it's just been so long since we've seen you. How are you doing?"

Part of me – the nicer part – thinks it's sweet of them. However, the insecure, inner teenager in me is skeptical. I go through the motions, exchanging pleasantries and saying the things people say in situations like these.

"I'm good, thanks for asking. Happy to be back and closer to my family."

"Will you be staying?" Brenna asks, twirling the straw around in her drink.

"That's the plan."

"Is Miles in town this weekend? Or maybe I shouldn't ask?"

And there it is. I wondered how long it would take for his name to come up. The last thing I want to talk about is Miles. I feel the need to protect what we have. It's obvious Brenna is interested in getting the scoop and nothing more. I take a drink of my beer and as I do I notice Cara's smirk. I can tell she feels the same.

"Miles is visiting soon." I leave it at that.

"You should bring him around here more. Introduce us to him." She sips from her drink while Taylor stands awkwardly beside her.

I nod but stay silent. They don't want to hear what I really want to say.

When they finally return to their own table, I am left thinking about what it must be like to be Miles. To never know if people like you for the person you are or just because you're a celebrity. My encounter with Brenna felt a little like that. It left a bad taste in my mouth.

When I'm paying my bill about an hour later, Miles texts, asking me how my night went. I stare at the screen, a jumble of emotions welling up inside me. Love, desire, longing, frustration. Most of all, I just want to see the man who makes my life sweeter.

Miles is happiness to me. And I miss him fiercely.

Chapter Thirty-Six

Miles

"Today's the day," I say as soon as she picks up the phone. "It feels like Christmas in July, Ryls!"

It's 8 a.m. in Los Angeles, which is 10 a.m. in Tennessee. It's been weeks since Georgia booked my flight to Deer Lake and I've been counting down the days ever since. I'm flying to Rylee first, for one day, before flying to Reed Point for my buddy's birthday.

I find a chair near my terminal gate and set down my duffle bag on the floor beside me. On instinct, I tug the brim of my ballcap down a little lower over my face.

"Why do you sound like you're out of breath? Are you feeling okay? Are you sick?" Rylee asks, concern in her voice.

"I'm fine, baby. Stop worrying about me. I just huffed it to my gate. We're boarding in five minutes, but I wanted to call you before I lost cell service."

I can hear the smile in her voice. "I can't believe I get to see you today."

"Believe it, Ry. I'm so fucking exciting," I say, listening to the flight attendant over the microphone announce they're boarding for first class. "But I gotta run, I'm boarding now. I'll see you soon, baby."

Hours later, I'm walking through the terminal doors when I spot her standing by the curb. She's wearing a pale-yellow sundress, cowboy boots and the biggest fucking smile. And she's mine.

I jog to her, flipping my hat backwards, dropping my bag at my feet. Rylee takes my chin in her hands, then leans in and kisses me. I take it a step further, deepening the kiss, my hand cradling the back of her neck. The second our lips touch, it's fireworks. Every nerve ending in my body lights up from the energy crackling between us.

She's in my arms.

I can breathe again.

We linger there on the curb. When I break the kiss, I drag my nose along her neck, inhaling her coconut scent. She smells so damn good.

"I missed these lips," I say, running my thumb along her bottom lip when we break apart. She tastes like peppermint from her toothpaste and her skin smells like the beach. I want my hands all over her, I want to make her remember why we're too good together.

The corners of her mouth float up and her cheeks are flushed, a light pink hue that matches the lip gloss she's wearing. "Come on, city boy. I wanna take you home. I want you to remind me what I've been missing," Rylee murmurs against my mouth before kissing me.

I can definitely do that. "Where are your grandparents?" I ask her.

"At a church luncheon." She winks, taking my hand and leading me to her car. "Perfect timing."

"Fuck." I groan, following close behind, feeling a little dizzy.

After what felt like the longest drive of my life, we are pulling into her gravel driveway. We both jump out of the car and I follow her into the old house. "How much time do we have?" I ask her, walking her backwards towards the hallway, slipping the straps of her sundress off her shoulders, pulling her hips into me.

"About an hour."

"Then we better make the most of it."

Taking her hand, I jog up the stairs to her bedroom, closing the door behind us. I push her up against the wooden door. "You are so goddamned beautiful, Rylee. I finally feel right being back in your arms."

"Me too. It's *you* that makes my life whole. I feel an emptiness when you're gone that nothing else can fill." She's kissing me as she says it. "It's only you, Miles," *kiss* "who makes me" *kiss* "feel complete."

Fuck. Her big, beautiful heart and the things she says to me. My breath hitches and then my mouth is on hers. I give her everything, kissing Rylee the way I've wanted to for the last two months, with heat and with passion and all of the longing that has built up inside of me. We kiss each other fiercely, my hands in her hair, hers clawing at my back. My tongue licks into her hers and she gives it right back. Stroke for stroke, we are desperate for this, to be back together, to erase the space between us that has been taking its toll. I want to show her that nothing has changed on my end. I want her just as much today as I did the day she left. But no, that's wrong. I want her more than that. She is all I want.

And finally, I have her.

The white-hot attraction we feel for one another is impossible to ignore. We're driving each other crazy, those long months apart driving us mad. Her hands find my ass while mine slip down her neck. I devour her mouth while my hands roam her chest. We're both breathing heavy, unable to get close enough. I'm so fucking worked up.

"Miles…" she whispers as she tips her head back and closes her eyes. It's an invitation to suck on her neck the way I know she likes it.

I kiss the smooth skin under her jaw, then her neck. "I'm going to remind you of all the reasons we are perfect together, babe. So fucking perfect." I growl, nipping her skin with my teeth.

"Yes," she pants. "Do that again."

I do what I'm told. Scraping my teeth gently over her shoulder, biting and nipping at her flesh while she moans and pants. I suck the silky skin on her chest into my mouth then watch her skin turn red, marking her, needing to feel like she's mine. "That feels so good."

I walk backwards towards her bed with her still in my arms and lie her down, hovering on top of her. In seconds I've tore off my T-shirt and jeans and I'm straddling her. Her dress is on the floor in a puddle too. I want inside of her so fucking bad, but I need to be open with her first. Honest and vulnerable, because that's what she deserves. That's how she is with me. "I've thought about you nearly every second of every day, Ryls, since you left," I admit, looking down into her big green eyes.

"I haven't been able to get you out of my mind," she says, her eyes flickering with want and desire and a million other emotions. I can feel them all over me, in me, like I am bathing in her.

"I'm sorry I haven't been able to visit more. It kills me that it's taken this long," I say, my hand moving up the sides of her body leaving flesh bumps in their wake.

"It's okay, Miles. You're here now. That's all that

matters. You're here with me now. I want to make the most of it."

"I've been miserable without you. I hate being apart." I drop down and kiss her, her head raising from the pillow to meet mine. Her eyes darken like they do when she's turned on.

Rylee's hand travels between us, gripping my hard-on, and it feels so fucking good. Her hand lets go. She's teasing me. I can tease her, too. I know how to drive her wild and that's exactly what I intend to do.

My arms are braced on either side of her ribcage, her chest rising and falling as her breathing speeds up. I bend down to kiss the space between her cleavage then drag my tongue up the center of her chest. Her breath catches and her eyes close shut. She moans a low and sexy sound as I make my way back down the same way I came, this time with the stubble of my jaw across her skin. Her back arches off the mattress, which gives me the perfect opportunity to slip one hand behind her back and unfasten her white lace bra. I throw it to the floor with the rest of her clothes.

"Yes, Miles. I love the way you make me feel."

"I'm only getting started." I plan on giving her everything I know she likes. Everything I know she wants. With everything I have. My hands, my mouth, my fingers, my tongue. We have so much time to make up for.

Her hands grip my ass over my briefs, and she squeezes, palming me, making me moan.

"Why are you still wearing these?" she huffs, sliding her fingers under the waistband of my boxers. "Off. Now. Naked. I want to feel every part of you."

I'm close enough to the edge of the bed that I can shimmy off the mattress and stand at the foot. I start to lower my briefs to the ground as she pushes up on her elbows to enjoy the view. I take my time pushing them down over my hips, freeing my erection while she watches with her lips parted. It's easily one of the hottest moments of my life.

Then she moves across the bed, looking up at me, from her hands and knees taking me into her hand.

Oh, I like where this is going.

She fists the base and gives me a slow stroke then takes me into her warm, wet mouth. Her tongue tortures me as she sucks me so good, while she strokes the base.

"Fuck, Ryls. So good." The room spins, and the only thing I hear is my pulse beating loudly in my ears.

I feel my dick swell and I know I'm gonna come but I need to be inside of her. "Baby, I need you and I'm almost there. Lie back on the bed for me."

She pulls off as I chase her onto the bed, kissing her and exploring her with my hands. "You're next, Ry," I tell her. eying her lace panties. She reaches for the lace, but I stop her. "I'll handle that."

She grins and I watch her skin pebble when my hands roam her thighs to her bellybutton. She shivers when the thin piece of fabric slips over her hips and I think I growl. *I fucking growl.* I want to devour her, to kiss and fuck her until everything else melts away and it's only Rylee and I left.

I pin her down to the bed with my hands laced in hers. She stares up at me with eyes that look drunk with lust.

"I am so happy you're mine," I say quietly.

Her expression shifts from desire to something softer as she releases her arms from my hold. She wraps them around my neck, pulling me down to kiss me. We kiss like this for a long while, taking our time and enjoying each other until I slide down her body and put my mouth on that spot. She moans, my face between her legs. I look up and watch her unravel.

I'm not nearly done when she reaches for my head and

tells me she needs me. "I can't survive another second. I need you now."

I go up on my knees and line myself up with her, pushing in, watching her hands fist the bed sheets. I pull back and push in again, back and forth until we are both writhing, coming undone. Her eyes on mine, never looking away.

I swivel, my hips sinking deeper, and I know we aren't going to last long. She arches her back and I watch her orgasm wash over her. I follow her, releasing everything I have into her, vibration after vibration sending pleasure through my body.

We both breathe out in relief. "Oh fuck yes," I pant. "I've been waiting for this. I don't remember the last time anything felt so good."

I feel happier and more relaxed than I have in weeks. A deep euphoria clings to my soul. I kiss her collarbone, her shoulder, then her jaw and I know it's not possible to live without her. I need to find a way to close the distance between us, and I will.

Waking up with Rylee pressed against me is a feeling I will never get tired of. Waking up knowing that I have to leave her in five hours to fly home to Reed Point is a different story. I could stay in bed with her all day. I could stay there for weeks.

We fit.

Once we dragged ourselves out of bed, we grabbed coffees and muffins and went for a walk. It was mid-morning and the sun had been shining for hours, the air warm and soothing like a balm to our skin.

We walk along the path to the lake and then keep

going. Neither of us seems to want to turn back, knowing that when we do it means our time together is almost over. My flight leaves for Reed Point at 2 p.m. I think we both feel the clock ticking.

"Are we good, Ryls?"

"Of course we are. Why would you ask?"

"I don't know. I guess I just need to make sure." My gaze rests on our intertwined hands. I haven't been able to stop touching her all morning. I am trying to get my fill of her, but I know that's impossible. I will never be able to get enough of Rylee.

The thought of going to bed tonight without Rylee curled up next to me makes my chest ache. It's a physical pain, one I've never experienced before. Heartache is a real fucking thing. But I brush the sad feelings aside and try to soak up this time with Rylee because that is the point of this whirlwind visit.

"I just want to be with you," she tells me. "I hate the distance between us, but I'll deal with it, to have days like these."

I stare at her, taking in the beauty of her face. Her eyes sparkle in the sun, spilling over with want. I lean into her, kissing the top of her head. She sighs.

"Same, Rylee. Same," I say into her hair.

We continue our walk without saying another word. On the property next door, Rylee spots a woman she knows – a referral from Gran, she tells me, she took pictures for her a few weeks back. The woman walks towards us with a handful of wildflowers in her grasp.

"Ah, it's good to see you, Rylee. I was just talking about you this morning." She gives Rylee a quick hug. "I was showing my sister the photos you took and she was blown away. She just got engaged and I told her she'd better call you up before the whole world discovers you and you're too big and busy for us here in Deer Lake."

"I don't think you have to worry about that," Rylee says, blushing. "I'm just happy you like them. Your family is so sweet, it was my pleasure. Sarah, this is my boyfriend, Miles. He's here visiting."

I hold out my hand. "Pleasure to meet you, Sarah."

"All mine. I'm a big fan," she says, shifting the flowers so I can shake her hand. "I heard you've been out and about in Deer Lake. The whole town is talking. It's not every day we have a celebrity around."

"I don't believe that. I've met Linda down at the Sunny Side Up, if anyone's famous around here it's her," I say, flashing a smile. "I definitely give that patty melt five stars."

Sarah's eyes go wide. "It's amazing, right? If you think that's good, try the mac and cheese next time. They put a Cajun twist on it. My mouth is watering just thinking about it."

I make a mental note about the mac and cheese, then Rylee and I say our goodbyes. I gesture to the path towards the house, but Rylee stays where she is, hands on her hips.

"What?" I ask her. "Why are you looking at me like that?"

"You are the most charming man I've ever met." She shakes her head. "You make everyone you meet feel at ease. I'm pretty sure poor Sarah has an even bigger crush on you now."

"She seems nice, but the only girl I have a crush on is you," I reply, grabbing her hand and pulling her in the direction of the path back to the farmhouse. "And on that note… have you given any more thought to starting your own photography business? Seems like you're a big hit. I knew you would be."

I can sense Rylee's hesitation. I wish she could see

herself the way I do. Her photography is better than any photographer I've ever worked with.

I tilt my head. "You're really, really talented. You know that, right?"

She's quiet for a few moments, like she's absorbing the idea. When she finally speaks, her voice is quiet. "I don't know. I've been thinking about it. I'm warming up to it."

"I'm glad. And I'm here to help you in any way I can."

"I know, Miles. Thank you."

We reach the end of the path as the farm and the house come into view. Rylee stops, pulling her phone out of her pocket. "Can we take a picture?"

"Absolutely." I want to remember this moment with her. A moment of bliss, pure happiness, *love*, before she slips away from me again when I board that plane in just a few short hours.

We turn our backs to the farm and Rylee's childhood home. I pull her to my side, clinging to her a little tighter, not wanting to leave her. I catch the scent of the beach that is so her. I close my eyes quickly. I haven't left and I already miss her. It's a beautiful pain.

I take it all in… tall grass, field flowers and my country girl with her arm wrapped tightly around my waist. Rylee snaps a photo. And another. Before she snaps the last photo I drop my lips to hers and kiss her. When I pull back from the kiss, she's glowing, a big smile on her face. It's how I always want her to look – like she's right where she belongs. With me.

"Hey, Ryls…?"

"Yes, Miles?"

"You've changed everything for me."

"Everything?"

"My priorities. My entire life. All the things I need to be happy. *You* are what I want most."

She goes up on her toes but doesn't kiss me. Instead, she cups my face and gazes steadily into my eyes.

Like I've given her the moon. Or maybe like she's just as in love with me as I am with her. My skin tingles. My heart skips a beat. Then she sweeps her lips against mine.

We walk the rest of the way back to the house, and I go upstairs and pack. Later, she drives me to the airport, and right before my plane is to take off, my phone vibrates with a message.

It's from Rylee. It's the photo of us we took today on the farm. The last one – the kissing one.

She follows the photo with a text. *My everything.*

My smile is instant. I fall for her even harder.

Twenty minutes later I'm on the plane, staring out the window as Deer Lake vanishes from view.

Chapter Thirty-Seven

Rylee

I'm going through the motions: breakfast, the market, taking Belle to school, making my grandparents lunch, doing a few loads of laundry. Later in the day I go to the cemetery. I bring my momma petunias, her favorite, laying them on her tombstone and place a painted rock that Belle made on my father's. I sit in the grass, filling them in on Gran and Gramps and my photography. I tell them how I quit my job and moved back home to be with our family. I tell them about Miles and how I think I'm in love.

The thought of them never meeting him crushes me. I wish they could see how talented and sweet he is, how witty and charming and handsome. I want so badly for them to know how much he loves Deer Lake, and Gran and Gramps. My momma, I bet, would get a kick out of the fact that he's a Hollywood movie star. My daddy would only care that he was treating his little girl right.

I spend a little more time under the sun, breathing in the clean, warm Tennessee air. Memories of my parents and my two older brothers and I flood my mind. Like the time my daddy tried to teach the three of us kids how to fix a flat tire or the time my momma drove me into Nashville to get my ears pierced.

Sometimes it still hurts to think about those happy times together, but usually the memories bring me comfort. I came to terms with my parents passing a long time ago. I found a way to move on.

My phone buzzes in my pocket but I ignore it, not ready for the memories to fade just yet. For a minute I can hear my daddy's voice and my momma's laugh. Closing my eyes, I allow myself to get lost in this walk down memory lane. It's peaceful and calm and quiet, except for the faint sound of the breeze through the tall grass. I suddenly feel so tired, and decide to give into it, lying back and letting sleep pull me under.

When I wake up I'm surprised to see that 45 minutes has passed. Gran and Gramps were at a church function this afternoon and I told them I would cook dinner. I rush home and head immediately to the kitchen, chopping the vegetables I need for the stew and getting a start on the dumplings. I set the lid on top of the pot so it can simmer just as my grandparents walk through the front door.

Once dinner is done, and the dishes have been cleared my gran and gramps settle in to watch an episode of Jeopardy and I finally have a free minute to dig my phone out of my pocket and check my messages. *Miles.* He's texted a few times. He's missing me, he's written. His day was long.

I walk outside to the porch and call him.

"Hey Ry," he answers, and I smile. His voice is exactly the sound I needed to hear.

"I got your message. I was going to text you then changed my mind. Hearing your voice is better."

It's been two days since Miles left Deer Lake. Being

with him for those 24 hours was amazing, but the distance is once again taking its toll. Now that we are separated again it's starting to feel like this might be impossible. Could this be the beginning of the end? The thought scares me. I can't lose Miles.

"I'm happy you did. Where are you?"

"I'm at home. I just finished the dinner dishes and now I'm sitting outside on the porch." The air feels cool, so I grab a blanket and drape it over my legs.

"Can you video call me?" he asks. "I want to see your face."

"I can. Give me a second."

"That's better," he says when his face appears on my screen. "Looks like a beautiful night."

Miles looks perfect, wearing a dark gray hoodie, his hair perfectly styled, and his jaw covered in dark-brown stubble. He's flopped on the couch at his parent's house, and I can hear his mom's voice in the background. My chest aches at the sight of him. It's a feeling I've grown used to – it never seems to go away.

I release a breath. "It is. Cole and Cara and the kids are coming over soon to sit around the firepit. The kids want Gran's famous s'mores."

"Sounds like I'm missing a good time. How was your day?"

"It was okay. I drove Belle to school in the morning and then helped Gran make a peach cobbler for her church luncheon."

"Sounds like Belle is loving having you around."

"She paraded me around her class like a show pony. She introduced me to her teacher like I was some sort of celebrity. It was cute," I say, tucking a few loose strands of hair behind my ear.

"Did she ask you for your autograph?"

"Belle?" I ask, confused.

"No, her teacher."

"Ahh. Her teacher is a he."

"Is he as handsome as your boyfriend?" he asks, and my heart does a dip. I'll never get tired of hearing that word. Miles Bennett is my *boyfriend*.

"Is my handsome boyfriend jealous?" I waggle my brows at America's sexiest man alive. His teeth scrape over his bottom lip, and I have to swallow a groan. Those soft lips that are like heaven on my skin. He's got to know what that does to me. What his face, his abs, his charm do to me.

"Maybe," he says, taking a swig from his water bottle. "Just thinking of you around another man makes my heart go all crazy."

"Don't be having a heart attack on me now," I say in an exaggerated southern drawl because I know what it does to him. "I'm finally starting to warm up to you."

Miles laughs effortlessly. He does everything effortlessly. His smile lights up across his face like a 10-foot-tall Christmas tree. He looks heart-stoppingly gorgeous.

"How's everything in Reed Point? How is your family?"

"Everyone is good. Not much new to report. I'm tired from the birthday last night so I'm staying in. Mom's happy about that." He sighs. "I miss you, Rylee. This whole long distance thing sucks. I hate going to bed missing you every night."

"I know. It's brutal. How many more days?"

"Twenty-four." He pauses for a second, his expression sad. "That's too many, Ry. I fucking miss you so much." There's a heavy weight in my chest that matches the sadness in Miles' voice. Why does our relationship have to be this hard? I stare at my phone, wondering how much to say. I could tell him that the distance between us is killing me or that I think about him nearly every second of every day. But would any of it make a difference? Or would saying it only make this harder on both of us? We've made the decision to live our lives thousands of miles apart. I left when all I really wanted to do was stay. But he never asked me to. So, here we are.

"I miss you too. How was your day? You said it was long. Are you okay?" I ask him, attempting to steer the conversation to less painful territory.

"I'm okay now," he says, leaning his head back against the leather headrest. "It was just one of those days where everything went wrong."

"Do you want to talk about it?"

"Only if you want to hear about how I sat around for an hour waiting on a producer who never showed for a Zoom call, got my ass kicked in a brutal workout that Georgia set me up with here and lost the part I auditioned for last week." He drags a hand down his face. "I'm looking forward to relaxing here tonight, watching the Yankees game with Dad and having a drink."

"I wish I was there to rub the stress from your neck. You look tense. I'm sorry."

"Don't worry about me, Ryls. Tomorrow's a day off, so there's nothing work-related on my calendar. I'm having lunch with the guys at Catch 22 before my flight."

"That sounds fun. You need it. Call me before your flight?"

"I will." He gazes at me wantonly.

"I better run. I can hear the kids in the kitchen and it's getting late. I better help Gran with the s'mores."

"Okay, babe. Say hi to everyone for me. I'll talk to you tomorrow." He takes a breath like there's more he wants to say. But he doesn't.

"Bye, Miles," I say, blowing a kiss into the screen and then tapping the end call button.

I force myself to get up from the swing and walk into the kitchen, where I'm met with Belle and Lainey, who wrap their little bodies around my legs.

My phone buzzes in my hand and I immediately swipe the screen to life hoping it's Miles. But it's not him. It's Meg. I stuff my device in my back pocket. I'll text her later tonight once everyone has left.

For the rest of the night, Cole, Cara and the kids, Gran and Gramps and I sit around the firepit eating s'mores. We talk for hours, about the kids taking riding lessons, about the photography sessions I have coming up, about Miles.

He is the only thing missing in an otherwise perfect night.

I hope we can get through this. We have to.

Chapter Thirty-Eight

Miles.

My morning started off with a 7-mile run. It wasn't that I needed the extra cardio, I get more than enough from the sessions with my personal trainer. What I needed was to blow off some steam, ease the ache in my chest, calm the frayed nerves in my body that felt like they were misfiring. I needed a distraction from the storm in my mind. In other words, I was a mess.

Seeing Rylee three days ago was supposed to help – it should have been the salve to the pain in my heart, but it only seemed to make things worse. It only left me wanting more.

I ran in the direction of the beach, adrenaline coursing through my veins. I pumped my legs as fast as they could go, past the coffee shop on the corner of First Street that I brought Rylee to when she visited last month. I shook the memory from my mind and kept running to the boardwalk and along the edge of the beach, hoping to escape my thoughts. But my mind continued to swarm with images of

Rylee. Her barefoot in that same sand, walking home after dinner at Catch 22. The night she met my family. All of a sudden, even Reed Point reminded me of her.

When I got back to the house I showered and changed then went down to the kitchen to make an egg sandwich. I check my emails while I eat, hoping for news from Action-Flix about the role I'm hoping to land. My inbox is empty. I refresh and still nothing.

My mom finds me there, sitting at the kitchen counter. Her shoes clack against the hardwood floor as she crosses the room to the stove and lifts the kettle from the burner to fill it with water. "Your sandwich looks good. I didn't know you could cook," she says, returning the kettle to the stove.

"I can't, but I've seen Rylee make these enough times so I figured I would try."

"And?"

"It's okay. Not half as good as hers are." The eggs aren't fluffy like she makes them, and the spice is all wrong.

My mom sighs, walks over to the island, and rests both of her hands on the counter. "What's wrong, Miles? I know you. You're not yourself. I hate seeing one of my favorite guys on the planet so sad."

Shaking my head, I look down at my breakfast. "I'm fine, Mom."

"Are you seeing Rylee next weekend?" My mom asks, the tone of her voice careful, like she is afraid to pry.

I shrug like an idiot. "Nope."

"Why not?"

"She's shooting a wedding which will take up most of her Saturday," I say, pushing from my chair, walking to the refrigerator, opening the door reaching for the orange juice. When I turn back I see my dad is in the kitchen doorway. He tops up his coffee and takes a seat at the kitchen table. In typical fashion, he will let my mom do the talking, then add his two cents worth at the end.

"You should surprise her anyways. I know she would love to see you."

She would love that.

"She has a lot going on, she doesn't need me there getting in the way," I reply, my mood getting the best of me.

She shakes her head. "Miles Michael Bennett, I'm surprised at you. Of course she needs you there."

"I doubt she would see it that way, Mom," I say with frustration in my voice, knowing it's a lie. I'm just in a shit mood and mad at the world. I'm on edge and I'm tired of this ache in my chest.

My mother crosses her arms and narrows her eyes at me. "Miles, this isn't you. My boy goes after what he wants. I've never known you to sit around and sulk."

"I'm not sulking, Mom. I'm just tired."

And I'm in love with her.

I'm also 100 percent sulking, but I'm never going to admit it. I'm pissed that Rylee is thousands of miles away and I can't stop thinking about her. I'm angry that my mom is right, and this long-distance thing is bullshit. And frustrated because I don't know how to fix any of it.

"Mom, I..." I start, then stop, not even sure what I want to say next. My mother suddenly covers her mouth with her hand.

"You're in love with her," she exclaims, her eyes instantly misty. "Miles? Are you in love?"

I try not to look surprised but can feel my cheeks heat up. There is no dodging this question. My mom has always been able to read me like a book. I sigh. "Majorly."

"Aw, son. I'm so happy for you," my mom says,

pressing her hands to her heart. "She is a great girl. Your father and I think she's wonderful. Right, Michael?" She looks to my dad for backup.

I couldn't ask for more supportive parents. I won the lottery being born to Michael and Grace Bennett. I don't take that for granted.

"We do. You picked a good one. You should listen to your mother. She's some sort of love guru. How do you think she landed a catch like me?" he teases, and my mom reaches over to swat his arm with a tea towel.

"Listen, sweetheart. It's time to stop sulking and do something about it. I can't stand to watch you moping around here all lovesick anymore."

"Are you done, Mom?" I ask, irritated, pushing my plate to the center of the island. She fills her cup with hot water from the kettle and sinks a tea bag into it. She rounds the end of the island, taking the seat beside me.

"I'm only worried about you, Miles. You've always been so stubborn. You love her, son. Don't let her get away."

"Mom," I groan. "I love you, but you don't know what you're talking about. Tennessee is her home. Her family needs her. She's happiest there."

I'm happiest with her.

"Says you, and that is not your decision to make. That girl didn't step out of her comfort zone for the whole world to judge her just so she could say she's dating a Hollywood star. She doesn't care about any of that. It's you, Miles. The real you. She doesn't love Miles Bennett, the movie star. She loves my boy, Miles Bennett from Reed Point. And I see the way you look at her. If you don't think that's enough of a reason to give this thing between the two of you a shot, then I don't know what to tell you."

I sit up in my chair, resting my elbows on the marble counter, my head in my hands. "I don't want to complicate things for her."

"You already have. You did the moment you decided she was worth risking your heart for. The moment you let her in and gave her a piece of the real you."

I blow out a frustrated breath, my gaze dropping to my phone and the lock screen photo of Rylee and me. It's the selfie we took at the farm. My arm is around her waist and I'm kissing her, a ray of sunshine cutting through the photo. She looks fucking breathtaking, and I would give anything to have her here with me right now.

"You have it all, sweetheart. The houses, the cars, the fame, the talent. Your father and I always knew you would. But none of that means anything without someone to share it with." She pats my knee with her palm. "I'm going to leave you with that."

She grabs her glasses and her crossword puzzle book from the counter then slips off her stool. "I love you, Miles, and I really like her."

"I know."

"I can see she means a lot to you. I hope she knows that. I hope you tell her. This can all be worked out." She kisses the side of my head.

"I love you too, Mom,"

For the rest of the day, I can't get my mom's words out of my head.

Someone to share it with.

I do want that, and I want it with Rylee. This distance between us is the definition of torture. Everything reminds me of Rylee. She's all I think about. Yesterday I struggled to learn my lines for a guest appearance I'm shooting, too busy remembering the feel of her lips when I finally kissed her. This morning I was 20 minutes late for a Zoom call with Matthew, distracted by a selfie she sent me. Then I spent the call in a daze, thinking about the constellation of freckles across her nose while Matthew talked to me about God knows what.

The truth is my heart is in Tennessee. My heart is wherever Rylee is.

Chapter Thirty-Nine

Miles

Twenty-four hours have passed since I've heard from Rylee. That may not seem like a long time, but it felt like an eternity. I've never been the type to text someone countless times a day – or even once a week – but here I am, losing my damn mind waiting to hear from her. I feel crazy, wondering where she was and why she hasn't returned my text. Is she having second thoughts about us? My mind feels like a blender, my thoughts spinning out of control.

I'm walking out of my personal trainer's when she finally calls. I pick it up on the first ring. "Ryls. Hey. I—"

Her soft voice interrupts me. "Hi. Sorry, I'm walking down by the lake so reception might be in and out."

"Are you okay, babe? I didn't hear from you and I got worried." The words fly from my mouth with zero chill.

"I'm okay." But there's a tone of sadness in her voice. *Fuck.*

She doesn't sound okay, and it immediately makes me

nervous. I would give anything to know what is going on inside of Rylee's head.

"Miles," she says, and the way she says it makes my heart sink. Something feels off. I have a bad feeling in the pit of my stomach. This doesn't feel like Rylee. Or like us.

Fuck. Would she really break up with me over the phone?

Break up? Why is that thought even entering my brain right now?

"Ryls?" I say, my voice soft. My pulse pounding in my veins. "I'm worried about you. Are you okay? You can tell me if you aren't."

"I don't want you to worry. I'm okay. This has… I mean… long distance isn't easy and lately, it's been really hard."

I wince, feeling like I've been kicked in the groin. She's not okay. "I know. I get it. I fucking hate it," I tell her, mad at myself for focusing so much on my own pain, for not realizing sooner how difficult this has been for her. I should have asked more questions. I should have been a better listener. I should have paid more attention.

"I'm sorry," she continues. "I'm the one who put us in this position. I feel like this is all my fault."

"Don't say that. This is not anyone's fault. This is our reality. It's not easy, but we are worth it."

"We are," she says quietly, and I pray that she believes it.

"I'm sorry this is hard on you. I hope you know it's the same for me. I hate being this far away from you. Please talk to me. I don't want you to shut me out." She's gone silent again and it's making me want to scream. I tell her what I think she needs to hear. "You mean the world to me, babe."

"I know," she says, another two-word answer.

"Tell me what's on your mind," I say. "I don't like it when you go quiet on me."

She sighs. "I think I'm just having a bad week."

"And why is that? Tell me so I can make things better."

"Truth is, I'm not really sure what is going on with me. I feel down and I shouldn't. I have so much in my life to be thankful for. I have my family, the farm, and more photo shoots booked than I can handle. And of course, I have you." I can hear the tears in her voice. My heart shatters.

"Miles, I'm going to be okay. I'm not broken. And I'm not going to suddenly decide I don't want to be with you. I'm just in a bit of a rut."

I unlock my car and slide into the driver's seat, yanking off my baseball cap and chucking it across the leather seats. I sink into the chair. My heart feels heavy. My biggest fear is that one day she'll realize she's had enough and want to end things. I wouldn't blame her. I know I don't deserve her. My life is chaotic. I'm not even sure when I will see her again, my schedule is so packed with promos and interviews. But I know now that I need to go see her. We need to talk. But when? My calendar is booked solid for weeks. I'm not sure how to fix this, and it scares the shit out of me.

Some days I want to scream or punch a wall at the thought of not being able to see Rylee. I'm starved for that connection. She's so far away. My head falls back against the headrest in frustration. There's no other woman for me. There's only Rylee. I am completely devoted to her, but I miss the touch of another person. Her hands on me. My mouth on her. Her heartbeat steady against my chest. I long for the intimacy that I only want from her.

There's only so much a man can take and I'm pretty sure I'm at my breaking point.

I arrive at Catch 22 to meet my brothers and my old high school buddies Dylan and Colten and Owen for lunch. I have to catch a 9 p.m. flight to Los Angeles later tonight, but it will be good to spend a bit of time with them. We try to get together whenever I'm in town.

A hostess greets me, holding open the door, ushering me inside. I follow her to a table on the patio where the guys are already seated. Liam looks up as I make my way toward them, nodding a hello. The waitress is at the table, handing out menus and taking our drink orders.

"I'll take a Coke," I say, sitting down.

"I'm starving," Liam says, opening up his menu. We all do the same.

While we're scanning the menu, we talk about work and families and give each other the gears, all of us catching up on one another's lives.

Dylan tells us about the girl at the gym who he's been wanting to ask out for forever. "At the pace you're going, D, I will have four kids by the time you ask this chick out," Liam tells him, rolling his eyes. "Man up. What the fuck are you waiting for?"

Dylan shakes his head. "You gotta make a girl want you. You can't rush the process. There are steps involved. You idiots could learn a thing or two from me."

"I'll remember that for future reference," Colten says. "If I want to die single and alone."

We all laugh. Catching up with these guys when I'm in Reed Point always reminds me how much I miss hanging out with them. It would be nice to just call them up for a beer after work rather than waiting for the three or four times a year I'm back in town.

My phone dings in my pocket. It's a text from Georgia

and I check it quickly in case it has something to do with my flight tonight. The good news – it doesn't. The bad news – Georgia has updated my calendar for the next fucking forever and left me with no free time at all.

I lean back in my chair, wondering where Rylee fits in to all of this. Maybe I should have known when I suggested long distance that it was going to feel impossible. Maybe I was too love-drunk to see it.

Parker looks over at me as I scrub my hands through my hair.

"By the way, you look like hell," my brother says.

"Thanks, Parks," I sigh.

I miss her.

"He has a point," Liam says from across the table. "You look like your dog just died." I feel five sets of eyes staring at me. My leg starts to bounce under the table.

Parker puts his glass of water down on the table and looks at me. "Okay. I've held back long enough, thinking you would figure this out on your own, but obviously you haven't, so here are my two cents." He taps the table with his index finger twice to drive his point home. "I've known you a long time and I've seen you with a lot of women. A lot is probably an understatement."

"Get to the fucking point, would you?" I warn.

"My point is," he starts, "I've never seen you act like this before. You're different when you're around Rylee. You're in love with her. Anyone with two functioning eyes can see that. And she loves you too."

"It's not that simple," I say, my voiced laced with frustration. "If it was, I'd be sitting here with her instead of you assholes."

"Maybe it could be. Does she know how you feel about her? Have you told her you love her?"

"No."

"Then you are an idiot. A massive, dense, incredibly stupid idiot. Why the fuck not?" my brother demands, giving me a verbal beatdown. I know the answer to his question, though it probably won't make sense to Parker. I haven't told her I love her because I don't want to complicate her decision to move back home with her grandparents. I'm making things easier on her.

"Because she left. That's why," I say, like the answer is obvious. "Her heart is in Tennessee with her family. She needs them. They need her too."

He scoffs. "She needs you, Miles. Most of all she needs *you*," he says, his voice softer now but no less insistent.

"She left."

I wanted her to stay.

I'm still so angry that she's gone. I'm hurt and sad and stuck in this terrible rut. Angry that she left and angry with myself for letting her go.

"She's probably scared. You never told her how you feel about her. Do you love her?" Parker asks, leaning forward in his chair.

I do love her, but I've never said the words out loud.

"Do you *love* her?" he repeats.

The table is silent for a minute. Simmering on the question, my heart sinks. I fucked up. I let her go. It's my fault that she left. I never told her how I felt. I never told her I was falling for her. The truth is, I've been falling for her for months. I never fucking told her that I *love* her.

I love her, I know that much, and I need her to know it too. To never doubt it. I've never been happier than I was during those days and nights with her in Vancouver. They were a dream. They were everything to me, and I want more of that. More of that magic we create whenever we're together. I need to fix this. Regret begins to claw at me, all the *what ifs* taking up space in my brain. What if I had told her that I was falling in love with her? What if I had asked her to stay? It's too late to go back in time, to do it differently. But I'm willing to do whatever it takes now for us to be together.

"I love her."

"Then you know what you need to do. Man up, M.B., and go get your girl."

Chapter Forty

Rylee

"Did you hear a word I just said?" My gran looks up from the kitchen table she's wiping, giving me a stern glare. She takes the empty plate from in front of my gramps, shaking her head at him. The gesture, I know, is meant for me.

"Listen to your Gran, sweetheart." My gramps sits back in his chair adjusting his glasses on his nose. This is how these two work. My gran tackles the hard conversations head-on while my gramps backs her up. They've been like this since I was a kid.

Admittedly, I didn't hear a word she said. I'm standing at the kitchen sink, washing the dishes and staring blankly out the window. I'm depressed and mopey and everyone in my family knows it.

"Rylee-Jay, we need to talk. We have news for you."

My heart jumps in my chest. What kind of news could they possibly have for me? What if one of them is sick? I grip the edges of the counter, soapy water from my wet hands dripping down the front of the cabinet.

Gran must notice that I've gone still, because she gives my arm a squeeze before handing me a dish towel for my hands. "No, sweet girl. It's nothing like that. Your gramps and I are fine," she soothes. "Now sit down."

She walks towards the table, taking a seat herself and crossing her arms over her chest.

Letting out a long exhale, I toss the towel onto the counter. I know better than to argue with her when she has something to say. I take the seat across from her. My gramps is at the head of the table. I have no idea what this is about, but they are making me nervous.

"We're moving," my gran blurts out of nowhere. "We're selling the farm."

"You're what? Wait… I don't understand."

"Gramps and I are moving to a seniors' place that we've had our eye on. A few of our friends from the church live there and they just love it. It's something we've been talking about for years and an apartment recently became available, so we took it."

I can't believe this. "Why is this the first time I've heard about this?"

"We didn't want to tell anyone until we found a place. And we knew you and your brothers would give us hell. We appreciate y'all taking care of us all these years, but we don't want to be a burden. Besides the farm is gettin' to be too much work."

"You two will never be a burden. I'm just sorry I haven't done enough," I manage to say. I can't imagine them anywhere but in this home, on this property. "Are you sure you want to leave the farm? You love it here."

"Never been more sure, honey. Wait till you see this place. They have bingo on Saturdays, ladies' night on Tuesdays and a yoga class three days a week. We can enjoy our lives instead of working our tails off around here. It's a good thing." Gran rests her hand over top of mine.

I can't help but laugh. "You're really going to go to yoga?"

"You bet I am," she nods. "You know your Gramps and I love you more than anything in this world but it's time you had a talking to. So listen up."

Taking his cue, my gramps stands up and presses a kiss to the top of my head before walking to the back door. "Listen to her, sweetheart. She's a smart woman." He winks at me before disappearing outside.

"Now, you listen," she begins in her *this-has-got-to-stop* voice. "I've let you wallow long enough. I've watched you mope around this old house for weeks. You don't go out. You're not seeing friends. You don't do anything for yourself. You've made it your full-time job to take care of your Gramps and I, and frankly, it's driving us a little crazy."

I sigh. I know she's right. My heart is broken in two. One half of it is barely beating in my chest, the other half is in Los Angeles with Miles. A tear slides down my face. When would this heart of mine stop hurting so bad?

"Come here, sweetheart." Gran stands from her seat, rounds the table and pulls me into her chest. Another tear slides down my cheek, soaking into her blouse. I'm not sure I will be able to stop the rest from coming. This cry feels like it's long overdue.

"You have a choice to make, Rylee," Gran says, pulling away from our embrace. "You can figure out a way to be with that handsome man of yours or walk away and find someone else who can make you happy. I'm sure there are plenty of nice men in Deer Lake who would love the chance to date you-"

"Gran…"

"Let me finish. This needs to be said. You deserve to be

happy and anyone who knows you, knows that you aren't happy right now. I know you love him, and I also know things are complicated. I'm not asking for you to explain any of that to me. I'm just here to tell you that there's always a way. Especially when love is involved."

Gran squeezes my shoulder one last time before walking outside to let me sift through my thoughts.

There are a million emotions rushing through me that I don't know what to do with. Maybe I'm having a panic attack. I'm not sure. But I *am* sure that I want Miles so bad that it hurts.

Maisy, my grandparents' dog, must sense my grief, because she moves closer to my chair, pawing gently at my thigh. It makes me want to cry even harder.

I rub behind her ear. "You want to go for a walk, Maisy-girl?"

I decide I could use the fresh air. I leash up Maisy and take her out the back door. We walk past the barn to the lake and keep going down the dirt path.

I want to call Miles and tell him the news about the farm, but I needed to think about what this means. How would this change things? I would miss the farm. It feels like the only place left that tethers me to my parents, and the thought of losing it causes a throb deep in my chest.

I take my time, letting the cool air soothe me. We take a loop of the lake before returning to the path. When the farmhouse comes back into sight I unfasten Maisy's leash, letting her run the rest of the way home.

I go into the kitchen to fill her bowl with water, then swing open the screen door to call her back into the house. I step onto the porch and freeze.

Miles.

He's standing in the driveway, a black duffle bag slung over his arm and Maisy right by his side. This can't be real.

It feels like magic. *He's here.* He looks more beautiful than I remember. He's wearing a gray Henley and black jeans, his ballcap flipped backwards on his head. I blink once, then twice, making sure it's really him.

He's smiling at me like he's the happiest person on earth and I know the feeling because that's exactly how I feel right now. His bag slumps to the ground and I don't think twice. I run to him and he catches me in his arms. It feels like home. It feels like I'm finally right where I belong.

All of the longing for Miles comes rushing at me, every single emotion I've hung on to over the last several months hits me like a Mack truck.

My legs wrap around his waist, my arms wind tightly around his neck. It feels like we're holding on for dear life. Afraid to let go. Finally, whole again.

When we finally pull apart and he lowers my feet to the ground, I just stand there staring at him. I must be in shock.

"Hi," he says, somehow managing to make one single word sound sexy.

"You're here."

"I am."

Is this real? Is this really happening? I must be dreaming.

My skin heats when his fingers tuck a loose strand of hair behind my ear. After all this time, it surprises me how much his touch affects me.

"I've missed you, Ryls."

"I've missed you too," I tell him, my eyes locked on his. "I can't believe you're really here. How?"

"I cleared my schedule. Georgia probably hates me right now, but I had to see you. I couldn't wait one second longer," he says. He's gazing into my eyes, and I'm totally and utterly lost in him. "You're the woman I want. I've wanted you since the moment I met you. I never want to go another day without you here in my arms."

"Oh, Miles," I whisper, running my fingers across his jaw, knowing what I need to do. I finally know exactly what I need to tell him.

"I hated every second being away from you. I need you, Ryls, with me. I don't think I could ever get my fill of you," he says, before he brings his mouth down on mine. The kiss is slow and soft and everything a kiss should be.

When the best kiss of my life ends, I know I need to tell him everything in my heart, everything that I haven't been brave enough to say until now.

"I was trying to live with only half of my heart," I confess. "But it was never going to work. I need you, Miles. You are everything I've ever needed. I can't live like this without you for one more second."

Sliding his arms around my lower back, he pulls me to him. Then his lips are back on mine, and he's kissing me until I can barely breathe. Soft kisses this time that taste like a promise of something more to come. Something that feels like forever.

When he breaks the kiss, his eyes gleam. My hands reach up and grip the nape of his neck.

"I want you with me wherever I am. That might make me a selfish prick, but it's the only way. I need you, Ryls. I'm all in with you. It's you. Only you."

"What are you saying, Miles?"

"I'm saying I can't live without you. I regret letting you go in the first place." He slides a hand behind my neck, looking me in the eye, "Be with me. I don't care where. Just be there and not thousands of miles away. My heart can't take it."

It feels like I'm floating on air. I steal another kiss before he finishes what he was saying.

"I mean it," he says, resting his forehead against mine. All of a sudden the doubt and frustration dissolve and I think maybe we really are getting our happily ever after. "Be with me."

It's everything I've longed to hear. My heart has wings, it's soaring. With astonishing speed, I answer him. "Yes."

"Yes to what, baby? Tell me… tell me we'll figure out a way to make this work where we can be together in the same fucking house, in the same fucking city."

"We'll figure it out," I promise. "I want to be with you. I've never wanted anything more. Miles, I-"

"I love you, Rylee. So fucking much. I've never loved anyone as much as I love you, and I probably never will. I'm sorry I cut you off but in case that's what you were about to say to me, I wanted to be first." He smiles the most beautiful, handsome smile, taking my face in his hands.

He said it. He actually said it. The three words I've been wanting to hear for what feels like three lifetimes. The same three words that have been on the tip of my tongue for so long. When he tells me he loves me, I feel those words. I feel them all over my body. Because I've realized that Miles is my heart and wherever he is, is where I want to be. We'll figure it out together.

"I love you, Miles. Loving you is as easy as breathing," I confess. And nothing has ever felt better. Love was the last thing on my mind when I ran into Miles on that rainy day in Vancouver. But that's what I found, and I plan on doing whatever it takes to keep it.

Miles closes his eyes and kisses me, and my lips are where they belong. When we break the kiss, I can't stop myself from asking: "You really mean it?"

"What? That I love you?"

I nod.

"I meant it yesterday and the day before that, and a month before then. I've known that I'm in love with you for weeks." Miles' smile is huge and brilliant and makes me tingly all over. His words are as beautiful as a sunrise. "You make me so damn happy, Rylee. I never knew I could feel this way. I need you, baby, now. But not here. We can't do all the things I want to do to you with your grandparents across the hall. I booked us a room for the night at an inn not too far from here."

"Mmm, it has been too long since you've touched me. I just need to pack a bag."

An hour later, Miles undresses me as soon as the door locks shut behind us. We spend the next hour in bed, gloriously naked together doing everything we've been longing to do to each other for so long. We make up for lost time in the very best way.

It took us long enough

Chapter Forty-One

Miles

"I want to move back to L.A. with you."

I freeze in place in the bathroom of our hotel room, finding her eyes in the reflection of the mirror. "But your grandparents are here. I know how important they are to you."

"They're selling the farm. They only told me a few hours ago and I planned on telling you but got swept up in your surprise visit. They've found an apartment at a retirement home. They seem really excited about it." She half-shrugs and sighs at the same time, wrapping a white, fluffy towel around her body. Her hair is still wet from the post-sex shower we just took.

"*You* don't seem that excited about it."

"I'm not sure how I feel about it. Losing the farm will be tough on all of us but on the other hand, my grandparents will get the care that they need, and I can stop worrying about them so much."

I reach for her hips and pull her body to me.

"My gran told me I need to get my own life," she says with a laugh, burrowing her face in my neck. "I'm pretty sure she insinuated I was smothering them."

"Well, your Gran wants great-grand-babies immediately. Maybe this is all part of her plan."

Rylee frowns. "I love you with my whole heart but that is not happening anytime soon. Just so we're clear on that."

"Ten-four. But one day, we will have mini-Miles' running around with your green eyes and my charming personality. Maybe six of them. Maybe an entire baseball team. You know me, Ryls. I don't half-ass anything."

She gives me her *you-are-from-another-planet* look. I've seen it plenty of times before, whenever I rile her up.

"Ryls, I want you to be happy. You know what my life in L.A. is like. You won't be able to walk freely there, not when you're with me. You need to think about that. You'll need a bodyguard whenever you're out. I won't negotiate on that."

"I'm okay with that. Being with you is all I want. The rest I'm willing to deal with."

Everything is finally feeling right. For the first time in weeks, my body relaxes, the tension in my shoulders melting away. We can figure out the logistics. I know one thing for sure: I want her to move in with me. I'm as impatient as they come, so I grab her by the hand and pull her out of the bathroom and onto the bed.

She giggles, holding her towel against her body. "I'm still dripping wet. What are you doing?"

We're both in only towels, sitting in the middle of our tousled bed sheets. Water drips down her chest into her cleavage, and I barely resist the urge to lick the beads of water off her skin. "I want to figure this all out now. Where do you want to live?"

She looks pensive. "Well, I have my apartment in Burbank, although I'm pretty positive I've been replaced by Meg's boyfriend. But I'm sure I could find something closer to you as long as I could afford it."

"Or you could move in with me?"

"Move in with you?"

"Yes, move in with me. Actually, it's non-negotiable. I want you to move in with me. Let's do this, Ryls."

She lifts her eyes to the ceiling and lets out a breath. "Miles, we've been together for all of three months. You can't suggest things like that."

"Why not?"

"Isn't it too soon? I've never lived with anyone before."

"Neither have I, because I've never wanted to. But even if you're a car ride away from me that's too far. You've seen what happens to us when we're not together. We're both miserable and nobody wants to be near us. Moving in together would happen sooner or later anyways. Let's just go with sooner."

"You're really sure about this, aren't you?" she asks, her voice soft, her eyes wide in disbelief.

I take her hands in mine. "I've never been more sure. Please say yes. Then we'll get your grandparents settled in their new apartment and figure out when you can fly home to me."

My heart beats double time waiting for her to answer. I don't think I've ever wanted anything more in my life.

"Okay," she says.

There goes my heart.

There are no words to describe how freaking happy I am. I'm speechless. So instead, I slide my hand along the back of her neck, pulling her in to me. Her legs straddle my waist, her towel slipping down her body. And I kiss her like it's the last time, knowing all the while that we have forever in front of us. She takes the hint and kisses me back the same way.

"I fucking love you, Ryls," I say. "I never want to love anyone but you."

***

Four weeks later, Rylee and I are in Los Angeles boarding a private plane to Reed Point. We're in a hurry to get home so I asked Josh Lucas for a favor. Three hours later his jet is fueled and waiting for us, ready for take-off.

Liam called me early this morning and as soon as I heard the nervous tone in his voice I knew why he was calling. Ellie went into labor in the middle of the night, so they rushed to the hospital. Doctors told them they would have a baby within the next 24 hours. My brother is going to be a fucking dad.

I had Georgia clear my schedule for the next three days so Rylee, who was sleeping soundly in my bed when I got the call, and I could be there for the birth. At least we're hoping to make it. This plane can't touch down in Reed Point soon enough.

Rylee follows me up the airstairs into the small aircraft. Her mouth hangs open when she sees the leather couches, boardroom table and mini bar. "How will I ever fly economy again?" she asks in wonder, running her hand across the plush leather seats. She looks like a kid in Disneyland for the first time. And I'm so fucking happy that I get to be the one who gets to spoil her for the rest of her life. No, I haven't asked her for forever just yet, but I've had a radiant cut diamond solitaire hidden in my gym bag for two weeks.

"I owe Josh big time for this," I tell her, setting her

carry-on bag down. We settle into two sizeable leather recliners near the center of the over-the-top aircraft.

"Yes, you do. He's a generous man. We'll have to think of something. Maybe I could do a family photoshoot for him and we could have a few shots framed?" she says before shaking her head. "Forget I said that. Why would he want my photos? I'm sure he works with the best."

"You *are* the best, Ryls. Don't sell yourself short. I'm positive they would love that."

When we finally touch down, our luggage is loaded into the trunk of a Suburban that is waiting to take us to Reed Point General. Ellie is still in labor, according to my mom. She has been texting me regular updates. Liam is apparently a mess seeing Ellie in so much pain.

Rylee insists we stop at a deli along the way to pick up sandwiches and soft drinks for my family, who have been sitting in the waiting room for hours. With our arms full of food and drinks, we arrive to find everyone sitting in a tiny waiting room. They're all here: my parents, Parker and Olivia and Jules. Ellie's parents, too.

"Did we make it in time?" I ask. "Has Ellie had the baby?"

My mother stops pacing to greet Rylee and I with a hug. "No sweetheart, but she's close. Thank you for coming. It means a lot to your brother and Ellie."

Two long hours later, my big brother is officially a dad when Ellie gives birth to a beautiful baby boy. Turns out Liam was right all along, it's a boy. I'm betting we'll be hearing about it from him for years to come.

Once we're allowed, we all gather in their private hospital room and crowd around Ellie, who is beaming at the bundle in her arms. Liam sits on the edge of the bed, gazing at his son who at just a few hours old already has a firm grip on my brother's finger. I can feel the excitement vibrating off of him, the pure happiness in his smile as he watches his son sleep.

"Liam had eyelashes just like his when he was a baby," my mom says, cooing over her first grandchild. "He's just perfect. Does this little muffin have a name yet?"

"He does," Ellie says. "Hudson Michael Stephen Bennett. His middle names after his grandpas."

I look over at my dad to see his eyes are damp. Thankfully Rylee brought her camera and is busy clicking away.

"I'm so happy you two made it," Ellie says. "Thank you for coming."

"Yeah, thanks guys. It means the world." My brother has been a father for all of five minutes and he already seems to be softening. I suddenly think back to when we were kids. Liam was always the serious one, the thinker who listened more than he spoke. Now he is a father, engaged to a great girl, surrounded by a family who love them and their new little guy.

"We wouldn't have missed it. You have a beautiful family. Happy for you, man," I say.

"Uncle Miles, would you like to hold your nephew?" Ellie asks.

My heart speeds up. "Please."

Liam takes the baby from Ellie and hands him gently to me. Rylee looks at me and smiles and I wonder what she's thinking. I've never asked her if she wants kids, although judging from how in love she is with her nieces and nephew and how she's staring at little Hudson right now, I am pretty sure I already know the answer.

"Hey, handsome," she whispers over my shoulder at Hudson. "He's beautiful, you guys, and so tiny. Congratulations. I'm so happy I'm here to meet him."

"I already see so much of Liam in him," Ellie gushes, her eyes glued to her brand new son. "He's definitely a

Bennett, which means we are going to have our hands full."

We all laugh, just as Hudson starts to fuss in my arms. I kiss him on the forehead and hand him to Liam. "Back to you, bro," I tell him with a grin. I can already tell I'm going to love being an uncle

Leaving Ellie and Liam to get some rest, we all say our goodbyes and walk to my dad's Bentley in the hospital parking lot. He offered his car to Rylee and I for the three days we're in town. My dad hands me his keys and then he and my mom hop into Parker and Olivia's car for the drive home.

After slipping into the leather seat, I turn my gaze to Rylee, who's buckling up her seatbelt in the passenger seat beside me. "You hungry, country girl?"

"I am."

"Tacos?"

"Sounds perfect."

We decide on take-out from Cocina Caliente, a Mexican place that's one of my favorite stops when I'm back in Reed Point. After picking it up, I drive us to the same lookout spot I had taken Rylee to on our last visit to my hometown.

"Are you taking me where I think you're taking me?" she asks, the window down, breeze blowing through her hair.

I wink. "That depends on where you're thinking."

I park the car and notice we're the only ones here. We find a spot overlooking the city, the ocean deep in the distance, and I lay out a blanket for us. I had asked my Dad to put one in the trunk of his car when we made the plan to fly out earlier today, knowing we'd end up here.

When we finish eating, I gather our trash in the bag it

came in and stick it in the backseat of the car, then walk back to Rylee.

She's standing, looking out over Reed Point. The rays shine across her golden-brown skin, sunlight beaming down on her like a lighthouse directing me home. That's what she is to me. Home. Wrapping my arms around her from behind, I pull her back into my chest and kiss her neck.

"Is it me or is the sunset extra beautiful tonight?" she asks, nuzzling her cheek against mine.

"It's got nothing on you, Ry," I tell her, unwrapping my arms from around her waist and moving to stand next to her so I can get her full attention. I reach into my pocket for the reason I brought her here tonight.

Rylee starts to cry the second I bend to one knee.

"Miles?" she whispers through tears, a look of surprise in her big green eyes. I flip the box open, holding out the ring. She gasps and her hand flies up to cover her smile. I'm smiling right back at her like a lovesick fool. "Let me love you forever, Rylee. You are the one for me. The only one I'll ever want. It's been you from the second I saw you and all I want is to love you forever. Will you marry me?"

Rylee lowers herself to the ground, taking my face in her shaking hands and kissing me. Then, as tears streak down her cheeks, she nods over and over, gasping out the word "Yes," and flings her arms around my neck.

Once we pull apart, I slip the ring on her finger. She stares at it, then up at me. "It's the most beautiful thing I've ever seen. I love it. I love it so much. But not as much as you. I could never love anything as much as I love you."

Her smile is bigger than the moon. I kiss my fiancée, and she melts against me. "I love you so much. I can't wait for forever with you."

"You know what?" she asks playfully.

"What?"

She smiles again and I feel it in my chest. "My heart was always set on you."

I kiss her, and I see stars, and maybe even fireworks too. The woman who makes my heart expand to twice its size is in my arms, and I know I'm right where I belong.

Epilogue

6 MONTHS LATER

Rylee

Spring has arrived in Los Angeles, but I'm too busy to enjoy it. I'm surrounded by boxes and more boxes and have a to-do list a mile long, but I forget about all of that when I look up and see Miles holding a bottle of champagne in our new house – yes, *our* house, which we moved into last week.

"We need to celebrate, Ryls," he says as he pops the bottle. The bubbly flows out, making us both crack up as Miles dips his head to drink it back. He gives it his best shot, but most of the champagne splashes to the kitchen floor.

"Celebrate?"

"Fuck yeah, we need to celebrate," he says, cleaning up the mess with the towel.

"How should we celebrate?"

"I want to make every memory here with you. So we're starting with today. Making memories, baby." He kisses me so fast I don't see it coming. "This calls for champagne and then you naked underneath me, or up against the counter. On the stairs will do too."

I laugh, giving him side-eye. What am I going to do with this man? "What does sex have to do with celebrating? Shouldn't we be eating cake or throwing a party? That's what normal people do when they have something to celebrate."

Handing me a flute, he clinks his glass to mine. "Insatiable, Ryls, when it comes to you. You said so yourself. I can never get enough. I'm just trying to decide where I want to have you first."

My cheeks start to feel a little hot and I'm suddenly thankful for the balmy breeze floating in through the kitchen window. I flash him a cheeky grin. "With a house this big, you have plenty of options."

Miles insisted we start fresh in a new house that we both chose together. The Bird Streets, where Miles lived when I first met him, were known for their parties, so we started looking in Beverly Hills for something more family-friendly with a big backyard.

Don't even get me started on the interior of this place. Open floor plan with light hardwood floors and vaulted ceilings with the most glorious wood beams. The back of the house is a wall of glass panels that open to a kidney-shaped pool with an outdoor kitchen and a stone fireplace. The house is set on a cliff with a view of the hills overlooking an entire valley. The view from the balcony feels like you are standing on the edge of the world. I look around in awe. How is this now my home?

It's not modest. A mansion is probably the right word for it. There's a theater room, of course, and two kitchens because apparently in a house this large, one isn't enough. I wonder what my mom would think of my six-burner stove or my sub-zero fridge with glass doors and a built-in ice-cream maker. It's wild.

But the very best thing about my new house is the memory wall of my photos that Miles surprised me with. Every one of my favorite memories are hanging in our front entrance, blown up and professionally framed. There are pictures of my parents, Gran and Gramps, my brothers and my nieces and nephew and the Vancouver sunset that will always remind me of when we first met. Then there's the photo that will always have my heart: The selfie I took of Miles and I on the farm, our kissing photo. Every time I look at it I remember how I felt that day, having just shared the best 24 hours with the man I was falling in love with only to have to watch him leave. I wish I knew then what life had in store for us, but I wouldn't trade our love story for anyone else's because this one is ours.

My eyes find Miles, who's across the kitchen. He's wearing a pair of gray sweatpants and nothing else. They're slung low on his hips so I can see the V of his abdomen and the sexy happy trail that disappears into his joggers. His hair is a mess, but somehow he still manages to look like he just stepped out of a photo shoot. I drink him in, not knowing how the man manages to look this good with zero effort.

I don't think I'll ever understand what I did to deserve him. Every day with him is better than the one before. They say that true love is meant to last a lifetime, so there's nothing wrong with being patient and making sure you get things right. I got things right. I found my other half and plan on never letting him go.

The fame I was so afraid of has become familiar to me. The attention I never wanted is something I've learned to live with. I continue to avoid the press whenever I can and rarely agree to comment on anything concerning Miles, but his fans seem to like me nonetheless. They like us together so much that they've merged our two names into one, so now we are Ryles. I think it's a bit ridiculous, but it doesn't bother me. Tabloids refer to us as America's Sweethearts. I'm good with that.

Gran and Gramps are happy in their senior retirement community. Miles and I video call them two or three times a week, but only get a chance to talk to them when they aren't too busy to accept our calls. They've taken to bingo nights and poker and as promised, Gran is a regular at yoga. I've been able to fly out to visit them at least once a month, staying with Cole and Cara since the farm went on the market last month. Last week we received the news that it had sold. I cried for the better part of that day. It was tough to see it go but I told myself I would create new memories with Miles and the family we hoped to have after we married.

Gran always told me love isn't something that you find, it's something that finds you. We found each other, Miles and I. A small-town girl from Deer Lake, Tennessee found her one big love in a Hollywood heartthrob. A beautiful man who has fought for me from day one. Before Miles, I never knew what it felt like to be put first, to be loved so fiercely. When Miles Bennett loves, it's with everything he's got. He lays his heart wide open. And I'll never take that for granted.

"The floor is sticky now. Look at the mess you made," I say, dropping down beside him where he's sitting on the floor going through a box. Miles grabs me by my waist and pulls me into his lap.

I giggle. "Can't get enough of me, can you?"

"Never," he says, sucking on my neck. We never seem to get enough of each other. We always want more.

"Same here."

I thought I had everything I needed, but boy was I wrong. My life needed Miles to feel whole. He's my other half. My one true love. When I think about forever, I think about him.

And I will spend the rest of my life loving this man with all that I have.

Miles

Three weeks after we moved into our new house, I had the number one box office movie in the world. It was an action flick I had filmed two years ago with an up-and-coming actress who the world had fallen in love with. I felt like a fucking king, but the high of being on top in my career paled in comparison to coming home to Rylee every day.

I'm in the back of a town car on my way home to her. I can't wait. I've been in London on a press tour for a week promoting the movie. The plan was originally for Rylee to join me, but her work kept her home.

She decided not to go back to work as a PA and instead focus on her photography. She brought it up over dinner one night and I encouraged her to make the change. I think she needed a gentle push, and I was only too happy to give it to her. Rylee is fucking talented and photography makes her happy. It also allows her a flexible schedule so she can travel with me when I'm shooting on location, which won't be an issue for us for a while since I landed the ActionFlix part I auditioned for that will shoot in L.A. *Fuck Yeah!*

As for my most recent co-star, Violet, I've heard through the Hollywood grapevine that she's single. Emilio broke things off with her shortly after filming wrapped. I felt bad for her, that Emilio wasn't the one for her, but that was life sometimes. Not everyone gets their happy ending. Hopefully she will find the one and get to experience what Rylee and I have one day. If she is lucky.

Thanks to the horrendous L.A. traffic, it's two hours later before I'm finally walking through our front door. Rylee greets me in the kitchen looking heart-stoppingly beautiful in a white tank and skinny jeans, a head band in her hair.

"Welcome home, baby. I missed you."

"It's so good to be home. With you." My hands grip her waist, then I pull her to me, inhaling her scent. I pull back an inch to kiss her, forgetting all about the jet lag that had set in, happy to be back in her arms. I will always come home to her, there's no place I'd rather be. My world spins around Rylee Brookes.

I'm lost in the kiss, I can't keep my hands off of her. She makes one of those sounds that drive me crazy and I moan softly. "Upstairs, Ryle. Last one up…"

The words die on my lips. Rylee dashes for the stairs to our bedroom. I scramble after her, listening to her laugh until I catch her in my arms. Somehow in our frenzy, we manage to make it onto our bed, Rylee lying underneath me, fully clothed for now but I'll be fixing that soon. But first…

"Fuck. There's nothing I want more than you right now, but it's going to have to wait. I have something for you, and I would like to give it to you now."

I walk over to the dresser and retrieve a small box from a drawer, which I hand to her.

"Miles, what did you do?"

"Open it and see." Goosebumps prickle my skin waiting for her reaction.

She slips the white ribbon from the box and opens it. "A key?"

"A key to the farm. It's your farm now. I know how much it means to you, so I bought the property from your grandparents. I talked to your brothers about it too, and they're happy it will stay in the family. I've been waiting until the deal went through to tell you."

Rylee's eye fill with tears as she clutches the key to her chest. Seeing how happy she is almost makes me cry as well. She looks up at me, seemingly speechless.

"I hope I didn't overstep. Do you like it?"

"Miles, I don't know what to say. You bought me my childhood home. You've given me the greatest gift of all. I think I'm in shock. Thank you doesn't seem like enough."

She wipes the tears from her eyes, then moves to her knees on the bed and reaches for me. Wrapping her arms around me, she runs her thumbs over the nape of my neck. "I love you, baby. Thank you. I hope you know how much this means to me."

"I do. I love you too."

There isn't anything I wouldn't do for this woman. She has me wrapped around her finger. This is only the beginning. I plan on spoiling her every chance I get.

"I'm going to love you forever, Ryls."

"That's good because I'm going to love you for the rest of my life."

She kisses me and I kiss her back with everything I have. I have my entire world in my arms, my one big love, and I'm a lucky man.

THE END

· · ·

Thank you for reading! Ready for the final book in the Bennett Family Series? Get ready for Jules and Beckett's rivals to lovers, forbidden and secret relationship, spicy romance next! Read one of my favourite scenes I've ever written (the pool scene at the hotel) in Crazy Over You now.

Acknowledgments

Thank you so much for reading this book! I hope you enjoyed Miles and Rylee's story. I'm forever grateful you took a chance on an indie author who loves this genre endlessly. It means the world. A special thank you to all the incredible readers who have read the Bennett Family series and have continued to support me.

Thank you to my Beta readers, ARC readers, bloggers and bookstagrammers for the unconditional love and support you throw my way every day. Every share, post, review and mention is appreciated more than you know.

A special thank you to my editor and friend, Carolyn De Melo, for sticking to impossible deadlines and talking me down from ledges- not to mention your incredible wit and insights. Thank you for always putting up with my last-minute changes. You are brilliant.

Thank you, Carmen, Janelle, Brandee, Mary and Leah for lunch dates, proofreading and your feedback. You each played a role in keeping me sane and bringing this book to life.

Thank you to my sweet friends and my author friends for listening to me complain about the shit I have to do, entertaining me with jokes when I need them and being there for me every step of the way. I hope you know who you are and how much you mean to me. I love celebrating each other's successes.

Thank you to Jayde Ubels for knocking another adorable cover out of the park. There is no one I'd rather design covers with! Working with you all is as easy as breathing.

Finally, thank you to my family, who make my dream possible. You put up with a mom/wife who brings her laptop everywhere we go and love me fiercely when I need it most. Your constant support means the most.

Lily Miller XO

Afterword

Thank you for reading! If you loved the story, I'd be so grateful if you left an honest review—it helps more than you know. Your time and thoughts mean the world.

Want to stay connected? Join Lily's newsletter to get the latest updates, special sales, audiobook news, and first looks at new releases.

Lily Miller Newsletter

About the Author

Lily Miller lives in Vancouver, BC with her husband—her real-life book boyfriend—and their two daughters. When she's not writing love stories full of heat, heart, and happily-ever-afters, you can usually find her in the kitchen cooking, sailing the Pacific Ocean, or with country music playing in the background.

A lifelong romantic, Lily has been hooked on happy endings since she was a kid, and now she channels that passion into writing small-town, contemporary spicy romance that celebrates love in all its messy, swoony, unforgettable forms.